The Soulweb

Steven M Nedeau

DEDICATION

This book was inspired by many hours spent in basements and dining rooms playing Dungeons&Dragons.

I dedicate this book to the friends that played:

Criss Bubacz,
Douglas Gale,
Michael Harpool,
Melissa Girard,
Sean Dwyer,
Shawn Girard,
Charles Andrews,
David Severance,
and Scott Nadeau.

You kick started my imagination.

Thank you

CONTENTS

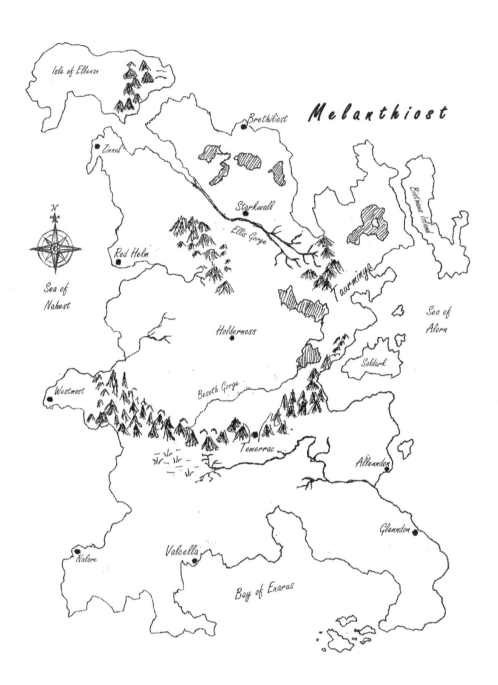

ACKNOWLEDGMENTS

Thank you
Christina L. Sage,
Dave Soucy,
Katie Skillings,
Heather Stein,
J.H. Macomber,
and Criss Bubacz

Chapter 1   Meeting

Ice ringed the puddles on the cobblestone street. The clouds, an angry grey earlier, shone in the sky in layers of crimson and yellow, brightening the heavens, but doing nothing to push away the chill.

Jaron watched his footing carefully. He had already taken a nasty fall, and his elbow ached with every bump. Not long ago, Jaron had been clearing away snow from the library stoop and breaking ice in the well water bucket. Now, it was warmer during the day, bringing hope that the winter was finally over.

Master Librarian Ceryss had ordered the delivery of a letter. As the sun had begun to set, he had come into the study to find Jaron, Ellian, and Keras arguing and laughing over the translation of an ancient tome. Ceryss had instructed Keras to make the delivery, but when Jaron saw the address, he begged for the task.

The letter, having only arrived moments before, still had an unbroken wax seal; two eagles facing each other and surrounded by a ring of leaves. With a black smudge, the address on the folded parchment read: to Arnor Ondstriker.

Popular at the library, Arnor was no stranger to Jaron. Quick with a jest and quicker to laugh at it, Arnor was always open for discussions and easy with his stories. For days, he would stay at the library, and with each of his visits, he would attend lessons, sitting in silence, scrawling notes into books produced from his pockets. Tall for a dwarf, at just over four feet, he still came to the height of only the fourth shelf in a bookcase. He was a scholar, a businessman, a fighter, a jester, and often a drunk. Jaron was eager to see him most of all because Arnor had been a friend of Jaron's father. However, of all the things Arnor might be, there was something he was not: here.

Jaron frowned, his eyes scanning over the faces in the market. Among the merchants closing their wagon shops, and patrons trying to make a deal on the day's unsold wares, a group of armored men caught Jaron's attention. It wasn't that armor was all that uncommon, but most people didn't strap it on to visit the market. Strangers were common in the port city of Westmost, but this group looked ready for a fight. Broken in, like a pair of boots that have to be worn to fit correctly, they stood in sharp contrast to the brightly clothed people of the city.

As if they were expecting to see someone, three of them were looking the crowd over. The fourth appeared to be asleep, leaning against a wall, his balding head down and arms folded on his chest in front of him. Jaron's eyes did a double take when he reached the fifth member of the group. The fifth member wasn't sleeping or searching the crowd. He was looking straight back at Jaron.

Unnerved at being on the receiving end of such a stare, and ashamed for having been caught staring himself, Jaron's ears reddened and he turned away to resume his search for Arnor. He looked down alleys, peered into shops, turned around more than one dwarf, and stood on his tiptoes to scan over the people of the market. So intent was Jaron in his search that he failed to notice the man walking up behind him, and started when he felt a hard poke on the shoulder.

"Boy."

Jaron turned and saw the warrior who had been staring at him. His deep brown eyes looked Jaron over.

"What is your given name?"

Surprised by the question, Jaron asked, "Excuse me, Sir?"

Another question came, "Your father, what is his name?" which was—in quick succession—followed by, "How old are you?" and, "Your mother, what is her name?"

Caught off guard by the personal questions, Jaron stared with his mouth slightly ajar. He had been expecting, from the force of the poke, a scolding about how he should be minding his own business. The man looked at him intently.

"Yaru, don't pester the boy," came a sharp voice from behind Jaron. Standing in the kitchen doorway to The Broken Horse was Arnor, blue eyes shining at Jaron. His black and grey beard hung low and in his brimmed hat was a long red feather. Striding forward, Arnor said, "Hello there, Jaron! Ah, I see you've a letter for me. And how did you know I was in the city?"

"I didn't know, sir," said Jaron, "I mean, until Master Ceryss instructed me to look for you in the market."

"Ceryss has his nose in more than is good for him. Very well, then, hand me the letter, boy," said Arnor, smiling.

Jaron held it out. Arnor took it and inspected the seal on the front. The smile left his face, but returned quickly.

"Just a moment..." Arnor said to Jaron and held out his hand to the warrior who had been questioning the boy. "Yaru, my friend, what are you doing in Westmost?"

Yaru took the hand of Arnor, but used the grip to pull the dwarf a short distance away, where the two held a conversation that progressed into a hushed, but heated, argument. Yaru grabbed Arnor by the shirt, lifting him off his feet, causing Arnor's hat to fall off his head. Yaru spoke quietly and put the dwarf back down. Glaring at Yaru, Arnor picked up his hat and brushed it off.

"Well?" said Yaru.

Arnor handed over the letter, placing the hat firmly back on his head.

Jaron watched Yaru's face as he broke the seal. Reading in silence, his expression of anger turned to sadness. After a few moments, the warrior, bending on one knee, reached into a pouch and pulled something out, holding it in front of the confused dwarf. Arnor snatched the item and held it close for inspection, his eyes widening to the size of silver coins. Yaru handed the letter back, and waited until Arnor finished reading it before he said, "I arrived this morning on a boat heading south from Brethiliost. I've been ordered east to Denshire. Goblins are crossing the Fortunal Mountains from the south and I've been sent to investigate. I expected you would be in Westmost. I was correct."

Arnor held up the item he had snatched from Yaru. "What about this?"

"Once I have made my initial contacts, I will try to find him," said Yaru, looking at the letter in Arnor's hand. Arnor nodded as

Yaru walked away and whispered with his companions. They were looking toward the inn, trying to get a glimpse of Jaron before they moved off, finally disappearing into the crowd.

"Come inside." Arnor pulled Jaron into the kitchen of The Broken Horse. "Listen to me, boy." Arnor shut the door behind them. "It is important that you do as I say. I'm going to walk out of the front door of this inn in a few moments. I need you to stay here, until I've been gone for at least two hours." He stopped and put his hands over his eyes for a moment, letting out a drawn sigh. "No. Wait until closing and then leave with the other customers. Then, go back to the library. I'll meet you there."

Arnor shook his head in frustration. "Broken Hammer! He shouldn't have sent you." He inspected the seal on the paper again and, with a glance out of the window, tucked it into his shirt. "It seems that there's more to this business than just a delivery and now you've been thrown straight into it, and sooner than I'd wished. There's much to explain."

"Why? What's going on?"

"You're going on a trip," Arnor said.

"Hmm?"

Arnor wasn't paying attention to Jaron's inquisition.

"Where are we going?" Jaron asked.

"I'll fill you in when we are both back at the library, but I must go now. Walk back to the library. Don't run. The less you do to attract attention to yourself the better."

"What are you talking about?"

"You wouldn't believe me if I told you, unless you saw them for yourself. And even then..." his voice trailed off. "Remember, walk. Don't run. I'll meet you at the library tonight if I can lose them." He started toward the door but stopped himself. "Eat something while you wait. Make sure you sample the ale. In fact, have two."

* * * * *

The streets were quiet when Jaron left The Broken Horse.

The temperature had dropped and he could see his breath as he exhaled. He stepped into the market square, now empty, and rubbed his arms against the chill. The company at The Broken Horse had been excellent. Patrons had talked about local problems, feuds between local businessmen and the guilds. He had enjoyed the food, much better fare than he was accustomed to as an apprentice of the library. The dark brown ale had tasted good, though bitter at first.

Jaron cursed himself for ordering a second flagon. He wasn't sure of his balance anymore. *Just concentrate,* he thought, *one foot at a time.*

The last two customers of The Broken Horse walked away, arm in arm, singing together as they held each other up.

> Walking into spider webs,
> And I cannot feel my legs,
> I hope I didn't take the spider,
> She was just protecting her eggs.

Walking the cobblestones of the square, Jaron himself, hummed a tune, one sung at the inn by a tanked-up priest. Jaron stopped short, remembering, *I didn't pay my bill.*

He looked behind him to find that the gas lamps of The Broken Horse were out. "Tomorrow," he said aloud to himself turning back to his path, only to stop again.

The street lanterns were dark. Walking by the moonlight so far, he had not noticed, but the lanterns in this part of town were supposed to be lit by dusk. He looked behind him. Yes, he had walked past two of them, both dark. Turning back toward the library, he picked up his pace. It had to be at least half past eleven. The lanterns normally burned away the night before their oil was exhausted. He had even seen some still burning after dawn. Either they hadn't been lit or someone had put them out.

Pushing goose bumps down his arms and spine, a cold draft hit the back of Jaron's neck. He shivered it away. His sandals interrupted the stillness of the night, scratching along the cobblestones, sounding as loud as booming thunder to Jaron's ears. A feeling that someone was following began to overcome him, but whenever he turned to look, the way behind him was always empty.

Arnor's having a joke on me! he thought, *spooked me.*

Jaron stepped between two buildings and looked behind him; no one was there. Feeling foolish, he leaned back against the wall of the alley and shook his head, smiling quietly at himself. Jaron could picture Arnor crying with laughter at the way he was jumping at every shadow.

Then Jaron bumped into one. It was cold.

*   *   *   *   *

"He's late, Ceryss." Arnor was pacing the office of the librarian. "I don't like it."

It wasn't like Jaron to be late. Ceryss summoned his second man. "I want you to send Ellian and Keras out to look for Jaron. He should be between here and The Broken Horse. Be quick." Thin and tall, Ceryss was more a man of brain than muscle. He had been the master librarian for twenty years. At not quite fifty years old, he was still a man that commanded attention when he wanted it. Ceryss strode back into his office. "Arnor, you should have come here first when you arrived in town instead of stopping for a drink."

"And you should have known I was probably being followed," shot back Arnor. "That seal on the envelope should have told you that. Are all of these books starting to clutter your head so that you don't recognize the seal of Keltenon when you see it?" Noticing the drop in Ceryss's posture, Arnor felt a twinge of guilt and backed off. "Anyway, the road was long and I was thirsty."

Ceryss smiled at the gesture but knew he had made a mistake. "It would figure, after all of these years I would send Jaron on an errand at precisely the wrong time. I should have made Keras bring it as I intended. Where is the letter now?" Ceryss asked.

"Here," Arnor patted his chest pocket.

"Have you verified the ring Yaru gave you against the seal?"

"Yes."

"May I?"

Arnor produced the ring from his pocket. "Yaru acquired it from one of his spies who said that she had removed it from the finger of a goblin near the city of Allenddon. He wants to head south to discover more, but Yaru has been ordered east to Denshire with four men. Apparently, the Markal goblins have been crossing the Fortunal Mountain Range. "

"That's odd. Why wouldn't they just use the Temerrac Pass?"

"Maybe they're planning an attack on the Nargesh goblins."

"Not likely. I would expect the aggression to travel the other way with goblins. Markal tribes have never been fond of conflict."

"When Yaru is finished investigating, he will head south to find word of that letter."

"You're headed north to Starkwall?"

"As soon as possible."

"I will send a pigeon to prepare for your arrival."

* * * * *

Jaron opened his eyes and found he was looking straight up. The stone blocks of the alley wall stretched up into the star-filled sky. Slowly, he rolled to his belly and pressed his hands against the ground to stand. His joints creaked like an old man's, or like one who has spent too much time outside in a winter wind. His head felt dizzy and tingled with a feeling Jaron could only equate to how your hand feels when it falls asleep, unattached and somehow alien. Bringing his feet under him, Jaron stood, stumbled, leaned against the wall, and fell back down again. He looked around him. Whatever he had bumped into was gone. At least he didn't have to deal with it, whatever it was. The only sound he heard was the calling of his name from far off. His friends were looking for him.

"Keras!" he tried to yell, letting out only a croak. "Ellian," he tried to say, but only vomited.

Digging deep, Jaron brought himself back to his hands and knees. Still trying to answer the call of his friends, he crawled out of the alley and lay there, out of breath, feeling the cold of the cobblestones before passing again into unconsciousness.

* * * * *

Sounds of a crackling fire and a muffled conversation woke Jaron. Ceryss and Keras were having a discussion or, from the sound, a disagreement. Looking around, Jaron realized that he was back at the library. He looked around again. This was the bedchamber of the master librarian. The fireplace glowed with a flickering light. Something was steaming in a pot near the flames, creating a smell similar to fall leaves being broken when they become too brittle and dry. His head still had the 'pins and needles' feeling but it was not as strong as it had been in the alley. Jaron sat up, swung his legs over the left side of the bed and tried to stand. He managed it, though the dizziness was still there.

"What are you doing up?" Arnor almost yelled at him as he entered the room. "Rest."

"This isn't my room."

Arnor smiled before answering, "I know that." He moved over to inspect the steaming black pot, "but we need the fireplace."

"This is the Master's room. I should go back to the dormitory."

"You'll lie back down and stay there. Master Ceryss hasn't slept in here for the past month."

"That's ridiculous. I brought him breakfast only this morning and set it on the table myself."

"That was a month ago."

"What...?"

"You really don't remember any of it?" Arnor said, wafting the steam from the pot with the lid.

"Any of what?" Jaron asked.

"For the past month, you haven't said a word, haven't left this room. You've been walking, and eating, and drinking, but it was as if you weren't here. It was like your body was here, but your mind was somewhere else."

Jaron sat back down on the bed. The steam from the pot on the fire smelled good, removing some of the fog in his head.

"What happened to me? After I left The Broken Horse, I was convinced someone was following me, but there was never anyone there when I turned to look." Arnor sat down in the chair near the fire and stirred the pot. Jaron continued, "I didn't believe you, you know? I thought you were trying to scare me for a laugh. But then, I bumped into cold, dark, well..." he stammered, searching for the best description he could think of, "air. It felt like walking into winter from summer all at once." Jaron took a drink of the water from the cup on the bedside table.

"That was a shade, boy," Arnor said without moving his eyes from the pot.

"A what?"

"Shades are the shadows of Demons. They come here to accomplish a mission of some kind. The ale dimmed its effect on you. Maybe that's why you're still here. You would have died, even from the minimal exposure you had."

"What is something so horrible doing in Westmost?"

"It was looking for you."

"Me? Why?"

"They don't know it's you they are after," Arnor mused to himself.

"What? Why is this thing after me?"

"I think that's why the shade left after touching you," Arnor said. "It didn't really know who you are."

"And just who am I?" asked Jaron, exasperated at not being answered.

Arnor stood, walked to the cabinet in the corner, pushed a stool into place, climbed up, and pulled down the bottle of brandy and a glass from the top shelf. He poured a generous helping and put the bottle back. As he climbed down from the stool he asked, "What do you know of your mother?"

"Just what I was told by my father; she died when I was one

or two, trying to have another baby. Her name was Halla."

Arnor carried the stool with him across the room and handed the glass to Jaron. He climbed up onto the stool and sat on it, his feet dangling. "And your father, what do you know of him?"

"A blacksmith by trade, he died of fever, seven years ago, when I was nine. I was already apprenticed to the library so I didn't get to see him much, really, but I remember him."

"Do you now? That's good," said Arnor, smiling and reaching for the glass. "Do you remember his name?"

"Loren." Jaron wasn't looking at Arnor and took a sip from the glass of brandy. It burned as he swallowed. He took a deep breath and exhaled it slowly, grimacing. "This is awful."

"The brandy was for me," Arnor pointed at the water on the bedside table. "That one's for you." Jaron handed the glass to Arnor and picked up the water.

"Anyway," Arnor said, shaking his head, "his name wasn't Loren, though we called him that. It was Lorenistal Keltenon. And he didn't die seven years ago."

"Excuse me?" Jaron asked, blinking.

"And your mother's name was not Halla. It was Estarial. She did not die in childbirth as you believe, but was murdered by the enemies of your father."

Jaron sat staring, mouth open, the water in his hand forgotten.

"You were nearly three then," explained Arnor.

"I don't understand. What? Why would a blacksmith have enemies?" The questions tongue-tied Jaron. "My father didn't die? Is he still alive then? Where is he?" Jaron stood up, feeling light-headed, but determined. Leaning forward on his stool, Arnor gently pushed Jaron back until the boy sat heavily on the bed again, nearly spilling his drink.

"It's a long story to tell, and it's late. Yes, he may still be alive. But I don't think so. That letter," he pointed to the bedside table where he had placed the piece of parchment along with a silver and red ring, "was written almost eight weeks ago by Loren. He was alive then at least. Tomorrow, we need to sneak you out of Westmost."

"Sneak me out of Westmost?"

"You already look too much like your mother, and you're even getting to look like your father as well."

Jaron's memory sparked. "That man at the market asked me about them."

"His name is Yaru. I still can't believe he picked you out like that. It's been fifteen years since he's seen you, though he was only ten at the time and you just a toddler. You do look like your mother. He," said Arnor, "is your uncle. Your mother was his elder sister."

Jaron was not any less confused.

"I don't have any family. My father told me I had no other family. Why would he lie?" The next question that came to his mind caught in his throat as he tried to ask it and his eyes blurred. "He left me. Why did he leave me?"

"Look, son, he did..." Arnor corrected himself, "we did this to protect you, and would have been successful for a good many years if..." he trailed off again.

"It's time to move you to a stronger location," Arnor said as he got down from the stool. "You need to sleep." He headed for the door.

"You're not making a lot of sense, Arnor."

"We've hidden you well up to now. Those shades are after you because of who you are, or more correctly, who your father is, and who his father was before him."

"And who am I?"

"You are Jaronthel Keltenon." Arnor opened the door and turned to face Jaron. "You are a king."

11

Chapter 2   Farewell

20 February 1108
They followed me from Lakewood, through the mountain pass to the middle road.
They set upon me last night. I am dying. I know now the steel that pierced me was
poisoned or cursed. I was dead the moment the edge broke skin. The fever is on
me. The last of my money has gone to pay a messenger to deliver this letter. Look
after my son. Please tell him I am sorry.

Farewell.
Lorenistal

*   *   *   *   *

The sun peaked over the mountains as Jaron lay in the bed, not sleeping. 'Not sleeping' was what he had been doing most of the night. When he did sleep, his dreams came quickly and they were not pleasant. Partly due to his own questioning, Arnor had thrust so much information at him the night before that his dreams were scattered, unsatisfying, and disturbing.

Jaron squinted at the sunlight entering the bedchamber through windows set high on the wall and stifled a yawn with the back of his hand. Sitting up in the bed, he was relieved to notice that the dizziness had gone, leaving only a light headache. He shivered as soon as his feet touched the floor. The spent embers of the fire had allowed the chilling hands of a dying winter to reach in through the open window and steal the warmth from the room, leaving the smooth floor icy cold. He used the washbasin and chamber pot in the corner of the room and noticed the clothes laid out on the table. A note read, 'Put these on.'

Under the note, the clothes glinted with intricate stitching. He held the shirt up to the window. It shimmered in the light and felt smooth to the touch. There were also pants, a pair of leather boots and a belt. Jaron pulled the brown wool pants to his hips and tied the straps at the side so they wouldn't fall down. He then pulled the shimmering grey shirt over his head, fastened the belt, and looked in the long mirror.

He didn't like what he saw looking back at him. His disheveled brown hair and green eyes decorated the face of a scared boy, smooth as a baby. He straightened, pulling his shoulders back as if he could will them to grow wide enough to fill out his new shirt. It looked too long. *A king, huh?* He sure didn't feel like one. He would feel more like himself in his own clothes, worn as they were. "I look a fool," he muttered to himself as he started to unbuckle the belt.

"Yes, I have to agree," said Keras as she entered the room. Ellian strode in behind her. His best friends at the library, Ellian and Keras always seemed to be together. Jaron turned to look at them and could not believe what he saw. Instead of their normal attire, each wore leather armor laced with steel rings. It fit them so naturally that Jaron remembered the men in the market.

"Armor, really?" Jaron asked, looking at his friends, and realizing that there might be more to them than just studies and books. Shouldn't they feel just as foolish as he? They did not appear to.

Keras, who looked more comfortable in her armor than Ellian did in his, sat down. "Well, we really didn't get much of a choice in the matter, though I like the look. Arnor insisted we wear it. He said the way..." Keras waved her hand in the air, "was going to be dangerous. We have some for you, too."

"You two are coming?" Both nodded. "Do you know where we're going?"

"Nope," Keras leaned forward, placing her hands on her knees. "You don't look much like royalty, you know? Don't let that get to you. They're goofy looking. I think it's because they keep marrying their cousins."

"Arnor told you, did he? I don't think I believe it myself." Jaron slumped on the bed, ears blushing red in embarrassment. The clothes and the attention made him feel awkward already, but being told 'he didn't look goofy enough to be royalty' was the closest thing in the way of a compliment he had ever heard from Keras.

Ellian spoke up. "No, neither of us heard from Arnor." He paused, running his fingers along his collar were the armor had left a mark on his skin. "I knew before I even met you. I was told eight years ago before I came here to guard you."

Jaron blinked in surprise. How many others knew of his secret? A woozy feeling came over him again. Was he still feeling the effects of the shade, or was this flurry of information causing this upset? One single thing fixed in his mind, holding him steady, keeping him from accepting. This story had to be untrue because of one undeniable fact.

"We have a king."

"And what is a king, really?" Ellian chuckled, "Seems we need protection from our own kings, lately. Gurrand calls himself 'king' and he is jealous of power. We need to hide you from him. If he finds out of your claim to the throne we will have trouble."

"I don't want to be the king. King Gurrand has no reason to fear that I might try to usurp his seat."

Jaron put his father's ring in his pocket. It didn't fit his fingers, but it did fit the seal of the letter still lying on the table. He had checked. *My father might be alive.* The thought put fire in his belly. *I might even get to see him again.* He had not seen him more than twice a year since his arrival at the library and that had stopped seven years ago.

Keras got up from her chair and opened a leather bag she had carried in with her. She pulled out a coat of thin chain mail. "It doesn't look like much, but it should protect most of your upper body, including your arms." She held it up and it reflected the beams of morning light against the opposite wall. "Arnor made it himself, and I suppose it might have some magical properties, though he denies it. It's stronger than it looks." Keras handed the coat to Jaron and reached back into the bag, this time pulling out a short sword sheathed in a leather scabbard.

Ellian and Keras fit the armor on Jaron, repositioning the belt so that it sat over the mail. They placed the scabbard and sword on his left hip. Over this, they dressed him in a hooded dark green cloak.

In the mirror, a brown haired boy of sixteen, both short and thin, stared back at him. *Yeah,* he thought, *this has to be a mistake.*

* * * * *

Filtering through the halls of the library, the smell of bacon drew Jaron, Keras, and Ellian to the dining hall. The creak of leather and rattle of steel, rarely heard within the library, echoed quietly from the polished walls of stone. Such a change from the slippers and sandals normally worn by apprentices, the hard boots hurt Jaron's feet with every step.

Jaron glanced toward his friends, Ellian, walking in front, and Keras to his left. He had never noticed how much larger Ellian was than he. Jaron, at five-six, looked insignificant next to Ellian's six-one. Even slender Keras stood and inch taller.

At the long table in the dining hall sat Arnor, steam coiling from the large cup in front of him. Piled around him on the table were plates with slices of bread and cheese, butter, one with bacon and sausages, fried eggs, and another overflowing with fruit. Arnor sat with his eyes closed, nearly asleep. Keras pulled a plate away from him and it slid noisily, waking the dwarf with a start.

It was not often that a large breakfast was available and Jaron ate his fill and more. However, no one ate more than Arnor. Even as tired as he was, he kept pulling the plates around him to eat more. "Another egg I suppose," he would say, or, "just one more grape." Arnor even put the leftover bacon into his pouch for later.

He had spent much of the night ordering the packing and provisions needed for travel to Starkwall. When Arnor wasn't locating the travel items needed, and packing, he had been checking on Jaron as he slept. His eyelids drooped and he let out a contented sigh after he drained his coffee cup. He was dressed in his usual attire but had added a brown cloak draped over his shoulders. He gathered his hat, checking that the feather was firmly in place, and stood. "Well, let's not be here all day. We are headed north by ship to Brethiliost," Arnor said to Jaron, "and then south to Starkwall."

* * * * *

Rows upon rows of shelves lined the large square room of the public reading hall, each shelf filled with books of history, adventure, poetry, science, and even magic. No patrons of the library walked the light and dark grey patterns of the floor today. The dark grey tiles extended out from underneath each massive bookshelf by a hand's length, while the lighter ones placed in the center of each aisle looked now like an arrow, pointing Jaron toward the center of the room, to the marble table set on a raised circle of dark stones.

At the table, behind a worn and cracked history book, sat Ceryss, Master of the Library of Westmost. He did not look up as the group entered. Ellian, walking in front, spoke, "Master, we're ready."

Ceryss addressed Arnor. "I have made queries about the sailings today. Only one ship sails north this morning. Go to the pier and find the Aquilo. She should be ready to depart within three hours." He turned a page of the tome set in front of him and lowered his gaze for a moment before rising and closing the book. Lifting it, he walked into one of the aisles and placed it gently back into its place on the shelf. As he did this, Keras and Ellian set their packs down and walked to the bookshelves on the opposite side of the table. They removed a piece of molding from the bottom of the case, revealing a secret compartment underneath. From this secret hold they drew two heavy iron bars, each an inch thick and ten feet long. These they placed into the 'decorative' holes directly under the marble tabletop. With effort, they pushed sideways on their individual bars. For a moment nothing happened, but slowly at first, then with greater ease and speed, the entire raised dais rotated out of the center of the room on a massive barrel hinge. Under the dais, a stairway wound down into the darkness.

Has anyone ever opened this door? Jaron thought. He was quite sure it did not exist on the blueprints of the library, having looked them over several times throughout the years since his apprenticeship began.

Striking a flint from his pocket, Arnor ignited the wick of a lantern. He took a small pouch from Ceryss, spoke a few quiet words, and having already shouldered his pack, started down the steps holding the lantern out in front of him. Ellian also approached Ceryss. He reached out, clasped Ceryss's hands, and descended behind Arnor.

Keras motioned for Jaron to follow Ellian. Still staring in awe at the secret door he had never imagined, wondering what other secrets the library held, Jaron took a deep breath and followed Ellian down the shadowed stairs. Keras watched Jaron walk down the steps until he disappeared from view.

Ceryss and Keras stood apart, remembering the fight from the night before. Ceryss finally said, "I don't agree with this decision."

"I know. I have to do this. I'm not afraid."

"I am."

Keras walked to the top of the stairs, where Ceryss stood, wringing his hands. She put her arms around the master librarian and pulled him close. Backing away, she wiped a tear from his face and said, "Goodbye, father."

The Master, teacher, protector, and father, feeling aged and tired, watched his only child walk down into the dark. With another tear rolling down his cheek, he strained against the iron bars, closing the secret exit.

*   *   *   *   *

The staircase wound down around the walls of a circular room. Light flickered from the lantern in Arnor's hand, cascading over stone blocks and bricks, rough-hewn and cracked with age. The walls bowed out in the middle and were closer at the floor and ceiling. *Much*, thought Jaron, *like the inside of a giant barrel.*

Keras crinkled her nose at the smell of mold. Ellian complained, waving his hand in front of his face. "Yeah, we should have opened this years ago and given it a good cleaning."

Jaron took a closer inspection of the walls. The stonework looked old, older than most of the city, certainly older than the library. Bricks came together to form intricate patterns of circles and triangles.

At the bottom of the steps, Arnor walked toward the wall and felt his way along it, running his fingers up and down, searching for something. Six feet along the wall, Arnor lay on his belly and inspected a brick in the lowest row. He stood back up, brushed himself off, stooped, and pushed on the brick. With a slight grating sound, it slid about a hand's length into the wall. Arnor stood straight again, motioning to Keras and Ellian to help him, and handed his lantern to Jaron. Jaron watched the three set their shoulders against the stones.

"And one, two, three." On 'three' they pushed hard against the wall. With a grinding noise of stone on stone, a section of the wall slid backwards and then to the right, leaving an opening large enough to fit through. If the smell of mold had been enough to make them gag, the new foul odor stole away the breath of the companions. Far surpassing the previous unpleasantness, the salty reek of a sewer made the mold stench of a few moments before seem like a spring breeze. Ellian gagged and retched at the base of the sliding door.

Arnor took a moment to compose himself, reached into his bag, removed three candles, and gestured for his lamp. Lighting the candles, he handed one each to Keras, Ellian, and Jaron.

"In addition to helping us find our way, the flame will help by burning away some of that stink," he said through the sleeve of his cloak. "Don't worry about the flame. The sewer is vented. The flammable gases go up the shaft."

"Doesn't do much for the smell," Keras said, coughing.

The way before them extended from the wavering candle light into inky blackness. Jaron could see that the tunnel was made of stone blocks arched at the top with a keystone so that the tunnel was widest at the bottom. He was afraid to touch the walls, fearing they might have a coating of slime that would refuse to wash away. The passageway branched off in three directions, left, right, and straight-ahead.

Keras pulled a map out of her pocket, held it under the candle, and pointed to the tunnel on the left. At every intersection, Keras reviewed the map. At the last turn, Jaron could see daylight reflecting off water at the egress of the sewer. The sound of the ocean was unmistakable, sliding out and crashing back in. As they got closer to the exit, Jaron could see that the ocean was actually entering the sewer.

"During times of high tide, the sea floods these tunnels, washing away the waste or the smell might have been worse," Ellian remarked as he blew out his candle.

A large, lichen-covered grate blocked the exit to the tunnel. Seaweed piled on both sides of the iron bars, which stood in eight-inch squares. A rusty lock held the grate tight. With a set of tools that appeared to come out of no-where, Ellian worked on the lock as the water of the bay rolled around their ankles.

Three minutes later, Keras said, "I thought you were good at this."

"I am," Ellian answered.

"The boat isn't going to be around all day."

"Do you want to try?" Ellian asked over his shoulder.

"I'm not touching that. Look how dirty it is."

"That's enough you two," Arnor interrupted.

After several minutes, with an exhalation of accomplishment, Ellian relaxed and handed the lock behind him to Jaron. He pushed. The hinges at the top creaked in protest and the gate swung up above his head. He strained under the weight. "Keras get the other side," he said through his teeth.

Keras squeezed in close to Ellian and pushed up on the grate. It was light as a feather. Ellian let go, smiling at Keras as he walked into the surf.

Arnor looked up at the sun and grumbled as he got his bearings. The sewer did not exit near the pier. They had to walk north in the water above the breaking surf for just under a mile before they could see even the sails of ships. They made the most of the walk, sloshing their boots in the light surf to wash away the grime, though they could still smell the stench for hours after. Keras kept looking at her hands and rubbed sand in with the salt water to clean them as she walked.

Westmost was the halfway point along the western edge of the landmass. Even locked between high mountains in the east and the sea on the west, it had become a major trading center. Ships from the north and south would trade their goods and return home laden with commodities from the other end of the continent. Ships also came across the sea, from Erlassen, to trade.

The pier was the heart of Westmost's bustling economy. The dock was thirty feet wide, and was long enough to allow four ships to be loaded at once. On their shoulders, men carried small barrels and some pushed wheelbarrows filled with provender toward the ships tied to the long pier. Nearly everything transported by the ships was stored within barrels. Due to their shape, they were easy to carry, roll, and stack within the hull of the vessels.

Shacks and carts lined the center of the pier. Fruit of every kind imaginable was for sale and some sailors were haggling over a price—with a young girl of about ten—for a basket of oranges. She was getting the better of them. Games of chance were running next to the fruit stands and a young man shouted loudly as he lost, pushing his opponent in anger before being set upon by others around the game.

The four cloaked figures received scant attention as they approached the hustle and hum of the pier. Wet from the waist down, they climbed the ladder and arranged their gear in a pile near the edge.

Perfumed and sharply dressed prostitutes, both male and female, flirted with the passing sailors, convincing many to part with some of their wages in return for some time well spent behind closed doors. The prostitutes glanced at the four newcomers. "No money there. Don't waste your time," one tall and beautiful woman in blue muttered to her girlfriend.

"Well, not today Charla, but next time, I promise," Arnor said and winked at them as they passed, catching a wide smile from the woman in blue. Ellian watched as they walked away and received a swat from Keras.

After a quick bite of the morning's bacon from inside his pouch, and a swig from a flask he produced out of a pocket, Arnor approached a man who was scribbling on a roll of paper with a sharp piece of coal, mumbling to himself. As Arnor started to speak, the man lifted his hand to ward off conversation. Finishing his tally, he turned his attention to Arnor and the negotiations began.

A few moments later, Arnor stormed away and returned to the waiting trio. "I should push him off the pier. The bastard raised the fee. Do you have any money?" he asked them. The four pooled their coins and counted, careful not to let any fall into the spaces between the boards of the dock. Arnor gathered the money and stood up. "Yes, this might do it."

Arnor approached the man again and, after a squabble, motioned them forward toward a ship. He grumbled as he led the way. "First-mate of the Aquilo, bet he doesn't live to make captain."

Chapter 3   Aquilo

Upon boarding the Aquilo, the passengers received a quick tour. Their cabin was two decks below and at the back of the ship. It was small but had two hard bunks, so called because they were rooted to the floor, with enough room for two to sleep above in hammocks. As the Aquilo rarely took passengers, the usual inhabitants of this particular room, the lower officers, would have to bunk with the rest of the crew near the forward part of this deck.

To Arnor's approval, the cabin had a door and a window. The door would provide the privacy needed to discuss their plans and travel routes, while the window would provide fresh air as well as an uncomfortable but convenient perch from which Arnor could dispose of his breakfast. He knew that it would come eventually. It happened every time he set foot on a boat. He did not like the sea.

One level above the hammocks of the crew was the long-weapon deck. Three ballista weapons consisting of weights, ropes, and tension planks sat spaced out along the front three quarters of each side of the ship. Iron balls and tools were stacked over the ship's keel behind the firing stations.

A crewmember, dressed in a blue shirt and baggy pants that used to be white, bragged as he noticed the visitors. "Ever seen one of these?" he asked. He cranked down a tension bar attached to the front of the weapon. "Me, Dimmie, and Virgil, over there," he pointed to a short boy piling shot, "can set up a hurler in under two minutes."

"So how does it work?" Keras asked.

"Well, you know, you have to be strong." The braggart flexed his bicep for her. Keras faced Ellian and rolled her eyes so only he could see.

"Watch it there, Bines," said Virgil. "Strong you ain't."

Bines answered Virgil with an obscene hand gesture. "We aim the ballista by hand. Look here," Bines moved to the back of the weapon. "The back here slides in this groove carved into the floor.

22

The front don't move but to pivot on that pin." He pointed to a pole that stretched from floor to ceiling. "We can cover an arc of twenty-nine degrees." Bines spun an x-shaped handle on top of a large screw at the back of the weapon. "We spin this to adjust the range."

"Ever been in a battle?" Jaron asked.

"Three skirmishes, and I hope it never happens again. Hurlin' is fun. Getting hurled at, ain't."

In addition to the in-place weaponry aboard, the Aquilo stationed men at the top of the three masts, both as lookouts and bowmen. Even the common members of the crew were armed. Every crewmember carried a long knife and kept an axe or a long curved sword readily available.

How often do these ships need to defend themselves? Jaron wondered. He really had no idea. The library had contained many books on seamanship and the economics of sea trade, but he had found these boring and long-winded. The stories from the sailors that ventured into the city from the dock were much more interesting. Sailors were a suspicious group and tales of great beasts rising from the deep to drag ships down were common. Pirates were, apparently, everywhere.

Jaron found it hard to believe that this could be a mere cargo ship. It looked plain to him that this vessel could survive a daunting battle against even the most fierce of foes. Perhaps the reason for such need for armament was that the Aquilo was, more often than not, a smuggler's ship. Maybe, this was the pirate ship. Whatever the scenario, the Aquilo would offer a strong defense.

The bottom deck of the ship held the cargo storage areas and kitchen. Food and beverage for the entire crew were stored in the rooms behind the cooking area. The stoves rocked with the ship, hanging in chains from the ceiling. As hot as they were, if they were to sit on the wooden floor, they could possibly set the ship ablaze. The cook, Sevaro, was a thin, short man with long silver hair tied behind him in a ponytail. He talked with anyone who came into the kitchens. Ellian had already begun to call him 'the long-talker.' He continued to talk even when it was apparent no one was listening to him. When visiting the kitchen, some men did not even extend a greeting for fear that they would be entwined in a lengthy discussion on the history of bread making or a twelve-point lecture on the intricacies of brewing beer, though, many others prompted the latter discussion in the hopes of scoring a cup.

Jaron found it odd that there was no brig aboard. He had read some tales of piracy and adventure, and he half-expected to see an area with two or three cells down in the bowels of the vessel. Apparently, in the event of a battle, the crew of the Aquilo did not take on prisoners or even survivors.

Discipline was harsh aboard the Aquilo. Most punishments consisted of a simple lashing, though the recipient probably would not consider it 'simple.' More serious crimes usually meant a sentence of death. Stealing or murder would earn the offender a rope around the neck. If the crime was especially heinous, the captain might order someone dragged. Sharks sometimes follow ships, due to the trash and excrement thrown overboard. Because of this, the crew came to call the dragging of a shipmate 'fishing.'

"The sea is hard. The Captain must be harder," had been Arnor's commentary on the subject.

Keras and Ellian lent their backs to the work necessary to run the ship. They followed the orders of the second mate, a large and leathery man called Kampson, pulling lines and hoisting sails. Jaron stood on the aft-deck, breathing in the sea air, and trying to keep out of the way as the Aquilo left port. Arnor was leaning on the rail. He didn't look well. His skin had a green pallor.

Seagulls called as they flew circles near the ship. Always present at seaports, seagulls were ever on the prowl for an easy meal, and could steal the bread straight from the hand.

As the sun set on their first day at sea, Keras, Jaron, and Ellian climbed down the steep ladder-stair to join Arnor in the private cabin. They could hear the crewmen snoring in hammocks that hung on pegs in the forward part of this deck.

The cabin door was slightly ajar and a cold salty breeze

brought the faint but familiar smell of vomit out to meet them as they approached. Arnor looked pale. He had refused to come away from the window to lie in a bed. Instead, he curled himself against the wall just beneath the sill, breathing in the open air. A brown ceramic jug of water sat near his hip and he caressed it. Every now and then, he would cough and take a small sip from the jug. He would not talk, merely grunting away any attempts to help him until the three resigned to leave him where he was.

Jaron removed his boots, stood on the bed, and gingerly settled himself into a hammock, pulling a thick wool blanket tight around his arms and chest. Ellian took the bunk underneath him while Keras climbed into the other hammock, leaving the other hard bunk for Arnor, should he feel well enough to leave his cozy spot on the floor next to the window.

Jaron lay awake for a long while thinking about his friends sleeping next to him, and he felt a sudden sting of doubt. *Are they my friends?* They were Royal Guards of the Kingdom of Melanthios, personal bodyguards to King Jaronthel Keltenon, if that was, in fact, his name. Had they ever been just his friends? Since age eleven or twelve they had been keepers of the Royal Secret.

Jaron had heard of the Royal Secret. He was, after all, a scholar, if only a mere apprentice at present. Up until these recent events, however, he had considered the existence of a Royal Secret to be only a dim-witted conspiracy theory. The textbooks alluded to it and always dismissed it as a minor fantasy to answer some random anomalies buried in the government's storyline.

Jaron had wondered where each of them went for months at a time every year. Ellian had told him that he left every fall to bring in the harvest of his family's farm, south of Starkwall. In the spring, Keras visited her uncle in Red Helm. *Useful,* thought Jaron, since Red Helm was their immediate destination. Only this evening did they confess that they both had lied. Each time one of them had left, it had been to attend training in the Kingdom stronghold of Holderness, at the garrison stationed there. Jaron, in a moment of clarity, realized that Keras and Ellian never left on their personal journeys at the same time as one another. One of them had never been far from his side since his induction as an apprentice to the library.

He didn't blame them for lying to him. Both were bound by some oath to follow orders, to defend him to the death if need be. Three years ago, Ellian had been reprimanded, though this was unknown to Jaron at the time, for not interfering when Jaron mouthed off to a bully in the market. The bully won himself a bloody lip. Jaron received a bloody nose and a black eye. Ellian received four weeks of stable duty when he reported for training that fall. But out of it, Jaron had learned a lesson, when to keep his mouth shut, and even more, how to take a stand. The cold breeze cleared the air from the room as they slept. Next morning, the three awoke to find Arnor, looking pale, draped across his bunk and snoring loudly.

Throughout the following week, when deck-duties did not keep Keras and Ellian entertained, they would teach Jaron the proper use of a sword. These lessons, taught with wide sticks instead of swords for obvious reasons, often left Jaron with bruises, scratches, sore hands, and bleeding fingers. More than one fingernail had turned a painful black.

"Try not to block it with your hand!" exclaimed Keras after having given Jaron a nasty crack across the knuckles.

"That's sound advice," said Jaron as he stuck an injured knuckle into his mouth.

"Swing across and parry with the tip pointed down so that you're in a position to attack as you come back," Keras said.

It seemed each lesson left more bruises than the last. By the fourth day of lessons, Jaron could—in an effort to avoid being stung—execute an effective series of parries, though his cuts and thrusts were slow and obvious.

"The strongest man does not always win the fight." Keras parried Jaron's slashes as she said this. "Often, duels end with the smaller of the two cleaning the blood from her blade," she said with a wink. "It is speed that wins fights. Decisions have to be made and anticipated. Quick hands and a quicker mind." With each reference to the word 'quick', Keras's wooden sword touched a vital killing spot upon Jaron, but only just.

Ellian and Keras were both well experienced with a wide variety of weapons. They often picked up items from the deck with which to spar. The crew sometimes neglected their duties to watch, placing wagers amongst themselves as to which one would come off the worse. It was often a comical selection of items. Ellian would choose a bucket and Keras a mop. Ellian would choose a net and Keras a belt. One time, Keras beat Ellian's sword using only a short rope with knots tied into the ends. Ellian suffered the jeers of the crew for hours afterward.

When not defending himself from the stings of Keras's wooden practice sword, Jaron found himself asking questions of his companions. "Why do you do it?" Seeing the look of confusion on Ellian's face, he continued. "You can't have been more than eleven when I met you and yet you were a guard even then?" Ellian nodded and threw the remains of the apple he had finished into the water. "So, why?" Jaron asked.

"My father," he paused, "I was eight when he died. I wanted to follow him, to be like him. I still remember when he would come home." Ellian looked out to the sea. "My father was a soldier. He was the one who first trained me. I was only a boy, and I couldn't even lift a sword. He taught me how to use my mind and my hands. After he died, they sent me to a special school run by dwarves where I studied for three more years until I came to the library. One of my instructors was my uncle. Another was my father's friend, Harnan." Ellian leaned on the railing, looking down at the water.

"How did he die?" Jaron asked. He had only been thinking about how this news had changed his own life. The news of Ellian's lost father opened his eyes to the sacrifices that hundreds must have made so that he could even exist.

"My father was the personal body guard to your father,

Lorenistal Keltenon. An assassin, who was trying to kill your father, killed him instead." Ellian straightened and turned away from the railing. "He guarded your father. And so I guard you to honor him." He unstopped his water bottle and took a small sip.

Keras let out a nervous chuckle. "That's a good reason. I didn't know that."

"What about you, Keras?" Jaron asked.

"My family aren't warriors. We're scholars." She started absentmindedly tapping the wooden sword on the deck. "I did it for a bunch of reasons. See, when I read one of the letters... Oh, sorry. Yeah, I read one of the letters that your father had sent with you to the library. So I, kind of, found out by accident, and well, once I knew, my father swore me to secrecy. Do you know what they've done to people who can't keep their mouth shut? He made me read about it. Not pleasant. Anyway, it was then that I decided that if I had to keep this secret close, I might as well be doing something about it. My father reads history books. Maybe, someday, my name will be in one of them. I just felt like I had to be a part of it. I knew I'd never be much of a scholar like my father, and I wanted to do something important... you know, to make him proud." She frowned, "I didn't figure on how much work it would actually be, though." She laughed. "You're a bit of a jerk."

Ellian shot the water he was drinking out of his nose in a sudden outburst of laughter, causing both Keras and Jaron to double over until they were crying and gasping for breath.

In between sword-practice, deck-duties, and spouting water out of the nose, Ellian and Jaron discussed how, without money, they were going to make the journey to Starkwall. Arnor had spent everything they had brought to procure passage to Red Helm, less than half the distance they needed to travel. When they arrived in Red Helm, there would be no funds to continue. Maybe Keras really did have an uncle upon whom they could impose. Arnor must have some sort of plan, but he had kept to himself for most of the journey, though he was no longer seasick.

One night, Arnor had taken part in a terribly lengthy discussion with Sevaro, 'the long talker.' While Arnor emptied a bottle of gold colored spirits, Sevaro had rambled on for an hour about mind control wizards attacking the free will of unwary travelers and prisoners. Up and down Sevaro paced, hands waving wildly in the air, spatula pointing to make his points as he spouted on about one conspiracy after the other, 'The Mad General' of the cellar, dead men walking around, or the secret dragon's den and its unclaimed riches. Arnor half-listened, half-laughed. Always entertaining, good information can sometimes be obtained from the ramblings of a wild, old, and well-traveled man. This did not appear to be one of those nights.

Arnor stumbled into the cabin after his three companions had taken their bunks, holding in his hand a small round bottle. As he closed the door with his elbow, he fished around inside his pockets. Unable to produce a cork from any of them, he settled for taking a long pull of the amber liquid rolling around within the clear glass. He squinted above him to Jaron, as if there were something he must know, regardless of his current condition. He reached up to wake the youth and, in doing so, he noticed the cork clutched within his fist. Lest he once again forget the whereabouts of the pesky thing, he pushed it into the neck of the bottle.

Seeing for the first time that the other occupants of the cabin were awake, and probably even sober, he asked his question. "What have you read of history, boy?"

"I've had lessons with Master Ceryss," Jaron answered.

"Then tell me some of what you know. Talk about the three founding nations if you know anything."

Jaron searched his memories and finally recalled. "There were three nations originally, the Dwarven underground realm of DaenDor, the High-Elven mountain kingdom of Taurminya, and one Human Kingdom, Melanthios."

"What do you know of Melanthios?" Arnor asked, bending down to take off his boots and striking his forehead on the bunk.

"What is there to say? It's the Human kingdom under King Gurrand."

"But it wasn't always so. Do you know the history of the war of 234?" Arnor rubbed his head, knocking his hat to the floor.

Jaron was silent a moment, pulling information from his daily hours of study back at the library. Looking away from Arnor, he shifted his gaze to the painted ceiling so as not to be distracted from his thoughts and began to tell the tale. "In the year 5706, the Human king of Melanthios, Hernan II, ruled from a city that served as the major pass through the mountains. It separated the northern and southern lands. Today, we call this city Temerrac. Hernan was blessed with two sons, each born to a different woman, concubines of the king, who had no wife. Loving his sons equally and having no other heirs, he divided his kingdom in half, naming one Eros and the other Elek, after his sons. This was also when he reset the year counter to observe the date of the split kingdoms."

"Wow," exclaimed Ellian, "you sound like you're reading from a book."

"Master Ceryss made me read the history out loud to the new apprentices. Had you been paying attention, you might already know some of this."

"Go on," said Arnor as he climbed into his bunk underneath Keras's hammock, still cradling the near empty bottle.

"The brother kings were fast friends and ruled the two kingdoms as one from Temerrac, but as their families lived on, generation after generation, the two kingdoms divided. There was peace between them for the first few successors. In 234, war broke out. The Southern kingdom, Elek, under the rule of King Deras, wanted to unite the land by negotiating a joint throne through a marriage of heirs. The Northern king, Mavius, had other ideas and poisoned King Deras. Mavius claimed lordship over Elek, announcing that a treaty had been signed by King Deras, who was now deceased.

"Some of the Southern knights accepted his lordship, but

others did not. War lasted for twenty years, with DaenDor and Taurminya coming to the aid of Northern Eros, for they believed the lie about the treaty. This was a chance to unite the Humans into a single realm again. They did not know of the treachery of Mavius. In the end, after two decades of war, the Human kingdom of Melanthios was finally united as the long dead Deras had wished. However, Mavius enforced horrible rules upon the Southern lands, further embittering them to their new oppressor. Several assassination attempts were made against him, but none were successful."

"Guy sounds like a real catch," said Keras, receiving a swat from Arnor lying in the hard bunk under her hammock.

"Mavius studied the dark arts, extending his life well beyond what is natural. After more than one hundred years of tyrannical rule, several Southern knights and lords formed an alliance against him. They brought their grievances against Mavius to DaenDor, as well as the other underground Dwarven cities, and to the Elven Kingdom of Taurminya, seeking alliances. The Elven Kingdom refused to help them, but the Dwarven king in DaenDor, having finally learned of the poisoning of King Deras, agreed to give them aid. The dwarves began forging weapons and smuggling them to the Southern knights.

"Unknown to the dwarves of DaenDor, or even the knights, Mavius's High Priest had made contact to the spirit world to gain information on the insurgents in his midst. It has been said that Mavius made contact with a demon. This demon's name was..." Jaron closed his eyes trying to remember.

"Are we discussing fairy tales now?" Keras interrupted.

"And what happened to these knights?" Arnor prodded Jaron while poking Keras in the ribs.

"The Southern knights drew up their armies and lay siege to the capitol city. During the attack, a devastating quake struck. This quake caused the valley to sink, dragging down nearly all combatants. The Southern knights lost most of their number but all of Mavius's armies and knights died in the quake with King Mavius. The castle and the surrounding towns and farmland were laid so low that water eventually swamped the area and it is now called The Lake of the Damned.

"Mavius's heirs eventually died out and a new king was chosen. Without contest, a general of the Southern knights became king and peace eventually returned to Melanthios. Trade opened up between the Human, Dwarven, and even Elven kingdoms. Travel between them was encouraged and the roads were made safe again from brigands. Law returned to the land." As he said this, Jaron heard the snores from Arnor's bunk.

Pondering why Arnor might ask all of these questions only to pass out, Jaron, in his hammock, closed his eyes and he too fell asleep.

Chapter 4   Red Helm

The call of the sailor in the high masts echoed over the ship. "Land! Red Helm on the horizon!"

All eyes turned east where the morning sun turned the clouds into a rolling yellow and red above the city of Red Helm. At first glance, it was as if the city itself altered the color of the clouds, for the tiled rooftops were made of the red clay native to the surrounding hills. The most common buildings were stone houses, two or three stories high, but fifteen or twenty towers stretched up above the general low-lying structures. Jaron gaped at the height of the towers and thought, *How far can those windows look out over the bordering hills onto the forests and plains?* He had read that the affluent families of Red Helm lived like kings. It appeared to be true.

The port of Red Helm was a wealthier community than Westmost. The mountains and dangerous paths that segregated the Westmost peninsula from the rest of the continent made land travel difficult in good weather, and treacherous in adverse conditions. This resulted in Westmost holding the economic strength of only a midway trading station. Red Helm, on the other hand, had access to the trade roads and inner lands and no major range along its edge. That made Red Helm, even with its shallow port, a key hub with travel to and from the port easier for merchants from several directions.

The wide dock, jutting out from the city's shore, had two ships tied along its sides with room for one more. The Aquilo, however, did not dock in Red Helm, its draft not being shallow enough. A longboat with four sailors at the oars brought the passengers and all of their gear to the docks, where after quickly unloading, the longboat made its way back toward the waiting ship before the dock master could levy a landing fee. The passengers, blending in with the crowd of sailors from the other vessels, shouldered their burdens and made their way down toward the low lying shops, taverns, and shipping houses that surrounded the port.

The air smelled of the open market. Spices, fish, fruits, oils, and perfumes filled the nostrils as merchants, each of them eager to make a sale, waved their goods with raised arms. Arnor led them to a quiet alley behind a butcher shop called Fawltey's and down some rough stone stairs to a door. Raising his left hand, he rapped on the door once. He then waited a few moments and rapped again. This went on for several minutes, knock, wait, knock, and wait. Finally, a short elderly man wearing a blood spattered green apron yanked open the door. From tallest to shortest, his gaze fell over the travelers and his grimace of annoyance became a smile in recognition of an old friend. He beckoned them inside. The old man waved his hands in the air and, stripping off the bloody apron, hugged Arnor.

The travelers followed him through a door and down a narrow hallway. The elderly man moved a table and chairs and opened a hidden trap door in the floor. A rusted metal ladder descended into darkness. Arnor started down the ladder grasping the old man's withered hand as he passed. Ellian quickly followed, but Jaron heard Keras mutter under her breath, "Not another stinking tunnel..." Jaron had to agree with her. He didn't want to enter another sewer. There had to be a better way to travel unnoticed. They looked down into the hole, leaning over it, smelling the air. Not happy about the situation, but having no other alternative, Jaron and Keras climbed down behind the others.

To their surprise and great relief, the ladder led not to a sewer but to a tunnel approximately thirty inches wide and eight to ten feet tall. This tunnel traveled, more or less, in one direction that brought them inland away from the sea. No one carried a candle, a torch, or even a lantern. The walls along the corridor gave off a greenish glow, enabling the group to see enough to squeeze through with their loaded packs.

Ellian reached out his fingers as his eyes adjusted to the dim illumination and brushed the wall. They came back glowing with the cool green light. "Lichen," he said. "It grows well here in the damp, though I doubt it would grow here naturally." He looked to Arnor,

"An old Dwarven trick?"

"You didn't think we could see in the dark, did you? Better than you, yes, but we do need some light, after all."

They came to another ladder, and next to the ladder, there hung a rope. Arnor gave a long pull on the rope and waited. He then pulled at it again and waited again. This went on for several minutes. Pull. Wait. Pull. Wait. Finally, a light showered down from above as another trap door was opened. A shadow of a head appeared in the opening. "Arnie! Hello, you old cotch! Is that a new hat? You've been gone long enough this time. I see you've brought some friends with you. Get up here and we'll open a bottle!" The head disappeared and the dwarf started to climb the ladder toward the light.

"I hate that nickname. C'mon," Arnor grunted over his shoulder.

* * * * *

Sitting in the common room of Edmund Samoss, the travelers were comfortable, having had the opportunity to eat and bathe. Their amiable host had ushered them off to his team of servants who made sure to provide all that they needed.

After bathing—in hot water no less—each of them found a set of new clothes to wear. It was clear that their host, as thin as he was, could not have worn any of them. Perhaps he knew of their imminent arrival, or perhaps he was just wealthy enough to have a few closets full of clothes he would never wear. Even Arnor had an outfit that fit him perfectly, as if tailored especially for him. The white shirt had ruffles at the sleeves, a wide collar, and a chest pocket.

"So much wealth," Keras said as she looked down, touching the dress Edmund's servants had provided. Ellian, Arnor, and Jaron had met her on the way to the sitting room. Jaron's breath caught in his chest when he saw her. Keras was beautiful. Her hair was tied up around the back of her head, showing off her long and slender neck.

"Edmund is a cloth merchant," Ellian said to her. Poking Jaron, he whispered, "Don't stare."

Edmund sat, rolling a dark red wine around within his crystal goblet, listening to Arnor finish the tale of their escape from Westmost. He leaned forward in his seat setting down his drink. "Have you sent word ahead to Starkwall?" Arnor grunted an affirmative. "The council will want to confirm his status. How long ago did Lorenistal die?"

Jaron quietly corrected him, "He might not be dead."

"Weeks ago, eight or nine," Arnor answered, "judging by the date of the letter. Jaron, do you have it handy?" Jaron rose from his chair, patted his pockets, and pulled out the page.

Edmund took the paper from Jaron and opened it under the oil lamp, examining the brown wax seal before reading it. "There isn't much information here. Where was it sent from?"

"The messenger that delivered it to Ceryss said that he received it in Nalore from another messenger. Where that messenger came from, I don't know. The last I knew of Loren's location he was in Nalore."

"You know the city of Valcella is making a move against Gurrand's holdings in the south?" Edmund asked.

Armor nodded, answering, "Their General Shale is pushing his weight around again."

"I think they are going to make a move against the Temerrac pass."

"I thought Valcella didn't have the manpower to take Temerrac," Arnor said, sipping from his glass.

"I think he has found them," said Edmund. "Most of the other Human cities in the south have fallen to him."

Ellian chimed in, "But, even that shouldn't be enough for an invasion of the North. We still outnumber his forces three to one."

"Well, something roused the Markal goblins and shook them out of their holes. Goblins have been filtering north through the lands. Are they fleeing war in the south? No one knows yet. Something big is happening."

"That's what Yaru was talking about, too," Jaron said.

"Has anyone heard if King Gurrand has mobilized his

knights?" Ellian asked. "Now that the coronation is over, he should be moving men to Temerrac. It's a long way from Brethiliost. The march will take months, longer if they are held up anywhere."

"Why did Gurrand make Brethiliost his capitol city? What a stupid and vain decision," said Jaron. "His hometown, sure, but Holderness is the central city. That should have stayed the capitol as his father had it."

"The new king wants a navy and Holderness doesn't have a seaport," Ellian countered.

"Starkwall then," Jaron suggested.

"There's no seaport there either," said Ellian.

"There's the Ellis Gorge in Starkwall," Jaron argued.

"And that water is only passable for small boats," said Ellian.

"Red Helm, then," said Jaron.

"Oh, no, not my city," said Edmund, laughing. "We don't want any kings here. A king's court is a dangerous place."

"I was thinking about the goblins. Strange," muttered Keras, sipping from her wine glass. "Here in the North the humans are peaceful and the goblins are quick to fight, but in the South the goblins are more peaceful and the humans are violent." She was not used to the alcohol and Arnor took the glass from her hand.

"Is this your third glass?" he asked. She nodded, smiling. Turning to Jaron, Arnor asked, "How much have you had, Jaron? Oh, I think that's enough." He took Jaron's glass as well.

"So will you stay with me for the week?" Edmund asked.

"No, we are not going to trouble you for long, Edmund. We are already a month behind schedule. Jaron had an unfortunate run-in with a shade."

"He survived a shade?" asked Edmund, looking at Jaron with new respect.

"Yes," Arnor answered. "I don't really know why, but I'm going to say it was luck, or the alcohol. In any case, we need to move on. Can you provide horses and gear to be on the road by tomorrow morning?"

"Yes. I might even be able to send an armed patrol with you."

"While I appreciate the gesture, I have to refuse. Better to go unnoticed if we can. What good would armed men be against a shade?"

Edmund laughed. "Well, if you have this boy," he gestured to Jaron, "some of them might live." Arnor laughed with him, but Jaron felt uncomfortable at the jest. After the last attack, he had spent a whole month in one room without any memory of it.

* * * * *

The night passed in comfort. Ellian and Arnor studied maps together trying to choose the best route to Starkwall. Where were the most likely places to make camp during the journey?

Keras spent her time laughing with a handsome servant boy that had helped her earlier with her dress. They soon made their way to the roof where, as the servant boy had suggested hopefully, the view of the stars had no match.

Jaron, not quite as brave as Keras, and much less brave than the servant boy, found Edmund's personal library. A prosperous man, Edmund had a great many books. Set on the top shelf was a book bound in green painted leather. Inside, the lines were written with care and proficiency. Jaron marveled at the quality. He had seen many books but this one was valuable beyond measure. In the pages, along the border, a scribbled passage grabbed Jaron's attention.

It is said, the power of the web spun was so great that even without the oath, some involved in the war with the oldest still walk the land, unable to die, either still under the influence of the Dark King, or hiding in dark holes, praying for forgiveness of their sins.

"Who would deface such a masterpiece?" Jaron said to himself in disgust as he placed the book back on the shelf.

* * * * *

"Easy there, Mindy," Arnor said to the pony as he led her

from her stall. Arnor had set up each of the ponies provided by Edmund to carry as much gear and food as might be needed for a trip of two weeks. While helping pack the ponies, Jaron asked, "That shade, it had me in Westmost. Why didn't it kill me then?"

"I haven't figured that one out yet." Arnor stopped working and looked Jaron straight in the eye. "You have heard of the Royal Secret—I know you have—a myth, a legend, a fairy tale? No. You are that secret." Arnor stopped filling his saddlebag, climbed down and sat on the stool he had been standing on. He reached into a pocket and pulling out a silver flask, took a long pull of whatever relief was inside. "Study has its merits, but there is still much you don't know. Books don't always tell the truth." Taking a deep breath, he continued. "Centuries ago, a king, Mavius, reunited the kingdom sundered in good faith by his own ancestor. Was it possible to do this through political genius, social strategy, or maybe even just plain old treachery? It might have been. The wheels of truce were rolling. Nevertheless, it might have taken a decade, even a century to consolidate power under a single king, and if that were to happen, he would not be that king. Lust for more power drove him. In his impatience, Mavius made a pact with a demon. The reunification had been a dream of his for many years and he studied the dark arts to attain it." Arnor rose again and resumed filling his saddlebag.

"You mentioned this demon in your history lesson a few nights ago, but only in passing. The extent of this demon's influence goes beyond what is available in your books. Mavius used the powers of the underworld to reunite the severed kingdoms of Melanthios. Spies, warriors, assassins, all came in the form of a cold wind to Mavius's enemies. That is how King Deras died, along with his heirs, not poison as you said the other night, though that in itself is as cowardly.

"After twenty-two years, a bitter peace returned to the Human race. Agreements were signed making Mavius king of New Melanthios, and all appeared to fall in line as relative prosperity crept throughout the once divided kingdom.

"Ten more years passed, twenty, eighty, but the king did not age, and the debt to the demon had not been paid. The demon reappeared, and in return for services provided, demanded that the newly reunited Human kingdom wage war to exterminate the elves." Arnor took another drink, coughing.

"So persuasive was Mavius using the dark powers that many joined him in this war against Taurminya: Goblins, Trolls, and, I'm ashamed to say, Dwarves.

"The Goblins were the first to turn on him, followed by the Dwarves, at least the dwarves above ground. Even the Trolls wandered away, climbing back into the great cracks and caverns. The Elves of Taurminya were strong. Mavius was forced to concede defeat and surrendered to the elves, giving up a large portion of his territory to buy his peace.

"On the Aquilo, you spoke of the quake that destroyed Mavius. It was no mere quake. When the king was unable to deliver the payment, the demon dragged him into the under-realm. Any who swore an oath to Mavius, servants, underlings, even his knights, were dragged down with him, held in the strands of the web the demon had spun around their oaths."

Arnor took another pull off the flask. "Edmund wanted to send soldiers with us, Bah! Do you think any soldier could stand up against a shadow? Those are only the lowly agents of the enemy. Since that day, the shadows have pursued your family."

"So, why is Mavius after me?"

"Are you that thick, boy? I thought they taught you better than that. You're his heir! Because of him, something from the dark place has been trying to snuff out all of you. We are only guessing why, but it is so."

Arnor sat down again, and took yet another long swallow from the flask. His eyes clenched shut, and he shook his head before continuing. "Mavius's son was crowned and days later found cold, with no visible reason for his death. His grandson was crowned, and one month later, he too was dead. Sons, uncles, cousins, again and again, one after another, no longer being crowned, falling to the sickness, or so it was thought. With this epidemic on the royals, no one wanted the throne. They felt it was cursed. The deaths continued.

"The situation was studied. They didn't know why your ancestors were dying, but they knew it wasn't disease. Necromancers captured a shadow. All it said, repeatedly, was 'Kill the heirs! Kill the heirs!' So, your ancestors were concealed. And undiscovered, the cold death passed them over. A new king was chosen from among the surviving generals of the Southern knights. He decreed that your family was to be hidden for its own protection. You became the secret. He formed a council to keep track of the family. He assigned guards. Your line is so far removed that in any normal world, it is inconceivable you should ever be king. Yet, here you are, heir to the throne."

Arnor hopped off the stool. He collected a few things and seeing that Jaron too had finished his work, started up the stairs to the main house, speaking over his shoulder as the boy followed.

"These necromancers are members of the council. They will attempt to hide your soul. It should confuse those looking for you."

"I don't think I like the sound of that. Why now? Why didn't they just do it when I was born?"

Arnor turned back and continued his climb. "You need to be the rightful king for the spell to work. I don't understand necromancy, something about the finger of the gods, or what have you, but that is why we fly to Starkwall. You need all the protection you can get."

Chapter 5 Long Road

Before dawn broke the horizon, the gates of Red Helm opened and four travelers rode out on ponies. No one stood inside the walls to wave goodbye and the riders did not look back. The stars of night faded away as they rode through the outlying communities and villages.

It was early May. Frost crusted the long yellow grass on either side of the road. As the sun rose over the mountains on their right, they could see the white blanket stretching over the fields.

Keras pulled her cloak closer about her neck and muttered under her breath. "We couldn't wait for eggs?" She bit off a piece of dried meat and chewed it, frowning.

"Maybe that boy from the roof should have got up early and made you something to eat," Ellian responded from behind her.

She turned around to look at Ellian. "What's that supposed to mean?"

"Nothing, I guess," Ellian said.

Keras faced front again and only a moment later turned back to Ellian. "If you were so upset about it, maybe you should have asked me first."

"Asked you what?"

Keras turned back to face front and nudged her pony forward until she was riding next to Arnor. They rode on in silence, the stride of the ponies rocking them gently, left to right, right to left, in their saddles.

The days grew warmer as they crossed the plain of Gurra, camping each night with laughter and stories. Keras and Ellian soon forgot whatever disagreement they appeared to be having, or at least they had forgiven each other. Keras had even offered to sit through the first watch with Ellian. By the end of the fifth day, they had reached the low-lying mountains of Melaral and set a camp at the base.

Though Arnor had claimed the duty, he was an excellent

cook; Keras announced she would prepare the meal that night. All day she had been hopping off her pony to cut herbs and pull roots. That afternoon, she killed three rabbits, using the bow gifted to her by Edmund. "Three should be enough, right?" she asked. Then, remembering how Arnor had eaten the day they left Westmost, she headed out to kill two more. As the others set up camp, she started a fire and prepared a coal bed to stew potatoes and roast the rabbits. All were surprised at their companion's culinary endeavor, and Keras beamed as she watched the others enjoy their meal. Jaron added cooking to the list of Keras's skills.

As they ate the most satisfying meal of this leg of their adventure, a point Arnor would argue against, conversation moved again to the possible reasons for the Markal goblins traveling so far north of the Fortunal Mountains. Markal goblins were, for the most part, timid and gentle. They were so unlike their Nargesh cousins that lived on the northern side of the Fortunal Mountains.

Humans and Nargesh goblins had fought skirmishes, battles, and wars against each other of course, but so had Dwarves and Elves, Elves and Humans, and Humans and Dwarves. It was a warlike continent, but more so the further south you went.

The morning came in warm and inviting, leaving behind the frost of the previous mornings. The path up the mountain was clear and wound back and forth across the face of a bluff as it climbed toward the summit. Leaves, wet from the morning dew, littered the path as green shoots of new plants broke through the layer of decay to reach for the spring sunshine.

Jaron expected that they would climb clear to the top of the mountain and anticipated the unobstructed view he would have of the landscape in front of them. It was not to be so. The trail crossed over to the other side of the mountain far below the peak, obscuring the view with heavy tree cover. He had read so many books describing the glorious sight from atop a mountain. He longed to discover if the beauty equaled the words on those pages. Now, finally here, he couldn't see anything.

As they traveled the northern side of the mountains of Melaral and the road before them wound downhill, they dismounted their ponies. Arnor did not agree.

"Why did we bring ponies if we aren't going to ride them?" he asked.

"Did you want to carry all the gear?" Ellian responded. "If an animal is injured carrying us down the hill you'll have to." Ellian insisted that the party lead the ponies through the tricky terrain. "An injured beast is of use to no one, least of all a rider," he said.

The path followed the line of a seasonal stream. Shrubs and grass gave way to sand, as if a giant plow had gashed the soil beneath their feet. The bones of fallen trees lay across the path. Roots lay painfully exposed in the sand and rock, tripping feet and grasping like fingers at the legs of the travelers.

Keras spied something white reaching up from the sand. Clearly, the trail held more than roots. This, she subjected, was a bone of some animal killed recently by a predator, but as she bent low for further inspection she could see that this was from no animal. There were orange rings of metal buried in the dust. Chain mail, rusted and broken, sheathed the grisly find.

Brushing away the dirt revealed a chipped and broken sword still clasped within the fingers of a warrior long dead. Only the hands were visible, and judging by the position of the dead warrior, Keras had been standing on the face. A chill ran up her neck, and she spoke a quiet apology to the soldier lying in rest.

Further along the trail lay a skeleton, rib cage wholly exposed. Tattered, the colors of his crimson cloak peeked out from the ground. The hillside revealed broken and crumbling coffins, but not many. Most of the men who had died here could not have afforded the luxury of a pine or oak box for burial. The custom was to wrap them in linen and bury them with weapons in hand. Grave robbers may steal a weapon laid on or next to a corpse, but the superstitious would not attempt to pry loose the fingers.

The whole area lay bare, exposed by the spring thaws coming

down from the nearby mountains and washing away the topsoil. Those without coffins had their bones strewn about the hill with bits of armor and cloth. The occasional grin of a skull, bleached by the light of day, stared past the travelers, transfixed by something beyond the painful world it had left behind. Ellian fell through the lid of a coffin that spanned the way. His silent apology for that misstep showed in the expression on his face as he extricated himself from the broken wood.

"How many are there?" Jaron asked, spying more bones lying in the brush. "What happened here?"

"This is the burial ground of the battle of Melaral," Arnor declared as he stopped and bent down to touch an oaken shield rimmed with rusted iron. "These men died defending these lands and were buried here in honor. Nature is cruel to their memory. Do not disturb the dust." It was a statement of respect for the dead, often used, but not completely fitting since none of the men had been reduced to dust yet.

Jaron recalled afterward the feeling that Arnor might not be just reciting historical knowledge, but recalling the events that led to this makeshift graveyard. Though unlikely, it was not impossible that Arnor had witnessed the aftermath of that battle and the tears that followed. The battle was one hundred and fifty years ago. Even Arnor, were he that old, would have been only a boy. But Arnor did not appear to have reached middle age, with only a touch of grey in his beard. Members of the race of Dwarves could survive the span of two hundred years. Jaron dismissed the thought. If Arnor had been there during the battle, he would be too old to be leading them anywhere.

Jaron reached into his lessons, and finding a contradiction he asked, "The flag of Melaral is blue with a green slash. Why are their cloaks maroon? I thought armies tried to match their colors to their home."

"Didn't read that one, did you?" Ellian answered from behind. "History books don't always tell the whole story. They are filled with glory and success, but never the despair and grief." He continued. "If you were a soldier who watched his best friend as he was cut down, a blue uniform would contrast sharply against the deep red of the blood. His injury would look to you as deadly as ever, and as a result, you might be inclined to flee. However, if his blood faded into the color of the uniform you would fight on, oblivious to the carnage around you. It is a cold and calculating move made by the men who plan wars, but leave others to fight them." Ellian's disdain for those often in charge did not just whisper in his voice, it shouted.

They soon left the burial grounds behind, but the sight of so many bones haunted Jaron's mind. He pictured the horrible and painful deaths of these men. *What had they faced in their last breath? Whom had they called to for help?* Jaron looked around at his companions and wondered at the battles Arnor had been in, at the extensive training Ellian and Keras had completed; preparing them for the inevitable skirmishes to come, and questioned if he would be able to survive his first encounter with an enemy.

* * * * *

Jaron could hear them coming. They walked in the light of the half-moon with nonexistent muscles, bone scraping against bone. Misery sounded with every step. The metal of their armor, corroded and damaged by severe rust, raked against itself, flaking away as a brown dust. In the air came the vile stench of mildew and decay.

They moved as a unit, not uniformly, but each soldier walking his path as part of the group. The bones of their hands curled around ancient swords, hammers, and axes, dulled in appearance if not in usefulness from centuries in the soil. The flesh of their faces, eaten away by time, revealed an ever-present and unnatural grin. The eyes that should have looked out from the skull were replaced with a blue glow, fading to black.

Jaron, terrified, closed his eyes and held his breath as they passed on either side of him, continuing on their terrible march. Footsteps shook the ground as he pressed himself deeper into it, trying to disappear from their sight, if they had any. A moaning wind accompanied them, reaching to clutch at the hairs on the neck. They walked on and the horrid echo of their movements disappeared into the distance.

Were they spirits? Looking down, Jaron inspected the ground where they had passed, running his fingers in the footprints. Doing so, he felt an itching sensation on the back of his hands and looked just in time to see the flesh falling away, revealing the blood and bones underneath. Pain splashed through his mind and became a crackling burn rising up his limbs. The moaning of the wind escaped his lips as he joined it in chorus. He watched in revulsion as the skin from his arms blistered away. Clutching his arms and breathing heavily, he snapped awake. A cold sweat surfaced, and he could feel the night's chill roll across his neck and down his back. Looking over to his friends, he was relieved to see Ellian and Keras sleeping soundly. Arnor was awake, it being his watch. He gazed at Jaron, having noticed him start, but he didn't ask about the dream that had woken the boy with such a fright.

Jaron closed his eyes again and pricked his ears to the darkness, hearing the noises of wind through the leaves. Bugs and frogs chirped in chorus to one another. Sighing heavily and rising from his blankets, he grabbed a stick and rustled the embers of the fire until the flames made the campsite visible. The ground showed no signs of anyone passing. The footprints were not there. He yawned but remained awake nonetheless, rubbing the back of his hands and keeping silent company with Arnor.

* * * * *

Next morning, embarrassed that he was still shaken from the visions of the Melaral burial grounds, Jaron told no one of his dream. After a hasty breakfast of bread and dried meat, they mounted the ponies and traveled to the foothills of Delhallen in short time. Narrow with drooping branches of ash and maple trees hugging the trail, the path was easy to follow. The hooves of the ponies rustled the leaves not yet decomposed from the previous fall. A stream rolled in the ears as it flowed alongside. The sway of the saddle hypnotized

Jaron after his sleepless night.

There was no warning, no slide of steel, no scream of attack. The goblin came from the trees, falling upon Jaron. In surprise and fright, Keras watched the black blade of the goblin plunge repeatedly toward Jaron's side before he fell from the saddle, flailing at his attacker.

The goblin's dirk came down a fourth time, but missed its mark and gored into the dirt as the gray-skinned goblin let out a pain-filled shriek. Arnor's silver throwing knife protruded from its back and it writhed about on the leaf-strewn floor of the forest trying to dislodge it.

Arnor and Ellian were now each struggling with an opponent of their own. A goblin landed on Arnor's pony wrapping its sinewy arm around the dwarf's neck and dragged him to the forest floor. More came out of the bush carrying cruel blades and surrounded the surprised travelers. Ellian dismounted, dropping the lifeless body of the goblin that had dared attack him. He drew his sword from the scabbard across his back. It sang as it twirled in his hands with deadly precision.

Keras, standing in the stirrups as her frightened pony danced in confusion, lifted her bow and launched an arrow into the chest of the leader who, with a yelp of pain, fell backwards onto the ground clutching the protruding arrow. He rolled in the leaves, groaning as he pulled at the shaft.

Arnor stood, pushing away the corpse of his assailant, and drew two throwing daggers. Two more fell from an arrow that glanced one goblin and struck another in the neck. The goblin that took the glancing blow from the arrow forgot his minor wound as Ellian's blade removed his head.

There were twelve goblins in the attack and the trio made short work of them with sword, blade, and bow. Keras rolled off her pony and hurried to Jaron.

Jaron pushed himself up from the forest floor, spitting out bits of leaf and dirt. The spot behind and under his right arm throbbed. Dropping back down to the dirt, he reached across with his left hand, expecting and fearing that he would pull it back sticky with blood. He did not. The mail shirt was tightly woven enough that the goblin's dagger had only scratched the skin, though the force of the blows left a hefty bruise. Jaron winced at the touch.

The sound of the dying goblins still surrounded him. They were a threat no more, but some of them still hung on to life. Jaron raised his head to witness Ellian quickly killing each of them in succession. Dropping his head again, Jaron retched.

"Look at this one," motioned Arnor to Keras. "This goblin is no more than fourteen years. True, they age quicker than Humans, but he is young to be in a scouting party."

"This one as well," replied Ellian, tilting the face of another for inspection. "It seems we've killed a scouting party of younglings." He bent to inspect the markings on the leather armor of the young goblin. "They are Markal, too, not a war tribe of the north."

Retrieving her arrows, Keras fitted them back into her quiver. "In another day these goblins might have been allies. Why did they attack?"

Having never seen a Goblin before, Jaron looked at the one that had attacked him. In death, his face stared out at nothing with wide yellow eyes. His hair, thin, wiry, and matted with mud, fell over his shoulders. Leather armor clung tight around his body and limbs but was open at the joints to allow movement. Painted on the leather across his chest were the colors white and red.

"These are Valcella's colors." Arnor retrieved his knives. "It is as Yaru was saying. Much is happening in the world. Have the Markal been pressed into service with General Shale?" He bent to draw Jaron to his feet.

Jaron looked around them. "Where are the ponies?"

Keras's pony, Big Red, stood munching on a turf of grass some yards away, and further out, Arnor's pony, Mindy, wandered, afraid to enter the clearing of the battle once again. The other two were harder to catch. Jaron and Keras, however, managed to do so.

"This was a scouting party. No doubt, the main part of their troop is not far behind. We must move and cover our trail before the larger contingent follows." Quickly, Arnor urged them to move the ponies off the road and up a steep hill through heavy brush and trees. He spent time with Ellian removing any marks on the ground and examining branches in the lowland brush for signs of their passing. Nothing was left that could point to the direction they had taken after the battle.

"Now we wait and let the larger force pass us by," said Arnor.

"Here?" asked Jaron, wide eyed.

"They wouldn't expect us to hang around. Any sane person would dash out of here. I'll feel better following a Goblin army than having it behind us."

"If we're discovered..." Jaron argued.

"I've done this before," Arnor silenced Jaron.

They led the ponies up over a small hill and down the other side where they were tethered and left to graze. Arnor, Ellian, Keras, and Jaron crouched on the hilltop, waiting and listening for the sounds of the approaching company of goblins. They did not have long to wait.

Forty strong at least, a group of goblins came running to where the ambush had taken place. They were not pleased at the discovery of their scouting party. Some cried. Some stamped in anger, and some searched down the trail for the slayers of their younglings.

Others stripped the bodies clean and began to arrange them for burial. Two had even started to claw the ground, digging the grave by hand when a large goblin came running up the trail behind them. He and the thirty others that ran with him were not of the same tribe, bearing markers of the Nargesh goblins. He slapped and yelled at the gravediggers. "No time, you filthy Markal! Run the road or you'll feel the sting of my whip or the cold of my steel!"

"But the scouts are dead," said one of the diggers. "Whoever did this must be near." He received the back of the larger goblin's fist

50

in reply. The leader then picked out twelve Markal goblins.

"You are the new scouting party. Double-time it to the front! You," he growled, pointing to three Markal who had been digging, "throw the bodies off the trail and conceal them." Grumbling, the Markal goblins obeyed his command and rushed up the trail to catch up with their fellows.

After the Markal goblins disappeared, the leader wrinkled his nose sniffing the air. "I smell pony." His eyes squinted, scanning the hill beside the trail. "No time," he raged, shaking his head and following his platoon.

Chapter 6   Goblin Bane

An hour passed as they lay there on the hill. Arnor looked out over the crest toward the trail. He was expecting to see stragglers or goblins left behind deliberately in an attempt to set up another ambush. Keras lay motionless, staring at the sky. Ellian rested on his back cleaning his blades and inspecting some damage to his armor.

Jaron felt a pit in his stomach. This had been his first taste of an actual battle, and he had failed. Were it not for his companions, he would be a corpse, reeking entrails on the stones of the road. He had feared that he would freeze in the face of combat. It had happened so fast, and he hadn't done anything.

He would spend more time practicing his speed and reaction exercises. He knew he would need that speed when the time to prove himself came again. However, there was more to it than that. He had to pay more attention to his surroundings from now on. Jaron closed his eyes to listen to the individual sounds of the forest. Birds called from far away. Insects buzzed loudly off to his right. The ponies stepped quietly in the grass, but he could hear it. Listening to the sounds around him, he heard Ellian snore.

*   *   *   *   *

Once Arnor was satisfied that all was safe, Ellian suggested that they travel, from here on out, without the ponies. The sounds of clomping hooves and creaking leather had lulled them into complacency with their surroundings. Perhaps on foot, they might have noticed the signs of the Goblin party that had traveled in front of them before it had circled back to attack. Arnor grudgingly agreed. It was still a long way to Starkwall, and he was not delighted thinking about the toll the distance would take on his legs. They would have to choose the best of their provisions carefully.

Keras fetched the ponies, unpacked them, and found a stone overhang to store saddles and provisions they could no longer carry. Keras and Jaron removed the bridles, and then unceremoniously set the ponies free. "Goodbye, Mindy. Goodbye, Red," Keras said, sadly.

Ellian selected the company provisions carefully. He stowed them into shoulder packs and bags attached to belts. The packs were much too heavy for Jaron's comfort. Nevertheless, he did not complain. Arnor, on the other hand, groaned as Ellian piled another strap over his head to rest on his shoulder. He grumbled and pointed out items that he didn't think they would need.

"We can leave this behind."

"Do we really need that pot?"

"What about all of this rope? We've been carrying it since Red Helm. We probably won't need it. There are bridges across the gorge, you know?"

"It might be warm enough to leave the blankets behind now."

Ellian didn't budge.

Once packed with food, bedrolls, and survival essentials, they strapped the weapons on last.

"Good luck swinging a sword carrying all of this," Keras noted.

"We're going on foot so that we can avoid having to swing our swords," Ellian answered.

They followed the path of the Goblin patrol, several hours behind and moving at a much slower pace. Ellian examined the trail as they traveled onward. Any deviation of the marks were tracked and analyzed. They did not need the goblins to circle around behind them, and so they measured their speed in favor of the additional precautions.

That evening, they made no fire and ate cold rations. The blackness of night fell around them, pierced only by the occasional stream of moonlight poking through the canopy of leaves above. The moonlight appeared brilliant in contrast to the utter darkness of the forest. As the night continued, low clouds draped the moon.

Rain was closing in. Arnor, glad that Ellian had not allowed him to leave it behind, rolled out a thin tarred sheet to cover the sleeping companions. Ellian placed a rock at each corner and wrapped the corner around the stone, tying it tight. This allowed them to stretch the fabric between trees without poking holes in it. Ellian chose a small hill off to the left of the trail. His forethought ensured that the ground they slept on was slightly higher than the main path. Their slumber might at least be dry.

By morning, the downpour had reduced the path to mud. Heavy rain drenched the travelers as they trudged onward, fighting the chill that reached in towards the spine through their waterlogged layers. Another wet night awaited them. They shivered with the cold, unable to dry out their clothing from the days march. At least there was no wind and the rain had stopped.

As the sun rose on the next morning, Keras was the first to notice the smoke. With the smell of burning wood swam the stench of decay. Unpleasant and acrid, it blended with pine, ruining the fresh scent that normally accompanied the morning after a shower. The reek varied in intensity, carried in as it was along a light breeze.

"Do you smell that?" Keras asked the others. "It smells like rotten meat. Is there a trash heap around here?"

The rising sun soon became warm, and the damp of their clothing chafed them viciously. After two hours, Keras could not keep silent any longer and requested a stop. Clothing layers were stripped and hung to dry.

Jaron tried not to look at Keras as she took off her clothing. She was his friend. The robes of the library had never shown any shape in her. Here in the forest, as cold as he was, he could not help but notice the way her pants fit her. He closed his eyes, quietly shaming himself for his thoughts, and blind, stripped off his wet clothes.

An hour they rested, drying in the heat of the daylight, when a voice fell on them from above. "Do not reach for your weapons or we will be forced to shoot." A slender elf dropped out of the trees onto the overgrown trail.

Jaron looked up to where the elf had been. A network of interconnected vines traveled from tree to tree. Was it a pathway hidden in the leaves?

"Who are you? What business do you have in the land of Velaress?" said the elf. He was dressed in the colors of the wood so that he blended in easily with his surroundings. His voice was not friendly, but he held his hand outstretched behind him, giving the silent command for any others in his party to hold their weapons. "Speak quickly."

"You know me," said Arnor. "Or you know of me, I'm sure. I am Arnor Ondstriker. I am known to the Timber Elves of Velaress."

"And your business?" pressed the elf.

"We travel through your land on our way north to Starkwall," replied Arnor.

"Yes, I know of you. Nevertheless, you do not have leave to pass. You must come with me." He waved his hand forward, and sixteen elves materialized out of the forest around them. Weapons were taken, and the travelers, still nearly naked, were escorted onward toward the tang of smoke and decay.

"At least they're taking us where we were planning to go anyway," Keras said. She turned to the elf nearest her. "Hey, as long as you're planning on carrying the weapons, don't forget to bring the packs. Mine is the one with the salt and herbs in it."

"Shh!" Ellian reprimanded.

Jaron recalled his lessons of Timber Elves and their culture. Their homes were in the leaves high above the forest floor. With nearly the same speed as one on the ground, they were nimble enough to pass from tree to tree. Their clothing mirrored the colors of the foliage. The stems of flowers or long grasses adorned the braids in their hair, and their eyes grabbed hold and refused to let go. Jaron was sure at first that they were brown, but as the leader of this band of elves stepped forward into the light, it became clear that a purple ring surrounded the black center, becoming brighter with the exposure to the light of the sun. His remembered ethnology lesson, however, was cut short by the gruesome sight of a bloodied battlefield.

A ghastly scene awaited them. The elves had massacred every single goblin. The stink of decay assaulted the senses and it stuck in their throats as they tried to breathe. Blood soaked the clearing, clinging to their shoes as they walked. Goblins lay disemboweled, or beheaded, or both. Pikes of wood were stabbed into the ground displaying grotesque heads, each twisted from the pain of their last moment. Carried by the wind, smoke danced along the ground. Tumbling up from the hundreds of bodies, it spiraled in the air until it finally dissipated. Elves were dragging the bodies of goblins and hurling them onto a roaring fire.

"From the smell," Arnor said to Ellian in a low voice, "this happened the day before last."

"Did they just start cleaning up?" Ellian asked.

"No, I don't think so," Arnor responded. "Look at the ashes."

Elves were here in large numbers. Two or three hundred were busy within the clearing. A forge had been set in one corner, a kitchen in another. They were going to make a stand here.

Their Elven escort brought them to the base of a large tree, no less than twenty feet in diameter. A vine ladder was lowered down from the boughs above. As they climbed higher, they saw that the branches of the trees were intertwined with vines and grasses from the ground below. Within the branches, the elves had made a room invisible to the passing denizens of the ground.

The ladder entered the room through the floor and continued to the ceiling where it blended out into the weave that made up the structure of the room. As each reached the top of the ladder, they sat near the access hole, exhausted from their climb.

"I have had word of your approach, Ondstriker," an elder elf declared from a chair woven up out of the floor on the other side of the large room. His dress was like that of the others, but his hair was unadorned. "I am pleased to see you." This elf's woven chair, unlike his person, was decorated with flowers and thorns.

Still out of breath from the climb, Arnor rose to a knee from his sitting position and bowed his head in greeting. "Lord Thorladel, thank you for your escort. It has been long since our last visit. Is my cell still unoccupied?"

Thorladel laughed. "Still holding a grudge, I see."

Arnor did not move from his position.

"It was necessary, Ondstriker, the escort today. These woods have become a battleground. I am surprised my scouts treated you as fairly as they did."

"Our weapons were taken; are we prisoners?"

"No, not for the present, but we shall see." Arnor grimaced, but Lord Thorladel laughed and smiled. "Arnor, you have become like stone. Our history together has been one of turbulence, but for now, we are not enemies. You are indeed 'not prisoners,' and your weapons will be returned." Thorladel stood and offered his wineskin to Arnor. "Drink with me for much is happening. Below us burn the corpses of three hundred Markal and Nargesh goblins. They came among us with death in their eyes or we might have let them pass."

"Until they attacked us I thought the goblins were only fleeing war in the south," said Arnor.

"So we thought as well. Many goblins had already passed through before any aggression was shown. Since then, we have shut our border. In our increased diligence, we have captured one of your kind. You may give us some counsel as to what should be done about him."

Arnor lowered the wineskin, swallowing hard and feeling the lump roll all the way down to his stomach. "A mountain dwarf? What has he done?"

"Nay, not one of the mountain, he is one of the caverns."

"A cave dwarf! Scum of the world!" Arnor waved his hand in the air. "Kill him."

"Ah, so I thought your answer might be. However, it is not so simple yet. He cares for a human with whom he traveled. The human is ill, near death. The dwarf is the only one able to give him comfort by means of some herbal concoction we have not been able to duplicate. The human wears the mark of Holderness on his arm. We have allowed them to remain with us for three days and nights for this reason only. The man claims to hold valuable information for the King himself. He will not divulge it and, being too ill to be moved, it appears that his message shall go undelivered."

"Why is this my business?" Arnor asked.

"Because he carried this." Thorladel handed a rolled parchment to Arnor. Jaron caught a glimpse of the signature as Arnor unrolled it to read its contents. The signature, written with large graceful circles, clearly read: Yaru.

A note from my uncle, Jaron thought in surprise and excitement.

In the message, Arnor learned the name of the man the imprisoned dwarf cared for, and he asked, "Harnan, where is he?"

"Harnan?" said Ellian. "He is here? Sick?"

"You know this man?" Thorladel asked. Ellian nodded sharply. "I am sorry, but I believe he is dying." Thorladel sat once again on the woven chair. "Our healers can find nothing wrong with him, but he continues to ebb away. Only the dwarf has been able to help him at all. He is in great pain."

"Please," said Ellian, "take me to him."

Thorladel picked up a staff from the floor beside his chair and rapped a hard knock on the trunk of the tree. Two elves appeared from a room above. The elves brought the companions to a higher level of the tree. This woven room was smaller than the last, consisting of a raised bed covered with straw. In the bed, dressed in a wool tattered shirt and clutching a blanket lay a man of fifty years. His beard was long and flecked with gray. He appeared to be in immense pain. Each breath came with great labor.

The room was stiflingly warm. A fire had been lit in a pile of rocks assembled into a fire pit. It had been burning for some time, and the coals had a red glow even as the flame hung low over them rolling lazily from blue to yellow. Jaron stared at the fire with concern. Looking at the wicker room around him, he could easily imagine a simple mistake lighting the entire tree into an inescapable inferno. As he neared the fire, he noticed that the flames did not rise in points to lick the air, but rolled back into the center. He reached to touch it, but Keras pulled him back.

On the floor, holding the hand of the sick man was a dwarf, dressed in black. Jaron was struck by how different this dwarf was from Arnor, or for that matter, any other dwarf he had ever seen. His hair was dark brown and cut short so that he was nearly bald, except his hair in back, which was long enough for the slightest of ponytails. It was pulled together high on the back of his head. His face was pale as if he avoided sunlight, but the beard surprised Jaron the most. Unlike most dwarves who took pride in the length and fullness of their beards, this one wore a goatee, braided and long. His eyes were brown, but at angles appeared to shine with a gray, almost metallic reflection. The strange dwarf noticed the newcomers and backed away to an empty part of the room.

Ellian was the first to Harnan's side. The man gazed wearily at Ellian's face and a smile shattered the pain from his visage as his eyes widened in recognition. "Friend, Ellian."

"I'm here," Ellian replied. "Are you hurt? What made you so ill?"

"I have been a guest of the Brindi. Cruel and evil as they can be, it wasn't them who did this to me." He broke into a fit of coughs and blood speckled his hands as he tried to stifle them. "It was my rescuers who damaged me so." Noticing Arnor's hateful glance at the strange dwarf, he added, "Nay not the Dwarves. It was the dead." Jaron, remembering his dream, jerked at the mention of the dead.

"They live again," Harnan continued. "They pulled me close and laid upon me a quest for my soul. Should I not complete it, my salvation from the under-realm would be forfeit." His eyes scanned the room as he spoke, stopping at each person before moving on to the next. "I was sure to fail. The touch cannot easily be shaken off. I have not much life left in me. I feared for my soul, for my body could not make it to Brethiliost. But," he broke a weak smile, "I see you have with you the son of Lorenistal and that may equal my salvation." His eyes slid again to Jaron and glowed with recognition.

"You have the look of your mother, but I see your father in you as well. Jaronthel?"

"Yes," said Jaron.

"Do you have news of your father?"

Harnan's eyes welled with tears as Jaron produced Loren's ring from a pocket.

Harnan raised a hand to wipe a tear, "It was your father I came looking for, but if he has sent you his ring, perhaps he is lost." He paused, in pain, breathing deeply. "The message I have is for you, then, not the king who sits on the throne in the capitol, not for Gurrand." Fits of coughing wracked him again, and sweat dripped from his face as he spoke.

"The war has begun. He has returned. It is because of this that shades move against you. They are only the first of many yet to come. He uses the force of his knights to unite the south under one banner. All are subject to him again, but without the dead the alliance will fail."

"His knights, William and Baros, have requested an audience with you," he said, looking directly at Jaron. "They wish the king to come to their tower at Sandy River. You are the king, aren't you?" A rasp had entered his voice making it hard to understand him. He reached out to the dwarf in black. "Thargus will be your guide. He has agreed."

At mention of his name, the dwarf sitting in the corner scratching his chest came forward. "He should rest. This is too much, straining him like this. Leave him be for a time." He pulled a cloth from his pocket and wiped the blood from the hands and lips of Harnan.

"Thargus, friend, this is the message I was quested to give. I am done now. But, you are right. I must rest. Bring them to the tower at Sandy River, to Sir William and Lord Baros." Thargus met Harnan's eyes, nodded his head, and left the room.

No one spoke. Harnan slept with hands folded on his breast. In sleep, the pain erased from Harnan's face and his breathing became easier, slowing until finally, it stopped altogether.

Ellian dropped his head onto Harnan's shoulder. Keras knelt to comfort Ellian. Jaron's heart broke for his friend and he took a step forward reaching to embrace Ellian.

Ellian finally let go of Harnan's shoulder and stood looking down at the man who had mentored him. Another father was dead.

Arnor motioned Keras and Jaron to the door to give Ellian one last moment. Outside on the deck, Thargus stood looking far out at the sunset. As the others passed by him, Arnor looked back over his shoulder and was surprised to see the cavern dwarf's face streamed with tears.

Chapter 7   Walls of Starkwall

Jaron broke the silence, "That note was from Yaru." Arnor raised his head to look at Jaron. His face showed no emotion, but his eyes, after meeting Jaron's, darted away to stare past him. "On the scrolled parchment you were given, it had his name."

"Yes," replied Arnor, tugging his beard.

"What was in the scroll?" Ellian asked. He was fastening his shirt and leaning back against a woven bench.

The elves had returned their packs and arms but they were not allowed to carry the weapons until their exit from the treetop village. Woven rooms, high up in the tree canopy, had been provided by the elves for their use. Though sparse in furniture, they were warm, safe, and comfortable. Timber Elves were, after all, not woodland savages like the thuran or minasts of the southern mountains.

"Yes," Arnor said again, gathering his thoughts before he said, "The scroll Harnan carried was written by Yaru. The scroll provides directions, written in his hand, and a map of our most likely routes to Starkwall." Arnor fingered the knife blade he was holding. "Was this map written under duress? That is a question I would very much like to ask someone.

"I don't think Harnan was yet aware of your father's death, but Yaru knew. He sent Harnan in our direction. Still, Harnan himself was, as you might have discerned from his ties to Ellian, a member of the secret guard that protects your line. I can't believe that either he, or Yaru, would knowingly aid our enemy."

Arnor made his way to his pack and pulled out his flask, recently filled by the Timber Elves. After a short sip, he continued. "As you heard Harnan say, two knights have requested an audience with you. Their names are Lords William and Baros. These two knights were, at one time, in charge of Mavius's armies. Personally, I think the journey to meet with them too dangerous. Sandy River is deep within the southern lands, and that is now well under the control of General Shale of Valcella."

"Mavius?" Jaron asked. "King Mavius?"

"Yes," Arnor said.

"They couldn't be the same men," Ellian said.

"I'm afraid that is exactly who they are," Arnor responded.

"Do you know why they want to see me?" asked Jaron. "Could it be a trap?"

"A trap? Not if I remember William correctly. Honor is a way of life for these knights. Still, it has been a long time since I've had dealings with them."

Ellian leaned forward to take some fruit from the bowl on the floor in front of him. "You know these men?"

"If these are indeed the same men, I did. William is a common enough name, but Baros? Many years ago we fought together and then against each other."

Jaron spoke to the ceiling, "What do we do next? Do we continue to Starkwall or take a detour south to Sandy River?"

"Detour?" Keras laughed. "It could take weeks, even months, to reach Sandy River from here. Right now, we are so far north that it would be silly to..." she looked at Jaron as if he were a moron and nodded as she said the next word, "detour in the complete opposite direction. The plan was to go to the council in Starkwall. We're almost there. We should stick to it. We sent word ahead. They will be waiting for us."

"I agree," said Arnor. "There is safety in Starkwall and the necromancers are waiting."

"But, what about Yaru?" Jaron asked. "We knew he was going south, and he connected with Harnan. Maybe there is news of my father."

"If these knights want to talk to you, it is because your father is dead," Arnor responded, "and that is all the more reason to get you to Starkwall."

"But Yaru..." Jaron began.

"Can take care of himself," Arnor interrupted.

* * * * *

Smoke curled out of the forge as the sound of the hammer rang through the air. Strong and deliberate, the arm that held it came down, striking the steel, flattening it into the desired shape. Jaron watched his father. The sweat dripped down the sides of his face, running into his stained shirt. Loren smiled back at his son. The hammer came down striking the steel, and the shower of sparks flashed in Jaron's eyes, blinding a white halo that obscured his father from view. When his eyes adjusted, his father was gone, replaced by the white marble desk of the library. Jaron was looking across it, tears streaming down his face. He jerked from his slumber, realized it was only a dream, and lay awake until the sun rose.

Early the next morning they made to set out, having informed the elves of their plans determined the night before. While they were preparing to leave, Keras pulled herself up onto the landing outside and rushed into the room. She was out of breath from climbing the ladders and ropes from the foggy ground below. "They are..." she placed her hands on her knees trying to gather enough air to complete the sentence, "...planning to execute the under dwarf."

"Good thing too!" exclaimed Arnor.

"But why?" asked Ellian.

"Cave Dwarves, they are murderers and villains all of them," muttered Arnor and, seeing the look on Ellian's face, insisted, "He was looking after Harnan, otherwise he would have been dead already."

Ellian scowled at Arnor.

"They're called Under Dwarves, Arnor," Jaron corrected.

Still breathing heavily from the climb, Keras explained the situation. "Were we to agree to follow him to Sandy River, he would have been set free into our keeping. They can't just let him go, and they don't keep prisoners for long. He can't go with us into Starkwall as a free man and would certainly be imprisoned or killed by the city guardsmen. So they are planning to execute him by beheading today."

"One down, one million to go!" shouted Arnor. "It won't

make up for the sacking of Mount Minnus, but it's a start."

"We can't just let them do it," retorted Ellian. "I'll take him as my prisoner. Prison at Starkwall is better than no life at all, and the guards at Starkwall won't kill him while I stand near. I will see that he is treated fairly until we can release him to the South."

"Your compassion will be the death of all of us, Ellian," Arnor spat.

"I won't abandon my principles for your prejudices."

"Mount Minnus, wasn't that three hundred years ago?" asked Jaron.

"Yeah, what's your point?" Arnor stared at Jaron until the boy looked away, then he turned his attention back to Ellian.

"He'll be your responsibility, Ellian. I'll have nothing to do with him." Arnor fingered the hilt of one of his throwing knives. "I almost hope he tries to escape." Then, seeing the look of reproach from the others, he followed with, "Well, I wouldn't wish prison on anybody." However, they weren't buying it.

*　*　*　*　*

Thargus looked at Arnor, Keras, Jaron, and Ellian and felt nothing. He had expected to experience something. He wasn't sure what it was he was supposed to be feeling, but there was nothing at all. His hand scratched at his chest.

He had been sure that Harnan would help him in accomplishing his own mission. Harnan had known one member of the four personally, and he had called the skinny boy out as the heir to Mavius. Thargus didn't see it, didn't believe it. *The answer is in the South.* Staying here would only hinder him, and if he could avoid being captured again he might succeed.

His hands bound in front of him, Thargus grasped the cord running from his wrists to Ellian's belt. He could not allow himself to accept the prospect of imprisonment either. There was too much to be done. There was too much at stake. He could see that, currently, this was the one option available to him. At least, with such a small party of travelers, he might be able to escape more easily. He had to.

He scratched at his chest, followed, and waited.

Harnan had made him promise to lead these four fools back to Sandy River. *Lucky for me,* he thought, *that they don't want to go.*

* * * * *

The road to Starkwall traveled through a valley carved by the waters of a glacier long gone. Rope bridges, some of them spindly and treacherous, others capable of allowing a fully laden cart to roll easily across, spanned steep trails and deep ravines. The road would, almost certainly, be watched.

Disturbed by his predictability and upset that Yaru—or anyone—could determine his plan of action enough to know his exact path through the wilderness, Arnor had now drawn up a different route, going over maps of trails with the leader of the Timber Elves. Some sections of the trail were no more than a rocky collection of hills that forced the use of one's hands. This was the reason Arnor had allowed Ellian to bind Thargus's hands in front of him.

The Timber Elves had allowed a great many goblins to pass through the forests before the invaders became aggressive. Signs of goblins were everywhere along the trail, and they came upon a few broken branches, spent campfires, and abandoned camps.

On the third day after leaving the elves, Ellian heard voices. He held up his hands for silence and they all held their breath listening, trying to gauge the distance to the speakers. Arnor motioned for Ellian, Jaron, and Thargus to stay put. He then signaled to Keras and the two of them crept ahead of the others and disappeared into the undergrowth. On hands and knees, they moved silently through the brush until they could hear the details of the conversation.

"We should send Murka out to forage. This bread is like sawdust. How do they expect us to be ready for battle on this?" The voice was hard and gravelly.

"Some meat would be better. I can't eat grass," came a more even-toned voice.

"Has Nerthy's crew been demoted, do you think?" asked a third and higher-pitched voice.

"Why's that, you say?" responded the first gravelly voice.

"Ordered to cut trees. His boys would rather be cutting bones, but they have to bring and haul the lumber."

"Somebody's got to do it, Murka, you loaf. Be glad it wasn't you," spat the gravelly voice.

"I hate this. They go inside the wall, and we spend weeks trying to bring it down. Not to my liking. Not at all." The even-toned voice was getting closer. Keras and Arnor backed away and returned to the group.

After explaining the conversation they heard, in a whisper, Arnor decided to try to circle around the trio of goblins and continue their journey. This was probably a guard outpost for a larger camp, and they did not want to get closer to the goblins, although they knew it might prove unavoidable, seeing as the camp was between them and their destination. They untied Thargus, and for the first time, Arnor spoke to him. He pulled him close by the shirt and stared into his eyes.

"We need to get past this post. You will come with us. If there is one false move from you, I will be right behind you, and I won't be happy. We will be forced to kill the goblins," he pulled Thargus closer, "and then I will kill you."

Wide and to the right, they circled the goblins, having to traverse a deep cut in the side of the mountain. Boulders towered on either side of them as they stepped through the icy cold of the fast moving stream that had made the hidden path. Centuries of nature's abuse had cut bowls out of the massive rock walls leaving them smooth on the sides. They came upon great caverns, created by the constant barrage of pebbles, sticks, and stones hurled relentlessly by the rushing current. The danger close by could not distract Jaron from the tremendous beauty before him. He gazed upward at the sight, reaching out to feel the smoothness of the rock. It was a hike of two miles before they emerged from the shadows of the crevice.

In another hour, they were back on their route.

Thargus traveled between Ellian and Arnor, single file, followed by Keras and last by Jaron. Jaron did his best to erase any signs of their passing, both when they entered the stream and also when they emerged from it, but he was no expert like Ellian or Keras, and Ellian was leading at a pace that did not allow perfection.

Once back, more or less, on their original trail, they traveled quickly. As they continued toward Starkwall, the number of close encounters with goblins increased. Finally, Arnor approached Ellian for a council. "There are too many goblins about to continue this course. You are familiar with this territory. What ideas do you have?"

"Maybe we should double back and try to come in from another direction."

"That is a long shot and you know it, a week backtracking, and then, what? East? Through the mountains? No good."

"We could go underground." It was Thargus. "There might be a way into the city from underneath."

"There isn't." Arnor's answer was firm. "We're not going underground."

We have, already, traveled underground twice on this journey, Arnor reasoned to himself. *But, that was before we had to look after a filthy cave dwarf.*

"Do we really know what we're dealing with? Keras asked. "Maybe we should head for higher ground. I was thinking Mantis Peak. We could take a good look around. Maybe there aren't as many goblins as we think."

"It's a good idea." Arnor turned to Ellian, "I thought you were supposed to be the bright one." Ellian rolled his eyes, and Arnor said, "All right, we sneak east to high ground." He bent down and drew a map in the dirt. "Our current location," he said, stabbing his index finger into the ground, "and through the Ellis gorge we'll have to make it under these three bridges unseen, and then finally up to Mantis Peak, barring any unpleasant interruptions."

"Those are main roads and wide bridges, two of them

anyway. What kind of cover can we expect?" Ellian asked as he studied the map on the ground.

"We'll have to scout as we go," was Arnor's response. "I've never been down the gorge, never had reason to."

"What if Mantis Peak has already been taken?" asked Thargus.

"Not likely," Keras said. "The peak is only accessible by the broken ledge path, and Movis Peak, on the northern side of the gorge, is much easier to take. Mantis Peak has been abandoned for decades."

The path down to Ellis Gorge was not an easy one. Many times, as it became too steep to continue, Keras would set up a series of rope loops that held their weight as they descended.

Looking up from the bottom of one steep slope, Ellian lamented, "Well that's a nice path to follow, if anyone is following."

"Don't worry your pretty little pants," Keras said as she looped the rope around her arm. "Watch this." She gave a yank, and the rope slid from the ledge above to land at her feet.

"What?" asked Ellian, shocked. "We just climbed down that. What if it had come loose?"

"Not with this knot, no way," Keras laughed until Ellian joined her. However, as they continued lowering themselves down into the gorge, Ellian was not his usual collected self.

Tired from the climb, they made camp. Here at the base of the cliff, overshadowed by boulders, they felt safer and relaxed, though it was a foolish thing to do. Eyes could still see from the cliffs above, if there was anybody to see, and having a fire would be unwise. For the night ahead, no watch was laid. Not even Arnor was capable. They tied Thargus thoroughly, though it was unnecessary. He too fell fast asleep.

Even in his slumber, Ellian was thinking about how to fool the eyes that might stare down from the bridges. He woke with the answer. The mud and rocks that filled the floor of the gorge were a dark gray, resembling the color of their wool bedrolls. Before starting out, he explained the idea from his dream. Bedrolls were removed from packs and rolled in the mud, until covered with more of the grey color. They were wet and heavy, but at a distance the company would look like rocks at the bottom of the deep gorge, at least while they were motionless. While the travelers were in motion, however, they would still be easy to spot. The bridges would need to be watched closely.

Ellis Gorge followed the path of the Ellis River that ran from the East to the ocean in the West. During the March thaw, this gorge filled from side to side with ice flows that tore cruelly at the stones and vegetation. By early May, the water and ice begin to subside and the water becomes low and shallow, never more than a few feet deep though ice cold, leaving plenty of room on either shore to travel. Arnor ticked off the days in his mind. Today was May 16th. If the flow in the river had lessened, they might be able to travel the gorge. As it was, neither side of the river would be an easy path. Walking the saturated sands would be tedious and draining. Obstacles came often in the gorge. Trees, knocked down or piled high by the force of the recent ice, meant half of their time would be spent scrambling over sharp stone and splintered wood. It would be slow going.

They approached the first bridge on one of the main roads into Starkwall. Large timbers supported the weight of the massive structure, reaching down the sides of rock. Traffic was low on the road above today. Ellian watched overhead as the rest of the party moved forward. Even from the distance, Arnor noticed a large red and white horn slung over the shoulder of one of the goblin soldiers. The pair of sentry goblins crossed from one end of the bridge to the other, but they weren't looking down into the gorge. They talked quietly as they scanned for anyone approaching. Underneath them, the group moved with care, eyes gazing upward as they inched forward under their blankets. Once reaching fair cover, well past the bridge, Arnor whistled three times, sounding remarkably like a quail. On hearing this, Ellian made his way to join the party, moving as the others had done.

Camp that night again had no fire. "At least our blankets are wet," joked Keras. Wool will still hold heat when damp, but that doesn't make it any more pleasant to be wet all night. Food was rationed, as it had been for the last couple of days. There was no game to shoot in the narrow channel, but Jaron managed to catch a large fish in the shallow pools of the river. They ate this raw and greedily, as it made up the best portion of their dinner.

The second bridge crossing looked much the same as the first, and they approached it with equal caution. Two sentry guards crossed back and forth along the length. Jaron and company crept forward underneath their mud-covered blankets, as they had done with the previous bridge, when the crisp sound of a horn filled their ears, followed by a fading echo. The party froze in place, eyes peering upward around the edges of their wet bedrolls. For several minutes nothing happened, but then came the stomp of boots, then dozens of boots. Then the sound of hundreds of boots rolled through the gorge like thunder. An army was crossing the bridge.

Arnor motioned for everyone to lie still. Ten minutes passed, then ten more. Boots gave way to wagons and horses. The group could not see the travelers above. Were those humans or goblins? One had to assume goblins. After the army had passed and the noise of their crossing died away, the journey to Mantis Peak continued, but now with more speed than before.

The third crossing was a narrow rope bridge that sagged down into the gorge. It swayed gently in the strong morning breeze, oscillating slightly as if the wind had plucked it like a stringed instrument. The eyes of the travelers scanned the length of the bridge and the sides of the canyon rim. With no sign of anyone above, the group continued with care.

"Ay, an animal! Something's down below!" came a cry from above.

The party froze, not even looking around their blankets.

"You've been in the ale again, Haga."

"No, I swear I saw something moving down there," said

Haga, followed by laughter. "I'll prove it!"

The sound of an approaching arrow sang through the air and a shaft pierced Ellian's blanket, striking the ground between his neck and forearm. He did not move.

Laughter rained again from above, followed by the second voice. "You're seeing things again, Haga. Move on. I don't like this wobbly bridge."

A third voice joined the chorus. "Good shot though. That rock won't be giving you any more trouble."

"Shut it, Bekkus," said Haga.

"Stuck right in the stone. That tip shattered," Bekkus guffawed.

"So why should I care. You planning on climbing down to get it?" The three voices traveled on.

Ellian pulled the shaft from the ground. "They left quickly. They must have been near the edge when they shot. Which way did they go?"

"North, toward the city," Keras replied. "But keep it down. Our voices might echo out of this hole we're in."

Two miles more and they were climbing out of the gorge and back into the sunlight. It was an unbelievably easy climb this time. Thargus had seen a path along the sides of the gorge that traveled up, cut into the stone. Only a few times were they scrambling up a steep spot. Once in the sun, they hung their bedrolls out to dry in its warmth.

Next morning, they followed the disused trail to Mantis Peak. Up and around the mountain it went under the shade of the trees, steep in some areas, with rocks laid to make an uneven stair, and calm and easy in others. One whole section around a cliff face had fallen away. Ellian led the way forward this time. He climbed unhurried and steadily, stretching out his long arms as he searched for purchase in the stone. Once above them, on a steady portion of the trail again, he lowered a rope, pulling Arnor up first. By the end of the day, they were at the peak, a bald face on the northern side of the mountain. Spread out before them was the city of Starkwall.

The old forest that had once surrounded the city had been cut down. Stretching from one side of the city wall to the other, a Goblin army of unbearable size surrounded Starkwall. There was no way in. The tents of the Goblin army covered the fields like flowers. Gray, white, and red, they fluttered in the spring wind as the goblins bustled around them, turning the newly felled Hinale forest into siege towers. Outside the stone walls of the city, the Goblin army had created a city of wood, with the sole intent of bringing down the stones of Starkwall.

Jaron looked out at the camp. His eyes traveled beyond the soldiers, to Starkwall and on to the horizon, to the clouds far away in the distance. The books at the Westmost library had been correct about the view. Even the army camped below, blocking their path, could not take that away.

Chapter 8   A New Direction

Long manned by soldiers, Mantis Peak was a lookout post. It was abandoned when the trail leading to it had fallen away, a casualty of ice and thaw. The door to the small tower remained intact after more than three decades of neglect with a complicated locking mechanism barring their entry to shelter. Even Ellian was unable to find a way past. They shattered the door.

Ellian tried to gauge the size of the army in the camp below. Eight hundred was as near as he could guess. He sat on the ground and buried his fists in his eyes. There was no way to get into the city.

Starkwall could last two months, three maybe, under siege. Longer than that, disease was sure to break out, especially if all of the outlying village populations were crowded within the walls. Water was a problem, even though wells existed inside the city. If the grain from the storage buildings fed the population now, next winter would be hard. It came down to the fortitude of the attacking army. Would their will to destroy be stronger than the health of Starkwall?

"This is where the goblins were going," Ellian said to Jaron. "All of those reports of goblins crossing the mountains... Edmund said they were filtering through the forests. Filter is an accurate word. They came here in small bands, avoiding most of the roads to make a sneak attack on Starkwall."

"But why come so far north for a sneak attack?" Jaron asked.

"The bridge," Keras answered, "yes there are three, but the main bridge across Ellis Gorge... Gurrand's knights and army are on the other side. If goblins control the bridge they can block Gurrand from heading south."

"Exactly," said Ellian. "The main attack isn't here. That General Shale of Valcella is smart. If the king cannot reach the Temerrac pass to defend it, then Shale will take it. Temerrac is expecting help from Brethiliost. They aren't going to get it. And from what I can see, they won't know until it's too late." Ellian pointed out the window. "Look." Circling in the sky over the Ellis Gorge, riding the air currents, were three hawks. "Starkwall can't even send a message," Ellian said. "The goblins planned this well. Those hawks will kill any pigeon they see."

Jaron stood, and taking out his knife, cut the cord binding Thargus's wrists.

"Are you insane?" Arnor demanded.

"If we're going to try to enter the city while it's under siege, we'd be stupid to try to do it with a prisoner. He might as well head south again on his own."

"He might just slit our throats when we sleep, too," Arnor stated.

"With what? We're all armed. He isn't," Jaron argued.

"Tie him back up."

"No," Jaron said, staring Arnor down. "This argument is over."

Arnor looked ready to say something more, but he did not.

Thargus, no longer bound by any cord, let his eyes walk over Jaron. *So young,* he thought, *Humans were always so young, even the old ones. What is he, less than twenty years, and a king so they say? But, not raised as a king.*

Because of the boy, Thargus sat cross-legged enjoying the sun through the window, still under the wary eyes of Arnor, but free. He could leave easily if he wanted to. He didn't think one of these men could stop him, but all together? *Yes, it might be possible.* He looked at Arnor, sizing him up. *He would be the most trouble.*

Thargus made a mental note of his provisions: a blanket, a cloak, a water skin, nothing else, not even a knife. He felt his pockets for anything else he might be able to use and found only a loose button.

Through the beams of sunlight, Jaron caught eyes with Thargus.

"How did you know Yaru?" Jaron asked.

"Who?" asked Thargus, still fingering the button within his pocket.

"The one who wrote the map for Harnan."

"The warrior?" Thargus prodded.

"Yes, how did you know him?" Jaron asked again.

"I didn't. Harnan did. The three of us were held in cells at Sandy River after we were captured. He pointed us in the right direction. We had intended to look for your father in the south, but with news from Yaru," he stopped, remembering with whom he was speaking, "Your father, I'm sorry." Jaron nodded, taking a deep breath, and Thargus continued. "We headed north to find you instead. Harnan said that Yaru was a man we could trust. I trusted Harnan like a member of my own family."

"Yaru's a prisoner?" Jaron asked.

"Yes, in Sandy River, south-east of Temerrac."

Jaron looked down at his hands and glanced over at Arnor and Ellian. They were making plans to enter the city. *Family*, thought Jaron. *They say my father is dead. My mother is dead. Yaru is my uncle, and he is in trouble.* He knew what he had to do.

"How far is it to Temerrac?"

* * * * *

"You want to go where?" Ellian stood up.

"Look," said Jaron, "can we get into Starkwall?"

"No."

"Should we go back to Westmost?"

"No."

Keras sat next to Jaron. "South is the direction no one is expecting," she entered.

"But if Temerrac is the target we'd be walking right into a war," Ellian argued.

"Temerrac doesn't know what's coming. If we go south, we could warn them," Jaron said.

"Or we could get caught in the attack."

"I can't do anything here," said Jaron. "We can't get into Starkwall. We can't stay here. We can't go home. I'm going to Temerrac and then on to Sandy River, with you or without you."

"You know I can't let you go without me."

Keras stood, stretching. "Then I guess we only have to convince Arnor."

* * * * *

When no one had wanted to travel to Sandy River, Thargus's decision had been easy, escape. There was the other business placed upon him. He had decided weeks ago to give the matter more thought, but now there was no time to question. His heart weighed heavy with his losses.

Listening to the others talk about their new direction, Thargus rose and looked at the position of the sun. Based on the shadows, he guessed it was around four hours past noon. "Too late to leave today," he mumbled to himself, "tomorrow morning." He started to draw in the dirt, marking major positions of landmarks and rivers between Starkwall and Sandy River. His drawing became so well detailed and accurate that eventually Arnor stopped glaring at him and took interest in the scribbles Thargus was making on the ground. He had given up using his fingers and was using a short stick in each hand to mark roads, rivers, mountains, fields, villages, towns, trade routes, and even some underground networks, although these were few and not well connected. Thargus's memory of terrain was uncanny. Arnor scoured the makeshift map for mistakes and could find none.

Thargus stood and quietly reviewed his work. He then made to call everyone over, but everyone was already standing there, amazed at his detail.

"This is our current position, Mantis Peak. This," he said sweeping his pointing stick behind him by several feet, "is where we are headed." He looked around to see the reaction on their faces, but there was none. All knew the trek would be long.

"I propose we move east, descending back into the gorge, and make for the village of Vesthall. Vesthall should be far enough from Starkwall to avoid running into any more of our little grey friends."

"How far is that?" Keras asked.

"About thirty miles."

Keras let out a long sigh. "That's a long road. It'll take days just to get to Vesthall. And then, what?"

"We could purchase or steal horses and take the mail road. We could be there in about six weeks." Thargus leaned back against the rock wall behind him.

"In six weeks it will be all over for Temerrac," said Ellian. "Why don't we just take the Holderness road?"

"Even that will take four or five weeks," Arnor said, "and we may have to duck and hide from goblins as we go."

Jaron gazed at the drawn map in the dirt and pointed. "What river is this? I don't know it."

"That's because it travels underground, from cave to cavern. It is called the Sotho Palala. We could get out of the underground near Temerrac in less than two weeks. From Temerrac, it is only three or four days to Sandy River."

"That could get us there a lot faster," said Ellian. "Why didn't you mention it before? It seems like the most logical choice."

"Arnor Ondstriker expressed his desire to stay above ground," Thargus responded. "There are rapids and calms all along the Sotho Palala. It would be quick, yes, but not perfectly safe. There may be other dangers along the river. I have not traveled it this far north before. There may be meetings with some of the people of the Sotho Palala. I don't know if we would be welcome."

Arnor stared at the map on the floor and said, "I don't want to take a month and a half on this trip either. Temerrac might fall in that time." Arnor looked pained at the thought. He had argued with Jaron about this decision to follow Thargus to the meeting at Sandy River, but had eventually backed down when he realized that Temerrac was under the threat of attack. If they arrived in time, they could raise the city's defenses. "Where is the entrance to the Sotho Palala?" asked Arnor.

An uneasy silence followed as Thargus and Arnor stared each

other down. "The closest entrance might be Blood Scar Mountain," Thargus answered.

"Friendly-sounding place," said Keras.

"The stone of the mountain is a deep red, resembling a scar on the cliff face. Distance is about..." Thargus looked back at the map and continued, "a little over a day from here, but we'll need to head south-east, and we may run into more of the armies camped below."

Jaron asked what he thought to be an obvious question. "There is also the matter of a boat. We can't float down the river on our backs. Is there somewhere along the way we could steal one? Though I don't know how quiet we could be trying to carry it."

"We'll deal with the issue of a boat when we find the river. I don't believe we'll have time to make an ideal water craft, but we'll do what we can with what we find," said Ellian.

"Broken hammer," muttered Arnor, "I hate the water!"

* * * * *

Smoke curled as it rose above the pine engulfed in the flickering orange of the flames. It popped and snapped as the wet wood surrendered to the heat. Mid-May nights were still cold with a biting wind out of the North. Ellian set the broken door in place within the doorway to both hide the light of the fire and to try to stifle the teeth of the wind.

At dawn, Keras had brought along Jaron for a quick hunting expedition. They had consumed their store of provisions from the Timber Elves and needed to restock their food pouches. The hunters returned with several squirrels and a bag filled with wild potatoes and onions. Jaron had not made any of the kills, and he had managed to lose two arrows.

Thargus was a good guide. His pace was easy enough that the group stayed close to each other. Arnor touched the trees as they walked, remarking on the straightness of certain varieties or the wide roots of others. He picked up leaves from the ground, putting them into his pockets after showing them to Keras or Jaron. Arnor even asked Thargus about the local trees. The topic of conversation soon rolled around to the underground river.

"Blood Scar Mountain," Arnor started, "why?"

"Why, what?" Thargus said, shrugging his shoulders and turning to look at Arnor as he walked.

"Why do you call it that?"

"We didn't name it."

"Who did?"

"Don't know," Thargus answered. "All I know is that the entrance we are approaching is a cave in the side of a cliff. There is a locked door we will need to pass through to gain entrance to the Sotho Palala."

Arnor was dumbfounded. "A door, and it's locked? Really? Who would want to break in?" He started laughing, snorting as he spoke. "Are they going to steal the rocks?"

Thargus did not answer. Maybe he didn't know, or maybe he didn't think Arnor deserved an answer. There was indeed much of value in the underground, but he could not expect this hill bumpkin to understand.

Their distrust of one another ran deep, for they came from different branches of the same tree. Each considered the other a traitor. The Mountain Dwarves and the Under Dwarves had been warring for centuries. At one time all Dwarves were the same. Some lived above ground. Some lived below ground. They had their cities in hard to reach areas to avoid contact with the other races of the continent of Melanthios.

The Mountain Dwarf city of DaenDor had entered into alliances with Humans and Elves, trading large quantities of Dwarven made goods. Dwarves are excellent artisans in all manners of steel, stone and wood. The dwarves of the undercity CalleDor, having made many of the goods, felt that the trade of these items, especially weapons, should be banned outside of the Dwarven kingdom. When CalleDor stopped supplying weapons to DaenDor, the Human king, Drewett II, invaded CalleDor, ransacking it and killing hundreds of dwarves, emptying the weapons house.

CalleDor was furious and demanded DaenDor end all ties with the Humans and Elves, but DaenDor refused. Their trade with the other races had made them rich, and DaenDor decided that the trade was too lucrative to abandon. CalleDor invaded DaenDor, recovering the weapons they had sold to DaenDor before the dwarves of DaenDor could sell the weapons outside of the Dwarven communities again. And so, about fifteen hundred years later, Arnor and Thargus watched each other carefully.

Jaron, who followed them, noticed their similarities in demeanor contrasted to their differences in appearance. He had known some people in Westmost to act the same way towards each other. He had never really understood it.

The walk to Blood Scar Mountain was not a great distance, but the terrain was difficult and required patience. The ground cover was a tangle of brambles, bushes, and shrubs. Ground that was firm softened and became bog. Even the trees hindered their advance. Bone-like limbs reached out to capture hood, cloak, and pack.

Their night was long and cold. They huddled together to conserve warmth and pulled dry leaves over their legs to try to insulate themselves further.

As they trudged along, the crimson cliff rose up before them out of the hills. Nestled between the mountains on either side, it appeared and disappeared as Thargus led the party over the swells of forest and fields.

"When I was a little girl," Keras said.

"You're still a little girl," Ellian chimed.

"Shut up," Keras laughed. "When I was a little girl, my mother used to take me out of Westmost on trips in the spring. We would take a wagon over the mountain pass to a fair on the other side. Sometimes, when we would come home the mountains would look like that." She pointed to the red mountain face ahead of them. "Blood Scar Mountain, what a horrible name."

"What was the fair like?" Jaron asked.

"Oh, the fair was beautiful. The colors of the ribbons stretched on the tables, there were so many. The dresses women would wear, I've never seen anything as beautiful. Even the wealthy ladies of Westmost don't dress like that. There were singers and dancers and jugglers," she smiled. "Juggling used to astound me and I would watch until my mother would pull me away. After watching enough, I learned how to do it myself. I even, once, saw a woman walk a tightrope.

"I wish I had gone to the fair," Jaron said.

"I went until my mother died. My father is too busy for all that. I'd like to go back. I want to wear one of those dresses. They were even nicer than that dress at Red Helm."

"You would go out in public like that?" Ellian snorted. Keras hit him.

"We used to have a fair that would put all others to shame," Arnor said. "Candy apples, roast pork, malted beer," he mused. "The land was ripe and wealthy. The women were thick and lovely." He looked over at Thargus. "One year we had some unexpected visitors. Do you remember learning of the slaughter of Fitzman's Fair?" he asked.

"You must have forgotten about the destruction of Bellcleg Den?" said Thargus.

Arnor fumed and spat, "Well then, what about the attack on Renston?"

"How many children did your people kill when they came to Gendron Hollow?" Thargus asked.

"Enough!" Jaron, Ellian, and Keras shouted together.

They came at last to the small lake where the base of the cliff sat on the opposite side. Far to the right, a marshy river emptied into the lake. On their left, the water passed through a narrow break in the stones before continuing away.

Arnor reached into his pouch and pulled out a worn spyglass. It had brass fittings, allowing it to view either long or short distances, but was made mainly from hard black leather. Extending the spyglass, he handed it to Thargus who put it up to his eye and scanned the far shore. Two minutes later, he finally lowered the glass, handed it back to Arnor and pointed out the location of the cave that was the entrance to the underground river.

"Well, here is where the fun begins," Arnor sighed. He held out a small axe to each Jaron, Ellian, and Keras. Then he explained to them the type of tree they were to cut, showing examples of the leaf and bark of each type. He had collected them on the long walk to the lake. "We are going to need thirty straight trees as wide as my fist and three times as tall as Ellian. I believe if we start right away we can be finished by tomorrow night or better." Arnor was already scanning the forest around them when he spat out, "Thargus, stay put."

"And I'm just supposed to sit here and watch you do all the work?" asked Thargus, rubbing his chest. "Arnor you cannot afford to be a moron. You will never finish before tomorrow night without my help. I can work just as hard as you can."

Grudgingly, Arnor removed an axe from his pack, and staring the cave dwarf in the eye, flicked it so that it stuck deep into the tree root next to Thargus's boot.

Without further conversation, they split into two groups, Jaron and Arnor in one group, and Thargus, Ellian, and Keras in the other. Off they went in search of suitable trees.

Jaron watched as a large chunk of the bark fell away at the first swing of Arnor's axe. "These axes weren't made for woodwork," Arnor said, sweating. "But you can throw them a mile." He smiled. "Still, if you swing something sharp enough times, whatever you're swinging it into will begin to take some damage. Once you have made a split in the wood, strike the haft of the axe, or back of the axe head, with a large stick or rock." Arnor took the rock Jaron was holding for him and smashed it into the back of the axe head. "This will drive the blade through." Two more strikes with the stone and Arnor could push the tree over. He held up the small axe. "Funny, how something so small can take down something so big."

When they had acquired the thirty thin trees requested by

Arnor, they started the work of stripping their bark. By the light of the fire, Arnor and Thargus lashed them together, using a good deal of rope made from the stripped bark as they did so. This, along with the rope they had been carrying in their packs, would tie the raft together.

It struck Jaron as funny that for one who did not have a strong affection for water travel; Arnor knew so much about making a watercraft. It wasn't really a boat. It fit the definition of a raft, but the poles on the outer edges pressed in to make an oval shape so that Thargus could direct the craft with a paddle at the stern. By morning, the work on the raft was finished and Arnor decided that they would rest in the shelter of the cave across the water.

On entering the raft, it sank just enough to keep their feet wet. Sitting down meant sitting in water, so they all stood.

Keras moaned at the design flaw.

"Well this is exactly what I had in mind," she said. "You're not in charge of building our next raft, Arnor." She mentioned that they would all be cold and wet for the duration of the journey. Arnor, of course, had foreseen this and two poles were already stretched tip to stern, bowed upward. This left a place to strap bedrolls and clothes well up away from the surface. Even so, the poles were awkward to move around, and ducking under them meant kneeling in the water.

Arnor and Thargus shoved away from the edge to begin the trip across the lake. The water was calm. The sun rose on their left between the peaks of the mountains and the birds sang in the forest behind them. A light breeze came from the south, crisp and cool. Makeshift paddles rose and fell into the clear water, driving them across.

"Will we be able to carry the raft down to the river?" Ellian asked.

"I do not know," answered Thargus. "I have never been here before. We might have to take it apart."

"If you've never been here, how do you know where the entrance is?" asked Ellian.

"I haven't been here, but I have been on this river, just never north of the Fortunal Mountain Range. We'll be getting off the river before the range so that we will approach Temerrac from the north." Thargus cleared his throat. "By the way, we are going to be stopping at a city underground."

Arnor grabbed Thargus by the wrist, letting go of the paddle. "You have something planned, have you?" he growled.

Thargus did not pull away from Arnor, but looked him squarely in the eye. "You chose the path, not I. The city lies on the river. We must stop there. None are allowed to pass the city without giving their names." Arnor let go of him. "This is the law."

Arnor picked up his paddle again. Thargus flicked his wrist, lodging Arnor's axe into the wood post next to Arnor's boot.

"I thought you might want that back."

Chapter 9   Sotho Palala

"Water logged boots and wet pant legs," muttered Keras. "This is gonna be fun. I can just tell." She did not sound convincing. Together, they pulled the raft onto the rocky beach. Arnor did not look well. He kept sipping the water from his flask to fight back the nausea of the short trek across the lake.

Thargus led the way, looking up at the rising stone cliff in front of them. The rock stretched high above their heads and far to both left and right. His eyes studied from the peak to the ground in front of him. "Ah," he said, and walked several paces forward, reaching his hands toward the wall. It appeared Thargus was going to give the wall a mighty push, but instead, Thargus vanished, passing right through. Astonished at first, the others inched forward, and one by one, followed him gingerly through the rock illusion. Each experienced a wet spongy sensation and the smell of oranges as they passed through to join Thargus on the other side.

Beyond the illusion lay a narrow path with high sloping stone sides. It meandered down and to the left, overshadowed by mammoth boulders that hung as if they were about to come crushing down. The entrance to the Sotho Palala was small, wider at the bottom and narrowing at the top.

"Jaron," Ellian said, "have you ever heard of the Lemon Squeeze?"

"No," Jaron responded.

"In Holderness, during training, one of our games was to see who could pass through the smallest opening. It looked a lot like this."

"I heard that you stunk at that game, Ellian," Keras added, receiving a wink from Ellian.

"You're going to have to turn your body sideways and crawl through headfirst," said Ellian to Keras. "I'll hand in all the gear to you and then we can all follow."

"Before Keras entered, she pointed a finger at Jaron, "Don't look at my butt," and then to Ellian, "Don't touch my butt."

"Wait," Ellian clarified, "so I can look then?"

She hit him, and squeezed through the opening.

Within the interior of the cave, the space opened up to almost four feet wide and six feet tall, but it was dark and wet. Arnor lit a torch. Cloaks, hoods, and hands came away from the walls slick with a blood-like black grime. The floor of the cave entrance had a slight incline, but thirty feet in, the cave wound down and to the right, like a spiral staircase without steps, down to a large set of doors. Twelve feet tall, each door consisted of diagonally slatted metal bolted to a wooden base. Two giant brass handles, roughly hammered, were set vertically, one for each door. The doorframe was wide, carved into the red rock itself. Flanking the door, two red stone statues of lions stood, each hair of their crimson manes flowing down to their chests engraved in exquisite detail. Jaron stepped ahead of the party to inspect them. The eyes were glossy red and reflected the flame of the torch in Arnor's hand. As he reached forward to touch the giant cat's shoulder, half-expecting to feel the soft touch of fur, the statue moved. Jaron jumped back in wonder.

The lion spoke.

"Alu ahn bukere an oth Palal?"

Arnor looked at Jaron, Keras, and Ellian. They all shrugged and looked at him. "What is your business on the Sotho Palala?" Arnor translated in the common tongue. "Seriously, none of you speak Dwarven?"

"We seek to travel your path," Thargus answered, in the common tongue, scratching his chest.

Arnor continued to berate Ellian, Jaron, and Keras. "I mean, you work in a library. You live in a library. Take a little incentive."

"You will stop at Sotho Entollo to register your names." The lion had switched to the common tongue. "Sotho Entollo will be watching for you. Do not defile the river."

Beyond the doors, the cave widened. The ceiling of the river cavern glowed bright with luminescent lichen, making the water shine a reflected soft green. The wide bank of the river was covered with small pea-stones, round and multi-colored. Growing sparsely out of the stone bed was a fine moss. Thargus walked to the water's edge and dropping to his hands and knees, drank deeply from the river, soaking his braided goatee thoroughly. Standing again, he drew a deep breath and sighed happily. "I missed the stone." He turned to Arnor, smiling, "Do you feel it, the moisture in the air?" Thargus filled all water skins with the water of the Sotho Palala. "This is the water of legend," he said. "You'll never taste better."

Arnor only grunted and piled his gear far from the water. "Come, we've work to do."

The makeshift raft was dismantled and ported into the cave, one skinned log at a time. Reassembly was time consuming, but in the end, all felt the vessel was a better one for the effort. The problem of wet feet and backsides was addressed, allowing one to sit or lie down without getting wet, although not comfortably.

Thargus and Arnor worked together on the raft, pulling lines of bark rope tight. "Do you always get sick on a boat?" Thargus asked.

"Every time," Arnor answered. "This is going to be a rough trip. Nevertheless, don't you get any ideas about my abilities. Even sick, I'll still cave your head in if I have to."

"Charming," Thargus responded. "I don't have any ginger, but we might find some birthwort growing under the trees above. Chewing that should help."

"Trying to poison me?" Arnor asked.

"Look, suit yourself. I just don't want you throwing up in the river. At the least, do this. Always face forward, downstream. Try to keep the banks up ahead in your vision. And steer or paddle as much as you can."

While Ellian and Jaron explored the riverbank, Keras produced from her pack a hook and line, and using stale bread for bait, left over from the provisions of the Timber Elves, was able to catch several small fish from the river. Arnor allowed a small fire from the trimmings of the raft and laughter came to each after the past few days of hard travel and toil.

The temperature of the Sotho Palala was warm and humid, causing the packs to fill up quickly with the armor, cloaks, and most of the clothing. All went barefoot. Only Ellian went shirtless. Arnor's brown shirt, though soaked with sweat, stayed on his back while his hat stayed firmly on his head. The red feather lay flat across the brim. At the stern of the raft with Thargus, Ellian pushed off from the shore, paddling slowly and making small corrections as the river carried them through the underground oasis.

The water mostly moved at the pace of a fast walk, but some areas of the Sotho Palala were dangerous. The walls crept in and the current increased, creating a ride that both thrilled and frightened all aboard. In sections of the river where the water was shallow, the rocks grated against the raft. Arnor and the others grimaced and winced as they imagined the damage to the ropes holding the raft together.

When the Sotho Palala ran wide and slow, it glowed blue-green from underneath. The luminescent lichen did not fade its energy at night and kept a constant shimmer upon the surface of the flowing river. "Look at the fish!" Keras said with a greedy look in her eye. The schools of fish contrasted as dark shadows against the glow from the bottom. "That one has to be at least five pounds." She pulled out her fishing line.

Thargus informed them that they had spent four days riding the river. Time was hard to discern underground for Ellian, Jaron, Keras, and Arnor, but Thargus always seemed to know the time of day or night.

Ellian wanted to spend more hours per day on the river but Thargus was adamant about breaks during travel to attend to necessary bodily functions. "Do not defile the river," he reminded them repeatedly. Some races, especially Humans, had a habit of using their rivers as both a toilet and a drinking supply.

Arnor did not complain about any chance to get off the raft.

His head ached and the ground spun beneath him. However, he was not as sick as he had expected he would be. Thargus had given him good advice. Keeping his eyes on the shores ahead and actively controlling the motion of the raft had reduced his level of motion sickness. He wished now that he had trusted Thargus about chewing the birthwort.

A low constant rumble broke against the walls and ceiling from downstream. "Sounds a bit scratchy up ahead," Arnor remarked.

Thargus raised his ear and closed his eyes, listening intently. "Good ears, Arnor. I had not caught that, yet. We haven't encountered anything too rough. Maybe this is not as bad as it sounds. Do you want me to walk the bank up ahead and scout it?"

"Nice try, skin-chin!" Arnor responded. "Ellian, Keras, walk around the bend up ahead and see what you see."

"I'll go!" Jaron offered. He had been bored on the raft. Though beautiful, the Sotho Palala was not really up to his tastes. He had no books, and there was not enough light to read anyway. He tried talking to Ellian, but all Ellian wanted to do was talk to Keras.

This made Jaron think of the girls in the square in Westmost. A beautiful girl had caught him looking more than once. One, in particular, had skin as dark as the night and eyes to match. Her smile ran chills up his arms, and her laughter, he had only heard it once, made his eyes well up with tears of joy. The next time he was in Westmost, he vowed, he would talk with her.

Very well," said Arnor, "Ellian, take Jaron with you. Keras, think you can land another fish?"

"I could try." She had already taken out the line.

Jaron ran ahead of Ellian, happily stretching his arms and legs. He stopped once or twice to reach for his toes, enjoying the uncomfortable pull on his muscles. Five days on a cramped raft had made his muscles ache. His legs yearned for freedom. The boulders and rocks on the bank became an obstacle course as he weaved and jumped among them. Out of breath finally, he waited for Ellian. The sound of the river grew louder as they rounded the bend, but there was still no sign of whitewater. Ellian gauged the distance to the next bend. *A tenth of a mile, maybe,* he thought. He turned around to try to get the attention of Arnor and saw daylight. A tunnel opened up on the other side of the river, invisible when looking downstream, but looking upstream, it was as clear as the sunlight it was letting in.

Recovering from his surprise, Ellian pointed out the tunnel to Jaron. "What do you think?" he asked.

"Want to go up and have a look?"

"I'm not sure. Maybe we should go and get everyone else."

Before they could decide, however, Jaron and Ellian found themselves pinned painfully to their stomachs on the ground.

"Well, well, what have we here?" croaked a voice in Jaron's ear. Water soaked through his clothing. Whatever was holding him down had crossed the river.

The pain in Jaron's arm rolled through his shoulder. He could see two large goblins holding Ellian down as well, though it took some effort. As far as Jaron could tell, there was only one goblin pinning his arm on top of him.

Ignoring the burning pain in his arm, Jaron shoved at the stones beneath him, grabbing a fist sized rock in the process, and rolled from under his opponent to over him. The rock came down with a sickening thud against the skull of the goblin.

Jaron rushed the goblins struggling with Ellian, tackling one of them off, so Ellian could overpower the other easily. When the skirmish was over, three goblins lay dead on the ground, one from a broken neck, one from a fractured skull, and the last from a knife wound to the chest. Jaron did not remember that part, but the knife was in his hand.

"Jaron, are you hurt?" Ellian asked.

"No, and you?" Jaron wiped the blood off his blade with his fingers.

"Just a bruise," Ellian responded, searching the goblin at his feet. They sported no armor, but wore dark leather breeches and thick wool shirts, emblazoned with red and white paint on the chest. "Valcella's colors again. They must have come from the opening we saw on the other side. It's about thirty feet wide here." Ellian looked across the river, and saw four water buckets. "The goblins must have seen us while gathering water and set up an ambush."

Ellian and Jaron came to the same conclusion.

"How many buckets are there?" Jaron asked.

"Four."

"One of them went back for help, back to the surface," Jaron said, panicked. There was no time to lose. They rushed back to join the others.

Within moments of rejoining the group, Thargus and Ellian were shoving the raft away from shore and paddling with all of their might downstream. As they neared the tunnel, ten or twelve goblins were rushing out. Jaron and Ellian had indeed missed one, and he had run back up the tunnel to collect reinforcements.

No spears or arrows were hurled at the raft or its passengers as they passed the goblins. Staring in disbelief, some of them laughed and shouted, "Ha, fish food!" The joke spread and they all laughed and jeered, mostly in their own tongue.

The sound of the river increased as the raft flowed downstream. Soon it became a deafening roar, echoing off the walls in a harmonic vibration. The raft rounded a large sweeping bend and lying long before them was a terrifying sight. A straight section of the tunnel held a frightening rolling of white water. Giant boulders lay just under the surface forcing divots and swells in the rushing river.

Thargus yelled instructions to the others. "Your pants, take them off and tie the legs together at the end." He was already doing this and the rapids were approaching with speed. The others followed his orders, unquestioning in their state of fear.

"Now pull the legs over your head to rest on the back of your neck with the pants waist open at the bottom." He was struggling to stand on the raft without hanging on, using his hands to demonstrate for the others.

"If you get tossed into the river, use the waist opening to gulp air from the surface. This should force air into the legs of the pants to help keep you afloat." The crashing waves of standing water were almost upon them. "Can any of you swim?"

"Yes," said Ellian.

"Yes," said Keras.

"Yes," said Jaron.

"No," said Arnor.

The raft pulled violently sideways around the first swell, and Arnor tumbled to the deck. Thargus pushed his paddle into the water, steering the raft as best he could through the challenges ahead. A large boulder hit the right side of the raft, breaking some of the lashings holding it together. Keras pulled on the poles, trying to keep the raft in one piece, but the next boulder broke a pole loose, throwing her several feet in front of the raft. She disappeared into the water. Ellian threw his arm out trying to reach her, but Keras was already following Thargus's advice.

Thargus was shouting to Keras, "Keep your legs pointed downstream! If you hit your head, it's over!" Ellian grabbed a coil of rope and threw a line to Keras. She could not reach it. Water was washing over her head with each swell, but the air in the pant legs kept bringing her back to the surface.

At the front of the raft, Jaron grabbed Ellian's paddle and was paddling with all of his might as Thargus yelled directions.

"Tell me where the boulders are when you see them!" Thargus screamed from the rear where he was attempting to steer.

"One on the left! Go right! Turn to the right!" Jaron shouted. He dug his paddle deep into the river, pulling the tiny vessel past the boulder lying just beneath the surface. More sharp and pointed pieces of stone blocked their path, but Thargus was able to steer around them. Several times, the poles of the raft caught on a boulder, twisting them violently in the process. If the passengers did not panic, the raft would soon correct itself under the paddle of Thargus to continue its journey. The deafening sound of the water became louder as they moved on.

Ellian was keeping an eye on Keras.

Thargus was steering the raft.

Arnor was helpless on the deck.

Jaron got a clear view of what was coming. "Oh, no."

Just past the succession of rolls and boulders were four, large drops of four to five feet each. After the last short drop was nothing, nothing at all but rising mist. The roaring of a large drop deafened them to each other's shouts.

Each held their breath as they fell through the short drops. The water held a moment of calm just before the raft reached the fall.

"Jump!" yelled Thargus, and they leaped into emptiness.

The fall was several seconds long. Jaron drove deep into the pool, feet first. Down, down, down he went. Then, he was swimming up to the surface, his lungs burning. With each stroke of his arms, he expected to break above the water, but there were always a few more feet. When he did reach the surface, he sucked in a deep breath of relief. Jaron's first thoughts were of the others. *Have they survived?* Looking around, he saw Thargus and Keras. Moments later, Ellian surfaced. The companions swam to the side of the pool.

"Are you hurt?" Thargus asked.

"No," said Jaron. Arnor's hat was floating in the middle of the swirling pool. "Where's Arnor?"

"He didn't come up," said Ellian.

Thargus was giving orders again. "Ellian, swim to the raft and drag it to shore. Unwind some rope from the raft. We're going to need it." Thargus was climbing the rocks along the shore, making his way toward the bottom of the waterfall. Jaron pulled on his pants, checking the pocket to make sure he still had his father's ring, and followed Thargus.

When Ellian returned, Thargus was naked, the center of his chest red with a circle of bloody scratches. Thargus tied the rope around his waist and gave the other end to Keras and Jaron. "Let the rope out as I swim down to him. When I give it a good yank, pull us back." He dove into the rolling whitewater. It had already been seven or eight minutes. There was just no way Arnor could be alive.

After a minute, Keras felt a pull on the rope, and she, Ellian and Jaron pulled, foot by foot, muscles straining at the weight of the two dwarves coupled with the weight of the falling water, until finally, Thargus reached the surface. He was alone. Pushing them away, Thargus gulped some air and returned to the bottom.

There was another pull on the rope, and the hauling began again. This time, Thargus had both arms and legs wrapped around a motionless Arnor. The Under dwarf sputtered and cursed as they all pushed and pulled Arnor onto the bank of the river. Arnor gripped his pants in one hand. Moments later, he was the one sputtering and cursing, rolling onto his stomach and retching water.

"What took you so long?" He retched up some more water. "You think I got all day? Like maybe I was just hanging out on the bottom for fun?" He looked at Thargus and coughed again—this time in surprise—"Are you naked? What the first layer of the under-realm happened to your chest?"

All the others could do was stare back at him until Jaron found his voice. "Ten minutes! You were underwater for ten minutes! How are you alive?"

"Would you rather I was dead?" He smiled, putting on his pants, "I got a few tricks of my own." Arnor found a large rock and sat down. "No wonder the goblins were laughing at us." He was now laughing himself. "I don't think we'll be followed."

"Still, we should recover and rebuild the raft as best we can, and soon," Ellian said. "There may be other openings from the surface. They may not follow us from that way," he pointed up to the waterfall's edge, "but we should not hang around to find out."

Arnor stopped, looking around, "Where's my hat?"

Chapter 10 Sotho Entollo

Gathering the scattered pieces of their makeshift watercraft took some time, but luck was on their side. Thankfully, the water in this area was clear. The bottom of the lagoon and basin consisted of relatively light stones and the luminescent algae bloomed. The packs and most of the poles had spun off into a lagoon on the side of the falls. The weapons and heavier gear collected in the center at the deepest point. Thargus's swimming ability was tested again as he gathered each item. Even Arnor's hat was recovered.

Reassembling the raft proved difficult. The improvised rope holding the raft together lay in shreds from the rough waters above the falls. They still had the rope from Red Helm, but it was not enough to make a sturdy vessel. Grudgingly, they climbed aboard the cross member raft. It dipped to just under the surface. They would all be wet until they reached Sotho Entollo.

This leg of travel, thankfully, was short, and soon the Sotho Palala widened with signs of civilization along the shore. Crops lined large areas along the sides of the cavernous tunnel.

Keras could not believe it. "Crops, underground crops. What grows down here? Is that corn?" Keras asked questions even though she knew the answer. It was, indeed, corn.

The colors of the lichen that had so effectively lit the Sotho Palala changed. The light produced by the lichen, a light green, sometimes rolling to blue, got brighter, until finally, it was a bright sun-like yellow. This yellow light streamed around the upcoming bend of the underground river.

Gradually, as the raft approached the city of Sotho Entollo, the subterranean sunlight grew brighter and the grass grew thicker. In bright red and yellow, flowers marked the walls of the cave, cheering the heart. Sotho Entollo was not the cave dwelling Arnor expected.

"A cave city," Jaron stated in awe. "It's beautiful."

Thargus spoke up. "We are not mud dwellers. We are not cave trolls. What Mountain Dwarves do with wood and bricks, we do with stone."

The dwarves of Sotho Entollo had carved each dwelling. Buildings were made of the rock floor of the cavern, carved down instead of built up. Underground, walls and roofs had a different purpose, privacy instead of protection. Rain, what is rain? Wind, there was none. Heat, the underground oasis provided. While most of the lichen around the city grew yellow, there was also some green and pale blue. Other colors were present as well. Pink, orange, and purple grew in gardens tended by the dwarves. Food had been Jaron's biggest question. By the look of the farms, he could see there was enough to feed several thousand. The city stretched away into the distance, and the cavern ceiling rose so high above that Jaron could not make out the details. "Sotho Entollo," he whispered to himself.

Dwarves, women and children, traveled on the banks of the river. Small boats with pairs of women rowed past them. Looking at Arnor and the Humans warily, they threw fishing nets into the wide river.

The companions paddled the raft as straight as they could towards several small boats moored offshore. On the center-most and largest dock, an old dwarf was waving to them with both arms. His mustache was long and white while the hair on his chin was cropped to about an inch. Like Thargus, his beard did not cover his cheeks. As the raft neared, he threw out a rope. Keras caught it cleanly and tied it to the pole at her feet. The dwarf tied the other end of the rope to a post on the pier and called behind him for help. Two other dwarves, also old, joined and the three of them reeled in the raft. It took much work to transfer all of the waterlogged packs up to the dock, but soon it all sat in a heap with the soaked passengers sitting exhausted on the wood beside it.

The sound of metal clanking against metal carried out from between the buildings on the mainland and a contingent of armed guards came marching onto the dock. Arnor counted them, twenty, and as they drew near, he noted that they also were dwarves of advanced age with long beards and deep wrinkles. Their armor was a collection of relics from bygone years, a mismatch of historic pieces. They stopped, while still thirty feet away, dropping to one knee in formation and leveled crossbows at the group. The dock-men moved to the other side of the dock to allow the guard to do as they needed.

The leader approached and spoke in Dwarven. Thargus responded in the same tongue holding out his hands in front of him, palms up. He was surrendering.

Why, thought Jaron. *What have we done?*

Guards from behind the crossbowmen came forward, two for each visitor, and bound them in iron shackles. The guards commandeered a cart from the angler's stalls to haul the packs and weapons behind the prisoners. The march through the city took nearly an hour. Children and women, both young and aged, peered out from the doorways as they passed. No others walked the street.

Like an abandoned city, thought Arnor. *Where are the young men?*

Each prisoner's room had a bed, table, and chair. The blankets were warm and made of fine wool. There were books and candles. If the door did not lock from the outside, Arnor would have sworn he was at the most expensive inn at Westmost proper. But lock, it did. A lovely cage it was, and he didn't like it at all.

All were roomed separately. Jaron thumbed through his room's stack of books. Philosophy was not really his subject. Darhall of Grondhill was a familiar author. When he had studied the philosophers, however, he had not concentrated, and all he really learned about Darhall of Grondhill was that the man existed long ago. What he really wanted right now was a map.

* * * * *

Nine sat in a semi-circle around Thargus. Dressed in robes, they stared at him disapprovingly under bushy grey eyebrows as they stroked the long silver and white hair on their chins.

The center dwarf, younger than the rest but still of advanced age, placed his hands on the podium in front of him and stood. A quill scratched loudly as the secretary of the nine council members, seated far to the right, recorded the encounter.

"Your name?" the head of the council asked in the common tongue.

Thargus was surprised. *This isn't natural for a Dwarven council. Why are they speaking in common?* Quickly, he controlled himself and answered.

"Hammerfist. Thargus Hammerfist."

"Your town of birth?" again, in common.

"Stenwood Den."

"Age?" again, in common.

Something is wrong. Hearings are never held in common. "One hundred and eleven."

"Occupation?"

Thargus did not answer. Something was moving in the hall behind the council.

"Occupation?"

It's cold in here, Thargus thought. *It shouldn't be.* Underground, variations in temperature were never this abrupt. Thargus heard a shuffling sound, ever so slightly. A shadow interrupted the light resting on the shoulders of the council members. *Shade!* Thargus thought in alarm. He kept his eyes and face stoic. He had seen them before. His thoughts traveled back to home, to the terror a shade had held there. He forced himself back to the present and answered the question.

"Cartographer and sage."

"I see. Explain to us the nature of your business and why you travel with such strange companions."

"I travel with the three humans as their guide."

"And the hill dwarf?"

"A mountain dwarf," Thargus corrected, "and a business partner to the father of these three."

"Destination?"

"We are bound for Calhalen in the deep south." The city of Calhalen was also on the Sotho Palala and seemed a plausible lie.

"Very well. This council hearing has finished. Hammerfist, Thargus, you are free to go. You have three days to make the necessary arrangements to leave Sotho Entollo. Collect your companions and go in peace."

Members of the council shuffled out as two dwarves approached Thargus to remove his bonds. Thargus was hesitant to leave. He could not lead the shade back towards the others and saw an opportunity to mislead this minor demon.

"Guard, where is the temple? I wish to pray. It has been a long time since I have had the chance to sit in a proper temple."

"It is under the rose colored stalagmite, near the center of the city."

* * * * *

As Thargus wandered the streets, he was disturbed by the lack of young men in the city. The women of Sotho Entollo were gracious and friendly to him as he passed, but he did not dare ask them what had happened to their husbands and sons.

Inside the temple sat one of the council members, the scribe. Thargus sat in the last row. The scribe turned around to see who had entered. He turned back to his prayer book for a moment before closing it with a deep breath. He stood and made his way to the last row.

"Greetings Thargus of Stenwood Den. I am Soukar Splintleg, and you have questions you wish to ask me."

"I do," responded Thargus. "Why was the council speaking in the common tongue of the Humans?"

Soukar sat down next to Thargus. "Did you not notice anything else during the hearing?

"There was a presence, something dark and unnatural."

"It was the presence of this thing that prompted our change in protocol. We did not want you to reveal the true nature of your journey, for we believe we know what it is. The shades are watching all roads to Sandy River. The hill dwarf in your party is Arnor Ondstriker." He brushed out the wrinkles in his robes as he spoke.

"Who?"

"Now is not the time to play stupid, Hammerfist. Many cities are under surveillance. This city is. Stenwood Den is." Thargus flinched. "All of the food grown by this town goes to support the armies above. Where are the men, you are asking? Slaves for the armies of Valcella, making weapons and handling supply lines, they are forced to work in return for the safety of their wives and children here in the city."

He paused and changed the subject. "We know of the fate of Stenwood Den. We know something of you. Cartographer and sage, true, but the bloodstain on the front of your shirt doesn't lie to me. Does it itch much?" Soukar looked at his own hands, at his nails. "Mine does."

Thargus's eyes went to Soukar's chest. "You're from Stenwood?"

Soukar nodded and said, "You have a mission. Who is your target?"

"I do not know. I am still waiting for confirmation. Until then I have been tasked to be a guide."

"One of the boys?" Soukar paused, "or the dwarf?"

"I do not know."

"I understand your drive to save our city." Soukar grabbed Thargus's hand. "If it is one of the boys, you must withhold your completion of the contract until after the boy has met with the knights at Sandy River."

*   *   *   *   *

Keras, Ellian, Jaron, and Arnor sat isolated in their locked rooms, wondering what was to become of them. The dwarves that attended to them did not engage in conversation and their meals were hard tack with water. After two days, they were allowed to meet in a common room with several chairs surrounding a table of dark wood. In this room, they found their belongings, which they greeted with relief. They opened bags and mentally cataloged to see if anything was missing or lost. Several items were still wet, but everything appeared to be present, save weapons and armor.

Not long after their reunion, Thargus joined them. He had shaved the stubble from his cheeks and braided his goatee. At his waist was a short sword, plain and worn, with a scabbard of thick leather. Arnor did not give him time to explain, but leaped at him as soon as he entered. Jaron and Keras held Arnor back or he might have wrung Thargus's neck. "Where in the second layer of the under-realm have you been? Now that we are in your city, we are the prisoners and you are our captor!" Arnor bellowed.

"Nice to see you too, Arnor," Thargus responded. He sat down. "I believe I stopped being your prisoner some time ago. And you are not mine."

Arnor pushed himself back from Keras and Jaron, straightening his shirt. He sat down across from Thargus. "Well? Answer my question. What the broken hammer took you so long?" Arnor demanded, his voice deep.

"I have much to say. I'm sorry that I have not freed you before this. It was my intention to do so, but I did not know how to sidestep the danger that resides here." Seeing Arnor's impatience, he held up his hands. "Have you seen a young able bodied male dwarf since we came here?"

Arnor backed off and looked skeptically at Thargus as the under dwarf continued.

"The guardsmen that arrested us on the docks make up more than half of the city's current defense force. The city is under occupation from above. Sotho Entollo and its reserves of food are a great prize for a standing or traveling army. Most of the Dwarven men are topside, working as slaves for a mixed army of brindi, goblin, and men. Valcella, it seems, can reach even underground." He let this information sink in. "The food is shipped to the armies of your enemies." He dropped his eyes. "This city's inhabitants are starving."

"How much have you told them?" Ellian asked.

"The council? I lied to them, as far as the official record is concerned. I told them we were merchants on our way to Calhalen. I was able to speak to one of them, Soukar, alone after the hearing. As you can see, he recovered our belongings. We will have fresh provisions as well. And our raft has been repaired and improved."

"The weapons?" Ellian asked.

"Will be available when we make to depart the city," Thargus answered.

"Why should he help us? Since when are the Cave Dwarves our allies?" Arnor asked.

"I'm a cave dwarf," Thargus said flatly.

"The enemy of my enemy is my friend," Keras reminded Arnor.

"How are they controlling the city?" Ellian asked. "Is there a foreign contingent of soldiers stationed here?"

"I wish it were only that. But there is more bad news." Thargus's gaze rolled over each member of the group, but finally rested on Arnor. "I have seen a shade." Arnor's face paled. "It controls the city, holding the inhabitants hostage under the threat of its icy touch. That is why I am late. It took some time for it to lose interest in me."

"Does it know about us?" asked Jaron, sweating.

"Yes. However, what it plans or believes I do not know. All I know is that we must go as soon as possible. We can leave when we wish but—the shade—it makes me nervous."

"The shade, how do you know about those?" Arnor asked Thargus.

"I've dealt with them before. They came to my town and forced us out. It's part of how I met Harnan, but it's a long story."

"We need to go," Jaron said, looking sick.

"We are at a disadvantage underground. Our path won't be hard to follow," responded Arnor.

"Can we get back above ground?" Jaron asked.

"I agree with Jaron," Keras said.

Ellian, planning in his mind already, spoke up. "We need to know where we are with respect to the towns and terrain above."

Thargus nodded in agreement and started to rummage his pockets. Thargus produced a map and spread it out upon the table. It was the strangest diagram ever seen by Jaron, Keras, or Ellian but Arnor and Thargus were familiar with the markings. It showed landmarks both above and below ground. The words were Dwarvish, written in several different colors of ink, with each one representing a separate level of elevation or depth.

"Which way should we go?" asked Keras, not really expecting an answer. Her joke went unnoticed. Arnor answered her question without a hint that he understood her sarcasm.

"Down river, I expect. It's the quickest escape, and if there is an army above us we should try to avoid it."

Keras rolled her eyes and smiled at Jaron.

Arnor read the map carefully, tracing his finger along the paths drawn on the paper. "Sotho Entollo is still some fifteen miles from Temerrac in a straight line."

"But," Thargus interrupted, "the Sotho Palala does not travel in a straight line. The closest exit from the Sotho Palala is another fifteen miles downriver. That exit will add..." He measured the distance with his fingers, "ten miles."

* * * * *

Several elderly dwarves brought the party's arms. It was time to go.

Jaron walked behind the group. He felt like an outsider. True, it had been his decision to take this road to Temerrac at the tower outside of Starkwall. Since then, the other members of the group had made the choices that would get them through the day. How was he ever going to be a leader of men? *Perhaps I never will be,* he thought. *I'm no equal to either Keras or Ellian. One is a natural fighter and the other is a natural leader. Ellian...* Snapped out of his glum state, Jaron watched as Ellian crumpled to the road. Keras joined him, unconscious or dead as a moment of darkness passed over her.

In a blur, Arnor's knife was hurtling through the air and then through the shade, only to clank uselessly on the road. Thargus drew a short sword and lunged at the shade with a blow that would have struck down a mighty warrior, but as he touched the darkness, he too fell.

Arnor drew an axe and stood in front of Jaron, but the minor demon reached out and brushed him away with the back of its hand. Arnor let out a gasp, dropped to his knees, and then to his face where he lie still on the underground road.

The shade advanced on Jaron. He knew he could not outrun this thing. He was facing death. As the darkness reached out, Jaron could see a pale red where eyes should be, a deep emptiness. He braced himself for the cold nothing that awaited him.

The dark shadow raised its arms, fingers outstretched as it moved ever closer. When it touched him, it was indeed cold, but there was something different about this shade that was not present in the last one to touch him, substance. Jaron could feel the icy fingers grasping at his shirt and reaching for his neck. He realized if he could feel it touching him, he could touch it, and hurt it.

He was not about to die quietly, to come this far for naught.

Jaron's fingers reached for the throat of the demon and he squeezed. With every ounce of his strength he pressed. A wail of despair echoed off the ceiling of the cavern, crashing back down with almost physical force. Still he pressed, pushing with all of his strength. Pushing it back onto the ground, he squeezed this thing that had no breath until finally, it was no more.

Chapter 11   Enter the City

Jaron woke. His eye was being propped open and a blindingly radiant light was passing back and forth in front of it. A spasm of pain rolled through his temples as he clamped his eye shut and pulled away. The brilliant intensity disappeared and he opened his eyes to a white dot that slowly became the face of a wizened old female dwarf smiling down at him. "You have slept long, my young friend."

Jaron turned his head, glancing around the room to determine his surroundings, but the space was spinning ever so slightly and refused to come into focus. His gaze returned to the old woman. She, at least, did not bob and sway.

"They call me Orsal. This is the house of healing. I have been here at your side since you were found." She took Jaron's hand in her own. "Sotho Entollo owes you a great debt."

Jaron heard the words, but they did not register. His mind was rolling, trying to fill in the gaps from his last memory. He stretched his thoughts out, not really listening anymore, looking for the series of events that led him here. It was no good. He was confused, and he did not know this woman. She stood and poured water into a cup from a steaming pot. The scent of endalil tea wafted around the room.

"Your friends," Orsal said, handing him the cup, "suggested this for you." At hearing the words, 'Your friends,' all of Jaron's recent memories came flooding back. His eyes widened in terror for their safety, and he made as if to stand up. Sensing this, the woman gently pressed him to lie back against the pillows. "Your friends have been eagerly awaiting your return.

"That shadow had been here to hold this city hostage." She took a deep breath. "It killed many children of Sotho Entollo until the men surrendered and were put into bondage." Her eyes closed and an edge of steel resolve held her voice from wavering. "And after the men were gone, it would come in the night, stepping into nurseries. It would visit the school. It would kill at random to hold us in line. It has been a year since I have seen my husband or son. My daughter Eleinai sang for our men as they were led away. My daughter will never sing for them again, even if they live."

* * * * *

Jostled by a Dwarven child, Arnor had been the first to wake following the attack. Looking around, at Ellian, Keras, Thargus, and Jaron, he finally focused on the young girl. "My friends have gone to get help." She looked over to the black stain on the road and smiled. "You killed it." To Arnor's great astonishment, she then hugged him with all of her might, crying. She smiled, cried, and hugged, pressing her face into his shoulder. The little girl, Caral, stayed with him until her friends returned with mothers and grandmothers.

The Dwarven women watched over them as they recovered. Thargus woke in short time. Several hours later, Keras and Ellian regained consciousness, but Jaron lingered near death for a day and then lay on the edge of wakefulness for another.

During the wait for Jaron's recovery, the city elders visited the site of the attack, spitting on the ground where the shade lay staining the road. The city's finest families clamored to house the heroes.

"Hey," exclaimed Keras in jest, "The lock is on the inside of the door this time."

The people of the city made some new additions to the company's gear, nothing too extravagant. These were poor people, after all, but they generously shared what they had available. Plenty of dried fruit, dried meat, and hard tack bread filled the packs. Soukar Splintleg even provided a boat.

Thargus looked at his new sword, a gift from the council. An inscription, 'Et alaes u tra,' emblazoned the center of the blade.

"What does it mean?" Ellian asked.

"In small steps," Thargus answered. "Who cares? Look at that blade."

At news of Jaron's recovery, Keras and Ellian were eager to see him. Arnor held them back. "He is still weak. I do not know how any of us survived, but he took the weight of the attack. Give him time. When he rises from the bed, you may visit him." Arnor, however, did not heed his own advice, and he visited Jaron within the hour of his warning to Ellian and Keras.

"My lad, are you awake?"

"Arnor! I am. Come in, please!"

Closing the door behind him, Arnor pulled over a short stool and set it next to the bed. *He survived again,* Arnor thought.

"I killed it? Can they die?"

"It's dead. I did not know it was possible."

"I felt it, you know, when it attacked Ellian. When it attacked Keras, Thargus and you. I felt it, deep, deep in here." Jaron touched the center of his chest. "It grew weaker with every hit, every touch. By the time it got to me it must have expended much of its energy."

"I don't know." It was the truth. "Before you, every person who has been the subject of a direct attack by a shade, every one of them, has died. Last time it was a glancing touch. This time, you survived a direct attack. And not only that, you beat it, killed it."

"I thought all of you were dead when I saw you fall. How did you survive?" Jaron asked.

"I don't know that either. Maybe, as you said, it was conserving its energy for you." Arnor poured himself a cup of endalil tea from the pot next to the bed and lifted his cup toward Jaron, "Do you want some more?" Jaron held out his cup for Arnor to refill. "Maybe, there's something about you that weakened it. This was your second encounter, most don't get that." Arnor sipped his tea, burning his lip. "The only reason you survived the first encounter, in Westmost, as far as I can fathom, was the ale in your system in conjunction with only a glancing curiosity of the shade. The one in Westmost had not known your identity. But this one here, this one had guessed it."

My identity, what is that, I wonder, Jaron mused to himself. *Son of a man; who was heir to a throne that is no more, orphan, bookkeeper, librarian, oaf.* He brushed aside his doubts for a second. "Arnor, these knights, the knights of Mavius's army, what do they want? I don't think Mavius would feel any great peace knowing that they seek an audience with me. Perhaps they don't follow him as strongly as one would believe."

"More than ever I begin to agree with the plan to meet the knights. If we can convince these knights to abandon Mavius, we might have a chance. Do you think you could face another one of the shades?"

Jaron's face paled as he asked, "So, you think there are more?" Arnor nodded. Feeling dizzy, Jaron said, "When it grabbed me, I felt its pain. But I also felt anger, deep and deadly, like it had been hungry to kill." His eyes closed, and he looked drained. "It's cold."

"It's all right, lad, rest. I'll just sit with you a bit."

*   *   *   *   *

Laughter filled the voices of the children around them. They were not to be shooed away by the elders of Sotho Entollo. When the shade had held their mothers in awe and fear, the children did not attend classes, did not attend prayers, and did not play. Now the children were free to be children again. Caral and her friends held dramas for Arnor and Thargus, acting the parts of animals and spirits as they told the tale of Gimmish the Grand, an old Dwarven hero. The children even convinced Arnor to play a game of cards.

Meals came from different houses each night. The cooks would stay to talk with the travelers and would loathe leaving them. More than one maiden dwarf made an advance on either Thargus or Arnor. One even had her eye on Ellian, causing him to blush in embarrassment.

Two days passed too quickly, and when the group made to leave this time, the city elders and a small collection of women and children gathered to wish them farewell. The boat was loaded with their packs and food. Keras and Arnor took the two front oars and Jaron and Ellian took the two rear. Thargus stood at the stern.

Arnor glanced back to see the city once more and instead saw the little girl, Caral. She was waving and smiling. Arnor found a smile of his own as his eyes welled. He waved back, and in that instant, for the love of a child, the long prejudice and hatred of Under Dwarves began to melt. *The City of Sotho Entollo,* Arnor thought. He would come back to this city in a time of peace, if he could, if it were still here after all of this mess.

After speaking with the elders, they had decided to use the exit at the ventilation tunnel named Pasir Ris. The distance was not far. Once there, they abandoned the boat, tying it to the service dock at the tunnel entrance. Someone from the city would retrieve it later. The Under Dwarves sculpted this bore as an airshaft to bring fresh air from topside into the Sotho Palala. Six foot round, a breeze flowed out of the opening, bringing the smells of living plants with it. Being underground for so long can have an effect on one's disposition, and it wasn't until this moment anyone let on just how much they were eagerly awaiting the touch of sunlight again.

After a quarter of a mile of walking in a winding line, the path started to rise, until the angle was too steep. Keras and Thargus used a rope and spike system to scale the walls, lowering ropes to those waiting below. As they neared the exit, the path became a natural cave, sloped and cramped. Feeling the wind on their faces, they crawled in single file through the natural cavity as it meandered left and right. The mouth of the exit was high up a moss-covered wall over a shallow and fast moving river. From the opening, there was a twenty-foot drop to the riverbed. Keras set an anchor spike in the rock just inside the crevice and used the rope to lower herself to the flowing water. "It's like ice!" she cried.

Trees and rock walls obscured the view on both sides of the river so that there was no clear way to determine direction. The group therefore had two choices: upstream or down.

Arnor produced a needle from his pack. After rubbing it across his clothing several times, he placed it on a fallen leaf in one of the stone impressions filled with water. It immediately spun around to point in the Northern direction. "Well," said Arnor, "the river is flowing south-east. Downstream it is."

The river wound its way between steep walls of rock. Walking would be difficult. Stones and ledges were plentiful on both sides of the river, but the path had to be chosen carefully so the route would not disappear. None of them were interested in swimming the frigid waters.

Some distance downriver, Jaron could not determine how far, as it was hard to count his steps jumping from rock to rock, the steep rock walls opened up to a field, filled with wildflowers, tall grass, and sunlight. Jaron closed his eyes and smiled up at the sun peeking out from behind the clouds. He took a moment to enjoy its warmth. Insects buzzed away in the afternoon heat.

"Can we stay here for an hour?" Jaron asked.

"Temerrac is about three miles southwest of here," Thargus said. "The Sotho Palala brought us south of the Besoth Gorge and we are now about a mile east of the Holderness Road." He rolled up the map and stowed it back in his pack.

"An hour is a long break," Ellian said, looking up at the sun and clouds. "If we press on, we could be in Temerrac by noon."

"Noon, one o'clock, what's the difference?" Keras asked, lying down.

"Look at the sky," Arnor said, helping Keras back to her feet. "This weather isn't going to last."

After the field, the path narrowed and the five of them traveled in single file. The trees were tall, straight, and slender. Old leaves and branches littered the sides of the trail. The clouds overhead began to darken and a light rain fell. The ground beneath their feet became soft with water that pressed up from underneath with every step.

To his left, through the trees, Jaron could see the tall buildings of Temerrac. Over the next clump of trees, rising high into the sky, a feat of engineering overwhelmed Keras, Ellian, and Jaron. They had never seen a structure so massive and clever. Temerrac had an aqueduct. The tubes, hollow and wide, stretched from far below the water's surface to the fill basin at the top. Within the tubes, giant screws, tight to the insides of the tube, forced water to rise at a continuous rate. The same river that provided the water drove the screws by way of a giant paddle wheel connected through a series of gears and powered by the current. From the fill basin at the top, the water flowed down stone channels to the next section where, two hundred yards away, another set of water screws raised it again. This system repeated itself until the water was raised to the city on the hill.

Jaron stared at it, mouth open in wonder and curiosity.

"You trying to catch mosquitoes?" Arnor asked.

"It's so tall. This brings water all the way up into the pass?"

"Well, there are several screw points along the way, but it does just what you said."

Jaron wanted to spend time inspecting the aqueduct, but the others would not wait. At least the sections followed the road to the city. The road wound back and forth as it climbed into the pass of Temerrac like the paths leading to the Melaral battlefield. Jaron shivered as he remembered the horrible dream after walking through that graveyard.

The walls of Temerrac reached high, connecting to the mountain stone on the sides of the pass. As they entered the city, familiar smells reminded Jaron of the market in Westmost. The scent of toffee apples and muffins filled the air.

"The Northern side of the city is the theater district. Best in the land, best in the world, probably," Arnor said. "Come this way." Arnor turned down a side street. He fluffed the feather in his hat looking truly happy. "This city has been my home more than once. I spent twenty years here." He smiled at the memory. "Those were good years."

The street narrowed. They were entering one of the older and wealthier sections of Temerrac. The buildings were modest but tended meticulously. Arnor stopped at a double-wide door with a rounded top and knocked. A small hinged door in the middle of the large rounded door flipped open and slammed shut again. The door was yanked open by a smiling man, rotund and large. His beard was cut short, like his hair, which was balding and brown. His clothes were well cut and expensive. He picked up Arnor in a bear hug.

"Arnie, you're back! Did you bring any of the Elven whiskey with you this time?" He put Arnor down. "Come in, come in. Who are your friends?"

"Jon," said Arnor, "we can't stay long, just a night maybe." Arnor stepped aside and introduced first Ellian, then Keras, Thargus, and finally Jaron.

"I am Woburn, Jon Woburn."

"Governor of Temerrac," said Arnor.

Jon laughed it off. "I wasn't always."

They walked into a sitting room where two other men were already engaged in conversation. One was tall, wearing a red jacket, and the other, like their host, had a belly on him.

"Where are my manners? I'm so sorry. This," Jon said gesturing to the tall man with the red jacket, "is Harris Tuno of the Mason's Guild. They've expanded since you were here last, Arnor."

"How so?" asked Arnor.

"We've moved to the old city hall building in the southern district." Harris smiled. "Recruitment is up and our projects are finally becoming profitable."

Jon pointed his finger at the other man. "And this is Verne Ringman of the Hall of Elements."

Keras found her voice first. "The Hall of Elements!" she said in awe.

All regarded Verne Ringman with renewed interest. Blond stubble adorned his cheeks and chin while a curly head-full of yellow golden hair fell onto his shoulders. Like the others of his trio, he was overweight and pale. Study of magic, obviously, did not afford one to spend much time away from the tomes of complex spell formulas. An easy chair and lack of exercise were surely the cause of this man's portliness. Verne met their gazes with humility. "I'm just an apprentice really."

"Go on," said Jon. "Show them something."

"It's nothing," Verne answered. Jon and Harris both prodded him until he relented. Verne took an ember from the fire with his bare hands. It didn't burn him, and using the glow, he created a small flame that danced across his fingers, sometimes rising nearly to the ceiling. He extinguished the flame and threw the still glowing ember back into the fireplace. Like children at a fair, Jaron, Ellian, and Keras applauded loudly.

"That's just magic," said Verne. "You should see what Harris has been working on."

Harris, smiling, was eager to reveal his discovery. He produced a small box and opened the lid, revealing a white and grey powder. "Get me a mug," Harris said to Jon. Harris placed a small bit of powder into the mug and set it on the table, clear of anything flammable. "Verne, if you would?"

Verne retrieved another small glowing ember from the fireplace and dropped it into the mug. A hissing and glowing pillar of flame erupted from the mug for a fraction of a second. Jon rushed to open a few windows to air out the smoke from the room.

Harris, waving away the smoke from the mug, smiled at the stunned looks from his audience. "We discovered the properties of this last year and we think it will have a great many uses: building roads through the mountains, excavating precious metals, maybe even weapons. We've been producing and stockpiling it in the Mason's Guild for further experiments."

"Jon," Arnor said, "this isn't just a friendly visit. We've..."

A horn interrupted Arnor, sounding in the distance, ringing out three times. The horn was followed by bells, loud and low in tone. The bells rang five times before the call was answered by other bells within the city. Jon listened to the horn and first bell toll before his face went pale.

"What's happening?" Jaron asked.

Jon grabbed his hat and headed for the door, "There is an army approaching the South gate."

Chapter 12   General Shale

A great distance to the south of the city, the glow of torches wound through the trees as a large army advanced, marching along the wide road. Bearing the colors red and white, men rode in formation. Oxen pulled covered carts filled with barrels and crates, armor and weapons, or tents and tools. They spread out into the valley between the mountain sisters of Gemisis and Gemore.

Jon looked out from the high walls of Temerrac. "White and red colors, Valcella is here. There are far more than we anticipated. We expected this might happen so close to King Gurrand's coronation. He pulled forces north for his own glory, but they should be back soon. We've received pigeons that they're on their way."

"They're not coming," Arnor said. "That's why I'm here. I just left Starkwall. It's under siege. The bridges are closed."

"But the pigeons, the messages..." Jon said.

"Forgeries," Arnor answered. "I'm sorry Jon. It took us too long to get here. I had hoped we could warn you in time."

Jon turned to one of his men, "Send pigeons to Denshire and Holderness. Inform them that Temerrac needs aid." He then added under his breath, "Stupid coronation." Composing himself for his men, he looked out over the wall again at the army making camp. "Still, the gate should hold. We knew Valcella's armies would try to pass through Temerrac eventually. They won't be able to take it. Temerrac has always been able to restrict the passage of armies through the mountains.

"You don't intend to let them through?"

"Valcella is a neutral city. If we let one army through, we have to let them all through. No, we will hold until help arrives."

Arnor frowned.

A horn call sounded from outside the southern wall, one long blast followed by three short. The pattern repeated. Jon pushed away from the wall. "Arnor, I would be a fool not to use your council while you are here. Come with me. Let's see what this general has to say."

Outside the south gate of Temerrac, four men on horseback waited to speak with an emissary from the city. Jon and Arnor rode out to meet them.

Tall on his horse, Valcella's general wore a black chain mail shirt, breastplate, rerebrace, and vambrace. His gloves were black leather and creaked as he gripped the reins of his steed. The horse bore black barding on its neck, shoulder, head, and chest. A long mustache of speckled grey fell from the general's face to rest on his breastplate. His eyes held contempt and arrogance in them.

"I am General Shale of Valcella. Who are you?"

"Jon Woburn, Governor, representative of the People of Temerrac. What is your purpose here?"

The general leaned forward, "We intend to pass through this city."

"We are a neutral city. We always have been, General. We'll send word north so you can hold a meeting with King Gurrand."

"Neutrality is no longer given to you. We intend to pass through." He said this flatly, turning his horse to leave.

"What do you offer in return?"

The general spun his horse back around.

"We may let you live. If you intend to stay in the city, I suggest you get the rabble under control. You are now subjects of Valcella. I will not tolerate incidents of disobedience. We pass through Temerrac tomorrow. Open the gate."

* * * * *

The darkness softened with the coming dawn. The Eastern Fortunal Mountain's high and naked stone peaks appeared black in contrast to the halo glowing from the rising sun behind them. As the first dazzling finger of sunlight reached past the mountains, General Shale lowered his spyglass. "The gate is still closed. Send the Pelmari and ready the battering ram."

The walls were no match for the pale-skinned soldiers. Their ladders weren't raised from the ground but lowered from the mountains on either side. For the past week, the Pelmari had been climbing the mountains that flanked Temerrac. They had only to drop into the city from above.

* * * * *

"How many?" Arnor asked.

"Eight hundred Pelmari soldiers have invaded the city," said Jon. "The guard heavily outnumber them. We should restore order soon."

"Eight hundred Pelmari soldiers might as well be ten thousand. We're talking about the Pelmari here," Arnor shot back.

"The guard will take them."

"It's the Pelmari," Arnor argued. "Have you ever seen the Pelmari in battle?" asked Arnor. "Skin as pale as a cloud. Their ears are round, but the eyes are Elven. Orbs of light purple, like the lilac flower when it blooms in late summer, they stare into your soul. No other Human on the continent has eyes of that color."

Jaron recalled learning of the Pelmari. The men and women were fierce. Born into a mercenary society and raised as soldiers, each boy and girl in their culture leave their parents at age nine to attend a fighting academy that pits them one against another. Before age twelve, all attendants of the academy have been involved in at least one sanctioned fight to the death.

Each warrior specializes in warfare skills and tactics. The students practice hand-to-hand combat, from basic grappling, to gravity defying kicks. They learn how to be lethal with any kind of weapon. A Pelmari soldier can make two hundred cuts, using a halberd of eight feet in length, until the unlucky victim dies of blood loss. They have the ability to kill quickly and without pain, but cruelly choose not to.

Jaron wondered, *how does such a society flourish? How do they overcome their cruelty to bear children with each other?* Jaron had not known many women, and fewer girls, in the library of Westmost. He had surely never kissed one. Every time he had the opportunity to talk to one, a knot rolled up in his stomach and somehow made him spout stupid things. Jokes, as old as the sea, or meaningless boasts overcame him whenever he opened his mouth, proving his idiocy. As afraid as he always was of women, he had never worried about actually being on the receiving end of bodily harm. Each Pelmari woman was as deadly as any male.

Jaron forced his thoughts back to the matter at hand. The Pelmari were killing and burning all over the city. How many were there, eight hundred? Each Pelmari soldier, wearing red leather, could best eight to ten of any warrior. Jaron looked around him and did not count many warriors. Ellian he could count as one, but Keras? Outside of practice on the Aquilo, he had only seen her use a bow. Arnor had proven himself in battle after battle, and Thargus; well that was another question.

We came to warn Temerrac, Jaron thought, *another failure. Can I do anything right?* He looked down at himself. He was skinnier than he had been in Westmost, but he was also stronger. His legs did not tire so easily and the pack on his back no longer felt a burden. Still, he was no soldier. With the Pelmari invasion of the city, and the army determined to pass through, Jaron had a hard time understanding how they were going to be able to get through to the south themselves.

Ellian joined Jaron in the common room. He was out of breath from running. "Jaron, there's a group of Pelmari on the way to this quarter. Arm yourself and get to the roof."

*   *   *   *   *

Most of the city guard were busy at the wall. Valcella's battering ram hung suspended from a wooden mount. The men of Valcella pulled it backwards with long ropes then let it swing against the door without exposing themselves to direct bowshot. It fell against the south gate shaking the ground with every hit.

Boom.

Boom.

Boom.

The people of the city had armed themselves with swords, axes, and bows. Some even used objects from their homes or professions. Pitchforks, knives, flails of wood, pans, all became weapons. Across the square, the butcher had armed himself and his sons with razor sharp knives. They carried thighbones of cows to ward off blows. The butcher carried a heavy wide blade, the muscles of his arms conditioned for swinging it through bone.

Jaron watched from the rooftop for any sight of the invaders. He had taken a bow from the wall downstairs. Ellian and Keras remained with him, but Arnor and Thargus had joined the fray on the other side of the city.

A wave of Pelmari came through the square, killing any in their path. Women and children fell as often as fighting men. Out of the reach of Jaron's bow, a Pelmari soldier was making a stand at the corner of the square. The bodies of guards and civilian men lay about him as trophies to his grisly skill. One after another came at him. One after another fell to him. He moved with a flurry of turns and throws, and his blade bit deep as it followed the arc of his momentum. As the onslaught of challengers thinned, he fought with less intensity, conserving his strength.

Keras, watching intently, could watch no more. Setting aside her bow, she checked the catches on the two scabbards that crisscrossed her back. The catch on each scabbard kept the short swords in place until flipped to the side with a flick of the thumb. This allowed her to draw her blades from underneath, instead of blindly reaching over her shoulders for them. She scaled her way from the roof to where she could safely leap to the ground.

"Where are you going?" Ellian yelled after her.

"I can help," Keras yelled back. Anger swelled within her as she walked past the dying men, women, and children, but she did not stop for them.

The Pelmari soldier finished his opponent, the butcher, deftly avoiding a wild swing and driving his blade up into the heart and lungs from underneath. He pushed the butcher from his blade with his free hand and looked around him to see if there were any more threats. Keras, at a distance, did not immediately register to him and he moved to leave.

"Hold, Soldier," Keras called as she approached. Still wiping his blade, the fighter turned and readied himself for another confrontation. Keras drew her short swords, reaching behind to her kidneys and flipping the catch on each. The blades were before her in one smooth simultaneous motion, with her left blade catching the first swing from the pale demon before her.

The two joined in a dance of attempted murder, each trying to gain the advantage on the other. Keras mimicked the circular fighting style of the Pelmari soldier. Her blade-to-blade parry accelerated, pushing the point of the attack away and nudging her assailant off balance by stepping into the wake of his swing. The soldier took a blow to the midsection as Keras raised her knee.

Jaron had never seen such ability. He did not notice as Ellian, following the same path down the front of the building as Keras, left him alone on the rooftop.

The soldier was back on his haunches, having rolled over backwards from the force of the knee. Keras stepped, left foot over right, circling her opponent, blades moving in a slow pattern like a coiled snake waiting to strike.

Other citizens of Temerrac entered the square and as they noticed the combatants they watched from a distance, fearful of the outcome. They gasped in alarm as Keras and the Pelmari soldier danced around each other.

The sound of the swords ringing together came to Jaron's ears an instant after his eyes registered the swing. Keras began to spin with her next attack. Steel whirled in patterns, creating a shield against counterattack. Blow after blow turned away as Keras deflected, parried, and blocked.

Keras read her opponent. She cataloged his moves and attacks and deconstructed his pattern of defense. She noted the flick of his shoulder, recognizing it as a prediction of the coming thrust. The movement of his upper body in conjunction with the speed of his footwork showed Keras a weakness in her opponent's core strength. Based on his prior movements, Keras reconstructed the Pelmari's attack pattern. She knew what he was going to do next. She knew where to strike to remove the soldier's strength. Parrying the Pelmari's surprise attack, she guided her edge to slash across his thigh.

Pelmari blood splashed, mingling on the ground with the blood of his victims. Keras slowed her momentum while still keeping the flow of her deadly routine. Another slash at the soldier's leg hit deep. He was bleeding into his boot, moving ever slower.

Keras's next attack followed a spinning parry, pinning her opponent's sword to his own side. Without the ability to stop the succeeding blow, the Pelmari soldier exhaled deeply, preparing himself for what he knew was coming. Keras's short sword entered his spinal column just above the shoulder. He shuddered and collapsed in a broken heap at her feet.

Keras dropped to one knee next to the paralyzed soldier. Wide and wan, purple eyes stared at her in amazement. Mouth agape in pain, the fighter's powerless hands released their hold of his weapon. Using the edge of her sword, she ended the soldier's suffering.

In the distance, the sound of the battering ram echoed.

Boom.

Boom.

Boom.

"Jaron, get down here!" Ellian called up.

Jaron shouldered his bow and carefully climbed down to the street.

The people entering the square were now increasing in number and they all came from the southern side of the city. Ellian was getting information from the youngest son of the butcher. He had left the square early and did not yet know of his father's death.

There was the smell of smoke in the air. All across town, buildings were burning. The Pelmari were lighting whole blocks of the city. Jaron could hear the crackle of flames inside the buildings as he ran past.

"Get Keras," Ellian said. "The last Pelmari are making a stand near the temple. We're going there."

* * * * *

The temple bridge was a bridge no longer. Mangled and broken, it had the appearance as if a pair of giant hands had grabbed it from the ground and twisted it. Within the fabricated pond surrounding the temple, fifteen-foot tall mounds of dirt rose out of the water. The last of the Pelmari soldiers had used the bridge as a defensive advantage. Setting their backs to the island, they had been able to repel attacks from their front.

They had not counted on either the temerity of the citizens of Temerrac or the power of the students from the Hall of Elements. Verne had cast a spell that forced the Pelmari soldiers backwards onto the bridge. Flames had spread from his hands down to the ground and across the bridge in a wall of fire and searing heat. Then, another mage had twisted the bridge to hinder their return. And so the Pelmari fell back onto the island until they finally retreated to the temple. The people of the village did not follow them, believing them contained.

The sound of the ram at the southern gate continued to ring.

Boom.

Boom.

Boom.

The people were taking advantage of the lull in fighting to tend to their dead. Jaron watched one girl. She cried at her mother's side, tears streaming over the blood that covered her face. Verne watched over another young girl that had taken a blow to her head. Blood caked around her left ear and down her neck. Verne would not leave her side.

Thargus and Arnor met him there. Arnor had cuts and bruises. He had taken two of the Pelmari soldiers with him down a flight of stairs. He walked away. They did not. Thargus had taken a slash across his forehead, not deep enough to break bone, but he would have a nasty scar to help him remember this day. Dirt and blood stained his hands. When asked about his wound, he only replied, "I did my share of damage as well."

Arnor, after tending to Thargus, visited Verne as he was telling his tale of the battle. "Harris and I, we were running from the group of soldiers that had been attacking the city hall. We were not prepared to fight any of them, and they knew it. As we turned the corner to the temple round, we met another two soldiers holding Neeva." He gestured to the girl. "I think they were going to kill her. They seemed to believe we were a bigger prize. Perhaps, they recognized me from the Hall of Elements. I used the first spell that came to mind and boiled their blood where they stood. Neeva took a nasty blow to the head from one of them. When our pursuers caught up to us, I corralled them toward the bridge by laying down a superficial, but intimidating, floor of fire. My master twisted the ground forcing them to retreat further." Verne brushed the girl's hair back. "Without my master, I swear, we would probably be dead."

"Your master, where is he?"

"It's her, Neeva."

Arnor, surprised, looked down at the girl. "Is this her, your master? She's not yet fourteen!"

"I know. She is the youngest master in the Hall, but her powers are formidable, and her memory is flawless for calculations."

Her dark brown hair was matted with blood. There were no shoes on her feet, and her soles were filthy with the dirt and dust of the streets. Dressed as one of the Hall of Elements, her wide-collared shirt was gray, to represent the stone. Her pants were black and cut short around the calves. She carried no pouch for spell components, and no spell book.

"Did she do that?" Arnor asked, incredulously, pointing to the contorted metal of the bridge and the giant piles of dirt and sand on either side of it.

"Yes, but because she was already suffering from the blow of one of the soldiers, she lost consciousness before she could do any real damage."

"She did that after he hit her? Are there any other Masters from this Hall walking around the city? We could use them." Arnor stared out at the destruction. "I hope she lives."

The sound of the battering ram changed.

Boom.

Boom.

Crack!

The Valcella ram had broken through the gate.

Harris came running from the south side into the round screaming at the top of his lungs. "We have to get out of the south end!" Harris yelled. "Everybody to the North!"

"What's going on?" Verne asked. "Is it the gate? They've broken through?"

"No, fire, the Mason's Guild is on fire! The powder..."

Verne's eyes went wide. "I don't think I can contain that."

"If you can't make the north gate, make way for the sewer and drainage system on the eastern side." Harris was frantic. He left them and tried to get people to understand. They needed to run before it was too late. He was interrupted by the sound of marching boots. Shale's army had entered the south gate and was headed this way.

A tremor shook the ground, accompanied by a thunderclap that left Jaron's ears ringing. The sound fell like a rolling boom that shook his spine. Immediately after, another thunderclap broke through the air as another tremor knocked them from their feet.

Dust poured like fog through the streets of Temerrac.

Chapter 13   Death at Sandy River

Sunlight pierced Jaron's sleep. Straining to withstand the brightness, he opened his eyes. Pain danced in his temples, stretching across the back of his skull. The world rolled around until vertigo pushed him to reach out his hands for support.

Under Jaron's hands, the floor of the wagon trundled, wheels maneuvering the uneven road. The iron bars overhead cast short straight shadows from the summer sun burning down high and bright in the sky. The wagon crested a hill in a wide-open field.

His tongue felt grimy and he wiped dry spittle from the corners of his mouth. He touched his left temple with his fingers and winced sharply at the pain.

That's a big bump, Jaron thought.

Four people were in the cart with him, a girl, a woman, and two men Jaron recognized as guards of the southern wall, Rennek and Jel. They were badly beaten, and Rennek looked either unconscious or dead.

Next to Jaron sat the girl Neeva. He had seen her before with Verne, but Verne was not in the wagon.

Jaron tried to catch her attention.

"Hey," he whispered.

There was no reaction from her.

"Excuse me," he tried again.

"Shh!" was all she said.

He sat for a minute or two, but he could not keep the silence.

"I know Verne," he said.

She glared at him.

Jaron thought to look behind him. There, on horseback, a sandy haired soldier in his red and white tunic rode alongside the cart. When the soldier moved ahead of them again, Neeva spoke.

"Don't talk to me. I don't want to know you."

Jaron glanced at her. Over her eye, half covered by her black tousled hair, was a nasty welt. Dried blood sat in one corner of her lip.

He looked away, trying to make out where they were. Staring out from between the bars as the field became forest, there wasn't much to see. The road was well maintained, hard packed with gravel and wide enough for two carriages to pass each other without either pulling aside.

"Where are we going?" he finally asked.

"South. Valcella, probably," Neeva answered after looking to see that the soldiers on horseback were far enough away. "Something you did, or said, or had, caught the General's attention and now we are all being carted south." She touched the bars in front of her with the tips of her fingers.

Then Jaron realized, "You're Verne's teacher, the stone mage?" *She's so young,* he thought. *Is she even fifteen?* "Can you get us out of here?"

"No." She looked perturbed at his questions.

"Why?"

"Because, I have to touch it," she hissed. "Don't you know anything of magic? Do you think I walk barefoot because I enjoy the sand through my toes? I need to touch it to control it."

"But fire magic doesn't need to 'touch it.'"

"It has to be close enough to touch, for fire." She put her slender arm through the bars, reaching for the ground. "Too far."

A whip cracked the air, and Neeva jerked her arm back into the wagon screaming in pain. Her brown eyes smoldered with hate at the guard. Surrounded by wood and iron there was no way for her to use her talents. A large welt took shape on her shoulder. Frustrated and angry, she craned her neck to search the other wagons for Verne. If he could get close enough to a spark or a flame, they could get out of here. Her view to the front was blocked by the tails of the horses pulling the wagon, and her view behind was obstructed by the horses pulling the next cart.

"Fire, stone, water," Jaron said to himself quietly, "what about air?"

"There are no air mages. We're always touching air and we

can't use it. Maybe we're not intended to." She traced calculations on the wood floor in front of her absently.

"But..." Jaron started.

"Shut up."

The only one in the cart Jaron didn't know was the woman. Her eyes met his. She was older than he by maybe ten years, and she had been crying recently. Dirt lines streamed her face, and her auburn hair hung flat, matted with sweat and mud. The woman asked, "What is your name?"

"Jaron."

"You have a strange accent."

"I'm from Westmost."

"It was you, wasn't it? You had the ring?" she asked.

"What? They found my ring?" Jaron searched his pockets.

"The General, when he found it, said you were a spy and asked everyone if they knew you or not. Nobody did, except for that tall boy they brought you in with. It didn't matter. He rounded up the twenty-five people found closest to you and put us in these carts."

"Ellian!" Jaron gasped. "Where is he?"

"He was alive when I saw him last, but they did horrible things to him. He wouldn't talk. The soldiers that brought you, of course, spoke plenty. They were given extra rations of beer and food."

"A lot happened in a couple of hours," Jaron remarked.

"You've been out for two days, stupid," Neeva said. She looked at the girl. "Anna, shut up. You're going to bring the guard back."

Jaron reached up to feel the swelling on his head, "That explains why I'm so hungry."

"You've been sleeping," Neeva said, scornfully. "We've been starving. All we've been getting is a cup of water a day."

"Except for him," Anna said, touching Rennek, "nothing at all. He called the guards on horseback a name, and they stopped the wagons to beat him. They stopped us again this morning and beat him again. I think they're going to kill him."

"How many people did they kill in Temerrac?"

She cleared her throat. "My son, he was almost ten." A tear rolled down the dirt path on her right cheek and she wiped it away, pushing the stain to her jaw. "Something terrible happened. Buildings fell. The ground cracked. I can't explain it."

"I can add another of you lot to the entertainment schedule tonight." The sandy haired soldier had ridden up to the cart to quell the conversation. His face was grim as he stared down at them. There was fire in his eyes. This man enjoyed his work.

Over the next hours, through scattered moments of whispered conversation, Jaron was able to piece together some of the events that had occurred after his blow to the head. The powder that Harris and the other masons had stockpiled caught fire and exploded, destroying the Mason's Guild and most of the other buildings in the southern end of the city. After the explosions, the Valcella soldiers came upon the hospital. Checking for survivors, or looting the dead, they had found Jaron's signet ring. The ring bore the mark of Mavius, and because of this, the soldiers believed they had apprehended a spy.

Better that they think I'm a spy than know who I really am, thought Jaron.

Lieutenants, under General Shale, had ordered that any found near Jaron should be taken prisoner as well. Verne, Neeva, Thargus, Arnor, and Keras were herded into these carts along with several Temerrac citizens from the makeshift hospital. Harris had somehow managed to escape.

The wagons rolled to a stop.

A man, far to the front of the wagon train, called out, "What business do you have on the general's road?"

A strong disembodied voice, carrying easily across the distance, answered, "You carry prisoners of great concern to our lord."

"You are blocking our progress. If you do not give way, then your life shall be forfeit."

Laughter, mocking and loud, rang from the front of the procession. The scream of a horse and the cursing of a man followed this laughter.

"You sorry son of a whore! What have you…?" He didn't finish his question.

The deep voice spoke again. "Go back to your General. Tell him who has his prisoners."

The guards drew their swords and advanced. Jaron, unable to see what was happening, heard the screams of dying men. The prisoners waited in fear. Were they being rescued or abducted again?

When the wagons moved on, they rolled past the bodies of the Valcella soldiers. The sandy haired man lay on his face, blood pooling under him, staining his red and white tunic.

*   *   *   *   *

Grass and brush grew up out of the center of their new path causing the wagons to shake and lean with the terrain. Trees blocked the way, growing so low that men in robes had to cut them back with axes. This was a road of little use.

So where does it lead? Jaron wondered. *And who are our new captors?* He just saw the robed and hooded men, and only ever heard the one man speak. They didn't wear the colors of Valcella. Their cloaks were grey and blue and they had their hoods up, despite the oppressive summer heat and humidity. They didn't ride their horses, instead walking along, guiding them with black gloved hands, and they said nothing. They intimidated even Neeva. She kept her hands and arms well within the bars.

In the waning light of the second day, the overhanging trees of the path gave way to broader roads and fields. The sounds of a metal hammer on steel rang out over the creak of the wooden wheels. The smell of stables and horses carried on the breeze. Jaron assumed they had reached a permanent settlement, but he soon realized it was a vast staging ground or outpost for yet another army. The wagons moved across a wide and recently built wooden bridge.

Their arrival at the camp went unnoticed by soldiers who

were busy training, working, or eating. Roads entered from several points around the perimeter of the camp. Their captors circled the outside, avoiding confrontations with anyone. *Too bad,* thought Jaron, *in one of these wagons is a fire mage. If we just drove through the middle of camp, he could roast everyone.*

The wagons rolled into the courtyard of a tall tower with men and goblins on guard duty. Jaron watched the bustle of the camp with interest. Like the robed figures leading the wagons, the men wore the grey and blue colors.

Jaron's eyes went wide at the next sight: brindi. There were brindi in the camp. *The enemy is in league with Brindi. How desperate—or crazy—does one have to be to do that?*

The Brindi were small, no taller than an eleven-year-old Human child, and they were slender. In fact, Jaron had confused them with children at first. However, these were not children. These were Brindi. Their eyes showed no compassion.

Jaron knew how unusual it was for Brindi to work with Goblins or Humans. Although they were beautiful in appearance, they were cruel and hard toward the twenty-five prisoners, particularly toward the dwarves in the last wagon, Arnor and Thargus.

Two of the cloaked figures carried Neeva, kicking and struggling, from the wagon to her wood paneled room. They were careful not to let her touch the ground. She, Anna, Keras, and three other women shared one room. The brindi separated the men into three groups. Jaron faced the little jailer as the door clicked shut. He was sharing his room with both Thargus and Arnor.

Thargus sat brooding in a corner. Several brindi had taken the liberty of showing him from the wagon cage to his room. For ones so small, they held great power in their punches. His eye had started to puff up almost as soon as he had entered the room. The violence of the past week showed on him. A long scar was forming on his forehead. Blood had dried into his black goatee and he brushed through the hairs with his fingers, littering his white shirt with the black specks of it. But the blood in his beard wasn't his own, and it didn't belong to the brindi responsible for his eye. This blood was days old from the battle of Temerrac.

Arnor sat on the bed of straw and wool, his blue eyes looking around. His hat was gone and he ran his hands through his black hair. He pulled off his boots, inspecting the sole. "Well that hole is almost clear through." He dropped the boots on the floor and lay down. "I've been here before," he said. "They didn't lock the door last time."

"You've been here?" Jaron asked. "Do you know anything about the area?"

"Not much, I traveled the roads mostly. The North and South weren't at war at the time. There was an attractive maiden living here, then. Her father and I had our differences." He winked. "I remember that the beds were a lot softer than this back then."

"So, where are we?"

"I'm sure the girl and her father are long gone," Arnor said before answering Jaron's question. "We are the guests, or prisoners, more likely, of Sir William and Lord Baros. This is the tower at Sandy River."

*   *   *   *   *

Dust and debris lay thick in the corners of the stairs, but the center of the tread was clear enough for sure footing. The climb up was long, ten levels high, and each floor had a ceiling height of twelve feet. At each curved twenty foot landing was a wide door.

There were window openings at every floor of the ascent, but they were thin and offered a limited view. The camp circled the tower. Rows and rows of makeshift structures and camp tents filled the view on all sides. Wagons traveled the roads. The smoke of smithies and the sounds of clanging metal carried up to the windows. The glass had long fallen out of the rotted frames and a breeze entered from the sweltering day outside, raising the temperature within the tower interior. Through the slit openings, sunlight on the western side of the tower created slivers of dust-filled rays.

In the higher levels of the tower, the doors were in decay, as if they had not been oiled or tended for years. Some doors were missing entirely, allowing Jaron to catch of glimpse of the gloomy interiors. The smell of mold was strong.

The Lords had summoned only Jaron and Arnor to make this ascent. The others sat below, locked in their wood paneled rooms on the second level. Arnor and Jaron's attending guards, walking in front of them, had not seemed eager to take this assignment. The first two chosen had refused, taking instead the punishment of lashes for disobedience. The two that accepted the task were clearly out of shape, their breath rasping with increasing intensity as they climbed.

By the eighth level, the guards pushed Arnor and Jaron in front of them. This did not bother Jaron, for he had been annoyed at following the overweight and slowly moving idiots. His pace quickened as he anticipated the coming introduction. Arnor did not hurry.

At the ninth landing, the guards refused to go any further. They gave instructions to continue up to the top landing and the door that accompanied it. They then made their way back down the stairs, unimpeded by their lack of breath any longer.

Arnor watched them scuttle down the cracked and broken steps, but Jaron's eyes were on the path ahead. He had begun to climb before Arnor even turned around. A light fog rolled down the stairs as the two took each step upwards. The temperature dropped, ever so slightly at first, but sharp as a blizzard as they reached the tenth landing. This door, unlike the others below, appeared to be in good condition with worn slats, centuries old, held together by iron bands. The door stood slightly ajar.

"Hello?" called Jaron as he pushed the door inward. Sunlight streamed from the wide-open balcony on the far side, illuminating the heart of the room and leaving shadows that reached out from the corners like arms and fingers grasping with menace. A smell of disuse and dust filled his nostrils and he wrinkled his nose. Interrupting the flow of the evening sunlight, a silhouette of a man sat bent over in a chair, studying something on the table in front of him.

Jaron called again, trying to make his presence known to the man, "Hello?"

The silhouette did not move or answer. Unable to help himself, Jaron approached curiously but cautiously. No movement came from the figure. Still unable to see, Jaron stopped advancing directly towards the silhouette and moved to the side, allowing the yellow light to reflect against the scene before him. As he neared, he discovered that this was not a man after all, but the remnants of a man, a skeleton.

The skeleton was resting on its forearms with its head bowed low as if to study the game in front of it. The dark blue and silver cloth of his clothing was worn and faded with age.

Did this man die here pondering the next move? Perhaps some morbid prankster set him in this position as a jest.

Jaron moved closer to inspect the board, leaning so far forward that he nearly brushed the deceased player. He did not recognize the game. The pieces were located on a hexagonal grid in seemingly random positions and were of various shapes ranging from a tall obelisk to a squat star shape. Two colors of each shape were present in this strange game of strategy. Jaron reached forward to touch one of the pieces.

"We have company," came a deep rumbling voice from behind Jaron. Intrigued by the skeletal gamer, he must have passed by the owner of the voice cloaked somewhere in the shadows of the room. He turned his back on the macabre figure at the window, letting his eyes adjust to the darkness as the voice spoke again. "It has been twelve months, Baros. You had all of the time you needed in Glenndon to ponder your move. You have lost the game. There is no move left."

Jaron whirled at the sound of wooden legs screeching against the stone floor behind him. Seeing the skeletal gamer rising from his chair, pushing the table away gently, Jaron jumped back violently in fear, fell down, and crab walked on his hands and feet backward away from the rising vision.

The voice came again, "Settle down, youngster. We are not dressed for battle. We have been away at the Eastern Coast managing some unpleasantness."

"It can't be," murmured Arnor. He had reached the doorway and was looking in. He did not appear alarmed and was trying to focus on the figure. The glare of direct sunlight hid the features of the knight, and so the reason for Jaron's terror was not instantly clear to Arnor. "Baros?" Arnor moved into the room, and the change in illumination made all clear to him as he saw the features of a long past friend. The brief moment of elation gave way to grief and a touch of sorrow filled his eyes.

Out of the gloom stepped a tall and cloaked figure. Like the skeleton standing on the other side of the room, his clothing was deep blue, embroidered with golden thread, but tattered. A golden falcon, grasping a spear in one claw and a helmet in the other, emblazoned his chest. A wide leather belt with a round silver buckle pulled the cloak tight around the waist, accentuating the width of the figure's shoulders. A cool blue light glowed from within the hood of the cloak. Fleshless hands rose up to pull back the mantle, revealing only bone and hair. A mustache and beard were all that remained of the face. The triangular opening of the skull replaced the nose. Within the eye sockets pulsed a dull blue light.

The skeleton spoke again, looking toward the door, the timbre of his voice reflecting off the walls to create an echo. "Arnor, old friend, enter and sit with us."

Arnor took a deep breath and made toward the voice, arms raised for embrace, but Sir William, for this was indeed the Sir William that Arnor once knew, held an outstretched skeletal hand, palm and fingers extended to ward off the advance of the dwarf. "You may not touch us, old friend. It could mean your death. We are cold, colder than the winter wind."

Arnor stopped and looked at Sir William and Lord Baros. His face filled with sorrow and pity. "What happened to you?"

"We have been many times to the darkest depth of the under-realm. We have fought the demons and the dead. We have longed for the rays of the sun."

Arnor looked sick. He balled up his fists in anger and grief, "So many years."

"Many lives were stolen. Do not measure your revenge on our loss." It was Baros who had spoken now, his voice was not as deep as William's, but held the same eerie quality.

"Arnor, we are not the men you once knew. No taste of food, no pleasure of warmth or desire of flesh remains." William spoke as he walked past a still prone Jaron to the balcony with the gaming table. "No bodily need has risen within us for time untold. We do not sleep. We do not dream. We laugh without joy." He turned to face them. "We hope, and plan, and plot. And that is why you are here." He sat down.

Arnor helped Jaron stand. They were lightheaded, their minds filled with fog thicker than the mist that had been rolling down the steps. Questions filled their hearts but neither could convince his mouth to convert the inquisitions to sound, and so they stood speechless and eagerly awaited for William to continue.

"You," William's bony index finger pointed to Jaron, "are meant to die. Our king fears you and has sent an assassin to dispose of you. We intercepted and repurposed this assassin. You know him, for he is a member of your party."

"Thargus," Arnor said under his breath.

"Yes," said William. "A curse has been placed upon him such that he must eventually complete his task. Mavius himself performed it."

"Look to the chest of your friend," Baros said, "for the web is there, attached to his soul, even as it is to ours, and yours. We are held beyond even the release of death to an oath taken. We are servants of our king Mavius. If he were to command, we have no option but to obey. We have fought his battles after life and for life. His body is intact, though his soul suffered the deeds he inflicted on his enemies and friends alike. No fear of repercussion clouds his purpose. He desires to be king again, an immortal king."

Baros stopped pacing and held out his arms. A shroud of darkness filled the room and became graphic visions of fire and blood, campaigns fought in the underworld, massive in scale and gory in detail. Armies of men rolled over hills of fire grass and battered doors of glowing steel, gaining entry to courtyards of devils and ghosts. The men became ruined bodies, scarred and bloody from an incomprehensible collection of wounds. The bodies reduced slowly, from skin, muscle, and sinew, to statues of bones and armor that moved as men. The dead armies followed Sir William and Lord Baros, conquering all before them.

William interrupted the vision, saying, "There are more than a hundred of us. We bled, but did not weaken. We fell, but did not die. We rotted, but did not feel. Our heroes became your villains, the shades, commanded to return from the depths to destroy your ancestors. They do the bidding of only Mavius and spy even on us. All in his line must perish before his return. For, one in line of his throne could rebut his efforts with a simple command to us."

The underworld landscape faded, becoming green grass, fields, and city walls. The band of skeletal soldiers marched across the paths and roads to towns and villages, killing as they went. Men, soldiers and civilians, women, mothers, daughters, sons, babies, all slaughtered as swine for the butcher, falling under the swords and touch of the grisly army. No remorse or pity did this army have. No hesitation held their weapons as they advanced unfeeling toward their commanded goal.

The cries of children filled Jaron's ears, and tears welled up in his eyes to flow down his cheeks, a stain to represent his weakness, his empathy. This army had none. *Do they have any weakness? Can we stop them?* So much death filled his vision that he shut his eyes to it. The play did not stop and Jaron raised his hands to his face in an effort to close it out.

Anger and hate replaced feelings of futility and despair.

Jaron's hands trembled in readiness to act, but he held them back. No, he would not allow it. He did not know how he would stop them, but he would do so. Fingers curled around an imaginary sword hilt and Jaron became part of the vision, swinging blade into action.

The first swing shattered the shoulder of a skeleton trying to enter a house. His second swing removed the grinning skull of another. He was not alone. Keras and Ellian were there. A pile of broken bodies surrounded Keras as she whirled a spinning dance of destruction, graceful and deadly in the blink of an eye. Ellian led a group of ten or more battle-hardened men, his commands pushing them to greatness as they flanked a regiment of fighters with Sir William's glowing eyes.

The visions of Lord Baros ended, and Jaron found himself back within the tower. Sir William had moved close, leaning forward as if to study him. "Mavius has set his eyes on you," Sir William said. "Therefore, we believe you are the one. Mavius has been to the under-realm. Is he dead or alive?" Sir William mused. "We do not know. As the heir to the throne of the kingdom he once controlled, your will may supplant his own. This is why he has hunted and destroyed his descendants."

"He, Mavius," said Baros, "has damaged his soul. He pulls on those of the poor wretches he deals with. It has made him weak. We escaped the under-world through a portal created by him, but he must return to the portal often to rebuild his strength, or he will perish." Baros paced the room slowly as he spoke.

William placed the back of his hand over Jaron's chest. After a span of several seconds, a tendril of smoke appeared, and then another, and another, until William held between the fingers of his skeletal hand, the center of a smoke web, its strands stretching to Jaron's torso. He held it steady for a moment. Jaron could feel pressure in his chest, and then with a jerk Sir William clenched his fist. Jaron gasped in pain but the web held him fast in William's powerful grip. Sir William pulled it upward, lifting Jaron off the stone floor.

Jaron's eyes went wide in pain. A crushing heat enclosed him. Arnor leaped forward to rescue Jaron, but Lord Baros, with a wave of his hand, swept Arnor aside violently. Arnor landed in a heap near the gaming table, but was on his feet again almost immediately.

William placed Jaron back on the floor and released his grip from the web before backing away. "The soulweb holds you tightly within it. Mavius is correct to fear you. More powerful than a demon, and yet he fears you. He fears that you could close the portal, the portal that is the source of his life, or that you could command his minions."

Baros, unable to contain himself any longer, said, "Waste no more time. I've had enough of it. Command us to stand down, to bear arms no more. Release us of this vow we must follow!"

"I," questioned Jaron, "command you?" His hands rubbed at his chest, easing the pain. His head reeled in confusion.

"Yes, bid us to stay our efforts!"

"What do you command?" asked William.

Arnor slowly joined Jaron in front of the knights. "Jaron, command them to lay down arms and return to the rest of the grave."

"I," faltered Jaron, clearing his throat, "command you, William and Baros, to lay down your arms. You will no more follow Mavius or his orders."

Silence held the room for a moment. Both Sir William and Lord Baros bowed their head and stood up. Baros turned and placed his grisly hands against his skull in despair.

"You," stated Sir William, "are not the one. I feel no compulsion to follow your command." He turned to the window. "There must be another. You are in line for the throne of Mavius's kingdom, but you are not the king, not yet. Our hope has failed us." The two knights walked away to the balcony and sat at the gaming table. Baros stared into the sun and William set the game pieces in their starting locations.

Sir William spoke to Jaron again. "You will return to your

cell." He set the pieces on the game board carefully in their places. The click of steel against wood echoed quietly around the room. "Your web is strong. Still, we may order your death to be carried out by mortal followers. Nevertheless, for now, you live. Your companions are under no such protection, however. They face execution on the morrow."

Baros stood at a nod from William. Stepping forward, Baros held the back of his hand over Arnor's chest. A web of smoke appeared within his fleshless hand as Arnor writhed in agony. "I'm sorry about this, Arnor," he said. "I'm afraid your time has come." Lord Baros reached in with his other hand to pull at the web, and with great effort from his wide shoulders, tore it in two.

Chapter 14   Broken Bars and Stone

Walking down the stairs, his eyes tight from the tears spent, Jaron set his will into place. No more would he question his ability. No more could he question his place in all of this mess. He found himself in circumstances reserved for heroes and great men. Somehow, he had to become one of these men. He must survive.

I am not the heir to Mavius. Someone else in line for Mavius's throne is alive. Yes, Jaron thought, *my father. He's alive.*

Ellian and Keras had come along from the safety of the Great Library of Westmost to protect Jaron. Now, they were going to die. How long had he known them? For so many years, he had thought them to be his only friends. Bodyguards they might have been, but they did seem to care about him. Now Arnor was dead and Thargus...

He took a deep breath.

Thargus accepted a contract to kill him, but was repurposed, William said. *How trustworthy is that? Does he still have the curse on him? Is the contract binding?*

Behind him, four goblins carried Arnor's body, shuffling the weight between them and cursing their lot.

After Arnor's web was broken, Lord Baros called for the goblins to take Jaron back to his cell and remove Arnor's body from the tower. Arnor had known both William and Baros. This thought harped on Jaron.

How long ago had they been pulled from this world into the torture that deformed them? Jaron did the math, his brain trying to remember all of the events. Mavius had been born in around the year 200. Mavius killed King Deras in 234, starting the war. The war lasted twenty years. Mavius ruled for over a hundred years. *No, that can't be right.*

He scoured his memory. *This year is 1108.*

Arnor knew the knights, personally, so logic has to hold that Arnor is either eight or nine hundred years old. Jaron turned to look at the body of his friend. The goblins held him unceremoniously, each bearing the weight as best he could. Arnor's body jostled with every step. Then, it spoke with a tone of sharp annoyance.

"Put me down you clumsy oafs!" Out of surprise and disbelief at hearing Arnor speak, the goblins did exactly as he asked, with a thud.

Falling down a flight of stairs never did anyone any good. Arnor fell down fifteen steps, knocking down Jaron as he went. Jaron had fallen down only half a flight and he lay in pain on the bottom rubbing his elbows and left hip. Up above him, Arnor was standing and pushing the goblins away as they hurried to catch him. New tears rolled down Jaron's face as a smile overcame him.

"Yeah, I knew them," Arnor answered the question that had been in Jaron's head only moments ago. He had pushed the goblins away after regaining his feet. This was enough for them, and they fled back up the stairs to cower in-between the horror at the top and the dwarf that had just returned from the dead.

Jaron just stared at Arnor, smiling.

"I can't die," said the dwarf.

"What do you mean you can't die?"

"I've tried but it doesn't happen. It's a long story."

"How could you possibly know these knights?" Jaron was incredulous. His mind reeled at the sudden return of his friend, and the grief let go its fierce grip on his emotions. He wanted to sing, to jump down the stairs, or run up and laugh in the fleshless faces of the knights. "Nine hundred years!" Jaron exclaimed. "That's how old you are. Most of the buildings on this continent are not that old."

"Some are. Most didn't last, shoddy workmanship."

Jaron just laughed, wiping the tears from his cheeks. Arnor took hold of Jaron's sleeve and guided him down the steps.

"I survive any attempt to dispatch me and I don't exactly know how. I was a member of the Dwarven contingent of the knights who tried to murder Mavius centuries ago. It was a wretched act. We had sworn fealty to him in the years before, and we broke those oaths. Something of his magic or darkness grabbed at us, and Sir William and Lord Baros fell to his will. I did not. Perhaps, I would be as they are today if I had."

They reached the third landing. Arnor continued his story while they were walking.

"After the destruction that took Mavius, his enemies, and his followers, I felt a tug at my chest and searching my flesh I found this." He opened his shirt to reveal a black spider web drawn across his chest. "It's not a tattoo. It doesn't wash off. Through this," Arnor clutched his chest, "I could feel the movements of those I lost. Sometimes I could hear their cries. Many years went by before I regained my sanity."

"It was then, I felt I knew what was happening. Your ancestors were dying off. Mavius was trying to get back. I tracked your family down and began to hide you. More than a century of wealth I had at my disposal. I built a force using the enemies of Mavius, underground of course. We hid your line from both Mavius and the sitting line of kings."

"What they said about Thargus..." Jaron started, but Arnor silenced him.

"Look," said Arnor, "we will confront him together."

"The knight lifted me. What was that thing on my chest?" Jaron asked.

"The soulweb," Arnor answered. "I knew that I had it. Until they grabbed yours, I didn't know that you had it also." Arnor pressed his hand to his chest. "Mine keeps me from dying, like those knights up there." *Will I wind up like them?* he thought.

"Does that mean I can't die?"

"No, I wouldn't count on it," Arnor answered.

Walking up the stairs, a tall goblin looked up, puzzled. He pushed back Arnor and Jaron to look up the stairs for his companions that had entered only minutes ago. Stepping back with a grunt he motioned for two others to bring the prisoners back to their room. In silence they walked, Jaron's mind racing with question after question.

In the hallway between the rooms, Jaron looked through the

barred doors trying to get a peek at where Ellian was. At one of the doorways, Neeva lay face down on the floor. She was searching for something through the cracks in the floorboards.

"She's up to something," Arnor remarked as he passed the cell, "I hope she does it soon."

Back in their room, Arnor and Jaron pinned Thargus in a corner. As the light dimmed in the sky, Thargus faced them unafraid.

"The knights," said Thargus, "sent Harnan and I to bring you here. They caught him in their search for the heir. Then they caught me because I was following Harnan."

"Why were you following Harnan?" Arnor demanded.

"I was sent by Mavius to kill the next heir to Mavius's throne. He gave me this." He pulled his shirt open, revealing the scratches across his chest. They formed a deep red web. Blood held on the strands like dew in the cool morning. Large sores sat over the lines and looked to be infected.

"That's not what I saw on your chest on the Sotho Palala," Arnor said angrily.

"It comes and goes. This," Thargus spread his hands out from his chest, "is connecting me to Mavius. When he touched me, it did something, made some connection between us. Oh, the visions he has, they terrify me."

"You see his thoughts?" Jaron asked.

"Sometimes images come to me, but they are hard to understand," Thargus explained. "I was supposed to feel an irresistible pull to complete the contract when the target was close. I never felt that pull when I was around you." Thargus did not look remorseful or contrite. He met Jaron's eye with steady resolve. "Harnan seemed to know where to find you. When he and Yaru were captured, it was only a matter of time before they got me."

"Yaru, he was here?" Arnor asked.

"This is where we started from. I haven't seen him or heard his voice, though. I think—maybe—he managed to escape."

"So, Mavius sent you to kill the heir. If that were me, would you still carry out Mavius's order?" Jaron asked.

"You're not the heir, not yet, or the knights would have freed you," Thargus said. "You're not the one I want. That's why I didn't feel any desire to kill you. My real target is out there." Thargus touched the sores. "We have to escape."

"So you can hunt down and kill my father? This is where our friendship must end, Thargus," said Jaron.

Arnor balled up his right fist and punched Thargus with everything he had. The cave dwarf fell limp to the floor, unconscious. Arnor knew two things. Thargus was a threat. Come morning and the executioner's axe, Thargus would be a threat no longer.

Arnor had no fear of the axe. If it managed to kill him, he might at last be free. Ellian and Keras still had no idea what the dawn was going to bring. How were they spending their last night?

Jaron squirmed and turned, snapping awake each time he started to fall asleep. He crept over to Arnor in the darkness and shook him. "If something were to happen to me, I want you to find my father. I don't know where to start. But you, you can't die. Use that to help him if you can." Arnor nodded and Jaron returned to his spot on the floor, where he finally slept.

* * * * *

As the sun rose, soldiers opened the doors and walked twenty-five men, women, and dwarves down the stairs and out into the courtyard. Confused and disoriented, the prisoners from Temerrac walked out into the daylight, realization hitting them as they saw the executioner and block in the middle of the yard. Neeva walked along with the others, her toes flexing into the cold dirt. Unlike the others, she was smiling.

The mysterious soldiers that had brought the prisoners to the camp had returned to their Lord after putting the captives into their rooms. Their new jailors were not privileged to the information about the limitations of mages from the Hall of Elements.

The ground began to hum, ever so softly at first, then with a frequency that intensified to a rumble, followed by a solid shake every second, as if a giant walked the ground nearby.

A spear of stone, slender as a blade of grass, shot from the ground underneath the executioner, impaling him. Another struck the guard holding Neeva, driving through flesh and bone like a needle through fabric. She was laughing, her hands weaving death around her.

Hands of sand formed around the legs of the other guards and slowly pulled them down. They let go of their weapons and cried for help. Neeva's magic held them fast, pulling them down into the ground. The prisoners found their voices gone at the shock of such a sight. None could say a word until the grasping fingers of sand disappeared.

With the abandoned weapons at their feet, Jel and Rennek, now recovered from their beatings in the cart, armed themselves. They tossed a spear to Arnor and one to Ellian. Even Anna grabbed a knife. Thargus did not pick up a weapon, but lingered back, separated from the others.

Verne embraced Neeva as the rumblings continued.

The whole camp was waking. Men rushed from barracks and tents, looking around for the source of the shaking. Desperate to escape, horses whinnied and ran in circles within their enclosures. Neeva brought the rumbling to a stop.

"We need to leave the camp, Neeva," Verne was saying to her. "There are too many of them here to try to take on. We will become weak, and they will overpower us."

"Weak?" Jaron asked.

"From the magic, it drains us," Verne replied. Then to Neeva he said, "You shouldn't have woken them. It will be harder now."

Her hands lifted palms up, as if she was trying to lift a heavy log. In unison with her motion, fingers made of stone broke through the ground behind them. A gigantic hand of broken rock knocked away the wood and iron of the gate. Forearms and shoulders of granite, wide as a city street is long, followed the hands. A back extended away from them, and a head, molded from the pressures of time, rose to face them. Neeva gave a silent command, and the golem stood, high as a five-story building and wide as the face of a cliff. It rose, stretching its hands into the air, happy to be free of the confinement of ages.

Alarmed, soldiers shouted to one another as they saw this threat rising within their midst. Others just stood staring, mouths agape at the unbeatable foe. Slowly, the golem strode toward them, its feet crushing anything that hindered it, men, horse, or goblin. All fell to its wrath. Neeva laughed in the spirals of her magical destruction.

"We must bring her!" Verne shouted. Neeva was entranced in her spell. Her hands weaved simulations in the air and she could not run. Ellian and Keras lifted her as they followed Arnor and Jaron away from the destruction of the stone giant. As soon as her feet left the ground, the golem collapsed.

"No!" Verne pulled at them, "Drag her! Her feet need to stay on the ground." They dropped her. Neeva landed on her back and the wind left her lungs. She gasped for breath, one hand clutching her chest, the other hand digging fingers into the dirt. Keras and Ellian grabbed her by the upper arms to drag her away.

In the confusion, no guard noticed their passing. No chase came from the army around them. As Neeva regained her breath, she lifted the golem again.

Men ran past them towards the monster. Others ran past them away from the monster. Pebbles fell from the giant fists as they swung into a man from above, crushing bone, smashing armor, and leaving only a pile of flesh that oozed out of the broken steel.

The golem roared, its voice a grating sound of unspeakable malice that shivered spines and quenched bravery in the ranks of the fighters rushing to meet it. Some men had the wit to arm themselves with an appropriate weapon. As the golem steadied itself to recover from a mighty swing, a boulder smashed into the left arm, knocking it off. The beast of rock fell to the ground only to reform and pick itself up again. Snatching up the boulder, it whirled the missile back to the catapult that delivered it.

Neeva guided the golem's attacks without needing to see them. The forest was only a short distance away. In the aftermath of the attack, a search for the missing prisoners was unlikely. It would take time to piece together the events inside the camp. Their escape seemed assured.

Arnor kept close to Thargus, always making sure to be between him and Jaron. He would not take his eyes off this one again. He had put his trust in the cave dwarf too quickly. When he was sure of their safety, he might even try to kill the dirty fiend.

A horn from the tower rang out in the morning air. The sound of battle continued behind them with a thunderous crash. Screams of goblins and men broke the air.

The horn sounded again.

No living member of the camp paid any attention to it. As they ran, the ground under their feet moved. Boots broke free from the soil around the escaping prisoners, kicking up. Hands without tendons scraped the dirt, digging for the surface only inches away. A knee bent up toward the air, pushing aside the weeds and long grass.

In shock and fright, many of the escapees cried out exclamations of despair and quickened their pace. Behind them, the creak of armor, long rusted and torn, rolled through the morning fog.

At the nape of his neck, a cold wind broke the summer heat, and sent a chill down Jaron's back. He knew what this was. He had seen it in his dreams. Behind him, several of the escapees stopped to stare, frozen in terror.

Helms rested on bone. Joints creaked without the muscles needed to support them. Hair and beard grew from fleshless faces, grinning the smile of certain death. More than one hundred such visions lumbered along, intent on murder.

Some of the fugitives fell at the sight of the dead rising to follow them. Those that fell, lay shivering in fright. They were, without mercy, dispatched by blade, or mace, or spear. This army of the dead had no malice, no empathy, or pity. Killing without compassion, they followed orders, the orders of Sir William and Lord Baros high above them in the tower.

Rennek held back with Jel in an effort to protect those cowering. His blade beheaded one of the skeletal warriors, but the bony hands reached out to place the head upon its shoulders once more. A mighty kick knocked another to its knees but it rose again to continue its advance.

The warriors circled a group of six. Diving, Jel broke through the gap. Out of breath from the sprint, he caught up to the others running away. There was no fighting these visions. Fifteen fugitives had so far fallen and died. Ten remained.

Neeva had collapsed from her magical exertion, and Ellian carried her over his shoulder as he moved between the trees. Chests heaved as they tried to increase the distance between them and the waking nightmare. They ran on, outdistancing the slow tortured movements of the corpses behind, but the dead do not tire as the living do.

Morning dew soaked through their boots. They slipped as they climbed the hill with their thighs burning in protest. The forest gave way to a small clearing and a path that allowed for easier travel.

Behind them, the dead continued their pursuit.

Over the next hill, a small contingent of goblins were surprised when a group of humans crossed their path. The sounds of battle had stirred them from their slumber in a distant camp and they were making their way to investigate. Blades already drawn, they quickly surrounded the escapees.

"Hello, hello," one said in the common tongue, his voice low, "and where are you going?"

"Something massive is attacking the camp!" Keras yelled. "Did you hear it?"

"Yes, we did. But, you are not members of the army." The goblin pawed Keras's torn and soiled shirt. "Prisoners, most likely."

A pipe in the goblin's left hand rose to his smiling mouth. "I believe we might be in for a rise in our wages, boys." He laughed cruelly, taking a long puff at the pipe, and squinted his eyes as smoke curled up and stung them.

"Nasty habit you have there," Verne remarked as he winked his left eye, "could be the death of you." The ember from the pipe burst into a bright torch of flame, rolling from the goblin's hand to his arm. Bright yellow and orange flames spun around him and consumed the smoker where he stood. The fire leaped, dancing from one goblin to the next until all were flailing about on the ground in an effort to extinguish the flames.

Verne turned and extended his hands toward the advancing ranks of bones. White-hot missiles of flame shot out of his fingers and encircled the slow fighters. It did not hinder them. Fire licked over chain mail and bone. Hair, wispy on the heads of the dead, crackled in the heat, adding to the stench of decay. Behind the dead soldiers, yet another Goblin patrol was gaining.

"It's no good, Verne! Run!" Jaron shouted.

Lungs were bursting and aching for air. Muscles screamed from fatigue as they climbed over walls and logs, followed always by the untiring dead.

"Is there no escape from these wretches?" Jaron gasped.

"We are tiring, and they are not. Fire doesn't harm them and Neeva is too tired to bury them," said Verne, breathless. "Maybe we could lose them if we had some other form of travel, horses, or a boat."

"No such luck, I suppose," Keras replied.

"How far behind are they?" Jel asked, breathing deep.

Keras looked back. Between the trees, the helms of the decaying soldiers rose and fell from view over the hill no more than a hundred yards away. "Not far enough."

"Ellian, put me down." It was Neeva's voice, weak and creaked with weariness. "Verne, come here to me." Verne rushed to her and she whispered into his ear.

"No, it's too much. There are too many of us," he said. She clutched his arm with both of her hands and closed her eyes in concentration.

They began to sink.

"Quickly!" Verne shouted. "Grab onto me."

Keras, Ellian, and Jaron grabbed Verne and Neeva to try to stop their descent, only to find that they themselves had begun to sink into the ground with the mages, and they could not let go. In panic, they thrashed about, but to no avail. Anna, Jel, and Rennek grabbed on to Keras and Jaron, but they were not sinking with the others. The ground parted their grip. Neeva's magic had reached its limit.

Arnor and Thargus shoved aside Rennek, Jel, and Anna, diving for Ellian's boots as they disappeared into the stone.

Chapter 15   Mark of the Spider

Arnor and Thargus rushed toward Jaron, Ellian, and Keras. Eyes closed, Neeva held Verne's hands. Jaron and Keras pulled to keep the two of them from sinking, each holding on to one of Verne's arms. Ellian joined, gripping Neeva's shoulders, and heaved for all of his might. The five of them sank into the stone.

As the hapless group submerged, into seemingly liquid rock, Rennek dove and threw his arms around Jaron's shoulders. Jel and Anna grabbed on to Keras, but Neeva's magic wasn't strong enough to bring anyone else with them. Rennek, Jel, and Anna were not descending with the others and were left kneeling and looking at the ground where Neeva, Keras and the three young men had been. The soles of Ellian's boots disappeared moments before Thargus was able to reach them. The dwarf bruised his hands as his palms skinned the stone. Arnor fell in a heap on top of him. They stared at the ground, pawing at it, as if to dig through to their companions.

"You lost them!" Arnor hissed.

Thargus kept searching the stone. "How did they get through that?"

"A spell! Where did she take them?" Arnor joined in the digging.

Anna, Jel, and Rennek gaped at the ground. Even living their whole lives inside a city that contained the Hall of Elements had not prepared them for the depth of influence upon the physical world that this magic contained.

Thargus sat back on his haunches, pushing himself up. "We cannot follow them," he paused, looking behind him, "and we cannot stay here. We have to move." He grabbed Arnor, and with much difficulty, for Arnor resisted, stood him up and spun him so they were face to face. "If we stay here, we die."

Arnor pushed him away. "Maybe you'll die, Hammerfist, I'm digging."

Thargus pushed back. "No, you will lead them to Jaron. This

will take you too long to get through."

The glare Arnor threw at Thargus overflowed with hatred. "And you care, why? The guards knew you. This is where you started. That beating you took, when we got here, wasn't easy, I bet. Why didn't they kill you? They wanted to. What stopped them?" Arnor demanded. He raised his spear. "I should kill you now. Is there a reason I shouldn't?"

"I can find Jaron's father."

Arnor balked in his advance to consider this, then he stepped forward again raising the spear tip.

"Loren is alive." Thargus's hands were up and he stepped backwards a pace or two. "I know he is, and I know where he is. I can't explain now, not here. They are coming." He ran backwards, away from the ghastly soldiers chasing them. When he saw Arnor, Jel, Anna, and Rennek start following, he turned and yelled, "Hurry!"

Moments later, the dead arrived at the scene of the mage's disappearance and stopped. They inspected the ground where Neeva's magic had allowed their target to escape. As they considered their next course of action, a patrol of goblins with dogs came up from behind. A bony finger pointed them in the direction of the remaining runners. The goblins followed the former prisoners, eager to leave the walking corpses behind them.

Arnor and Thargus broke through the low dead branches of pine trees as they ran. The branches snapped, stinging the runners with every crack. Jel, Anna, and Rennek had outpaced them and the dwarves could hardly keep up. The sound of howling dogs behind echoed in the distance. Arnor's lungs ached to bursting, but he knew he could not stop here. Capture would not improve the situation. Thargus looked as though he knew where he was heading, and he stopped short when he reached the top of the slope. Waiting there, chests heaving, were the three humans.

Thargus breathed deeply, panting his words to Arnor as he pointed toward a break in the foliage beneath them. "There, that is the way."

Arnor could hear a waterfall. In disbelief, Arnor shook his head, but when Thargus ran on, he followed. Down they went, and the trail became so steep at times that they held onto the trees to slow their descent.

Birds in the trees hushed as they passed. Every sound fell upon their ears, their senses heightened by the adrenalin rush. Snapping twigs, the rustle of leaves, the roar of the nearing waterfall, all came clear. Over the level of these came the voices of their pursuers behind them. Thirty goblins came crashing down the hill, breaking every branch or tree that stood in their way.

Rennek leaped from the waterfall's edge into the pool below, surfacing a few moments later. Anna jumped next, barely waiting for Rennek to swim clear. Jel and Thargus pushed a panicked Arnor off the edge, and he landed with a painful smack against the water. Thargus jumped in immediately after, and he pulled the floundering Arnor to where he could stand. Jel, after a quick look behind him, threw himself off the edge. It soon became apparent that he could not swim either. Rennek rescued him, dragging his flailing friend onto the bank.

"Girl," Thargus shouted to Anna over the din of the cascading water. "Venthaer, the plant, do you know it?"

"I do. It grows here?"

"It does. Take those two," he pointed to Jel and Rennek, "show them what it looks like, and gather as much as you can. The goblins, I think, will not jump. Goblins do not like heights. They will try to climb down. I do not envy them. That rock is a little slippery. If any of them do decide to jump, they will find two angry dwarves down here."

The venthaer plant had long and thick leaves. When bundled together they floated quite easily. Thargus wove them quickly into long pontoons, and by interweaving the pontoons together, he made a flimsy but buoyant raft. It took fifteen minutes to gather the venthaer leaves and complete the raft. The goblins shouted from the ledge above. Some threw rocks. Small stones hit both Rennek and Jel, but the goblins never made it down into the bowl of the falls. Three had tried to climb down and fallen to their deaths on the rocks below.

An arrow hit the ground next to Anna, nearly hitting her leg. She ducked behind a large stone. The goblins had an archer. She yelled and everyone took cover behind the rocks, everyone except for Arnor. He was finishing the last ties on the raft. The shaft of an arrow was sticking out of the raft where the goblin had missed him.

"Let's go!" shouted Arnor.

The escaped prisoners hurried to their raft of grass. The water still drenched them up to their stomachs while seated, but their craft allowed them to sink no more than that. Jel and Rennek shoved them off just as an arrow struck Arnor in the side of the neck. He slumped into the pool. A second arrow hit Arnor in the back as he lay sprawled in the water.

"Go! Go! Go!" Anna shouted, paddling with her hands. They all paddled as hard as they could to escape the range of the Goblin archer, leaving Arnor behind.

The river flowed swift and hard across rocks and bends, ferrying them away from their Goblin pursuers. Rennek stood to reach for an overhead branch and snapped it off to push them away from dangerous obstacles and strong dips. Rennek did the best he could to aim for the 'V' present in the flow of the water. After an hour, the river began to widen and slow. The trees overhung the water on both sides, casting shadows to turn the bed of the river into patterns of cascaded light and dark brown.

Thargus assessed his situation. This was Sandy River. He stared at the river bottom, which he could now reach with his fingertips. Pebbles and grit came up in his fist. His mental map spread out before him. They were traveling southeast towards the coast. That was where he needed to go. He scratched at the lines on his chest.

They paddled their makeshift raft to the side of the river where Jel and Anna set off to find wood for a fire. Rennek pulled the raft onto the shore and stripped off his wet clothes to wring them out. Before long, they sat before a raging fire, wearing as little as possible as their clothes dried in the heat.

"So, I don't know where you plan to head," Jel started, "but I want to go back to Temerrac. Just south of the city, on the edge of the valley, my family had a home. If I can get there, maybe I can get some clue as to where my sister is."

"I know Helen," said Anna. "She was a good friend to my sister."

"Will you come with me?" Jel asked.

"Temerrac is nothing but pain to me now," she said, "but I want to pay back some of the hurt done to me."

"I just don't want to be captured again," Rennek entered, "but the pull to return home is great."

Jel stood and stirred the fire. He had already made up his mind. "I'm going. Who is coming?"

"I am not," answered Thargus. "I'm headed south. What you three do is of little concern to me. I don't care. If you are captured and let it be known where I have gone, it will go ill for you when we meet again."

* * * * *

Thargus watched Jel, Anna, and Rennek cross the river and disappear from view as they went up over the hill. Temerrac was a dangerous road, one he would not be taking. Finally free of Arnor and the Humans, he could continue his mission. He was alone again.

"There you are!" came a voice from upriver. "I've been following you for miles." It was Arnor, the arrow still lodged in his back. He looked sweaty and out of breath.

"You were floating face down in the river!" exclaimed Thargus. His surprised look turned into a smile. "I thought you were dead."

Arnor walked the last fifty feet between him and Thargus. "Why didn't you pull me up on the boat?"

"You were dead," said Thargus, turning him around to

examine the arrow sticking out of his back.

"I had to walk the whole way," complained Arnor.

"You were dead," said Thargus.

"I know," said Arnor, turning back around to face Thargus.

"What do you mean, you know?"

"I mean, you're right. I was dead."

"Dead."

"Yeah, are you hard of hearing?"

"I saw you take two arrows."

"Yes, and they stung like crazy. Here, pull this out." Arnor put his hand behind him to touch the arrow.

"Where's the other arrow?"

"Oh, I pulled that one out; hard time breathing with it in there," Arnor explained. "I couldn't reach this one." Arnor pointed to his back. "Do you mind?"

"Pull it out?"

"Yes."

Thargus spun Arnor back around, gripped the shaft, and pulled. The arrow came out and Arnor gave a cry of pain. Blood started gushing from the wound. The arrow in Thargus's hand had penetrated Arnor by at least four inches.

"Why aren't you dead?" he asked.

"What's the problem? You've seen this before."

"I have?"

"At the falls…"

"Where you got hit by the arrows?"

"No, the other falls, on the Sotho Palala." Arnor sat down. "Where did the others go?"

* * * * *

Arnor scratched at the web stretched across his hairy chest and looked at Thargus. *Thargus never felt the 'pull' to kill Jaron. Does he feel a 'pull' to kill Lorenistal?* He reached across to Thargus. "Your web, let me see it."

Thargus opened his shirt.

"My web doesn't have those sores. Is it from scratching?" Arnor asked.

"I thought so at first, but they never went away, and they moved, very slowly. The sore migrates along the strands, like a weevil under the surface. No, it's not from scratching. I think my web is different from yours. Your web is a part of you. I have only had mine for a year. I think it might be a map."

"To what?"

"To you," Arnor only stared back so Thargus continued, "and others that have the web. Does every member of Mavius's line have the web?" Arnor shrugged. "This is why the shades can find them. If I read this correctly, I can see how far away the knights are. I can—maybe—figure out where Mavius is. I think I can even use it to figure out where Jaron's father is. His name is Loren, you said?"

"Lorenistal, but we call him Loren."

Arnor inspected the sores on Thargus's web closely. They were not overly large, but there were clusters of them so close together that they looked as if they were a single large sore. "Which one is me?"

"We are in the center of the web. I am the center, you are the sore."

Arnor laughed. "Sounds like the worst opening line ever."

Thargus joined him in laughter and pointed out the sores over to the right side of his chest. "These are the knights from Sandy River. The small one near them is Jaron." He reached up to his collarbone. "This is either Mavius or Lorenistal." He pointed again to his upper belly. "This must be also either Lorenistal or Mavius. Before I met you, I was following a large sore that, I thought, was Loren, but it turned out to be you and Jaron combined."

"There's another on your ribs." Arnor pointed out. It was smaller than the others, hardly breaking the skin.

"I don't know that one. It hasn't moved close enough to the center, which is me, where I could make contact," said Thargus.

Arnor had an idea as to whom that mysterious sore

represented but he kept it to himself, saying instead, "So where do we go? I threw Jaron into all this, don't forget, I promised to protect him."

"Yes, but that was when you thought Loren was dead. He is still alive somewhere. Protecting Jaron was the job of both Keras and Ellian. They are still with him, just as before you began this journey. Jaron is not the king, not the one to stop Mavius's knights. His father still lives. Loren is alive," said Thargus.

"All right, what now?"

"The knights had a plan to interrupt Mavius's chain of command. Can we find Loren? Would we be able to get back to Sandy River with him?" Thargus asked.

"We almost killed everyone we traveled with trying to get there the first time," Arnor said, "and that was without you trying to kill Jaron. I don't know if I want to try again to make the journey while, at the same time, stopping you from killing the one person who could save us."

"I'm supposed to kill him, but I might be able to hold back."

"Mavius's magic is pretty strong. I don't think I want to test it," Arnor said, stirring the fire. "You said Mavius sent you to kill the heir."

"Yes."

"Why you?"

"I was there when he arrived," Thargus answered.

"Where?"

"Stenwood Den. It is where he entered back from the under-realm. A massive sinkhole appeared inside a hall in the center of town," said Thargus, remembering. "Mavius and his soldiers climbed out of it. That is where he found me, and others. In Sotho Entollo I met one of my townsfolk, one of those chosen."

"How many secrets do you own?" Arnor scowled. "You are like an onion, layer after layer stinging the eyes."

"I am caught in the web, Arnor, just like you."

"What was this man sent to do?"

"I do not know everyone's purpose. I can guess that he was only a spy, but he knew my errand."

"Well, I don't want you around Loren. I think it's too tempting for you. Here's my idea," said Arnor. "Mavius passes through the portal to rebuild his strength. That means when he arrives there, he is weak. We need to get there before him and close it."

●

Chapter 16   Tunnels of Darrod

Through solid rock they sank, descending as though it were only a fog. In an instant, their speed increased. They fell into darkness, a jolt of pain announcing that they had reached the bottom. A drop of only eight feet felt like twenty. Blind, slow, and deliberate, they extricated themselves from one another.

"What was that?" asked Keras. "I feel like I could use a bath."

"Well, you are correct," said Ellian flatly.

"Verne, can you make a fire?" Jaron asked.

"I can't make fire. If there was a fire here, I could make it do amazing things. No, I can't make fire out of nothing. My magic doesn't work like that."

"Can anyone see anything?" Ellian asked. "I think I see a glow in that direction."

"What direction? We can't see you, blockhead," Keras stated the obvious.

Exasperated, Ellian continued, "Spin around and keep your eyes open. Remember the Sotho Palala? There's a green glow over there."

"Neeva?" Verne tried to wake her. She was cold and barely breathing. "She's spent from the magic. We need to warm her up."

"Say that again," Jaron requested.

"We need to warm..." A shirt hit him in the chest, stopping his sentence. Jaron had focused on the sound of Verne's voice, and just threw his shirt in that direction.

"Got it?" asked Jaron.

"Yeah, this will help." The shirt was still warm from Jaron's body heat.

"Hey Arnor, I've got an idea," Jaron said.

"Arnor didn't make it through with us," said Ellian.

"He's still up there with those things?" Jaron asked, alarmed. "We've got to do something to get him down here!"

"She's way too spent to be able to do that," Verne argued. "Any more from her right now could kill her."

"There's nothing we can do for him," Ellian stated reasonably. "Calm down, Jaron. Arnor and Thargus are resourceful enough to get out of this. What's your idea?"

Jaron took a second to compose himself and relax. Ellian was correct. Arnor and Thargus were good at handling whatever came at them, and he reminded himself, Arnor couldn't die.

"I've read that you can use echoes to determine direction." He waited for a response. None came, so he continued. "If we could bang two rocks together then maybe we could listen for the echo and figure out what direction we should be traveling. The echo will return quickly from areas that get smaller and will take longer if the area gets bigger."

"Not sure how that is going to help us figure out where we're going," argued Ellian.

"We should try anyway. Feel around on the ground for some stones."

They all bent to the ground, save Neeva and Verne, and began to search. Mostly they found just stone dust and gravel. Before long, Jaron had two stones, one he had found, the other Ellian.

"I suppose these are big enough. Keep looking though, these feel broken. I imagine round stones would be easier to get a good sound from." He cracked them together and listened to the echo.

"Hey, I found something," Keras said, "mining tracks."

A grunting sound came from behind them. It was a snort, a forced exhale of breath from something large in the dark. Green light illuminated their surroundings faintly, and revealed a large hulking shadow, then another, and another.

Large hairy hands picked up Ellian and hurled him into a wall. Jaron felt a sudden blow to his midsection, and he fell back several feet to lay gasping for air.

Her eyes finally adjusting to the low levels of light, Keras stepped to the side as a gnarled fist swung at her. Her right hand slid down the forearm attached to the fist and pushed the elbow upward as her own left elbow connected with a set of large ribs.

A cry of pain alerted Keras to the location of the beast's head. Stepping under the hairy arm, she brought up her right hand, thumb clenched tight, to connect with the side of its neck. Whatever this brute was, it went limp and collapsed to its left.

The other two, sensing the threat, tried to come at once in an attack, but Keras used their immediate sense of alarm as an advantage and dropped to her knee. She drove the palm of her hand up into the genitals of the closest one. The beast stopped with a groan, hindering the advance of his compatriot.

Keras, in her prone position, had no trouble sliding between the legs of her second unlucky opponent to attack the third from its right side. A well-placed kick to the inside of the left knee dropped number three down to its right knee. Keras followed up with a spinning heel kick to the back of its head.

In the increasing light, she surveyed her handiwork, two unconscious, one rolling in pain. Not bad for six seconds.

Jaron gasped on the floor. Ellian pushed himself up and rubbed his head. A trickle of blood marred his face and his eyes looked foggy.

The sounds of a group approaching showed the reason for the increased illumination. Each individual of the approaching group carried a small glowing stone, covered in the algae similar to that of the Sotho Palala. One of them carried an oil lamp, burning bright and adding a yellow glow to the green.

The lights fanned out to cover the width of the cavern. Brindi soon surrounded them. Jaron recovered his breath and sitting on the floor, got his first look at the Brindi of Darrod.

Their faces were grimy with dust and sweat. Sleeves were rolled up to reveal slender arms. Each of them gripped a shovel, chisel, or pickaxe.

A black-haired brindi, dressed in bright colors, appeared to be the leader or supervisor. He made his way to the three fallen attackers. Keras retreated several paces to allow him to investigate. The only conscious beast, recovering from the debilitating strike, stood and made as if to attack Keras again but stopped with a hand gesture from the black-haired supervisor. The would-be attacker backed into a wall and sat down heavily, brooding.

The leader held the back of his hand over each of the mouths of the splayed out attackers and felt for the pulse in the necks of the hulking beasts. "Still alive," he said in a strong voice.

With the newly available light, all could see what had attacked them. They were nearly seven feet tall. Their shoulders rippled with muscle, visible even through the long heavy fur that covered them. Short legs, relative to their overall size were thick and strong. A pair of short pants was all that each wore. The faces were striking. A thick hairy brow rested over solid black eyes. A protruding mouth with large canine teeth gave the face a dog-like appearance, made stronger by the pointed ears.

"How did you enter this tunnel?" asked the black-haired supervisor. "We were working at one end, and these thuran were working on the other."

"We fell from above," responded Keras. All eyes went to the ceiling except for the inquisitor's. His gaze was steady.

"There is no opening above us. Explain."

"We have a stone mage with us," Verne stated from the floor. "She's here. We fell through the rock."

"From the camp?" The brindi dropped their light stones to the floor, preparing to attack. The black-haired brindi drew a blade and lunged at Keras.

With no discernible effort, Keras disarmed him and twisted back the brindi's wrist, causing him severe pain. With her other hand, she held the tip of the blade to the brindi's throat.

The area burst into flames, blinding everyone present. From the floor, still cradling Neeva in his arms, Verne had used the flame of the oil lamp to create a ring of fire between them and the rest of the brindi. He did not use it to attack, but only as a barrier.

"Are you in league with the forces above?" demanded the brindi held by Keras.

"We are not," said Keras. "Put away your weapons and we can discuss our situation."

The brindi relented. Verne lowered the shield of flame and Keras released the black-haired brindi, but held onto the blade.

"You have a stone mage and a fire mage," stated the brindi leader, "decent bargaining chips. We may have use for a stone mage. Still, you could be spies from above."

"I'm awake." Neeva, in the arms of Verne, was pushing herself up. "You have need of a stone mage? Why should I help the Dark Brindi? You're in league with the forces that destroyed my school, took me captive, starved me." She could not stand and defiantly glared up at the brindi.

"I may be able to spare your life in return for your abilities. Otherwise, I can guarantee that we will be forced to kill you all."

Neeva laughed, glancing at Keras and the three massive thuran. "You could try." The brindi looked at the beaten thuran before meeting Neeva's eyes again. "Down here, I have no equal," she said. Neeva gestured to Keras, "She's strong, but I could bury all of you, every last one."

"Point taken," said the brindi. "We will escort you, under guard, to our manager."

"We are not prisoners and will not travel as such," said Neeva.

"Nevertheless, you must be escorted. Without us, someone else would attack you again. It is wise." The black-haired brindi extended a hand to Neeva. "I am Uhra."

As they walked, Jaron could see that the brindi were digging enormous bores. The sounds of pickaxes, shovels, and mining carts must have subsided during a lunch or a water break. It was because of this that the party had not heard the brindi at work. The brindi, however, had heard something fall during their break.

"What are you mining for?" Ellian asked.

"That's not really for me to say," Uhra replied.

They passed several other mining groups who looked at them with intense curiosity.

The mining manager did not have an office. He didn't even have a desk. On a large flat stone, scrolls rested in piles. A short brindi sat studying a map. He was definitely older than any brindi they had yet seen, and in his face were the wrinkles of deep thought. He addressed Uhra in fury.

"Who is this?"

"We found them in the section seven tunnel. They had fallen through the rock above with the aid of a stone mage."

This changed the manager's tone. "A stone mage? One of you is a stone mage?"

"I am," stated Neeva weakly.

"Interesting," he pondered. "How did you find this underground?"

"I felt the vibrations in the stone above. They travel like sound waves. I can hear them."

"Who else knows?" the manager asked.

"That's a good question to which I do not know the answer," replied Neeva.

"You're just a child. You couldn't possibly be a full mage." He turned to Uhra. "Dispose of them."

Neeva, who by now, had managed to recuperate, clenched her fists and then flattened them with her fingers fanned out. The makeshift desk became a pile of pebbles that spread out on the floor so violently that they washed up the wall like waves crashing on the shore.

The manager looked abashed, and he nodded to Uhra, giving a silent apology. "Ah, I may have been mistaken," the manager said to Neeva. "We may have business to discuss with you. Please allow me to summon Darrod, our leader." He looked around at the remains of his desk. "Uhra, get some blankets and food for our guests."

* * * * *

Darrod, having already seen the rock pulverized to pebbles and gravel dust, spoke plainly with Neeva when he came to meet with her. "I want you to help us finish the excavation under the Sandy River camp."

Neeva exhaled in disgust.

Darrod ignored this and continued. "The general in charge of Mavius's army, Shale, has ambitions aside from procuring Mavius's throne. He has a sore spot for Brindi."

She laughed, "Everyone has a sore spot for Brindi. Baby killers," she added.

Darrod continued, "Apparently, we wronged Shale long ago and he holds a grudge."

"So you plan to wrong him again?"

"Yes." He smiled. "We've been mining these tunnels to attack the encamped forces at Sandy River." Darrod chuckled at his duplicity. "He used the threat of the dead to force our alliance. The Brindi are subservient to no-one."

"So why help King Gurrand?" Jaron asked.

Darrod's chuckle became a laugh. "Gurrand can rot in the ground. Shale is the target. I really don't care who wins, as long as he loses. If the tunnels were complete, any who fell into the underground would never return. Without reinforcements from Sandy River, Shale of Valcella will fall to King Gurrand's army."

"Why should I help? I don't care about politics."

"Well, there is the whole 'death' thing."

"Seriously? You underestimate me. Do you know what I could do to you without any effort at all?"

"Maybe," said Darrod, "but your magic weakens you. When that happens, rest assured, whoever was left would kill you." He waited for her to register this. "Anyway, what we want from you is very simple. Dig out the area from under the camp until it collapses. It is taking us too long. We need to catch Shale undermanned. General Shale is already at Temerrac. He'll be facing Gurrand in four months at the least."

"What about the dead?" Jaron asked. "The men in the camp above, the goblins, you can kill them. You cannot defeat the dead."

"We are still working on that," Darrod responded.

"I have a way," Jaron suggested. "Your tunnels, do they reach under the Sandy River tower?" Darrod shook his head. "Don't try to kill them," Jaron said quietly. "Trap them. Excavate a cavern under the whole camp and drop it all at once."

Darrod's eyes lit up. He continued to expand on Jaron's idea. "If the tower collapses, the leaders of the skeleton soldiers would be trapped under ground."

Jaron completed the plan. "If Neeva can separate the void under the camp from the adjoining tunnels, the river might fill the collapsed area into..."

Darrod finished the sentence, "a lake of death for the living, and a watery trap for the undead."

Hearing this idea, Neeva, smiling savagely, dropped to the floor drawing diagrams and calculations in the dust.

"I take it you agree to help, then?" Darrod laughed.

"If I can stop General Shale... There must be no opening between your tunnels and the collapsed area," Neeva said.

She lay flat on the ground and stretched out with her hands, her eyes closed tight. "The work will take two and a half months. The depth will be one hundred feet. The width will be ten yards wider than the camp. Arches will support the camp. The arches connect back to the supports that currently hold up the tower. The tower supports are made of iron driven deep into a large mother lode of silver. I can't cut these." She frowned. "I need something for this plan to work." She looked up at Darrod and Jaron.

"Bring me Harris Tuno."

Darrod looked confused, but Keras understood right away. "The powder!" she exclaimed.

"What?" Darrod asked."

"Harris is a mason," Keras explained, then to Neeva, "How

could we possibly find him? If I were him I would be a hundred miles away, after what happened to Shale's army."

"Why, what happened to Shale's army?" Darrod asked.

"An invention of Harris's killed over a thousand of them," Keras answered.

Jaron's eyes went wide. He hadn't known that. "The powder," he said quietly.

"He has family in the fishing village of Hooksett," Verne said. "I have heard him tell of it before, a small farm."

Darrod spoke up, "We can't just let you leave. We'll send a group of our own to bring him back here."

"By force?" Jaron asked, stunned. "How do you think you'll get him to cooperate after that?"

"You'd be surprised what we are capable of," Darrod said.

"Send someone with them, then," Verne said. "But we can't use force. We need to convince Harris to return with them. He'd be more inclined to help with your plan if he were approached gently." Verne sounded convincing, but even he still had his doubts. They were, after all, asking Harris to aid Brindi.

Darrod considered this, scratching the beard on his childlike chin. "It is a risk, but it is worth it. I will send twenty brindi with you under the command of Behra. But if you can't convince him, we'll do it my way."

The twenty brindi selected by Behra were a motley bunch. The males, bearded and scarred, the women, hard and stern, they looked like children dressed up as adults, out collecting candy from their neighbors on the 'night of ghouls' in late fall. Among them, no one smiled.

"We are going where?" one named Dillog asked, as she tied her hair into a ponytail.

"We're going up. Gotta travel north of Temerrac to a village named Hooksett," Uhra said.

"Been there," a female brindi named Chelle said. "Boring as rain that place is."

"Why are we going? Don't we have work to do here?" Dillog asked.

"We're looking for a human. He could keep the skeletal army from joining in the invasion of the north," Uhra said.

Jaron ran his fingers along the shoulder of the leather armor provided by the brindi. It had rough edges and smelled like body odor.

"I didn't think I would miss that chainmail shirt Arnor made," Jaron said to Ellian.

"You'll get used to it. Look at Keras," he said, "it always looks like the armor was made for her. She wears it like she was born in it."

"Ellian, if you really like her, you have to tell her."

"I don't know what you're talking about," Ellian said, feeling his neck start to get warm.

Weapons selected for the trip were small. They were not preparing for a major battle so they selected only the basic and lightest weapons. Some had bows, for both fighting and hunting. Others had small swords or long handled knives.

Keras held no weapon. The brindi gave her a wide space even so. Ellian and Jaron carried packs. On foot, the walk to Hooksett would not be a short one. It was at least a week to Temerrac. Then how far it was to Hooksett Jaron could not say. The slope of the path climbed upward, and the stars became visible as they got closer to the exit of the underground maze.

Jaron stopped and just looked up at the beautiful night above him. A sound to his right jerked him back to the present. He sighed in relief. Walking toward him, led by brindi, were horses.

Chapter 17 Stenwood

"Six miles, no further," Thargus said. "Do you see that mountain there? That is the Peak of Patrice. My village is south of that, closer toward the coast." He stopped, catching his breath in surprise. "My, how lovely. The sun turns the peak gold at sunset."

"Yes, it's lovely," said Arnor. "Keep jabbering and I'll put a knife in you."

"Two problems, you haven't got one, and I'd like to see you try."

"Well you may be a good fighter, but eventually you would get tired." Arnor laughed at his joke. "I have a habit of not staying dead."

"Maybe next time I'll leave you underwater and save myself the aggravation."

"In three or four days, I might have learned how to swim." He had forgotten that Thargus had risked his own life to rescue him.

"Does the river bring us closer to your village than this?" Arnor asked.

"No, we will have to walk from here."

"Walking, arghh! I need new clothes. Look at the hole in this." Arnor stuck a finger through the fabric of his shirt. "I would like a new pair of boots," Arnor shaded his eyes from the falling sun, "and a hat."

"There is a trapper along the Attas road. We will come to it tomorrow. And we could get you a knife to test my theory."

Thargus looked around him and spotted a heavy stand of bushes, overhung by mighty trees, thick and tall. "We can rest here for the night. There is plenty of firewood close at hand, but we are to go hungry again, I am afraid."

"This trapper you mention, what have we to trade?"

"Nothing," said Thargus.

Clearing a spot on the ground, he piled dry sticks within it. Snapping twigs, Thargus set them in a ring. Round and round he placed them, winding them together into a circle. "This would be a lot easier if we had a flint and blade." Thargus shaved a stick against a rough stone on the ground, turning it into a spindle, and began the work of making a fire.

*   *   *   *   *

The Attas road was hardly that. Deep ruts from wooden carts and the hooves of countless horses scarred the ground that wound through the low hills and trees. They had finished fording a stream when the smell of pony's dung drifted to them from ahead. A small stable, housing two ponies, sat just around the corner, tucked in between the trees.

The trading post was a small house. Piled high, surrounding the weathered porch, sat the skins of every beast imaginable. The windows of the house were covered with wooden shutters to keep out the morning chill. Sitting on the porch, sipping from a steaming cup and watching the oncoming dwarves silently, was a bent old man. So like to his surroundings was he that the dwarves almost walked past him on their way toward the door.

"Good morn," said the man, taking a sip from his steaming cup.

"Ah, yes," said Thargus, "good morn, sir. How are you today?"

"As good as the brew allows," said the old man. "How can I help you two? You don't look as if you've anything to trade."

"Right you are, sir," said Thargus.

"Then be off." The man took another sip of his cup.

"We have need of food, water, and news."

"With naught to trade for it?" asked the old man.

"We can trade work."

"Well, that is something." The old man thought for a moment. Thin and wiry, his arms looked like twigs and his hair and beard were white and unkempt. His clothing was modest, a pale yellow shirt and brown pants over short leather shoes. He winked an eye as he found a solution, and his long eyebrows flipped down with the closing of his eye. "You can start by cleaning out the pony stalls. Food will be waiting when you've finished."

An hour later, sweaty and reeking of dung, they came back to the porch.

"Finished already? Excellent! There is a stream behind the house here. Head back and you'll find soap. Wash your clothes, too."

He gave them some time and came around as they were wringing out their clothes.

"Now that you're clean," he held out his withered hand, "name is Billy."

The food was good, and the dwarves were soon satisfied with the old man's end of the bargain. Butter over hard bread was more luxury than either had enjoyed in many a week. Apples, wild carrots, and smoked squirrel rounded out the table.

"Where are you two headed? Are you going to Stenwood? Not sure I would, if I was you."

Thargus asked, "You have news of Stenwood?"

"No one has come out of there in near two months. Can't remember the last time I seen a dwarf. A strange curse has fallen over it. If I were you boys, I would head for another town."

"I have family there. What is this curse?"

"I don't really know. They call it 'the still.' I am not going anywhere near there if I can help it. Ain't been nothing but soldiers, Human, come through here in a while now."

* * * * *

This Dwarf city was not underground. Burrowed into the side of the mountain, the main road into Stenwood Den was a crack in the mountain slope. The way was empty. Lookout posts for the town sat as quiet spires into the morning sky. No sign of movement appeared over the high walls. It was very different from Sotho Entollo. Even so, much of the architecture reminded Arnor of the underground city.

Stacks of round logs littered several areas of the street. Each was about four feet long and most were thicker than two feet.

"There's an awful lot of wood," Arnor remarked. He had been glancing at them as they walked past empty shops still filled with wares.

"It's not wood," said Thargus stopping to look closer. "Look, it gleams in the sunlight. These were not here when I left." He ran his hands along the shape. "It feels like glass." His hand wiped away some of the color. He wiped the color onto his shirt. Then, as he realized that the object was transparent, he wiped until the light of day could penetrate deep enough to make out a shape, a foot. Startled, he moved away from the glass.

"What?" Arnor asked.

Thargus walked into a shop, returning with a bucket of water and a dress. He poured the bucket over the glass and scrubbed. Encased within the material was a Dwarven woman. She looked to be in great pain and did not move, her face frozen in a grimace. Thargus looked around. How many logs had he passed already? His eyes wild with panic, Thargus jumped up from inspecting the woman and ran further into town, followed by shouts from Arnor.

"Where are you going?"

Arnor, wheezing, followed the sounds of Thargus's footsteps, soft as they were. Up a long flight of stairs, across landings, and through small courtyards they led, until Arnor could see Thargus in the distance on his knees before a pair of small logs. He wiped frantically at them, clearing the color away to see inside. When Arnor arrived at Thargus's side, the dwarf had given up.

"What's going on?" Arnor demanded.

Tears streaming freely down his cheeks, in between deep shuddering breaths, Thargus answered, "These are my children."

Arnor's heart broke for Thargus. "Did you know that this would happen?"

"No."

Arnor placed his hand on Thargus's shoulder. "We need to find out more if we are going to help them. Where is the portal?"

* * * * *

"This is where they came out." Thargus was looking, craning his neck, one foot in front of the other, so as not to accidentally fall over the edge into a deep vertical shaft.

Arnor walked to the edge and looked down, unafraid, but saw nothing: no light, no bottom. The shaft just fell away into darkness.

"How deep is it?" He asked.

"We've dropped rocks, but we have never heard them hit bottom."

"Has anyone tried to climb down?"

"I don't think so."

"Well, no time like the present," Arnor said. He swung his legs over the side until he was on his belly with his feet dangling over the drop.

"Wait!" shouted Thargus, alarmed. "There is some rope here. At least use it as much as possible."

Arnor looked at the cracks and crevices available for purchase during his descent and agreed. "How much have we got?"

Thargus guessed at the length, "Sixty feet." The drop was far longer than that. Arnor harrumphed and started to climb down.

Sweat poured off his forehead. He forced a fist into a crack and rested. Looking up he could see Thargus as a small dot on the edge of the lit circle that was the top of the shaft. Turning his head, he looked down into the blackness, still unable to discern the bottom.

Frequent cramping muscles forced Arnor to rest often. His hands were bleeding and raw. For two hours he had been lowering himself slowly down, winding around the shaft to the easiest routes. He looked around himself in disgust. His current path of descent had led to a dead end. The climb back to begin another branch could take fifteen minutes or more. Reaching up, he grabbed onto the edge of a crack. It let go, causing him to tumble away from the wall.

A gasp of sudden fear escaped his lips and he threw himself away from the wall with his feet, hoping to catch himself on the other side of the shaft, six yards away, before he gained too much momentum. To his surprise, he was able to hang on to the other side of the tunnel easily. He had not fallen far at all. He stayed there breathing heavily, wishing he had considered Thargus's suggestion of using ropes. His shoulder muscles locked together in pain and discomfort. Closing his eyes in determination, Arnor stuck his hand deep into a crack and made a fist. Secure in his position, he forced himself to relax.

His mind pieced everything together, replaying the short fall in his head. He had caught the outcropping on this side with the slightest of efforts. Looking up, he was able to make out the dislodged rock that had caused him to fall. *Where is the crumbled piece that came off in my hand?* he asked. It still had not reached the bottom.

Looking down, he found another irregularity in the wall and guessed the distance to it at five feet. *I could probably stand on that,* he thought. Bracing himself, he aimed at the outcropping, and keeping one hand on the wall, let go.

He did not crash onto it, but fell slowly down like a feather, meeting the surface gently. His fingers ran along the rock wall. Standing on the small ledge of rock, he looked down for another. Twenty feet below, on the opposite side of the shaft, was another break in the wall's uniformity. Aiming once again, he threw himself at it, to crash into the wall on the other side and fall gently to the ledge.

Is this shaft controlled by some magic? Looking down he saw another opportunity to test it, finding that, yes, it did have some quality that allowed him to control his fall. He took a deep breath and let go of the wall. The opening at the top began to get smaller and smaller until he was unable to see it, while, at the same time, a red light appeared below, and it was approaching with alarming speed. In a panic, he reached for the walls and his descent immediately slowed to a crawl, allowing him to touch gently down.

The bottom of the well was a half sphere shaped room with a flat floor. The source of the light turned out to be six glowing rectangles spaced evenly around the top of the round ceiling. A thin line that also glowed, though it was much dimmer than the rectangles, connected them.

A cracked and broken door lay on one side of the room. Wide and once majestic, it rested awkwardly on its hinges. Arnor ran his fingers along the wood and stepped through the doorway. If only he had his gear, knives, axes, and his hat. His red feather always made him feel stronger, as if it had some magical properties of its own.

The heat intensified through the doorway. He was already sweating from the exertion of the climb down. He wiped the sweat from his forehead and knocked off his hat in the process.

My hat!

Arnor reached down to pick it up. *It is my hat.* Placing it on his head, he set his hands on his hips to try to make sense of it, rubbing his thumb on the leather belt.

My leather belt!

Whoa! he thought. Running his hands over himself, he made an inventory: five throwing axes, five throwing knives, one short sword, a fine shirt, blue trousers, and boots. His hands went to his head again. *Still there, my hat, and a fine red feather.*

Arnor stepped back into the round room and rechecked his gear again, *still here. Something about this passage must,* he struggled to put the thoughts together, *must return lost possessions. On the other hand,* he thought, *perhaps it sees you as you see yourself, and makes it so.*

He yelled up to Thargus. There was no answer. *Well, how do I get back?* he asked himself. The ceiling here was so high that he could not jump up to it. Looking over his shoulders at the doors, he had an idea.

Before long he had both doors off their hinges and had wedged them up against each other in the center of the room under the shaft. He had reconnected the hinges to the top of the doors so that the two worked as a standing A-frame together. Using his axes, he climbed to the top to stand precariously on the pair. He could not reach the bottom of the shaft wall. He could try to jump. His fingers were only six to ten inches out of the shaft.

Arnor jumped for the shaft bottom lip, and kept going, rising up. Soon after, he stepped out onto the ground next to Thargus.

After much haggling—and after two demonstrations—Arnor convinced Thargus to jump into the shaft along with him. They floated down with varying speed, touching the bottom as lightly as the feather in Arnor's cap brushed the air.

Arnor watched Thargus as he passed through the open doorway, expecting to see a plethora of weapons materialize on him, armor, and dark clothes with lock-picks embedded in the sleeves. What he saw astonished him more than anything he had expected. Thargus wore a long brown cloak over an inner tunic of white silk. His boots were tall brown leather and had no shine to them. In his hand was a long staff of unworked maple. These were the clothes of a simple man, a holy man, not an assassin.

"You're not...."

"A scoundrel?" Thargus finished for him. He took a moment and inspected his attire appreciatively. "Thargus Hammerfist, sage of Stenwood Den, nice to meet you. I'm not one of the town elders and I'm not a priest. I was never wealthy and some of my skills are less than respectable." He looked Arnor up and down. "So this is the real you? Quite a few weapons there, mate. Stick a lot of people, do you?"

"I do what I need to, no more."

"You still look like a cheap merchant. Nice hat."

Arnor brushed the feather. "I like it. Where's this portal?"

Thargus became serious again. "I suppose if we follow this tunnel it will become apparent to us."

Together, they trod along the passageway until it came to wide stairs that climbed up to another doorway. This doorway vomited colors onto the landing in front of it, swirling in a round pattern, like paint stirring in a can, red, grey, yellow, orange and blue. Flashes of light accompanied the colors, breaking through with a mixture of intensity, piercing the eyes like painful pins. Around the door, blurred with the mixture, tendrils, brilliant in color, reached to pull at the stairs and walls around the doorway. There appeared to be nothing to close. No structure that would shut away the fantastic display sat beside it.

"Looks more like a hole than a door," said Arnor, climbing the steps slowly as the tendrils of color and light spun around him. Perhaps, the door itself was on the other side of this opening. If he could merely reach through and pull it to, he might be able to shut it. His arm passed through the doorway obscured by the swirling colors. Waving it around, he felt nothing, not cold, not heat, and no door latch on the other side.

He pulled his hand back, dismayed, but his hand came back changed. Blackness clung to it. It was cold. Startled, he fell back down the stairs, pulling at the blackness with his other hand. It clung tight.

Thargus came to Arnor's assistance, and under the effort of both dwarves, the blackness let go to stand before them. In a movement like to the unfurling of a flag in a strong wind, the blackness rose to tower over them. Tall and imposing, claws outstretched, in stark contrast to the brilliant color display behind it, was a shade, larger than any Arnor had ever seen.

A dark hand reached out for Thargus, and under the grasp, Thargus screamed in pain. He screamed, but he stayed awake. Dropping his staff, Thargus gripped the fingers and curled them away from his shoulder, falling to his hands and knees.

In a moment of anger, Arnor leaped at the shade, wrapping his arms around it, and squeezed. The shade shrieked in panic, struggling to escape the grasp of the dwarf. The burning cold was too much for Arnor to withstand for long and he had to release his grip. Sensing the opportunity, the shade withdrew and fell into the color swirl behind it.

Arnor glanced at Thargus. He was unconscious or dead. In fact, he himself didn't feel well. With a single step away from the doorway, Arnor swooned and fell into darkness.

Chapter 18   Meals for Minasts

The brindi prepared the horses for travel. Saddles and blankets waited in a barn no taller than Ellian. An hour passed with nothing more for Jaron to do but look at the constellations above him. He lay down on his back to further appreciate the moonless sky, brilliant with starlight.

The Cask of Castas shone with its seven bright stars. Below that, and upside down, was Anost the sailor. He tried to remember all of the constellation patterns from his lessons, but these two were always easy to pick out. That he could be so calm astounded him. Only months ago he was studying under Ceryss in Westmost, studying the deeds of others, some great, some terrible.

How will my deeds appear in the history books years from now? He laughed and answered himself. *I guess it would depend on who wins. That powder might keep the skeletal army from joining in the invasion of the north. It might not. Finding Harris is not going to be easy,* Jaron thought.

The grass was cool in the warm night air. He had filled the pockets of his new pants and shirt with dried fruits to tide him over until mealtime, which was not to come for several hours. He savored the flavor of a dried apricot.

Uhra, Jihe, Hahre, and Chelle had the horses ready before long, and the lot of them traveled in single file, with Behra in the lead. For two hours, they traveled in darkness, snagged by the occasional branch. The trees here were maple and grew so close together that they had to stop several times to allow someone to clear a path.

Finally, they broke into an open field. A short rest for the horses came with the rising sun. Clear and cold with a mud-silted bottom, a trickling brook sang, winding through the valley of grass.

Behra, sitting on a boulder near the water, studied a map. They needed to cross the mountain range without going through Temerrac. Snowy even in the heat of summer, the pass was windy and narrow, winding back and forth across the rocky face of the mountain. It could be done, but it would not be easy. If they were not able to bring the horses through the narrow pass, they would have to acquire others on the northern side of the mountain range. She looked at the map and measured the distance to the pass through the mountains. *Three days to get through,* she thought to herself. She added up the list of supplies. What she feared most were the minasts.

She had only encountered minasts once in her life. Tall and lanky, their muscles wiry and corded, they had enormous strength, lifting trees out of the ground by their roots and hurling boulders down on unwary travelers. Cloven feet climbed nimbly the sheerest surfaces aided by hands as dexterous as any Brindi. Tusks protruded from their lower jaws, curling up beneath eyes hidden under a heavy brow. A strong square nose looked in contrast to the floppy and long ears. They prowled this range and guarded the stone itself as if it were made of gold.

The party still had two days riding until they arrived at the base of the mountains. First, the forest of Dinna sat in their path, followed by the Dinst marsh on the other side. She did not like the marsh.

The forest of Dinna was dark and humid. Heavy boughs hung over the narrow trail, blocking out the sunlight while holding in the moisture. Swords could not break through the vines that hung across the trail, and the brindi pushed or pulled them out of the way so that the march could continue. In six hours, they reached the other side of the forest.

The Dinst marsh took much longer to cross. The water was shallow but the horses found deep mud along the path that made it hard to continue. Several times, they had to work together to pull a horse free of the suction. No one was dry. The gnats and mosquitoes were merciless, and no one looked forward to the stings and the itch that followed after. As the ground rose out of the muck and grime that was the Dinst marsh, the riders breathed a sigh of relief. They rode for another two hours to put distance between themselves and the quagmire.

"I don't care how far we need to ride to get away from those mosquitoes," Keras said. "I could ride forever."

That night, they lay out the bedrolls and lit no fire. Behra gave the order of the watch and all, save the unlucky owner of the first shift, fell fast asleep. The next morning, after a hasty breakfast, the travelers abandoned their single file configuration in favor of one that allowed conversation.

"I can still smell the marsh in my clothes," Jihe complained.

"A bath," Dinna said closing her eyes. "I want a bath."

"How many days until the knights in the tower leave to join General Shale?" Behra asked.

Jaron calculated in his head. "Four months, maybe less."

"Let's hope it is not less." She sniffed the air. "We're coming into summer. If we haven't found this Harris of yours before the end of July, we should go back and aid in the attack on the Sandy River camp."

Jaron did not want to return to the tunnels of Darrod. His only experience underground that he had found enjoyable had been the time traveling the Sotho Palala. The tunnels of Darrod were no Sotho Palala. Escape entered his thoughts. The brindi were many and they were well armed. *If we don't find Harris, Keras could probably take most of them,* Jaron thought, smiling.

'Baby killers,' Neeva had called them. Jaron remembered the first story he had read about the Brindi. *Everyone hates the Brindi.* The city of Castas, named for the constellation, once had an alliance with the Brindi during the war of Castam Pelmari. The Brindi felt cheated when it came to the division of spoils, believing that the city of Castas had not upheld their end of the bargain. The Brindi entered Castas while the army was away and killed the children, all of them.

Now, the Brindi were fighting for the same side as he, if only in secret. Nevertheless, he must be careful. Their duplicity in dealing with the knights at Sandy River could result in the loss of advantage for Shale's army, but it could also strike back against him. Brindi were a dangerous ally.

The grassy incline continued until midday and the vegetation gave way to ledge and stones. The air became thinner and the horses breathing became labored. They rested more often. Frosty air and a biting wind replaced the warmth and humidity of the marshes. The cold breeze tore through the layers of clothing. Each rider layered every piece of material they possessed about them, and some even wrapped themselves in their blankets.

Left and right, the road meandered around the face of the mountain, climbing higher and higher. Ledge rock overhung the trail, looming above, poised to crack and sweep travelers off the bluff. To one side, the drop into canyons and cliffs clouded the head and made some dizzy with fear. To the other side, marks of hammer and chisel showed where the stonecutters ground the path into the face of the mountain. They dismounted and took their steeds by the reins to guide them more safely.

Fighting against the wind as they were, they continued into the dark, walking by the light of the crescent moon until, frostbitten and miserable, they came upon a wider landing where they decided to spend the night. Air currents spun over the outcrop of the rock above, whistling shrilly, but twisting away without offending the group of weary men, horses, and brindi. Here, it was cold but the wind did not bite. Still, with no fire building materials available, they slept huddled together to share warmth with the horses.

Morning came with a dusting of snow and flakes sparse in the air. Jaron's fingers were cold, and he shook his hands to drive blood into them. A quick meal of dried meat and fruits did not satiate his hunger and cold water did nothing to warm his belly. A cup of coffee was all that he really wanted. How long had it been since he had bitten into a slice of apple or had a taste of pepper.

The day was spent snaking back and forth, ascending the stone path. By midday, they were passing around the mountain to the other side of the range. Still guiding the horses, they made slow progress, but the trail on the other side sloped down at least half of the time, and that was encouraging.

As the sun fell from the sky, a glowing orange filled the horizon in the west. They found the trail widening. This spot chosen for camp looked similar to the resting area of the previous night. The shape of the ledges nearby lessened the wind here as well. *Whoever built this road must have planned this,* Jaron thought. *We walk the distance between camping sites in under a day. This must have been well traveled at one time.*

They slept much as they had the night before. The chill air stung them even outside the reach of the wind. Snow, once again, began to flurry over the sleeping brindi and men.

Ellian took the third watch and he shivered under his blanket as he leaned against his horse. In the darkness, as one cloud blocked out the light, a call resounded over the whining of the wind.

"Owooooa!"

Not very loud, it must be coming from a great distance away, Ellian thought.

The call repeated, "Owooooa!"

This call came from a completely different direction than the first.

Ellian reached to Uhra and nudged him.

"Listen," he said.

The call repeated again from the original location. "Owooooa!"

Uhra started and grasped his spear, before waking the other members of the party. Together they listened and discussed their options.

"Triple the watch," Uhra said. "Those of you who have not heard them before, those are the minasts. They are nearby, and—most certainly—watching us. You on watch, keep your wits about you. They're out looking for a meal."

"Wait, these things eat people, like you or me, and we're going to go back to sleep?" Keras asked, stunned.

"We'll be moving faster in the morning. The minasts will try to cut off our escape as they bring in greater numbers. Could you hunt them down and fight them now?" Mocking her, Uhra feigned relief. "Good, we can all relax," he called out. "The great Keras is going to make the monsters go away." He laughed coolly, looking sideways at her. "No, we all have to be at our best, and our best bet is a quick escape with the rise of the sun."

No more calls came from the minasts, but Jaron and Keras had trouble sleeping. At sunrise, they all pulled their blankets off to discover that one of them was missing. Jihe was gone. The minasts had taken him in the night. Their brazen affront could only mean that there were more minasts around than they had originally believed.

Minasts, in small numbers, picked and poked at travelers, taking one or two members of large groups, but minasts in packs greatly outnumbering a traveling party would leave no one alive. Behra ordered everyone to pack up to continue the march. Chelle cried in anguish. Jihe was her mate, and she did not wish to abandon him.

They led the horses into the wind that whipped around the rock face of the mountain. The sun was just beginning to show full in the sky when Uhra, looking behind for pursuit, noticed three minasts trailing stealthily, using the stone side of the trail for cover when available.

"Owoooooa!" Their call came from behind.

"Owoooooa!" It repeated from below the ledge path.

Jaron stretched his neck out to look over the edge. Fifty feet below, climbing with remarkable dexterity was a group of forty minasts. Jaron jumped back in surprise, startling his horse and gaining the attention of the others. Quickly, one after another, they looked over the edge to see what had jolted Jaron so. Realizing the precariousness of the situation, Behra made a desperate decision. "Mount your horses!" she commanded. "We need to ride, now!"

Jaron looked down at the width of the road and the unnerving drop beside it. Behra scaled the saddle on her horse and threw her leg over the top. She took one last look behind to assure that the others were following her orders and spurred her horse down the trail as fast as the beast would travel. In fear, the horse charged down the trail at astounding speed.

Sweat, cold with the wind, beaded on Jaron's forehead as he guided his mount down the trail trying to keep up with Behra. Her moves, left and right, kept her horse from slipping over the edge, and Jaron was doing his best to mimic her in every step. Behind him, the impact of hooves sang like a thundercloud as it echoed off the rock. Ahead, minasts were starting to pull themselves over the cliff edge onto the trail. One minast lost its balance, bowled over by Behra's horse, and fell screaming from the drop. At the cliff edge, the hands reaching up from nothingness were followed by wide shoulders and heads adorned with fierce looking tusks.

Jaron pulled his horse left to avoid the outstretched hands of one shrieking minast, and nearly missed a turn that could have sent him hurling through open air to his death. Screaming in fear and whinnying in protest, Behra and Jaron's horses trampled the assailants. Jaron turned his head, hearing a loud yell behind him, to see a rider and mount falling together into the shadows.

Down the path ahead, minasts were setting up for an ambush, curling their bodies into the stones, setting themselves to spring out and grab. Jaron yelped in surprise as, ahead of him, a small minast leaped for Behra from the rock wall and missed, only just catching itself on the trail edge as Jaron rode past. He turned his attention to the wall next to him. It was moving, writhing with limbs and bodies ready to spring. They had set up their attack.

One or two of the fiends leaped at each rider. Jaron, having seen the failed attack on Behra, was ready and swung his fist as the beast came at him. His hand swung out, connecting with the jaw, cutting his knuckles on the protruding canine teeth, but stopping the attack before strong hands could grasp at him.

Two horses toppled over the edge, taking one rider and minast with them. The second rider, Uhra, was able to leap free. He reached up for Ellian as the human rode past, and Ellian threw the brindi up behind him. Uhra took advantage of his position. With his hands free and leaning against the bigger human in front, he reached for the bow and quiver attached to the saddle. Aiming deftly from the moving rump of the horse, he shot three of the minasts from the wall ahead as they were about to attack the riders in front.

Behind Ellian and Uhra, Chelle had dislodged her attacking minast with the aid of her long knife. She looked behind her to Hahre. The girl was struggling with her own minast, and she was about to lose control of her horse. Chelle reined her horse and flung herself onto the back of the beast accosting Hahre. Chelle's long knife came out again and with one hand on the thing's chin and her legs wrapped around its hips, she drew the blade across its throat. It released its grip on Hahre and collapsed from the moving horse, taking Chelle with it.

Chelle rebounded to her feet on the road and swung the blade into a new attack. She was buying their escape with her life. She would be with Jihe, and her sister Hahre would survive.

Still high in the mountains, the end of the stony pass was wide, allowing the horses to run hard without fear of falling. After reaching the safer road, they did not stop to rest for another ten minutes. When they did stop, they made sure to water the horses and rub them down. If it had not been for the strength of the mounts, they all surely would have endured a nasty end.

The call of the minasts was harsh and angry from high above. They had lost a large meal and lamented with loud yells that echoed from far away. "Owoooooa!"

Chapter 19   Slaves to Soldiers

Runoff from the mountain formed the cold stream that wandered away from the north side. During the rest, the horses drank long and deep from the stream. The brindi took a list of whom they had lost. Chelle, Jihe, Jidda, and Nisse had all perished. Jihe had disappeared during the night somehow. Nisse had fallen with his horse, misjudging a turn and plummeting to his death when his horse lost its footing. Jidda had lost control of his mount when a minast leaping from the walls had landed on him. Chelle was a huge loss. Her bravery had allowed the rest of them to make it down the mountain safely.

Jaron had only come to know a few names. Uhra, he knew from their first encounter in the tunnel. Behra, he knew. It was she who controlled the agenda for the group, and she made sure everyone knew it. Jihe and Chelle had been mates and were young. Had they been Human they might have been in their early twenties but for Brindi that could mean anywhere from thirty to forty years old.

He now made an effort to learn everyone's name, at least to hear them, for it would take some time to learn so many.

Working on her horse diligently, though tears streamed down her face, was Hahre, Chelle's younger sister. Danos, Kenda, and Rissa were members of the group that had accompanied Uhra in the tunnels when Keras had been teaching the thuran a lesson. Jaron had not heard their names then. Four girls, tougher than the boys, Gehne, Dillog, Dinna (named after the forest), and Joalle ate quietly next to the stream, arguing over who should be filling the water pouches. The last six, Kenast, Engle, Lurhe, Sindas, Mennas, and Joahe were working on practicing joint locks with Keras. Keras was thoroughly enjoying this teaching moment.

How would he remember them all?

The minasts had not pursued them into the grassland although the elevation was still high. *Are minasts an intelligent species?*

Jaron asked himself. *Are they just animals? They don't wear any clothing, even in the cold temperatures of the high mountains. Whatever they are, I hope I never encounter them again.*

Behra, calling for them to move out, interrupted his thoughts. The ride down into the valley was gentle and easy, a pleasant contrast to the last two days. Behra was not pushing the horses hard. The three lost in the mountains during the chase had been strong steeds. Behra had broken them herself. She did not want to lose any more of them.

She made the decision to travel Holderness Road now that they were north of Temerrac. Any encounter with General Shale's troops required the performance of a minor charade with the humans posing as prisoners.

"You can still ride your horses, but we'll lead them," Behra said to Jaron, Ellian, and Keras. "I need your weapons." They stared at her. "These ropes will easily slip off your hands, but to the casual observer, they will appear binding." She handed over three sets of previously tied cords, looking up at their skeptical faces. "Taking the road is the fastest way to get to Hooksett. Time is precious."

They did not like it. Ellian concealed a small knife in his sleeve instead of handing over all of his weapons. He looked at Jaron as he did this, perhaps implying that Jaron should do the same, but there was no time and Jaron did not attempt the minor subterfuge. Keras did not complain. She didn't really need a weapon anyway.

They connected with the Holderness Road several miles north of Temerrac, where Keras, Jaron, and Ellian were excited to see the aqueduct again. It stood parallel with the road, though some distance off, a miracle of engineering. It lent an aura of permanence to this land that, in reality, was only an illusion. Even Temerrac, one of the oldest cities on the continent, could be destroyed by a single incident.

The first travelers they encountered on the road were Humans, pulling nearly empty wagons and heading south. They stopped to discuss events of the past week in the war and to trade worthless trinkets, or so Jaron thought. They laughed, making cruel jests at the prisoners of the brindi.

"Oh! Did you get a boo-boo in your fight?" One of them poked Keras savagely.

"It's like getting caught by children, isn't it?" another of them chortled. Fifteen wagons passed, and every one of the drivers had a remark dripping with scorn and disdain. The 'captured' humans took no notice of the insults, but the brindi were seething. After the men driving the empty wagons were out of earshot, the brindi began.

"Children!" Danos complained to Joalle. "Road peddlers! Not one of them has ever swung a sword. I'd surely love to drive mine up into their rib cages."

Joalle spat on the ground after the wagons had passed. "They would sure look funny wearing their tongues as neckties."

"How can you tell a Human's boots from a Brindi's boots?" Joahe started, but halted the joke as he remembered their guests.

The small villages on the main road lay in waste, deserted and burned. Jaron realized that famine would visit this land. An army, especially an invading army, takes what it needs, and it needs everything. Some villages had even lost important buildings to scavenging, as soldiers had dismantled them to send the lumber north, where building materials were becoming scarce.

The next encounter with a wagon train was with a supply chain heading north. There were fifteen wagons, just the same as before, but now there were men riding alongside who were armed with long spears. The carts were filled with animals and food looted from the farms of the lands close to Temerrac.

"How is there so much traffic on this road? I thought the passage through Temerrac was closed," Ellian asked Behra.

"As did I, and I asked a wagon driver that." She took a drink from her flask. "Apparently, Shale has some wizards of his own, a student of the Hall. The student cleared debris that would have taken a thousand men over a month's time, and he did it in a week."

On the third day, while heading north, they overtook another supply train at the Besoth Gorge suspension bridge. The supply train was sending one wagon across at a time. As wagons reached the north side, they unhitched and watered their horses at the stream that emptied into the gorge just west of the bridge supports. After the last wagon reached the north side, the brindi and their 'captives' crossed the bridge as a group.

The same general banter passed between the brindi and the humans waiting by the wagons. One of the soldiers approached Jaron, Ellian, and Keras. He grabbed Ellian by his shirt and pulled him from his horse. "Hey!" he called to Behra. "We're carting slaves north. Do you want me to take these three off your hands?"

"Why are slaves needed in the north?" Ellian asked and received a fist in the eye. The soldier laughed.

"Well," the soldier said, changing his tone to resemble a caring teacher, "You see, we use slaves and worthless scum, like you," he winked, "when we need to ransack a castle or a keep. You take the oil and tar to the door where you will set the door on fire. Now, it's true that while you are doing this, the men protecting the very place we are trying to burn down will shoot at you. Of course, if you refuse, we're the ones that will shoot you. It's not a nice job, but better you than me." He took Ellian by the arm.

Ellian drove the concealed knife through the man's throat. Gurgling, the soldier collapsed to the dirt. The brindi pounced on the other soldiers and wagon drivers. Seconds later, blood pooled with the dust of the road, and twenty-five men lay dead.

Keras forced open the slave carts with a large axe. Twenty-two were in the carts, fourteen men, and eight women, among them Anna, Jel, and Rennek.

Anna embraced Keras as she jumped from the wagon. "What happened to you?" Anna asked. "We watched you fall into the rock. Where did it take you? Where's Neeva? Is she with you?"

"Neeva is fine. We left her and Verne behind. They had some work they wanted to accomplish. Where are Arnor and Thargus?"

Anna hugged Keras. "I'm sorry, honey. Arnor is dead."

Keras was stunned. "Dead? How?"

"He was hit by arrows during the escape. After he died, we split up with Thargus. I don't really know where he is going but he threatened us anyway about telling anyone. We headed back to Temerrac." She gestured to the bodies of the soldiers. "They picked us up just outside of the city," she said. "They didn't even ask questions." Anna leaned in to Keras. "Where are you headed and," her voice dropped to a whisper, "why are you traveling with Brindi?"

"The Brindi are going to try to destroy that camp at Sandy River," Keras said.

"The Brindi double-cross," Anna said. "Are you sure they're not double-crossing you?"

"I think it's our only chance to stop those skeletons."

Anna shivered, rubbing away the goosebumps that had run down her arms at the memory of the revenant soldiers.

The prisoners collected the soldier's weapons. The carts carried more weapons and armor. Within thirty minutes, the ragtag collection of slaves had transformed themselves into a formidable looking force. The men lying dead on the road were stacked into the slave carts and driven down a side path by Rennek and Jel, who returned thirty minutes later riding bareback on the horses that had been pulling the carts. They were dressed in the uniforms of the soldiers and carried their weapons and a horn.

The brindi were deep in discussion about the next course of action. Behra was furious. The trip to Hooksett was supposed to be secret and quiet. It was not so anymore. The newly liberated humans stood apart from the brindi, not trusting the 'sour children,' as they were called. A group of twenty-three had first reduced to nineteen, and had now swelled to forty-one. She called Ellian to her.

"This is your doing. Our mission may be over. I do not know how this can be hidden and this road may be impassable herein."

"I don't believe it will be as bad as all that," Ellian answered.

"What do you propose?"

"We take them with us. If we come upon another supply

train, we have no need to worry. We are merely members of Valcella's army. And if it came to it, we could fight."

"These aren't warriors you've rescued." She pointed to Anna. "That one is a housewife if I've ever seen one, probably from a rich family, no less. You've risked my mission with your impetuousness! Leave them and let them go where they will, but they do not come with us."

"I have seen some of these men in action. They fight well enough to hold their own."

She laughed, but it turned cold. She poked him hard in the chest. "Are you getting too big for your shoes? I won't have it. These people are not my responsibility. We are going on to Hooksett without them. I think maybe we should even dispose of them."

"Kill them?" Ellian said, shocked. "If you do this, you will have to kill us as well. Now it's me that won't have it."

Behra, reached for her sword. Anger filled her from this display of independence. She glared at him. Her hand stopped short of drawing the blade. She still needed the humans, at least one of them. She pushed the sword back down and pointed at Jaron. "He stays with me. I need him to convince this 'Harris' to come with us."

"I can't allow you to take just him," Ellian said. "I'll be going with you too.

Ellian looked back at the people he had rescued from certain death. Fourteen men and eight women were now armed and waiting for these two to decide the next course of action.

Ellian watched Keras practice some wrestling moves with Uhra, Dillog, and Danos.

"I need to speak with my friends."

Behra threw her hands up in disgust and walked away.

Keras, Jaron, and Ellian stood near the food carts.

"Arnor is dead," Keras said.

Jaron laughed, "No, he isn't."

"But Anna said he was hit by two arrows in the river as they escaped."

"I know it sounds stupid, but we've seen him survive drowning already. I'd wager he's still alive."

"I don't know, Jaron," said Ellian. "Anna was pretty certain. We're on our own, now. We have to decide what to do. The brindi still need Harris, but we can't all go to Hooksett. I have an idea." Ellian drew a map on the ground. "Over here is Hooksett, where we're headed. It is some twenty miles east, off this main road here. The blond one," he pointed to a pretty girl from the first cart, "says she is from a village, Denshire, about ten miles south of that."

"Denshire was one of the townships that Yaru was going to," interjected Keras.

"Yes," said Ellian, "that is where I want you to lead them. The village should not be deserted but it's far enough from the main road to hide you from any forces heading north, and there may already be a resistance building there."

"And what are you going to be doing?" Keras asked.

"What we promised the brindi we would do," Jaron said. "That has to be done first. Neeva is waiting for us."

"Neeva could care less about us," Ellian interjected. "I wanted to take them with us," Ellian said looking over at the freed prisoners, "but Behra is set against that. If you can, hide out with them in Denshire. I can come and get you on the way back to the tunnels."

"Don't take too long."

"Promise me you'll be careful," Ellian took Keras in his arms, hugging her tight.

"I don't know if that's a promise I can..." Her sentence was interrupted by Ellian's kiss.

* * * * *

The Valcella wagons filled with food, wood, nails, and canvas, were fitted with new drivers. The prisoners now wore the uniforms of Valcella's soldiers, those not soiled by the blood of their previous owners. In all appearances, they looked like any wagon train traveling the road.

"If we are to pull off this disguise, we have time to make up. We are a full day behind schedule," Rennek suggested.

"No, we won't rush," Keras replied. "Better to say we had trouble with some locals."

"But what if they send a patrol back to check it out?"

"I'm hoping they will." Keras rubbed her finger against her blade. "I've got my sword back." Then she smiled, remembering the kiss. "Today is a good day."

Chapter 20   Assassin's Redemption

The sun stretched its fingers into the valley containing Stenwood Den. White granite reflected the morning's rays, allowing the dawn to come early to the only two inhabitants of the village. Arnor squinted his eyes, forcing word associations to roll through his mind: light, colors, darkness, door. Arnor sat bolt upright. *Where am I?* he panicked. *The door, where is the doorway?*

A bowl of water sat on the floor next to him. *Water!* he thought. *When was the last time I had water?* He lifted the bowl to his lips and smelled it before tasting, clear, cold water. He drank it down. Next to the bowl of water was a jar. Picking it up, he inspected it closely, *peaches*. He opened the jar and pulled one out, enjoying the flavor and sweet juices.

Hey, he thought, *the floor is clean.*

Everything was dusty in Stenwood Den.

Blinking his eyes against the light, he stood up and stretched. *Where am I?* The walls were white. "Is that plaster?" he asked aloud, walking over to run his fingers over it.

The rooms around him received a quick inspection. In one of the rooms, set in beds, were two of the glass logs he had seen throughout the village. He moved closer to one, regarding the cleanliness of the glass and the clarity with which the child inside could now be seen. This was one of Thargus's children, a girl, beautiful in her innocence. The other child was a boy of maybe four years. The tears on the child's cheeks showed clearly through the glass. *Are they dead, or is this some type of suspended animation?*

"Arnor? Are you there?" Thargus was calling from the main room of the house where Arnor had woken up.

"I'm in here," Arnor called, feeling his voice hoarse from the dryness. "I'm in the bedroom."

Thargus came into the room and placed his left hand on the glass containing his daughter.

"I could not find their mother. I cleaned the house and set

them here in their beds. What good is it to hope? I don't know." He looked over at his son. "So young. I don't know this magic." He sat down on the bed. "When I woke, you were still out cold. I don't know how long I was unconscious, but you were out for a whole day after I brought you here. I decided to move you away from the doorway in case anything else came through the door."

"Wise move," Arnor said.

"Then, I started cleaning. I started with my children, then their bedroom." He stroked the glass covering his daughter. "Before I knew it, the whole house was clean again. I left you the peaches from our larder. I've been trying to find my wife."

"I'm sorry, Thargus. Your village may be lost." Arnor touched the glass. "Your children may never recover from this."

The fist that landed in Arnor's jaw came from underneath, throwing his head back, causing him to careen into a wall.

"This is my payment," yelled Thargus, "for failing!"

Anger burned deep within the under dwarf. Arnor was a cog in the wheel of this misery. *Can he also be the way out?* Thargus reasoned to himself. *Arnor cannot be killed. Could he be lost? What reason could there be to travel with him? I could do this myself. I can find Loren. I can kill Loren and then maybe this horror would end, but maybe not.*

Arnor spoke from the floor, rubbing his jaw. "You can stay here and live with them like this, maybe even become a glass statue yourself, or you can come with me and take vengeance on the one who did this."

"Is it possible?" Thargus left the room.

"We could kill Mavius," said Arnor. "You want to. You can track Mavius's movement," Arnor said following Thargus. "He continues to return here. When he does, he is weak. He enters the portal to replenish his power."

"Then we stay. We wait for him and kill him before he can enter the portal," Thargus suggested.

"One problem," said Arnor, holding up a finger. "He may not be alone. If the knights are with him when he returns, we are done, you anyway. They tried to kill me once, didn't succeed." A silence fell on Thargus and Arnor spoke again. "If we have Loren, we hold all the cards. He can stop the knights. We can stop Mavius. If he is still alive, he is the answer."

"I don't want to admit that you are right," said Thargus, "but you are. I don't like you anymore than you like me, but I trust you. Lead and I will follow, for now. But, be warned," Thargus continued, "the only reason Jaron couldn't command the knights and why I felt no pull to kill that boy, might be because I'm supposed to kill Loren."

*　*　*　*　*

In silence, Thargus and Arnor walked, each involved in his own thoughts. The road to Glenndon traveled the eastern coast, not on the shore, but not far from it. The smell of salt in the air, of the marshes, of sweet decay, rolled memories through Arnor's mind. Westmost, he was there not so long ago.

Arnor had talked Lorenistal into leaving Jaron there. Jaron had been just a child then. *He still is a child, almost my child,* thought Arnor. *Where is he? Is he still alive?* Ellian and Keras were strong protectors, but even they had limitations.

Thargus did not change to travel clothes, instead continuing to wear the long robes to which he was accustomed. His staff clunked against the stones of the road as he walked. His eyes were set on his goal ahead, always around the next bend in the road. The laughter of his children played on in his head, burning fuel for his determination. Visions of Mavius danced, teasing him. Were they happening now or were they memories of the man himself?

The seagulls overhead called to each other, curious of the travelers. Their chatter mixed soothingly with the sound of the waves along the rocky shore. The broken seashells and dust that made up the composition of the road shone white against the grasses and wildflowers lining it.

So much beauty here in the south, thought Arnor, *and so much violence. Snow and cold, maybe they limit a man's ambition to conquer up north.*

Here, in the heat of the south, there is such angst. Still, a person can be wrong. Arnor looked ahead of him to Thargus, leading the way. *Have I been wrong about Thargus?* He had questioned himself before on this, but had never allowed his prejudice to waver. *What else have I judged poorly? I can believe Thargus. There is no question that something happened in Stenwood Den, something evil. Mavius could do that without qualm, without conscience. How is Mavius traveling? Where is his center of operations? What does he gain by returning to the door at Stenwood? When will he make his final move?*

"Are you sure that we'll find Loren in Glenndon?"

"No, I'm not," said Thargus. "I know that one or the other is there, Mavius or Loren."

"How much food is left?"

"Are you hungry? We are four days from Stenwood. We should be in Glenndon today and have eaten half of the rations we brought. We should save something for the way back."

They sat under the shade of the shrubs and ate the dried provisions Thargus had packed from the larder at his home. The ocean ebb and flow carried its music to them, but the gulls had gone. Thargus noticed this first, and though he was glad to be free from their racket, he realized that when food was present, it was only natural for gulls nearby to make their presence known. He made Arnor aware of his observation and the two retreated deeper into the shrubs.

For a few moments, there was nothing to suggest why the seagulls had retreated. Arnor and Thargus did not move. A sound, faint and far away, reached their ears, a shuffling like someone dragging his boots as he walked, lazy and purposeless. Then, it became louder and more prominent over the sound of the waves, as if many beasts were dragging themselves along the road.

Through the branches and leaves of the bushes, they saw mighty lizards, long and low to the ground, walking in single file. Slime hung from their reptilian lips. Short powerful legs propelled them forward, splayed out such that their stride swung both head and tail side to side. Riding upon the backs of these fifteen-foot long beasts were men, lightly armored, but armed with spears and swords. Each also had on his arm a small shield, round with a half-moon cut out of one side. No footmen accompanied them. Arnor counted nine lizard riders. Why did the seagulls avoid these beasts? Perhaps they had long tongues, like frogs, and could catch birds out of the air. Two more patrols of lizard riders caused the dwarves to take cover. They were coming from Glenndon and wore the markings of Valcella.

In the distance, Glenndon was an empty husk of its former self. Spread across the beaches and hills surrounding the city roamed the stench of death and decay, with areas stronger, or not, based on the ocean winds. It caught in their throats, threatening to bring on spasms of retching, enveloping every sense in its aura. Arnor's temples ached, and the pain sat dully in the back of his head. His ears rung, pricked by the horror of his surroundings, to ring a note higher than any organ could play. He became dizzy and sat down.

On giant poles and crossed beams, hundreds of people hung crucified. Some, impaled on the poles, held the expressions of pain and surprise in their faces. Many of the crucified remains sent a smell of charred flesh on the breeze, having been set ablaze. Arnor had no doubt this had occurred before the unlucky victim's death.

No one was spared, not even the babies and infants. A large pit had to be rounded, and in it were the charred bodies of the smallest children, thrown into the fire, either alive or already dead.

Reaching up, Thargus brushed the feet of a child. The poor young boy hung lifeless and stained with dried blood. Thargus's face hardened. Arnor could not hold back his grief, though he had survived centuries and witnessed death on a scale never before suffered by any dwarf.

"Who would do this?" Arnor muttered in disbelief. Valcella was never capable of such cruelty before. Had General Shale grown even more hideous and heartless? Then he remembered the words of William in the tower. *"You had all of the time you needed in Glenndon to ponder your move. You have lost the game. There is no move left."* William and

Baros had done this. *Is this how they are building Valcella's army? Join us or die?*

Thargus pushed Arnor to get his attention. "What?" Arnor asked as he brushed him away. Thargus put his finger to his lips and pointed to the bottom of the hill ahead of them. Twenty lizard riders were climbing the hill.

Thargus and Arnor backtracked. There was no-where to go. The land before them was barren. Thargus pulled Arnor into one of the smoldering pits. They covered themselves with the ashes of the fallen. While they waited for the patrol to pass, Arnor was eye to eye with a little girl, her face untouched by the fire, her brown eyes gazing away unseeing, but her body charred and blistered.

They rose like ghostly avengers after the patrol passed, angered, and driven to seek revenge for the helpless that had, in their deaths, managed to offer them the gift of temporary invisibility. The soot became dark with the passage of Thargus's tears and he spread them across his cheeks. His robes of white became bands of gray. As he climbed out of the pit, his hands absorbed the charcoal so that he left fingerprints on the railing around the top. He would not hide from the next patrol.

He did not. The next patrol was not a lizard patrol, but two goblins and four men carrying a large chest on poles. Two each held the fore and aft ends of the supporting poles while a goblin walked in front and another in the rear.

Arnor and Thargus had no mercy; killing each the front and rear soldier at the onset of the assault. The porters dropped their charge and drew short curved swords. They had not expected an attack and could put up no adequate defense. They died within moments of one another.

From within the chest, Arnor pulled a book. "Fire magic," he said. "And this one is water magic." He flipped through it and tossed it to Thargus.

"First year studies," said Thargus, examining the spine. "Did these come from the school in Temerrac?"

"That would be my first guess," said Arnor, "but why would they want so many books for beginners? There are no advanced books in here."

"Maybe they've already moved those."

"Here's one I've never heard of." He examined the book's cover. It was plain and made of stiff brown leather. Burned into the cover were the words, "Current Studies." He turned it over to look at the spine but no other words were present.

They pushed the crate full of books into the ditch beside the road, and pulled the bodies of the goblins to the other side of the path, stacking them without ceremony.

"I'm taking this one," said Thargus, pulling out the leather bound book. "If I ever see Neeva and Verne again, they might want it."

"Why?"

"Look at it," Thargus lifted it up. "Does it look like those? This is a notebook. Those are textbooks. Trust me. I'm a teacher. If you're working on something new, this is how you would write it up. 'Current Studies' is a strange title though, water magic I would guess." He flipped through the pages slowly.

"Are you a mage?"

"No." Thargus opened his pack and placed the book inside. "Which way do we go now?"

* * * * *

No guards stood on the walls to the city proper. Where Arnor and Thargus were standing, the stones, as thick as three feet square, had toppled like building blocks in a nursery, leaving enormous gaps in the city's protection. Within the walls, entire city blocks lay as rubble. Larger buildings and towers stood, some severely damaged and leaning dangerously. The stench on the hills outside was nothing in comparison to the reek that hung within the walls of Glenndon. Arnor vomited, losing the nourishment he had so needed earlier in the day. He took a long pull off his water skin, washing out his mouth.

"This is the place?" he asked, still spitting.

Thargus put his hands on his chest and closed his eyes. A moment later, he answered. "Yes, and it's not Mavius here. He is somewhere else, training." He closed his eyes again. "He's training something big."

"So long as he's not here," Arnor said. "Loren is somewhere inside? Can you lead us to him?" Arnor readied himself for the smell to overwhelm him again but he was able to bear it. He pulled his shirt up over his face.

Through the streets and rubble they walked, seeing no signs of any corpse or means for the horrible smell. Something was there. The smell came and went, although it never went away completely. Shops and homes lay in ruin. Wares and rotten food lay in upturned carts. Blood that had pooled in the gutters had dried to flakes.

"Here," said Thargus, "I think this is it."

The tower stretched up into the sky at least ten stories. Fifty yards round at the base, it was an imposing sight, even with the holes smashed into the side, exposing the staircase in more than one area.

"Well, up it is," said Arnor.

As they climbed, they noticed the air becoming clearer. The staircase spiraled up, circling around the center rooms, and Arnor remembered the tower at Sandy River. What waited for them at the top of this one? Lord Baros and Sir William had once been close friends of his, now they were unhappy servants of the long dead king, enemies that had to be stopped.

He looked at the doors at every landing. There were several at each, and none had bars. He pulled open the door on the second landing, finding just a room, a bed, a desk, and a wardrobe. The next door had much of the same thing. The third door was also once a bedroom, but the exterior wall let in the wind from outside. The hole in the wall offered a view of the southern side of the city and the soldiers camped there. Almost five hundred men milled about. It looked as though they were trying to fix the walls. *What is there left to defend?*

Arnor looked again and called Thargus.

"Do you recognize the flag?" Thargus asked.

"No, I don't," said Arnor, "but the colors look like Valcella, red and white."

"Shale is behind this, this genocide." Thargus was disgusted, Humans killing Humans.

"No," Arnor corrected. That army is only arriving. William did this." He spat on the floor. "Sir William and Lord Baros."

They left the room and continued up. "We must be nearing the top," said Thargus. "My legs are like pudding."

The last landing brought them a surprise. A young human, wearing robes of grey, sat with his back to a door. Seeing them, he rose to his feet and pulled out a sword, preparing himself to attack, but when both Arnor and Thargus grimly pulled out their weapons, he changed his mind and drew a horn from his belt.

A blow from that horn would carry across the whole city from this height. As he raised the horn to his lips, an axe, small and slender, crashed into the horn, knocking it from his grip.

A look of panic came to the face of the sentry, and he bolted past Arnor and Thargus for the stairway. He was fast, much faster than either dwarf, even wearing long robes, and soon he was lost to sight.

"He's going for help. We'll never catch him," gasped Thargus.

Arnor pushed Thargus. "Go up, up, hurry!" They reached the landing at the top of the tower in a matter of moments. Arnor pulled two knives from his belt, stepped onto the parapets, and looking down tried to determine the location of the door out of the tower.

"We're ten floors up. If you try to hit him from up here you're just going to lose a decent knife," said Thargus.

"I know," said Arnor, and with a knife in each hand, he leaped from the edge out into the air.

Thargus, stunned, ran to the parapet to see Arnor falling away toward the running figure of the sentry, on whom he landed with a sickening thunk.

Arnor did not move for a moment, then he rose, wobbled on his boots, and fell over again.

Reaching the bottom of the stairs, Thargus found Arnor wiping blood from his eyes.

"I never would have thought of that," said Thargus.

"Remind me, would you," said Arnor, "not ever to do that again?"

Chapter 21   Hooksett Village

Hooksett sat in the crook between a lake and the river that fed it. One at a time, the brindi walked their horses across the short and narrow bridge. The road wound up and turned left to reveal a line of business fronts where customers and shopkeepers haggled prices. Further up the road, a blacksmith worked his bellows and the smell of smoke was sharp in the air. The brindi brought their horses to a small inn at the end of the lane. There was no name on the sign, only a carved mug made of wood hanging from the door.

Jaron and Ellian were not with the brindi. Brindi were, in all appearances, members of Valcella's forces. The ease with which they had been able to fool soldiers of General Shale's army held a blade with another edge.

"We'll have a better chance of finding Harris if we do not immediately appear as spies from the south," Ellian said to Behra. "If you insist at staying in the same inn as us, we shouldn't arrive at the same time." Jaron and Ellian watched as the brindi approached the inn, secured their horses, and entered the establishment.

An hour later, they followed the path of their small companions. The smell of cooking wafted from the door and was so inviting that they could not help themselves. They tied their horses and entered the inn.

"Ah, hello! Welcome to the Hooksett Mug." A man, tall and slender, cleanly shaven and smiling broadly, greeted them as they entered. "My name is Henry. Is it a meal or a room you'd be interested in?"

"Both," Jaron said. "Our horses are tied outside."

"And how many would be in your group?"

"Just the two of us," Ellian answered.

Henry did some arithmetic in his head. "Eighteen guests in one day. My, that's more than I've had in some time. Come in. Another group came in just about an hour ago, big group of brindi. Only passing through, I hope. Still, they paid well. Do you mind sharing a room?"

"With the brindi?" Ellian asked, feigning disgust.

"Oh, no!" the innkeeper said putting his hands to his chest, "just the two of you in a room."

"That will do fine," Jaron said.

"All right then. Sandy!" the innkeeper called out to the back. "Get old Joe and care for those two new horses. Put them in the stable with the others."

"You can place your belongings in your room, weapons too, please." Henry winked an eye at them. "You'll be brought a washbasin and soap so that you can wash if you wish. Dinner will be served at the bell in the common room."

Ellian and Jaron took a room together on the second floor. They soon learned that Behra, Joalle, Mennas, and Uhra took the room closest to the main door near the common room. Kenast, Engle, Lurhe, and Sindas all claimed one of the other upstairs rooms, these being larger with more beds. Hahre, Dillog, Dinna, Joahe, and Gehne took another of the upstairs rooms. Danos, Dinna, Kenda, and Rissa slept in the last room adjacent to the common room.

Anticipating how their presence in the common room would be received, the brindi decided to take their meals in the largest of their rooms.

Jaron pitied Keras for missing the meal. The long strips of beef came apart easily. The spiced potatoes, fried to a crisp, and eggs slow cooked and mixed with cheese tasted delicious. The best of all was the bread. Jaron could not remember the last time he had tasted bread. It was hot with a hard crust, and the butter melted inside when spread. They did not hurry and took several fillings of each plate.

The common room was 'full to the brim,' as the local saying went. The Hooksett Mug was a popular destination for the many inhabitants of Hooksett as its ale was unparalleled in excellence this side of the lake. Several men from the village had come in for a drink. "Like a meal all to itself," some said, regarding the ale.

The locals collected themselves around tables, and they

smoked, and drank, and told stories of strange things. The fireplace cracked and spat as it chewed through pine logs.

"I tell you," an old fisherman was saying, "not a man left in the village. And the houses all burned to the ground. I'd never seen anything like it."

"We saw the smoke from here. Where was the fire?" a young farmer asked.

"T'other side of the lake, on the southern edge, Wayford," the fisherman answered. "I was pulling in my nets, mind you, and caught the scent of smoke on the air. Looking up I saw a great rolling black, high as the eye could see."

Nods of agreement came from others at the table.

"Aye, I saw that as well," said a red-haired youth. "I was fishing with my dad and we could see, smoke rising way in the distance. We thought it was too much smoke to be normal."

"Well, I pulled into the cove, you know," said the old fisherman, "and tied off the boat to a dock some ways north of Wayford. Walking into the town, I saw nobody nowhere; like they had all ran off. The fires that took the buildings must have most died off for there was just ash and smoke left with some embers. I went to the main square and just stood there, my eyes burning from the smoke in the air, and don't you know what I found?" He waited to see if he had their proper attention before continuing. "Tracks, large and deep, this wide!" He held his arms out to show a three-foot space between his palms.

"Pond scum," a dark youth retorted. "You're making up stories again, old netter."

"No, I swear!" the old fisherman said.

"What did these tracks look like?" asked the youth.

The old man cleared a spot on the table in front of him and, after dipping his thumb in his mug, traced out a shape.

The dark youth laughed. "That looks like a giant chicken foot." This caused a roaring of laughter from the others at the table. "You're full of lily pads, old man. You probably never set foot on the shore."

"But where are the people?" the old man implored.

"Any news on the road?" a well-dressed young man asked.

"Well, most of that southern army is camped in and around Holderness. I don't know how many there are, two or three thousand I suppose. Wagon trains keep bringing supplies north to them, but they don't appear to be traveling any farther. They wiped out the food stores of several towns along the road, and burned some whole, leaving their garbage behind and the stench of their passing." The farmer drained his mug and swallowed hard. "It is only a matter of time until they drain their supply and begin looking further than the towns on the road for more food."

"Any word from the militias? Denshire, Benson?" the well-dressed young man asked.

"Some have offered resistance, but there are so many and the militia is scattered, ten here, thirty there. I heard tell that there might be some organizing by Belanton and some down near Denshire."

Jaron drained his mug, remembering the ale from The Broken Horse in Westmost. Ellian had asked one of the men at the table about the Tuno family, but the man only looked him up and down and brushed him off to continue his conversation with a cute red-haired girl in the chair next to him.

As the crowd in the common room dwindled, Jaron and Ellian retired to their room. *A bed!* Jaron thought. *When was the last time I slept in a proper bed?* There was even a feather pillow. They would find Harris here. He was positive of it, and with that reassurance to himself, he closed his eyes and slept until the sun rose again.

Jaron woke to someone shaking him. The early rays of the sun revealed Behra sitting impatiently on the edge of his bed.

"We are going," she said.

"Already? But we haven't even looked for him yet," Jaron argued.

"You're not going. We are. On the road and dealing with the forces of Shale, we have an advantage, but not here. Some of us are going to meet with Keras where she is waiting for you."

"From the sound of it," Jaron added, "you're going to have to approach Denshire with a white flag."

"Popular, we aren't." She frowned. "Harris may refuse to go if he sees us. We are going to be on the outskirts of Hooksett. We'll be watching the roads. When you leave town with Harris, we will join you. If you leave town without Harris, we are going to follow through with Darrod's plan. If that happens, you would be wise to avoid us. They all call us the 'sour children.' Imagine what they'll call us if we have to fight our way out of Hooksett."

The brindi left as quietly as they had come. Few in town made any notice while they were staying at the inn, but as soon as the 'sour children' left, tongues started wagging.

"Little sneaks. Bet that was a scouting party for provisioning that army up in Holderness."

"There was only sixteen of them. Why didn't we just lock 'em up?"

"More'n come looking for them, I'd wager."

The talk was more like that, until Jaron wanted to burst out that nobody knew what they were talking about. *It's a good thing the brindi aren't hearing this,* Jaron thought. Sindas had a stable enough disposition but Hahre might be hot headed, especially after the loss of Chelle and Jihe.

Henry did not recognize Harris's name when Jaron asked about him, or perhaps he did, and was holding out for proffered money to loosen his tongue. The cost of the inn was reasonable enough, and Ellian thought they could spare it with the money left behind by the brindi, but he did not offer any additional incentive. They would handle this on their own.

Jaron and Ellian spoke to group after group of townsfolk as they came to the inn, and the conversation always turned to Harris Tuno. The citizens of Hooksett were increasingly less friendly, pushing the topic away. So far, no one knew or wanted to say they knew Harris.

Each night, the men from the village returned and the talk of events outside Hooksett were the conversation of choice. More men had visited Wayford and confirmed the old fisherman's sightings. Something big was walking the other side of the lake. The town was burned and everyone was gone, not found dead, but gone.

"All gone, I tell you. I went clear from the shore to the farthest farm. Not a soul was found," a young fisherman named Gil explained to the others at his table. "It was just as Mister Hanford said it was."

"The question is; did they leave before trouble, or after?" asked the woman next to him. She wore pants instead of a dress and had the sun weathered look about her. "Wilson up on the Casset Ridge says he was visited by a young man from Welston over on the other side of the lake, just yesterday. Said people on that side of the lake were visited by some militiamen last week, or the week before, and began to move people out. Said something awful was coming."

"Well, where is this man?"

"Wilson says he just took some water and food and went south."

"Militia from Northwood headed south yesterday. Apparently there's a massing for a resistance army in one of those towns," said a man from the end of the table. "I'm planning to join them myself. My village is closer to the road between Holderness and the mountains. Empty. Valcella took everything, even pressed some people into service."

"Fire! Fire in the north!" came a call from outside.

People poured out from the inn and surrounding shops. They looked north and pointed at the smoke rising. A small group of the younger and stronger villagers found buckets, and filling them with water from the small stream, moved off toward the rising smoke in the distance.

Jaron and Ellian joined them, walking in the back of the group, a bucket filled to splashing in each hand. It was obvious as they neared the source of the smoke that the small buckets of water could not weaken the blaze that was engulfing the farmhouse. Orange flames curled around in a vortex spewing black smoke at the top. They put the buckets down and called for survivors.

"Hello!" the villagers yelled over the roar of the flames. "Hello!"

From behind the burning building, a woman was running toward them. Her clothes were soot covered and riddled with red. Her mouth open in panic, her eyes wide in terror, she ran with every ounce of strength within her.

Blood, thought Jaron. *That's blood.*

From behind the house and flames, a great green serpentine neck lifted up a long and horn crowned head. Mighty wings spread, reaching out to point to the east and west ends of the sky before pushing down to lift the heavy body from the ground. Through the flames and smoke flew the dragon, terrible and fierce, its scales shimmering green. Over the house it came, claws extended to scoop up the woman, and then it was over them, rising and circling back the way it had come.

Fear overtook the brave firefighters, and they dropped their buckets to flee back to the center of the village. Jaron and Ellian, afraid as any other, did not move but watched in disbelief. A dragon, they had encountered a dragon. Finding their senses, they dropped their buckets and followed the example of the villagers.

Back at the inn with Henry was Gillis Weldon, the mayor. The men of the fire brigade were yelling in a frenzy to try to get the point across as to what they had just seen. Gillis listened intently and tried to calm them down. People had heard the news, and many were rushing home to collect loved ones, belongings, and prized possessions. They would have to leave. There was no fighting a dragon. Teeth like knives and claws like swords, dragons were not to be meddled with.

Where did it come from? There hadn't been dragons known around these parts for hundreds of years. The stuff of legend they had become.

Echoing through the trees and across the lake, over the commotion in the village, a great horn call sounded. People stopped running to their homes and gathered in the village street. They had all heard the call. Someone had blown a great battle horn.

In the distance, soldiers rode, four abreast. A standard-bearer for the army of Valcella accompanied the men in white and red armor. The barding worn by the warhorses matched the colors of the men. The great beasts snorted in the warm air, fighting the bit, eager for confrontation. Astride them, the knights rode across the bridge one at a time, waiting on the near shore for their companions, and coming as one up the hill toward the crowd. They raised their visors and waited there for someone to speak.

"Greetings, and welcome to Hooksett village," the mayor said as he stepped forward.

"We are the emissary of General Shale of Valcella," said the knight on the far right. His eyes were hard and his beard was long and blond, but he was obviously the youngest member of his party.

"Greetings."

"Yes, you've said that." The knight smirked and glanced at his companions. He removed his helmet, shaking out his blond hair so that it draped across his shoulders.

"My name is Gillis Weldon. How may we be of service? I must apologize for the haste of our formalities, but as you are probably aware from the smell, we have had a fire. An entire family has perished."

"We know."

"About the fire?" asked Gillis Weldon.

"About the deaths, it is our doing." Handing his helmet to the knight next to him, the blond dismounted. "We have terms for you. Do you wish to hear them?"

"Terms?"

"Half of your catch from the lake will be delivered to Holderness for the health of the army and the glory of Valcella." Smiling, the blond held out a rolled parchment tied with a red ribbon.

"And you started this fire, did you? The Welss were a great family of high renown in this village. It was you who caused their deaths?" Gillis did not take the paper.

"Yes."

"We heard that a dragon caused it."

"That is correct." The blonde knight held out the scroll. He was not smiling any longer. "Are you going to take this, or is this discussion about to get messy?"

Gillis took the paper and the blond resumed his smile.

"See? That was not so difficult, was it?" He turned toward his horse but stopped short and drew his sword in a flash, pointing the tip toward Gillis. "I asked you a question."

"Leave him be, Nick," said another of the knights.

The blond lowered his blade and returned it to its scabbard, smiling all the while. He turned his back and remounted his horse. He shouted to the crowd. "Have you been to Wayford lately? I wonder if your response will be the same as theirs," he laughed. "We will return in four days. Have carts and drivers ready."

They did not cross the bridge again but rode north toward the burning house.

"Follow your noses, boys," the blond laughed.

Chapter 22   Bones of the King

"One guard, they only placed one guard here," said Thargus. "I don't like it."

"Well, it works for me," Arnor responded opening the door again.

"Listen, there are hundreds of men at the south side of the city, and I don't know how many goblins are lurking around." He spread his hands, pleading with Arnor. "One guard, it doesn't make sense. Why aren't there more soldiers in this section of the city?"

Back up the stairs they walked, Arnor constantly rubbing the blood out of his eyes and wiping it on his shirt. They sat and rested about halfway up, forcing their way into one of the rooms that had windows overlooking the south side of the city. Arnor set the broken doorknob on the windowsill as he looked out.

"It looks like they've looted the city. Look at the wagons," Arnor said. Stretching out from the southern edges, a wagon train traveled away from Glenndon. Men loaded more carts far in the distance. They could not see the goods being loaded, but they could imagine them, coffee, cheese, and bread. Arnor would fight ten gladiators for a single cup of coffee. A slice of cheese, any cheese, would seem like heaven.

"I say we bar the door in case of any intruders and take a nap," suggested Thargus. He reached into his bag, pulled out a jar of preserved fruit, and held it up to the light. "Apricots?" he asked.

"Yes," said Arnor, "but no nap. There was one man in here. I don't know if he was on duty or goofing off, but I don't want to take the chance that someone is coming to relieve him soon."

They passed the bottle of apricots back and forth, sharing them until only the juice remained, which Thargus drained with a gulp. Leaving the room, they climbed in silence, flight after flight. Six flights from the room, Thargus sat on the landing, breathing heavily. "How many floors are there to this tower? We've been to the top already. It didn't feel like this many before."

On they climbed, each stair seeming taller than the last, their legs burning in protest. Arnor reached out, using the walls to prop himself up. His breathing became ragged. Had he hurt himself in that fall? This was not the time to break precedent. On all fours, he climbed the stairs. Thargus suffered next to him.

On the next landing, catching their breath, they entered one of the rooms, its door mangled and broken, but to their relief the door opened easily. Thargus threw himself on the bed and sank into a deep sleep. Arnor sat in the chair before a desk. The chair creaked across the floor as he drew himself up to the desktop. There was a scrap of paper, a quill pen, and an almost empty bottle of ink. Weary with fatigue he held up the paper and read the writing on it.

Too often, the time is slowing.
Too many the climb has dropped.
Two more of them pass not knowing,
Once written what time has stopped.

The warmth of the sun poured through the window. He turned away from the light, letting it warm his back and looked at his shadow on the floor. The sun created a long rectangle throughout the room, interrupted by his shadow and a small round object.

What's that? He turned his head to see what the object of the shadow was, and saw that it was only a doorknob on the windowsill.

He looked at it again. *Yes, that's a doorknob.* Wearily, he walked to the window and picked it up, inspecting it. This is where he had placed it on the windowsill seven floors below.

He had placed it there, seven floors below, when they were halfway up the tower, halfway up the ten-story tower. He turned to point out this oddity to Thargus, head spinning with weariness. Thargus was fast asleep.

Arnor fought the sleepy feeling beginning to grab him. *Don't lean on anything. Don't sit down. Don't lie down,* he warned himself. Arnor shook Thargus awake, and he was not happy about it, trying to push

Arnor away, but Arnor persisted.

"What in the land of darkness is your problem?" Thargus shouted.

"Wake up! You can't sleep here. There's something odd happening." He held out the doorknob to Thargus.

"So, what? You broke that a long time ago."

"Yeah, I know, but I didn't bring it with me." Arnor answered.

"What do you mean?" asked Thargus, yawning.

"I left it on the windowsill downstairs, and when we got here, here it was."

Thargus was awake now, pondering the information. "Did you find any writing here?" Arnor produced the paper and Thargus read it quietly. "We're lucky you didn't fall asleep. We have to get out of this room." He climbed out of the comfortable bed as Arnor made his way to the door.

"No, not that way."

"Well, how the blazes are we supposed to get out, the window?"

"Yes," said Thargus. "Open your pack and give me the rope I stowed there."

Thargus took the rope and made his way to the window, where he dropped it on the floor, picked up a chair, and shattered the glass panes and wooden frame of the window. He handed the end of the rope to Arnor. "Tie this to the bedpost and drag the bed over here."

"Are we going down a floor?"

"No, we're going up."

Thargus stood up on the chair and lowered the rope out the window, leaning out and looking down. Arnor leaned into Thargus, trying to see what he was doing. While Arnor was looking down, a rope fell down from above, hitting him in the head.

When Thargus saw the rope from above, he reached up and pulled it in, letting go of the rope he was lowering. The cave dwarf then hauled in the rope that had appeared from above the window. As he did this, the rope, still tied to the bedpost, slid out of the same window, as if a great weight pulled down on it.

Thargus pulled all of the rope, the rope from above, in through the frame. Arnor pushed him off the chair and looked down out of the window. The rope, tied to the bed, went down to another window and disappeared within. Turning his head, he looked up to see the rope that was lying in a heap on the floor, going up to disappear into the window above.

"Thargus?" he asked.

"Yes, I know." Thargus grabbed the parchment, inkbottle, and pen, throwing them out the window. He shouldered his pack, and gestured to Arnor. "Climb."

Arnor made the climb easily, though he wished he could have done it without his pack. Wouldn't it have just been here waiting for him when he reached the next level? Thargus didn't want to take the chance. Maybe Thargus was right. When he reached the window, he had not found Thargus there waiting to help him inside. Nevertheless, the rope was there, tied to the bedpost, just as he had tied it below. His head was cloudy with the inconceivability of the situation.

"We're not the only ones here, are we?" Arnor asked as he pulled Thargus in through the broken window frame.

"No. I never thought we were the only ones here. Something was nagging me." Thargus pulled the rope into the room, and coiling it, stowed it back in Arnor's pack. "There are mages here, maybe something else, too."

* * * * *

The darkness of the doorway seemed to fall outward, making the hallway almost as dark as the room on the other side, like there was something in the room that pulled the light inward, leaving only the inky blackness in its place. Thargus felt his way forward through the door, waiting for his eyes to adjust, knowing that they may not. He felt behind him for the doorframe. Arnor was there.

Opening the door to get into the room had required some skill. Arnor had been able to pick the lock with a slender nail pulled out of the floor, but he grumbled and complained the whole time about how, had he been a common thief, his life would have been much simpler.

They worked their way into the room, and to their dismay, the door shut behind them. The air was icy, colder than the hall had been. Laughter spun from every corner. Arnor could feel the frigid touch as it circled around him, brushing up against him, a shade. Thargus gave a yelp as another shade touched him. How many were there?

Thargus wrestled with darkness, blind to the room around him. Then, he realized he could feel the frosty villains. Gripping with his left, he balled up his right hand into a fist and swung with everything he had.

At the impact, a bright glow of red filled the room like lightning, showing a glimpse of what they had to deal with, five shades of varying sizes. Thargus's hands stretched out in front of him, and feeling a moment of substance, he grabbed onto it, driving his weight on top of it, pushing it into the floor.

Another flash of red light filled the room and Thargus realized that the color was coming from him, from his web. Thargus pulled off his robe and shirt underneath, letting the glow fill the room. Arnor used the light to survey the space and pick his targets. A slide of steel against steel echoed from the walls. "They feel our fists. Let's see if they feel our blades."

Arnor threw a light axe in the direction of one of the shades as it moved to attack Thargus again, and the blade went clean through, just missing Thargus to clatter off the wall behind. The shade fell back in a scream of pain. It whirled on Arnor, rushing him, hoping to knock him off balance and keep him from hurling anything else. It was not a wise move for the shade. Arnor used the small axe in his other hand to strike it in the upper torso. This time the blade did not travel through, but held fast with a satisfying thunk.

The wail of the darkness traveled far outside the room. Inside, Thargus and Arnor fell to the floor in pain, grasping their ears, trying to deaden the sound that assailed them. It seemed to last an eternity though only a handful of seconds had passed. The silence after the scream deafened them, allowing them to hear the ringing tones echoing in their ears.

The glow from Thargus's web faded, leaving them again without light. They didn't find the door quickly, but Arnor eventually managed to reopen it, lighting the room and giving them the opportunity to inspect their surroundings.

Loren's unconscious form lay sprawled on the floor. They rushed to him. Had the shades touched him? Was he breathing? Was he dead? His breathing was so faint that it was almost imperceptible. Only by holding his hand a hair's breadth away from Loren's nose could Arnor detect any change. He put a finger to Loren's neck, searching for a pulse. The man was thin and gaunt, but he was alive.

"Well, can we move him?" Thargus asked.

"I don't know. I think we have to. How far do you think you can carry him?"

"Away from here," Thargus answered. "He's naught but skin and bones."

At that moment, Arnor fell backwards, tumbling until he struck the wall with a cracking sound.

Two figures stepped in from the hall, men of short, thin stature. Their clothing suggested scholars or mages, comfortable robes of elegant grey silk, like those of the boy Arnor and Thargus had encountered on the landing, but embroidered with patterns and swirls in white thread.

Thargus closed the space between him and the two robed men. A mighty wind rose out of the corners of the room and pushed him backwards with enough force that he fell back onto his rump.

"We are not as weaponless as we appear," said the mage. "Your physical attacks will gain you nothing." He raised his hands.

Arnor had regained his feet and a wind began to spin about

him. The swirling air currents lifted Arnor off the floor and spun him as a ball tossed into the air. He gasped in surprise but no air entered his lungs. Desperately, Arnor tried to inhale but there was nothing to consume. The mages had created a vacuum around him and Arnor spun in place as he suffocated. Finally, when it was clear that life had left Arnor's body, one of the mages lowered his hands, allowing the dwarf to crumple to the floor.

Thargus watched as the mages turned their attention to him. The wind grew. A spiral of air lifted Thargus's feet off the ground and he could no longer discern up from down. He could not breathe. *Is this it?* he asked himself.

Thargus fell to the ground landing on his shoulder, where, thanks to his combat training, he was able to roll to his feet. Taking stock of his surroundings, he saw one mage opening and closing his mouth, like a fish trying to breathe the air.

Behind the mage, Arnor, back on his feet again, had forced a knife into the lung of the mage holding Thargus in his spell. The other mage spun his hands in the air, reciting the calculations to try to suffocate the dwarf again.

Thargus did not wait. He leaped onto the second mage's back, and wrapping his arms around the unfortunate man's neck, broke it cleanly.

"What was that?" Thargus asked Arnor.

"Air magic. Don't know how they figured it out. It wasn't pleasant. I felt like a fish, and then I blacked out."

"Let's get him out of here before any more show up." Thargus hoisted Loren up onto his shoulders. *Now, all I have to do,* he thought, *is remember not to throw him off the ledge.* The urge was heavy. The web burned. This was indeed the man he had been sent to kill. Somehow, he knew he must not.

Out in the hall, the wind whipped up the stairs blasting Thargus and Arnor with sand carried in the air. They closed their eyes, warding off the storm with their hands. "This is not a natural wind," Thargus said. "There must be more of these mages. Hurry!"

They made their way down the stairs as quickly as they could with Thargus carrying Loren.

Outside the wall of the city again, they looked up at the tower. A great tempest brewed around the peak. If this did not bring the attention of that army on the south side of the city, what would?

Arnor hurried them to the road north, carrying both his and Thargus's pack, while Thargus bore the still unconscious Loren. Once past the remains of the former residents of the city and the stench of decay, they stopped to assess Loren's health. He was breathing on his own, deeper than he had been in the tower. His arms looked alarmingly thin, like there was only skin covering the bones. He had no signs of bruising or injury, but he was so thin.

Arnor scattered the packs looking for food and water. The contents of Thargus's pack fell in a heap next to Loren.

The under dwarf climbed up on a large boulder and was looking back at the city. "Do they even know we were there? No one seems to be following. Valcella doesn't often let anyone escape. General Shale isn't known for mercy."

"Nice hat, Arnie." Loren had spoken.

"Loren!" Arnor could not contain his excitement at hearing the voice of his friend, even if he did use the hated nickname.

"Easy," said Loren, pushing Arnor away gently. "Easy, I'm still weak, too weak. We need to escape by the fastest way possible. A boat, get us a boat."

"Thargus," shouted Arnor, "get a fishing boat, something with a sail."

"I don't know how to pilot a sail boat," Thargus protested, picking up his empty pack and refilling it.

Loren's hand fell to his side, where Arnor had emptied the packs, and landed on the book Thargus had rescued from the cart earlier.

"What is this?" asked Loren, lifting it to his face. "*Current Studies*," he said. His eyes went wide and he smiled, laughing. "Make sure we take this with us. I'd like to read it."

"Sure, ok," said Arnor. "A boat, "I'll get one and return just after dark. We don't want to alert anyone to our presence with a bright sail." He hurried off, his elation at the ability to communicate with his old friend giving his weary legs speed.

Thargus watched Arnor run away back towards the city, and then he looked down at Loren, thin, gaunt, and weak Loren. One hand went to the knife at his waist as he reached up with his other hand to scratch away the burning at his chest.

Chapter 23   New Allies and Enemies

The Hooksett Mug was awash with townsfolk that evening. They had come from the surrounding towns to hear the news of both the dragon and the soldiers from Valcella.

"Them foul Brindi are behind this, I'll wager," an old farmer from the east hill was saying. "Little sneaks were here only a day before clipping off quietly like."

"Looking at our larders, perhaps," said his son as he drained his beer.

"Now, there were others that came in around the same time as those sour children," Henry piped in. "Two boys in their mid to late teen years. They, of course, are still here and I don't expect any ill of them. But, I've got to wonder if they seen anything on the road before they arrived."

"Nasty runts," said the farmer and seeing a start from the innkeeper amended his statement, "Brindi."

Talk of this type rolled on all evening and Ellian and Jaron retired early to bed. In the morning, Harris Tuno, upon hearing that a dragon had attacked the village, had come to speak with Gillis Weldon at the town hall. Looking out the front window of the inn, Jaron noticed him right away. He approached hesitantly, unsure whether he should interrupt a conversation between a town leader and a mason. His concerns were unnecessary. Seeing Jaron, Harris remembered him, saying, "Hello, boy. You were a friend of Arnor?"

"Yes, I am."

"Any news of Temerrac?"

"I'm sorry, no." Jaron pulled Harris away from Gillis Weldon. "Can you spare a few minutes to talk?"

They collected Ellian and sat in the Hooksett Mug discussing all that had occurred in the time during their separation. Harris's guilt over the damage to Temerrac was lessened with the news of the toll his powder had taken on Shale's army.

"How many men is Shale rumored to have?" Harris asked.

"Three thousand," Ellian coughed, "following an unfortunate accident that claimed the lives of about a thousand men."

"Shale lost a thousand men in the explosion?" Ellian nodded. "So, Shale has three thousand," Harris said. "Gurrand should be able to repel them."

Ellian broke the bad news. "Shale has another army, maybe two."

"What? There are more?"

"We saw a camp, south of Temerrac. It was filling when we arrived. I thought it was, at first, just a supply camp. There might be three thousand more men there and...." Ellian faded off, unsure if he should continue.

Harris looked at him in confusion waiting for him to say more. Ellian did not.

"One of the armies," Jaron said, "is dead."

"So what's the problem with that? Good luck for us."

"Dead, but they're still walking around."

Harris stared at them. His expression said it all.

"I swear it is true," Jaron said and continued filling in Harris on the events that had occurred at Sandy River. Harris was dubious about Sir William, Lord Baros and their army. Dragons were one level of believability, undead another.

"Neeva is digging out under the camp," Ellian said. "She's going to trap the whole army, undead and all. She needs your help."

"My help?" Harris laughed. "You're talking about the most powerful stone mage alive. Why would she need my help?"

"She found," Jaron said, "a pillar of iron under the tower at Sandy River. She can't cut it. She can't crack it."

"And what will I do about it?"

"It's not what you will do; it's what your powder can do."

"That powder is dangerous. It took down half of Temerrac," Harris argued.

"Yes," said Jaron, "and that was only an accident. Imagine what you could do if you planned it. With this invention you could stop an entire army of reinforcements."

Harris smiled weakly. "I hadn't thought of it that way."

"So you will come and help Neeva destroy the camp?" Ellian asked.

"Yes," Harris hit his hand on the table. "It's better than hiding out here. Where is Neeva?" Harris asked.

She's under the Sandy River camp with the Brindi." Jaron had slipped. He had not intended to mention the Brindi yet. The hostility toward them in the town was too severe and it showed in Harris's response.

"Brindi!" He almost shouted.

"Shh," Ellian hushed him and lowered his voice. "They've allied against Shale, not officially, but in deeds. That group that was here was with us. The underground system is theirs."

"Will you come with us?" Jaron asked.

"I will. Though I do not," Ellian held out his hands palms down as a silent suggestion for Harris to keep his voice down. Harris complied and continued, "relish the thought of working with Brindi. They are a terrible enemy to oppose, cruel and inventive in their tortures. Nevertheless, I see the need to cut Shale's advantage over King Gurrand's army. Gurrand has, I hear, over two thousand men marching south from Brethiliost to face Valcella. The elves of Taurminya have pledged to aid him, for the time being, in exchange for permanent borders and the cessation of settlements into their territory."

"Shale has a dragon," Jaron said.

"The scales fall ever hither and thither. Where there is one dragon, there are bound to be more. What color was it?"

"Green."

"Well for us. I feared it would be a blue dragon, or black. Green dragons are dumb and hard to control. Valcella may lose as many men to that dragon as King Gurrand."

* * * * *

Men walked the road to Denshire. Those young enough and

strong enough, or those ornery enough to fight, left Hooksett before even Jaron and Ellian. Word had come through the Hooksett Mug that an army was forming in Denshire, and militias from all around were traveling there.

A driving force behind the young men of Hooksett was the arrival of a dragon under the control of Valcella's army. The Welss family, killed by the dragon, had many relatives.

As they left Hooksett, Behra and the brindi under her command joined them on the road. They had removed all colors of Valcella. Harris looked uncomfortable around them, even though he tried to hide it, and some of the young men of Hooksett made snide remarks and even threats.

Five days it took to travel to Denshire, and as they neared, Jaron was surprised to see hundreds of men walking about as if on errands, practicing swordplay or running spear drills. A patrol of men wearing grey tabards stopped them on the street.

"And where do you think you are going?" one of them asked. He had a shaved head and a heavy scar across his neck. "We don't allow Brindi here."

Kenast, Engle, Lurhe, and Sindas slid off their horses with weapons drawn. "You don't like Brindi here in Denshire?" Engle asked.

The men in the patrol drew their weapons, squaring off.

"We're looking for your lord," Ellian jumped into the conversation hoping to avoid a fight.

"Well, you can go ahead, but the brindi can't go," said the scarred man.

"We're traveling together," said Ellian. "I'll take responsibility."

"If I let you through, then it becomes my responsibility."

Ellian considered this. "Behra, will you agree to wait here?"

"For how long?"

"I don't know, half a day?" Ellian guessed.

"So be it. Harris Tuno stays with us." Harris did not look

comfortable with that arrangement, but he conceded.

Jaron and Ellian rode on toward Denshire, watching the training of men taking place in the fields around them. Knights, in full armor, swung swords with their squires. Archers stood in rows aiming at grass targets. Rows and rows of men filled one wide and grassy field. Every man held two wooden flails, one in each hand, and in unison, they spun in a pattern that would have injured anyone close enough to be a threat.

Jaron had seen that move before. Keras had done it in Temerrac with dual blades. *I wonder how well that will work against armor,* he asked himself.

The walls of Denshire were black with age and forty feet tall. This area had not always been peaceful, and some town lords had a history of attacking rival towns, especially wealthy ones. Scarred and weathered from long past battles, the gates were open. The road crossed a drawbridge that spanned a moat. After entering the gate, a young man with a book greeted them. The young man looked perturbed, and closing his book said, "You were the men that came with Brindi?"

"Yes," said Jaron.

The young man made a motion to four soldiers who had come up behind them. The soldiers drew their weapons.

Ellian reached for his waist but someone grabbed his sword hand and dragged him from the saddle. He landed sprawling on the ground. Jaron found a spear tip inches from his chest.

"State your names," the young man with the book said to Jaron.

"I'm Jaron Keltenon and that poor fellow on the ground is Ellian Wallace."

"Purpose in Denshire?" the young man asked.

"We are looking for a friend of ours. She might have arrived two or three weeks ago," Ellian said. "My friend is named Keras Alestan."

"You're a friend of Keras?" It was clear that the name was

familiar to him. Looking abashed, he called off the guards.

Their escort brought them into a tall imposing building in the middle of town. Within the walls of the city, paved roads and stone buildings showed a level of wealth Jaron had not seen since Red Helm. The buildings were tall, but always shorter than the city wall, with the exception of the keep located in the center.

Seated at a table in the keep were twenty men. They faced away from the door, using the light from the stained glass window to illuminate their work.

Pointing out something on the table and arguing with the man next to him was a man of about six feet tall. His brown beard was short, like his hair. At the far end of the table, listening intently, was Keras.

One of the guards escorting Ellian and Jaron approached her and whispered so as not to disturb the meeting. She smiled, looking in their direction, and after some words from Keras, the men from the gate left the room as quickly as they could, apologizing profusely, but quietly.

"So, did you find him?" Keras asked after leaving the table to join them at the door. She ushered them out into the hall as she spoke.

"Harris is outside the city with Behra," said Ellian. He looked at her and hugged her tight.

Jaron stood awkwardly for a moment, looking away before he finally asked, "What's going on in there?"

"Oh, it's a war council. The knights of all cities north of the Fortunal Mountain range and their lords have traveled here. The inns and castle are full. Did you see the men training on your way in?" She held Ellian's hand as she spoke. "They're going to make a stand against Shale." She let go of Ellian's hand and hugged Jaron. "I missed you. I had no one to pick on."

"Why are you sitting in on a war council?" Ellian asked.

"Well, I've done some teaching, small at first, but it has caught on, and now my name has been traveling around."

"Teaching what?" Jaron asked.

"Fighting techniques," Keras answered, "but, swords are hard to come by. Spears are easier. Still, I'm trying to teach anyone who joins that anything can be a weapon. I started with the men and women we rescued on the road. I taught a few of the brindi before that," she recollected. "Anyway, they taught a few and then those people taught a few. When we arrived here, those that had been traveling with me were still awful, but getting better at it. The ranks swelled a bit when we got here, but none of them are a match against any of the knights."

"You've been busy," Ellian commented.

"And you will be," Keras said. "I've been telling some stories of our studies, about some of your theories on warfare, and your designs for war machines."

"That was just kid stuff, untested. All of those ideas are just childish fantasies."

"Well, it piqued their interest, and they want to hear more."

"When? We need to get Harris back to Darrod," Ellian said.

"Why us?" asked Keras. "We found him, as we agreed. We can be useful here. Without us, the brindi can march him straight through Temerrac as if he were a prisoner."

"Ha, not too sure he'd agree to that. His opinion of them is not stellar," Jaron laughed.

"Rennek might go with him," Keras suggested. "Good guy, Rennek. Harris has known him for years. Perhaps he could convince him."

Keras cocked her head toward the door, listening. "I think they're finishing up. Let me introduce you." Keras led them into the room and toward the table where many men shuffled maps and papers. The tall man in the center turned at Keras's cough. It was Yaru, Jaron's uncle.

* * * * *

Harris, Rennek, and nine of the brindi would return to Darrod. Seven of the brindi had chosen to stay behind in Denshire.

Uhra, Joalle, Mennas, Dinna, Joahe, Gehne, and Rissa would learn some fighting skills from Keras and become ambassadors between the Brindi army and the increasing force of the humans.

Ellian, Jaron, and Keras would also stay behind at Denshire, where Keras would continue to train the men in her fighting style. Meanwhile, Ellian would speak to the leaders about tactics in battle.

What would Jaron do? He decided he would continue learning from Keras while trying to keep out of the way. He was staying anyway, although it would have been nice to see Neeva again, he mused. He had not wanted to return to Darrod. He had no desire to pass through Temerrac in its occupation or face the minasts again. He had met dead men and fought goblins, but minasts still haunted his dreams.

Behra led them out. Hahre, Engle, Dillog, Kenast, Lurhe, Sindas, Danos, and Kenda followed in single file. Bringing up the rear were Harris and Rennek.

Yaru had been happy to see Jaron. He looked much different than he had during their encounter in the market of Westmost. A long fresh scar crossed his face from the hairline on the right side of his forehead to his left cheekbone. His eye, thankfully, was undamaged. He embraced Jaron tightly and held him at arm's length, looking him over.

"I see my sister in you," he said, smiling, "and your father. You've become a man, but I still see the toddler who ran with me as a boy."

Jaron smiled back, uncomfortable and sad that he had no memory of the joy Yaru was expressing, but he was careful not to show it.

Jaron spent a good deal of time by himself. With Ellian and Yaru involved in the planning of attacks—there seemed to be one every day of some kind—and Keras designing training techniques for the army, Jaron seemed to be in the way.

Anna, whom Jaron remembered from the trip in the slave cart to Sandy River, was becoming quite adept at the maneuvers taught by Keras, and she was passing on her lessons as well. The swirl of steel around Anna, as she danced through the scales of attack and defense forms, reflected a shimmering of light in the morning sun that was blindingly brilliant and beautiful. Her face, still lovely, was fierce in determination, emanating the fire of hatred that burned within her. Jaron remembered the despair within the cart, the pain Anna suffered after the loss of her son. Driven by hatred, anger, and love, she excelled, pushing herself beyond limits.

Riders came into Denshire from the north on the first of August. They made their way to the war council room, and Ellian summoned Jaron. When he arrived, he found Keras seated at the table along with Ellian, Yaru, and the rest of the war council.

The morning light filtered through the tall and narrow windows of stained glass. It painted a color pattern on the table and far wall. An aged man, bent and frail, stood from his seat at the head of the table, his shadow blocking out the colored light. He made a search of the faces around the table and confirmed the identities of his fellows. His eyes rested on Jaron and he made as if to order him out, but Yaru stopped him.

The old man cleared his throat before addressing them. "Word has come down that King Gurrand has left Brethiliost and broken the siege at Starkwall. He is marching south; personally leading his army to face the forces of Valcella encamped at Holderness."

Yaru stood and spoke to the group. "Estimates are that King Gurrand's army should arrive by the first week of September. They are marching hard and fast with two thousand men.

"We have been attacking the Valcella supply trains between Temerrac and Holderness, but we have not always been as successful as we would like. Last night, a patrol came down from Holderness and killed forty of our men along the road. They know we're here. Do they know the number of men we have at our call? I don't know."

Ellian looked to Keras. "How many men are training?"

"Numbers, as I last looked, came to one thousand eight hundred. They are spread over the hills surrounding the city."

"This is my plan," continued Yaru. "I want to squeeze Valcella's army between Gurrand's and our own. Last we knew, he had about three thousand men."

"Things have changed," Jel spoke up. "As ordered, I visited Temerrac. More forces have filled that city, Pelmari, there must be four hundred more. A Goblin horde of several thousand also filled the streets. They are making arrangements to join Shale."

"We'll either have to hit them on the road and hope we can overpower them, or wait until they are in the city of Holderness."

Over the conversation, the city bell rang. A messenger came running in and whispered into the old man's ear.

"We may have started too late. We have received a pigeon from Temerrac," the old man said, standing from his seat. "The bell calls our soldiers, located in the fields around the city, to enter and begin fortifications." He looked up at Yaru. "An armed group is approaching along the western road, Pelmari. It appears that the new forces in Temerrac were not reinforcements for Shale, but were building to quell any meaningful attempt at resistance. Today, that is us."

*   *   *   *   *

The outer walls of Denshire had a commanding view of the western road. Luckily, the road was the only passable path. Even so, the army would be there within the day.

Ellian held a spyglass up to his eye, scanning the hills around Denshire. "Are all of the soldiers and men training within the city?"

"No," Keras answered.

"I have an idea. Do you remember the battle of Littleton from our history lessons?"

"Yes," said Keras, "but didn't they all die?"

"This time it will be different."

Ellian grabbed a piece of paper from one of the other members of the war council and a piece of charcoal. He drew furiously on it, talking as he did so to Keras.

"Find Sir John and Sir Wald, have them gather their men. You'll need two teams of horses. Drag each of the trebuchet up onto the eastern hill. Send some men around and try to collect those still outside under your command. Follow the pattern of the battle of Littleton. We're going to use the fields, swamps, and pits to our advantage. To coordinate the timing, we will use colored flags over the wall."

Ellian handed the paper over to Keras, who examined it, nodding her head.

"Yes sir, commander." She saluted. "I think this might work. We could even survive this."

"Enough of your sass. I'll clear this plan with Yaru. Go."

She leaned in to him, wrapping her hands around his waist, kissed him and left. Ellian watched her walk away and turned to see Jaron smiling at him. "What?" he said, before he smiled back.

*　*　*　*　*

In the same fields where the Denshire troops had been training, the Pelmari set camp. There were about four hundred, but four hundred Pelmari soldiers were more than equal to the task of laying siege to a city the size of Denshire. If those within could hold the walls, they might last several days, even two weeks. The city had several wells within. The grain from last summer was still enough to last a while. Time, however, was the issue. King Gurrand would reach Holderness by the beginning of September. If the battle for Holderness began on that day, then a long siege here would mean that aid would not come from Denshire.

Yaru looked out from the battlements at the surrounding hills and swamps. If Ellian's plan worked, then they could move out before the end of the week to catch Shale unaware.

Gurrand would need aid. If the attack against the Sandy River camp failed, then the army building there would pass through Temerrac to join forces with the Humans and goblins holding that city. Together, they would travel north to increase the strength of

Shale at Holderness. They might even be accompanied by a troop of skeletal warriors that could not be killed.

King Gurrand was not much like his father, King Roland III. When Gurrand was the prince, his destruction of the Eastern Coast was legendary, as was his desire to consolidate power over the lands north of the mountains. However, that was many years ago. King Roland had held a system of taxation that was not overbearing, and had pledged that his troops would come out of the central city of Holderness to protect the citizens of his realm. He had thwarted and fought back several invasions from both the coasts and from the south. Roland had brought stability to the warring cities and united them under one banner. Gurrand did not have as good a reputation. His first mistake was moving the capital city to Brethiliost, far in the North. Even so, Gurrand was a better choice than Shale of Valcella.

With the sun going down, torchlight flared up among the camps outside. Men in those camps moved with purpose, constructing long ladders. Archers on the battlements took aim and dropped any Pelmari soldier foolish enough to enter range.

The drawbridge added another obstacle for those wishing to enter the city. Inside the city walls, the men and women were preparing for the coming siege. Water filled every bucket available. Children were escorted inside, and doors locked. At sunrise, the attack would begin. Meetings continued through the night, but the attendance was minimal. Ellian and most of the knights had left the city on horseback before the Pelmari arrived.

Jaron watched the first glimpse of the sun break on the horizon before becoming a glow across the eastern sky. A cry erupted from the fields. It was the Pelmari shouting together and then going silent. They were coming.

On the battlements, men ran in a flurry to staff the walls, firing arrows at the attackers and ducking to avoid a missile aimed from below. Men, both inside and outside the walls, fell screaming as shafts pierced flesh. Some made no sound at all, but fell dead.

Jaron took a position on the top of one of the walls. He had been practicing the bow, and finally felt like he was a help and not a hindrance to those around him. In all likelihood, they would not be able to hold off the Pelmari.

During The War of Broen, more than one hundred years prior, the Pelmari had crossed the southern continent. Any castle that did not offer them food and shelter had been invaded. The people inside were killed in the most gruesome fashion. Pelmari threw children from the top windows onto the cobblestones below. Men were dissected, their organs pulled out while they still lived. They skinned the women. Some of the books in Westmost proposed that the leather armor of the Pelmari had been made from the skin of those women. Jaron shivered at the thought.

Archers had shot a few of the Pelmari as they attempted to put the long ladders into place. The ladders, wide across the bottom, were long enough to reach the top of the walls even though the base of the ladder was outside the moat. At such an angle, they were difficult to erect, but once in place, the ladders could not be pushed away or pushed over. In horror, Jaron realized that the moat and the fortified main gate were not going to stop the Pelmari. They were all going over the top of the walls.

No soldier began to climb until all of the ladders were in position. The majority of the attacking force sat just outside of bowshot, laughing, drinking, eating, and shouting jeers at the defenders inside. Every so often, an arrow would catch a lucky breeze and fall among them, but the Pelmari ignored them. Even if the missile struck one of them, they would not cry out, but would pluck the arrow out of their crimson armor.

The Pelmari erected five ladders across the front wall of Denshire. Shields were hoisted and blades unsheathed as the Pelmari readied themselves for the slaughter they had come for. No demands were called. No terms of surrender would be accepted. They were here to destroy hope, to remove all thought of resistance.

A shield wall readied itself at the base of the ladders, blocking shot after shot from the shouting archers above. Then, as a wall of one mind, they started to climb. The first Pelmari to climb each ladder wore a strong helmet and armor such that it spread far on either side of their shoulders, creating a moving shield for the warriors that followed behind. Any exposed Pelmari were shot. They fell into the moat below. Others, knocked off the ladders by falling wounded, came up out of the waters of the moat rubbing their skin and wiping the thick water from their eyes, only to realize that it wasn't water at all. So confident were the besiegers of their success that they failed to notice the firelight that appeared on the distant eastern hill.

A fiery ball of straw and dung struck the base of the center ladder, toppling it broken into the moat, and causing the moat to erupt into flames that rose in a sudden rush up the stone walls of the city.

Men fell to their deaths climbing out of the flames, unable to extinguish them. Fiery missiles rained down until all of the ladders lay collapsed and destroyed.

The Pelmari soldiers were not daunted. Sixty of their number they had lost so far. They had enough men still, they believed, to handle this city. They pulled away from the moat, letting it burn, and turned their attention to the force on the hill. They would have to destroy the forces outside the city before attempting to breach the walls again.

That is when the cavalry, led by Yaru and Ellian, struck from around the south wall. Across the back of the camps they rode, driving the Pelmari toward the burning moat and the archers atop the wall.

Three hundred and eighty-eight Pelmari died in the attempted siege of Denshire.

Of the defenders, only seventy-three were lost.

Chapter 24   Clash of Stones

Neeva rolled the pebble around the floor with her magic, taking pleasure in the tiny echo it made as she lay in her bed with one foot in the dirt. Her excavations were complete. The supplies Harris needed to make his powder had been surprisingly simple to obtain. She was able to mine some of it out of the walls of the same tunnel she had excavated. Now, all was ready, and at dawn they would carry out their attack.

She felt the tension in her neck and rubbed at it, her fingers tingling. *Should I enjoy this feeling?* she questioned herself. Before the escape from Sandy River, she had never used her magic for malicious intent. She found that, she was not only competent, she was good at it. Though the realization of what she was capable of scared her, she enjoyed it. Neeva fell asleep, still rolling the pebble and smiling at the sound it made.

*   *   *   *   *

Harris, Rennek, Verne, and most of the brindi remained underground within the protected tunnels, separate from the hollowed out bowl underneath the tower and camp of Sandy River.

Neeva, along with a guard of four brindi, had climbed a knoll that afforded a view of the entire Sandy River camp. Her work was finished. The attack could proceed without her aid. The camp was larger than she remembered it. The movement of the men at this distance reminded her of ants dismembering a corpse in order to bring it back to their nests.

A beacon of power for those underneath, the tower loomed strong and tall in the morning sunlight. Steam rose from the roof as the morning dew evaporated. Dirt rippled underneath her feet with the shock wave of Harris's powder explosion. The tower fell, collapsing straight down upon itself, forcing a billowing cloud of dust into the sky. Neeva heard the rumble of stones as it all fell into the excavated bowl.

From the hole where the tower once stood, the ground failed.

The circle of falling support expanded outward with increasing speed, collapsing into the pit. Caught off guard, men, goblins, and horses fell to their deaths. Buildings crumbled piecemeal, breaking into large sections as their foundations disappeared beneath them. On the hill, Neeva heard the surprised shouts. Unable to outrun the falling ground, men shouted ahead of them, "Run!" It did not help.

Some men died from the fall. Others died from the debris. Those that lived had another horror to face. The sound of the water rolled like thunder as it fell into the bowl. Sandy River had redirected itself to the lowest elevation point and it was crashing over the edge, striking the bottom of the giant hole, the sound reverberating around inside of the cavern. There was nowhere for the water to go once it fell over the edge. The bowl was beginning to fill.

Of the few hundred men and goblins that survived the fall, none could find an exit. They grabbed broken sections of wagons, boards, and timber from the wrecked buildings to stay on the surface. Without them, drowning was a certainty.

Some of the men could swim, but for how long? Floating on the surface, perhaps they could wait for the water to reach the top of the bowl. With the water around their knees, they began to build rafts out of the floating materials. They guessed at the time it would take the diverted river to raise them to the level of the camp and worked together, putting as many of them on the rafts as possible.

Twenty-four hours into their ordeal, with the water forty feet deep, they saw their first sign of life from the rim above them. It was a dozen brindi. The men shouted in relief and called for the brindi to throw down ropes. The brindi smiled and waved back, taking out their bows.

* * * * *

From the hill in the north, Gurrand looked out over his army. Rows of archers stood stretching out far to the east and west, like grey pawns waiting for command. Behind and over the crest of the hill, hidden from the view of the enemy, his cavalry waited. In front of them, also in grey over their chainmail, infantrymen held their pikes upright and straight. On top of each pike sat a terrible display. Carried from the liberation of Starkwall, the heads of goblins stared unblinking.

The fog sat thick in the center of the plain, watering the half-empty wheat field that grew there. The invasion had interrupted the harvest. The sun sat low behind the mountains in the east, its rays lighting the sky but not yet the ground. Holderness glowed a golden hue, its spires just touching the sunlight.

Behind those dark walls, Shale would have some surprise for his opponent, just as Gurrand had his cavalry behind him. The southern lands were famous for their war engineering. Although the inventiveness of war would cost the lives of his soldiers, Gurrand was anxious to witness Shale's machines.

At the base of the walls of Holderness, the main gate began to rise. Soldiers poured out like milk into a basin, their white and red uniforms grasping at the rays of the sun as it climbed over the mountains.

*   *   *   *   *

Men ran out of the north gate in droves, not all of his men, but most of them. He was gambling heavily on the outcome of this battle. Shale looked down from the highest tower, and surveyed the courtyard just inside the main gate. Ten trebuchet units sat ready for the cavalry charge that was certain to come. These machines had been decisive in the taking of Holderness. How effective they would be against an attacking force of cavalry was yet to be tested. Each machine had a unit of twelve men and six shot, low in comparison to the number of horsemen with Gurrand's cavalry.

The south gate, locked tight, was guarded by four hundred men, fighters from the road campaign. They had fought bandits and rebels to fortify the supply train coming from Temerrac. Some of his Pelmari soldiers had carried out the destruction of a local collection of lords to the east and returned triumphant to swell his forces even more.

He ran a hand over his long mustache. His reserve armies had not arrived yet: six hundred brindi, three thousand goblins, three thousand more men from Sandy River, and of course there were Mavius's knights. He need only hold out until they arrived. When they did arrive, he would route Gurrand easily. Shale laughed quietly to himself. Success was assured. Gurrand did not even know about the dragons. This would be a slaughter.

He watched the King's emissary gather under Gurrand's standard and trot their horses toward the center of the field. They remained within shooting range of their archers. His emissary rode out to meet them. There would be no agreement. Regardless of the demands of King Gurrand, Shale had instructed his man to demand all lands south of Holderness be subject to the command and taxation of the City of Valcella. King Gurrand would not give up so much territory without a fight.

After a brief conversation in the center of the field, Shale watched the representatives of the opposing forces ride back to their respective lines. Thanks to his high vantage point, he could just hear the commands of his lieutenants.

Bowmen trotted forward and set arrows to string. The armies traded volleys. The silence seemed to last an hour as the shafts of death arced across the center of the field to force screams out of the enemy.

Shale smiled at his men hidden below in the courtyard. He would hold these back until King Gurrand brought his cavalry within trebuchet range. While the trebuchet rained fire on the horsemen, his dragons would then swoop down on the king and his closest knights.

His smile faded. Looking down, he saw a member of his Pelmari attack and kill two soldiers operating one of the trebuchet. The Pelmari were dismantling his victory, one by one, setting the trebuchet to flames.

* * * * *

On the field, following the volley of arrows, each side's infantry advanced toward the fog. As a slow moving line at first, and then with increasing speed, they ran into the mist. The enemy came into sight less than twenty feet away. Those men who were prepared, survived. Many fell at the meeting.

From outside the fog, shapes struggled and fought. Cries of both triumph and terror filled the air, mingled with the clang of metal on metal. King Gurrand endured these sounds for four minutes before motioning to his flagman to signal the next wave of the assault.

Gurrand's cavalry charged with shields up and lances raised. The mist had begun to dissipate. Hearing the approach of hooves, those not engaged with an opponent, made every effort to dodge the warhorses.

*   *   *   *   *

Keras held her breath. The uniforms captured from the Pelmari soldiers that had tried to sack Denshire were ripped and bloodstained. No one had the right color eyes. An alert captain could bring the whole subterfuge to its knees. Fifty men from Denshire had infiltrated the army of Valcella. They shared a code word among them for easy recognition, "Sotho." Four at a time, they had entered with caravans as soldiers from the south. The supply caravan's original drivers, replaced by the Denshire militia, lay dead, hidden in a dozen or so towns that made up the rebellious forces.

On the south gate, Denshire had fifty of the four hundred working for them. Taking the gate would require both excellent timing and bravery.

With a crash, ten Denshire men kicked in the gatehouse door and rushed in to take command of the room. Ten more, including Keras, held the door against the surprised Valcella soldiers nearby. The inner portcullis rose.

No call came from the men trying to retake the gatehouse as more militiamen joined the fight. When Ellian and his troops entered the city of Holderness, all was quiet once again. With silence and control, they brought eight hundred of their forces inside the city walls and closed the portcullis behind them.

To determine the enemy locations within Holderness, men

who knew the city scouted ahead. The first reports came back that the dragons were located in the western courtyard of the city. One of the dragons had a saddle attached to its back. The other two were smaller, but still had the strength needed to crush a man with either a swipe of a tail or the grip of a talon. The trebuchet were located in the northern courtyard, where they could get the most direct aim on the battle in progress.

"We will start with the dragons and trebuchet," Ellian told his patrol leaders. "Anna, you and your patrol have the trebuchet. Jel, your patrol, Keras's patrol, and Rissa's Brindi patrol will take out the dragons. I will take Jaron and his patrol and take the officer's tower."

*　*　*　*　*

Lances at the ready and swords on their hips, the brindi were on the northern side of the western courtyard. On the southern side, Keras and Jel waited with their patrols. Seven or eight dragon handlers were preparing to release the dragons from their chains.

Each dragon was larger than anything Keras had ever seen walking. Three dragons waited. The scales on one were as green as the fields. Another was blacker than the night sky, and the third and largest dragon had scales as blue as the retreating night at dawn. The sunlight had not yet reached this side of the city, but Keras thought, *they must shine like mirrors in the light.* They were beautiful and deadly. Their necks were long and muscular, and their wings folded tightly to their sides. The thought that she would have to kill them filled her with regret.

Keras raised her spear and gave the signal to the others. They broke into a run as fifteen spears sailed through the air to strike the blue dragon, only to bounce away. The dragon turned its head in their direction and screamed in anger. It spread its wings to escape. The sound of breaking steel rang as the dragon launched itself into the air, snapping the chain like a thread. The other two dragons tried to follow the blue, but the brindi were on them. Rissa clung to the neck of one of the giant beasts. It shook its black head back and forth, flinging Rissa against the walls of the courtyard with a sickening thud.

The blue dragon was climbing up and away from its attackers as the chain swung under it wildly. In fright, the green dragon pulled against its tether. Cornered, it would soon turn to fight. The black dragon that threw Rissa was crawling with brindi. They had small sharp knives and gouged bits of flesh off as the dragon shook and scratched, trying to dislodge them.

The green dragon spread its wings and brought them down with such intensity that those near her fell back with the force of the wind. Keras sailed fifteen feet, losing her grip on her sword and shield. In pain, she found herself looking up at the mighty underbelly of the monster.

She heard a great intake of breath as the dragon spread its wings and raised its head to the sky. The green beast was preparing to incinerate its enemies and her wings unfolded as her body braced to exhale. At the last moment, the dragon coughed flames into the sky, screaming in pain. Mennas had climbed onto her back and had driven a Brindi blade into her spine.

The green dragon railed in fury, coughing flames as she spun to dislodge the little menace. With a ringing, her chain snapped, and she rose from the ground, taking Mennas with her. She did not fly away, but slammed her body into the nearest tower, smashing Mennas, who fell thirty feet to the cobblestones below. Freed from her pest, she turned on the five brindi attacking the black dragon with ferocity. She swooped down to grab Joalle and Dinna in her massive claws, bringing them high into the air before letting them go. The swords and spears could not pierce her, and she reveled in her destruction.

Gehne and Joahe scattered under the onslaught, and free from her tormentors, the black dragon snapped her chain to escape into the air.

Shaking off the buzzing in her head from her fall, Keras made her way to the top of the parapets as quickly as possible. Without information on the position of the dragons, they could be taken completely unprepared. To her relief, the dragons were not circling back for an attack. The two dragons that had been hurt were visible in the sky, far to the south, leaving. She could still hear their cries of pain and anger echoing through the air. The larger dragon, the blue one with the saddle, was flying over the men on horseback, regardless of army affiliation, and picking them from their mounts.

* * * * *

As the trebuchet burned behind them, Ellian, Jaron, and their men were trying to gain entry to the city central tower. A battering ram was fashioned out of the remains of the war machines.

Shale looked down at the destruction of his plans. Out on the plains, his men were fighting Gurrand, but without his dragons and trebuchet he would not be able to hold Gurrand at bay. Shale could still win. He had not yet called forth the rest of his forces hidden within the forest to the west. Now it was time.

He picked up a blue flag and waved it over his head. It was large and billowed hard in the light wind. Men high in the other towers of the city took up the signal. Shale drew his sword and made his way to the stairs. Losing this first assault of the battle did not worry him. He still held the city. The small bands of insurgents below were not enough to force him to retreat.

Joined by his personal guard as he walked down the stairs, he smiled. These men would die to protect him; such was their belief in the cause. Many, many more were still within the walls.

On the first landing below the tower peak stood a barred wooden door with two guards outside. This wooden jail cell stood within the center of the tower.

Shale opened the door. "Are you ready to perform again?"

"I won't do it," said a small voice from within.

"Pity, I was beginning to like your mother's company."

"No! Please, don't!"

"No, is not a word I enjoy hearing. Something about it grates on me. I'll ask again. Are you ready to do your duty?"

"Yes." The child from within the cell walked to the door. He was thin and hungry, his clothes the tattered remains of fine silk. A large welt covered the area of his right cheek, but he was not dirty. Shale motioned a warding hand to one of the guards and drew his blade. Shackles were not necessary, but the boy had no defense against a knife in the back.

"Your mother, as you are aware, will suffer if you do not follow my commands."

The young boy looked up at the general, tears streaming down his face. With a look of pure hatred, he stepped barefoot out of the wooden cell and onto the stone floor.

From the balcony, they could see that the battle was not going well for the men of Valcella. The sun had burned off the fog and revealed the thousands of bodies of both King Gurrand's men and Valcella's. Those in grey uniforms walked among the bodies, looking for the faces of those they cared for, and killing any of Valcella's men that were still breathing. Even the dragon had flown off, seemingly disinterested in the carnage.

King Gurrand and his knights were riding down the hill to claim victory over the center of the field. They were a hundred horsemen of privilege from northern castles. Clean of bruises and bloodstains, they rode as if they personally had won the assault.

The boy ran his hands along the floor of the balcony, caressing the tiles. He stood wiping his hands together, feeling the sand and particles of stone between them.

King Gurrand had reached the center of the plain and was speaking to ranking members of his cavalry there.

"Now, Justin," Shale commanded.

The child held his hands toward the sky, palms up. He reached down and repeated the gesture. His small frame strained as he appeared to pick up a great weight.

The ground around the battle plain began to tremble and rise. It cracked in a large circle that encompassed the King and his remaining men. From his position in the tower, Justin wrenched the stone out of the ground. Dust shot up into the air as the battlefield sank in the center and stone rose around the outside, sharp and jagged, like splinters of wood. Horses and men looked around in confusion and terror as the ground around them came alive to trap them in the center of rocky peaks.

The child collapsed in exhaustion. Shale grabbed him by the neck, forcing him to stand again.

"More."

The child put his hands together and a form started to appear in the ground within the circle. First, a massive hand, then an arm, then a head and torso started to pull itself out of the ground, a grey stone golem. The stone giant, thirty feet tall, roared at the sky and attacked King Gurrand and his men.

* * * * *

From out of the western forest, rode the horsemen of Valcella, five hundred men in white and red. The horsemen were approaching the outer ring of stone holding King Gurrand and his knights and nobles in place. They were able to ride up the steep slope from the outside to gaze down on the captured enemy.

A trumpet sounded below and the northern gate of Holderness opened again. This time, it was not Valcella's soldiers joining the battle. Yaru led the Denshire charge. They rode out to fight the Valcella horsemen, filled with the determination of those fighting not for conquest and plunder but for home and hearth.

The clash of steel rang as both sides volleyed for advantage, riding round their enemy or dismounting finally to finish off the battle on foot.

Shale watched his horsemen. "Boy, new target," he pointed at Yaru's standard-bearer, "them."

The grey golem climbed out of the crater and stood on the precipice preparing to enter a new fray. Behind it, there was no movement from either horse or man. With mighty blows from its stone fists, it crushed any who stood before it. Horsemen fled the reach of the mighty statue, skipping at just near the edge of its swing.

Mighty hands grabbed riders from their mounts, turning the

tide against Yaru's cavalry. The golem withstood sword, spear, and lance attacks without damage. Stones rippled under the hooves of horses, throwing them to the ground, breaking their legs so they could only scream in pain or hobble away ruined.

From the ground below the trampling horses, another golem formed, rising into the sky, even larger than the first, its fists shimmering with malachite.

Justin cried in terror. He had not called this new golem. He must not let it stop him. Justin spun his creation around to push back the malachite golem. High on the tower balcony, his eyes darted around the battlefield looking for the other mage that could bring forth such a monster.

The malachite golem pounded the ground before itself in challenge and charged. Panicked, horses and men tried to dodge the terrible sight. It struck the grey golem, throwing away chunks of stone and malachite, and the air filled with the sound of grinding rock as the two grappled. Then the golem of malachite struck with such force that it removed the upper torso of Justin's stone golem from the lower half.

With a sigh of despair, Justin fell forward, his strength depleted. Unable to catch himself, he slid off the balcony. Disgusted at the boy's failure, Shale didn't try to catch him and only watched the small body plummet to the stones below.

* * * * *

Raising the large black horn to his lips, Shale gave a loud call.

Flames rolled up the sides of the tower, burning nothing, but driven by the magic of a fire mage below. Out on the field, that was the work of an opposing stone mage. Justin hadn't been strong enough. He would have to find himself another.

Blood trickled down his side from the arrow that penetrated his armor. He had no more men to call. The Brindi had turned on him and the army of Sandy River had not arrived. He blew the horn again. The wind of massive blue wings pushed him away as he heard the grunt of a dragon landing.

Reaching up, he placed a bridle over the head of the blue beast and settled himself on the saddle between the wings. He stroked its neck and the dragon leaped into flight.

* * * * *

"You could not have made your way here so quickly." Ellian said, incredulous. Neeva, smiling gleefully, was covered in grime and blood.

"We took the short road," she replied.

"Through Temerrac?" Ellian asked.

"Through the mountains."

"But the minasts..."

Neeva grabbed him by the shirt, pulled him down to her level, and spoke each word slowly, "through the mountains."

"Through..."

Chapter 25   Wind and Breath

They were sailing north, back towards Stenwood. "We'll stop at Allenddon, sister city to Glenndon," Thargus said. "There, we can buy horses if Loren is well enough to ride. If he isn't, we'll get a carriage."

Loren sat propped up on the nets at the front of the boat. Repeated assaults by his captors as they attempted their magic had damaged his lungs. Speaking at all was a great undertaking and he could only say a few words at a time in a low whisper.

"Shale of Valcella has been keeping you all this time?"

"Yes," wheezed Loren. "His men attacked me. I sent that letter. I thought I was dying. They kept me alive."

"Those mages we killed," Thargus said, from the rear of the boat, "air magic?"

"Yes, it was," said Loren. By manipulating the air inside his lungs, they had kept him breathing, even when he was so close to death. Loren had been living in torment. Every day, the mages had attempted to make him speak with their magic, folding the air against his vocal cords, trying to form the words that came out of his mouth.

Arnor looked at his hands as he spoke, feeling guilty for his part in the misfortunes of Loren's family. "Mavius has returned," said Arnor. "He is in league with Valcella."

Loren's eyes went wide and the tendons in his neck flexed sharply.

"Now I know why," Loren said. "General Shale intends to betray Mavius. He wants to control the knights, through me." Loren tried to sit up straight. The nightmares of his childhood had finally materialized.

"Who knows what Mavius intends when he is through with Shale? Betrayal might be in his mind as well," said Arnor.

"The knights, Mavius's knights, can we intercept them?"

"They were searching for you," said Arnor, "but they found Jaron."

All of the color left Loren's face and he broke into a fit of coughing. "Is he with you?"

"No. We were separated after he met with Sir William and Lord Baros." Arnor drank from his waterskin and offered it to Loren. "Jaron couldn't command the knights. But, he isn't the heir. You are. You are the only one who can override Mavius's command to them."

Arnor told Loren the tale of himself and Jaron in the tower at Sandy River, of the confrontation with the undead knights and their eventual escape. Loren became distraught at hearing that Jaron had been through so much pain and despair. Anger roared in his eyes.

"Where is that book that fell out of your pack?" Loren asked. His face was grim. Arnor and Thargus busied themselves with piloting the small boat while Loren read, his lips moving silently.

For two days, Arnor and Thargus sailed the small boat north, resting in turns. The mist from the bow splashing through the water kept them cool in the August heat, and they used their cloaks to ward off the biting rays of the sun. Loren began to move about the boat, holding himself against the side rails with increasing steadiness. His strength was beginning to return, though he still looked sickly. He ate and drank what he could, slowly and painfully, but with determination.

Allenddon appeared around the bend in the shore. It was much smaller than Glenndon, there being no outer wall of defense. Arnor had never been to this city. He tended to visit the larger and more exciting places of the world. This wasn't one of them.

There was one dock jutting out into the sea. A ship as large as the Aquilo could not have berthed there, but this small vessel was no problem. One problem they did have was a lack of money to pay the docking fee. Thargus resolved the issue by selling the vessel to the dock manager for one-sixth its price. They removed their packs from the boat and helped Loren ashore.

"Good thinking, Thargus," said Arnor.

"What else had I to do for two and a half days at sea?"

Allenddon was a town of short white buildings and narrow

cobblestone streets. The beach made it an ideal fishing town, and although the township was small, merchants came daily to haul the catch to neighboring towns and cities. The men of the village were dark-skinned and hardworking. They went about with no great hurry, but their wives bustled about, running the sale of fish or bargaining with merchants.

The attitude of the town folk was one of apprehension. The news of Glenndon's destruction weighed on them, for news of such magnitude traveled fast, haunting the nights of those that heard it. Merchants carried the news, as did seamen, and the inns of the town were full each night with the tales of the smoke and massacre that befell there. Doors and windows closed to travelers. People whispered to each other in the streets, and many refused to answer simple questions. These people were afraid.

With a good deal of searching, the three found an inn, Old Tommy's, near the dock. It was small and had only two rooms, of which they hired one. A merchant from Temerrac, pushed out by the violence there, rented the other room at Old Tommy's. With him were his wife and two young children. The children played, but their parents were quick to look over their shoulders at noises and hugged their children more often than usual.

The three rested and let Loren build his strength. His breathing was becoming stronger. His appetite had improved, and he did not look nearly as ill as he had before their arrival at Allenddon. The diet of meat and fish allowed him to increase his activity and his speech became louder, if only slightly.

Thargus counted out the money they had left from the sale of the boat. There was enough to purchase three small ponies, but not enough for a cart.

"Do you think Loren will be strong enough in another week?" Thargus asked Arnor.

"Do we have enough left for both the ponies and lodgings?"

"For another two weeks, yes. I wish we had enough for a cart and a pony. I do not want Loren to fall off a pony. That would cost us even more time. Mavius is growing weak. He's going to return to the portal soon. I want to be there before he enters, not after."

Three men in grey robes came to the inn that night. There being no available room, they made way to another public house across the town. They did not inquire after anyone at the desk as far as Thargus, who was sitting in the common room, could hear. He listened to them discuss the inconveniences of traveling as they left through the front door.

Arnor discovered that the robed men had taken residence in another inn called The Cellar across from the town hall on the northern side of the town. They had begun meeting with public officials on the day after their arrival. They did not make inquiries for two dwarves and a human, which was puzzling to Arnor. Maybe they hadn't come from Glenndon, after all.

Loren would have to stay in his room until it was time to leave. He sat near the open window listening to the sounds outside, holding down the pages if the wind tried to turn them. Many times, he would fall into fits of laughter as he perused the book, closing it to catch his breath or wipe away a tear from laughing so hard. Other times he was serious, engrossed in the words before him, as if solving puzzles in his mind.

Thargus spent the week visiting the other inns of Allenddon. There were only three others, The Flying Fish, Gertie's, and The Cellar. He drank a beer, or two, at each and mingled with the patrons. He sat in dark corners and whispered to both dwarves and men. Some left laughing at him. Others stood, solemnly meeting his gaze, shook his hand and left quietly. Before the end of two days, Thargus had sent word out through merchants to find some of his town folk. He was building his own web. He asked questions, and even told his true name to some of the people he met.

Arnor shut the window, wary of eavesdroppers hanging outside. "You can't go about spreading your name or giving these people information about where we're going," he said.

"We are returning to Stenwood Den," stated Thargus. "We

are going there to kill Mavius. He won't be alone. We will need soldiers, dwarves from Stenwood Den. The merchants I've sent have to give credible information to the dwarves they encounter, or their word will not be trusted. My people would kill them if they said the wrong thing. I will not lie to these men."

"But, what about those men who did not agree?" Arnor asked in exasperation.

"I give them three days. No way, they could hold on for four."

"What do you mean?"

"I play to win, Arnor. I don't think it would be wise to leave loose ends. I think you know what I'm getting at."

"You won't lie, but you'll murder?" Arnor was cold with his gaze at Thargus.

"These men that you're so concerned about are not good men. They were mercenaries, available to the highest bidder." Then, seeing the look on Arnor's face, he asked, "What are you prepared to do?"

Arnor lowered his eyes, remembering his own actions when he was allied with Mavius. How many men had he killed? How many families had he destroyed? As a General of the Dwarven forces under Mavius, he had brought the sword to city after city, following a king he knew to be unjust, if there ever were such a thing as a just king.

In two days' time, Thargus held a meeting with four dwarves from Stenwood Den, Beshaa, Nuala, Sarmas, and Mennan. They were leaving ahead of Arnor, Thargus, and Loren to meet up with them again at the trapper's shack. They would recruit more dwarves if they could find them.

＊　＊　＊　＊　＊

The storm came from the ocean and the wind whipped wildly through the streets of Allenddon. The storefront awnings snapped loudly as the bursts of air rippled across them. Some awnings tore from the sheer force of the gale and others were ripped from their support bars to career down the street. Dark and menacing clouds rolled in during the previous day, prompting Arnor to suggest that they withhold their departure for another day or two, but Loren would not have it.

Lightning filled the sky, breaking across the ocean tempest with a beautiful fury. Loren reached his hand out to catch the mist as he spoke. "They are still here, those air mages. This is their doing. They seek to hold us here until reinforcements arrive. That is why we must leave at once. The air currents rolling through the streets of this town hold the footprint of the man they're looking for. They're tracking me."

"How could they know you're here? We could've sailed almost anywhere," Arnor asked as he tied his pack to his pony.

"Air magic can sense air magic." Arnor and Thargus just stared at him, dumbly, waiting for him to make his point. "The book," he continued, "I've been studying air magic. That's why my breathing has improved. My health hasn't improved. My magical ability has."

"If they can sense you, can you sense them?" Thargus asked, helping Loren up on to his pony.

"I can feel the effects of their magic in the wind. It isn't natural, and by recognizing this, I can tell their level of instruction. They are novices; no more learned than I. The book," he touched the outline of *Current Studies* under his shirt, "was a very fortunate find. Where did you come by it?"

Thargus told the tale of the goblins carting a large quantity of books outside of Glenndon, and Loren was not surprised. "So the master had called for his research materials. I wonder what else he had in store for me." He removed the book from his shirt, opened it to its first page, and pointed out the name, *Istilia Chonos*. "The master of air magic," Loren explained, "this is his book, his diary of the steps of discovery."

"Was he one of the two we killed in the tower?" Thargus asked, mounting his pony.

"No." Loren held his chest in pain. This long discussion was

254

taxing his strength. "He knew of your arrival, but he trusted his best two pupils to contain the threat. He's still out there, teaching his students."

Outside the stable, the rain crashed down sideways in waves that followed the gusts of the wind. Trees in the distance were dark outlines that swayed and creaked under the onslaught of the weather. The wind whipped, spraying mist at the three as they prepared to leave the protection of the stable.

"So we go," said Loren, leading the way.

The water and wind did not touch Thargus, Arnor, Loren, or even their ponies as they rode out from under the roof. The wind halted in momentum as it approached them to whisper through their hair gently, pushing aside the rain as it did so.

Loren had a smile on his face as wide as a canyon.

*　*　*　*　*

"Mavius can move between the planes," Arnor explained as they rode, "and is doing so to increase his power and influence in this plane."

Thargus spoke up, "The knights in Sandy River, William and Lord Baros, talked of stopping him."

"They had hoped that Jaron was the heir and that he could command them to stand down. We all know that wasn't the case," said Arnor, pulling his pony to the side so that Thargus could ride next to him.

"We have the heir now," Thargus said.

"However, they also spoke of closing the door," Arnor continued, "and that the heir might be able to do it. This would trap Mavius in this plane, diminishing his power. If Mavius is partially in the under-realm when the door closes, then he will again be weakened. Best would be, if you could get Mavius through the door, and then close it. You could trap him again, for centuries, maybe forever. Without his knights he would be in great peril."

"So we shut the door," said Loren.

"After we kill him," said Thargus.

"But we don't have to kill him," said Arnor.

"Yes, we do," said Thargus. "If he lives, then so does the web, along with the mischief he has caused in trying to come back. My best bet in destroying the effects of his spells is to destroy him." Thargus stared past Arnor. "I want my children back."

They rode in silence for the next few hours. Although the trees lining the path rattled in the wind of the terrible storm, it was as a warm summer day to the three riders. A stone outcropping provided shelter for them overnight, enough to keep them and the ponies dry and warm beside a fire. Loren did not eat, but he fell asleep almost in an instant, having maintained a spell consistently for a full day. Along with the magic he used to keep them dry, he was also using other spells to aid his breathing.

Morning came with a fog, heavy, wet, and as thick as soup. There was no breeze, a point noticed by Loren, who was much refreshed from the long sleep he enjoyed. Thargus and Arnor had taken turns on the watch allowing Loren to regain more of his strength.

The lack of wind on a foggy morning was not unusual. In fact, neither Thargus nor Arnor could recall there ever being wind on a foggy day. It would blow the fog out. However, Loren remarked, yesterday was a major storm, so there should be some wind still blowing out as the weather cleared away. Something was amiss.

They packed their ponies and rode on, paying close attention to the edges of the road. They could not see more than fifteen feet ahead of them. As the road came to cross a wide and shallow stream, the sun broke through the fog. Ahead on the other side of the stream, barely visible, were three robed figures astride horses.

"Stop, Loren," they commanded.

Loren pulled back the reins, and brought his pony to a halt. Thargus and Arnor came to a stop on either side of him. Loren found his voice and spoke louder than either had heard him since they found him in the tower. "I am no longer your prisoner." His voice echoed in the distance. He appeared to do this without effort, the muscles of his thin and gaunt face relaxed, as if he were only carrying on a quiet conversation over tea.

"Your companions are not needed," the figure in the center stated. A wind fell on both Thargus and Arnor, ripping around them, pulling the two dwarves from their ponies, and pinning them to the ground. Arnor's hat rolled away into the brush. "Come with us willingly and these two half-men will live. Refuse and they will die."

"I wasn't finished," said Loren, his voice still reverberating against the stones around the stream. "I am no longer your prisoner. You are mine."

Great gusts of air exploded on the shallow water, parting it to reveal the stones on the bottom. The stones rolled against each other in the gale, moving in the direction of the three robed figures until they lifted out of the stream bed to pelt the two robed mages on the outside of the trio.

The two men fell dead from their horses, bloodied and pierced by smooth round stones.

The wind forces holding Arnor and Thargus subsided. The dwarves stood slowly, trying to understand the pressure that had held them. Each gave Loren a look of surprise and respect as he stared down the remaining foe. Arnor retrieved his hat and at a nod from Loren, they remounted their ponies. Loren held his bony hands up in front of himself, palms out, fingers spread, and he whispered to the wind, eyes never leaving the figure on the other side of the stream.

The remaining mage spun his hands at the air, chanting at the top of his lungs, demanding that the atmosphere align to his commands. The horses on either side of him started and ran away from him, panicked. His horse shook its head back and forth, wanting to flee, but not knowing where to go.

Loren brought his heel back, nudging his pony forward. He crossed the stream, Arnor and Thargus following behind. The water around them shuddered as the mage attempted the same spell that had killed his two companions. The surface of the water rippled with the circles of tiny raindrops, but no water fell from the sky.

Reaching the other side of the stream, Loren approached the mage, looking up at him. "I remember you," he said. "How many of your spells did you practice on me?"

The mage only steeled his gaze, staring back, defiant, a spell brewing within his mind, something that would destroy this upstart, regardless of the order to return with him alive.

Loren spoke again. "Here's one I've wanted to practice." His hands turned from palm out to palm in, and he pulled them to himself quickly.

The mage started gasping, his mouth opening and closing. His hands went to his robes, reflexively pulling them from his neck. His gaze traveled from Loren, to Arnor, to Thargus, eyes searching for the answer from Loren, and then searching for help from Arnor and Thargus. A light blue color entered his face and he fell from his mount.

For the next six days on the road, they met no other. Loren had taken the horse of the last mage. The saddle was far more comfortable than the one on his pony. Arnor and Thargus still rode their ponies, not wanting to climb any higher in order to ride the beasts of the other two mages. They tied the two horses and Loren's pony to leads and made their way through the trails in single file.

The deep ruts in the Attas road were a welcome sight. The small stable appeared through the trees, and behind that sat the trading post of the old man.

No skins sat on the porch. No fire came from the small stone chimney. On the porch next to the broken chair was a dwarf. Hearing their approach, he turned and went inside only to return a moment later followed by four more dwarves.

"Ho, Thargus," said one, recognizing his friend. "I'm sorry we can't offer you coffee yet this morning, we've only just arrived ourselves a day ago."

"Aye, Beshaa, where's Billy?" asked Thargus smiling.

"He's dead."

The smile faded from Thargus.

"When we arrived, he was lying here on the porch. We buried him out behind the shed. I'm sorry, Thargus. I knew him well. Did you?"

The old trapper had been living on the outskirts of Stenwood Den for twenty years. Thargus felt a pang of guilt for not speaking to him more than he had. "No," said Thargus. "How did he die?"

"Mavius's men, I think. They ransacked the place, too. Took everything."

"Any idea, how many there were?" Arnor asked.

"A hill dwarf!" Beshaa shouted. "You didn't say anything about a hill dwarf." He shoved Thargus to the ground and drew his short sword, glaring angrily.

The sound of steel against steel came from the porch as the dwarves drew their weapons. Thargus scrambled to his feet to stand between the dwarves and his companions, hands stretched out. "Wait, Wait, Stop!" he shouted to hold them back. "This hill dwarf is risking his life to help us regain the town."

"How can you trust him?" Beshaa asked, fingering his axe. "When was the last time he shaved?"

"Hill dwarves don't shave, you know that," Thargus said. "Listen, Beshaa, he has ridden with me for many, many miles. He is trustworthy, I assure you. We need him, and the human."

"You'll answer for him?" Beshaa did not look convinced.

"I will. And by the way, he's a mountain dwarf."

* * * * *

As the sun set behind the hills, causing the sky to glow pink and orange, Beshaa and Nuala sat around a small cooking fire with Thargus and Arnor. Many dwarves had joined them over the course of the day. Holes littered the woods behind the shack as the dwarves dug themselves in. They laughed and jested with each other in quiet voices.

"What do you know of the men that passed through here?" Arnor asked.

No one answered.

This feud between the dwarves was getting to Thargus. First Arnor had been insufferable, and now his kin were being just as bad. In exasperation, Thargus repeated the question. After a brief hesitation, Nuala answered, staring at the fire. "Between thirty and forty men passed along this road, near as I can tell. The road was still wet from the rain last week, but I'm sure. I entered the town last night. They're guarding the well. Men are spread around the town. Sarmas and Mennan snuck in with me to take a look around, and they said that the men are waiting for something or someone." Nuala looked at Thargus. "Are you sure the fiend will show his face?"

"We brought eleven other dwarves with us," said Beshaa, "Mennan brought forty. More are coming from the surrounding hills. Nishan says he has a small patrol from Kellerton. Dwarves have been waiting for a chance to strike. We total our tallies at around two hundred, so far, for the assault on the town." Beshaa stoked the fire, standing up. "They have forty men inside. They're outnumbered."

"The entourage sounds small for Mavius," said Arnor. "This group is here to secure the town. The 'fiend,' as you call him," Arnor looked at Nuala, "will bring more men with him when he arrives." Arnor pulled a pot of steaming water from the tripod over the fire and poured some into a metal cup, which he after handled with some care. "If we kill all of the men inside the town now, then Mavius will be spooked, and we will not be able to trap him as we hope. I suggest we hold our assault until he arrives."

"But then the number of men in the town will be more than doubled," Thargus argued.

"And," said Loren, appearing out of the darkness to sit with them, "we still have to be at the bottom of the gravity well when he arrives. We're going to have to sneak in there, and we may need a few extra dwarves to subdue any personal bodyguards he allows down there with him." He took the cup from Arnor, and said, after taking a sip, "Thank you, Arnie."

Arnor frowned.

Chapter 26   Forces Opposed

"Yaru, a runner has arrived from the battlefield," Jaron said as he opened the door. The man who followed him sucked in heavy gulps of air and glistened with sweat. Yaru looked up from the captured battle plans of Shale.

"Sir, we've sent men to search the crater for wounded. King Gurrand was among them. He was sorely hurt and is not conscious."

Yaru pushed away the plans and stood up from the table. "Take me to him."

The crater created by Justin in the center of the battlefield was over thirty feet deep. Even from the outside, the walls of the crater were tall, rocky peaks stretching skyward. Neeva used her magic to smooth out an entrance to the depression in a matter of minutes. She was frail from the overuse of her magic in the past week, but the path was clear enough.

Men and brindi were walking among the dead strewn across the red stained loam. They checked each for signs of life. Those found were carted to the makeshift hospital in the center of the crater.

The hospital was not a place of peace. Men lay in rows as they were attended by the healers. The screams of pain rang out as the doctors plucked arrows from flesh. In one corner, a man, held still by his friend, swore loudly as a doctor cauterized his wound with glowing steel. Those that the staff were unable to save lay outside of the sheltered tent to die alone.

Badly bruised, the right side of King Gurrand's face had turned a dark shade of purple, and his right eye was swollen shut. The lines of his helmet were imprinted in the bruise from the mighty blow. Had he not been wearing the king's armor, he might not have been recognized. His right arm was most surely broken near the shoulder, and doctors were rushing to put the splint in place while he was still unconscious.

Many of his knights and nobles were awake and spoke with

awe of the giant fists of stone that had laid waste to those trapped in the crater. "It did not matter what weapon was in your hand. We could do nothing about the moving statue. We tried to distract it from the king, but we failed."

Yaru made sure that King Gurrand was going to survive before he addressed the head doctor.

"How long before these men can be brought within the city walls?"

"The King can be taken now," the doctor responded, "the others soon after. We need men to transport them, though. It will take some time."

"I will see to it that you have the men you need." Yaru motioned for his guards to pick up the king's litter and ordered them to bring it to the high tower where Shale had been defeated.

*　*　*　*　*

"So, you are the boy I've heard so much about. Did you lead the attack on Holderness from the south?" The king sat propped up on pillows and sipped at a cup of tea. His face still showed the imprint of his helmet, a scar he would carry until his death. A full three days had passed since his injury on the field. Doctors had tended him in the tower, and he slept for most of those hours. Now, he was alert and in command.

Ellian chose his words carefully. "No, Your Majesty, I was not in command of the attack. I led the assault on the rear gate."

The king turned his attention to Keras and then to Jaron. He looked them up and down, assessing them. He did not seem impressed. "What are your names?"

"My name is Ellian Wallace. That," Ellian pointed, "is Keras Alestan, and that," Ellian pointed again, "is Jaron Keltenon."

"Keltenon?" the king asked.

"Yes, Your Majesty," Jaron responded quickly.

"I've heard that name a lot lately. It is an old name." The name Keltenon he recognized. Of course, anyone with knowledge of the ancient kingdom, something a king would surely have, would know it. *I will have to remember this one,* he thought.

Each youth had two names. First and last names meant that each of these youths had come from families of renown. One name, for sure, he knew. "Alestan, are you the daughter of Ceryss, head of the Westmost library?"

"I am," Keras said bowing.

"Your father sent me many books at my request. I have longed to visit the Westmost library. It has a long and interesting history. I believe it was even a stronghold for the city armory, before it fell nearly to ruin. It is a fine library.

"Thank you, Your Majesty."

"Are you all library apprentices? Have you studied?" They all nodded. "Tell me of your dedicated fields."

Keras spoke first. "My studies were supposed to be world geography, but I never excelled at it. I was more at home studying training techniques for hand-to-hand styles." The king nodded and moved on to Jaron.

"History," Jaron blurted out. "I studied history. The lands within your kingdom have each written their own. They don't always agree with each other."

Gurrand nodded and turned his attention to Ellian.

"I studied battle tactics of the known and past kingdoms. I research the old battles and try to learn from the mistakes of the commanders involved."

"Is this how you managed to take the city?" The king took another sip of his tea.

"Not really, Your Majesty. We didn't use an open assault. We were able to infiltrate as some of Shale's men. It was Jaron's idea." Ellian looked back to Jaron.

"Battle of Sascity," Jaron said hurriedly. "I remembered it from my lessons."

"You did not, however, travel all of this way to join a small militia in Denshire. Why have you traveled so far east?"

"They came for me," Jaron said, thinking quickly. "I'm

looking for my father."

"Lorenistal Keltenon," The king added.

"You know my father?" Jaron said, and then remembered, "Your Majesty."

"I know of your father," the king corrected.

A cold sweat formed under Jaron's shirt.

The king finished his tea and set the cup down. "How many men have you?"

Ellian closed his eyes adding the casualties from the city ambush, the horsemen lost during the attack by the golem, the Brindi reinforcements, and the scattering of men and women from Holderness that wanted to assist in the effort. "I would say, after our casualties, five hundred footmen, one hundred-thirty horsemen, and about five hundred brindi."

"Brindi!" the king exclaimed. "You're trusting Brindi? I may have heard many things but this is out of the question. I will not have dealings with Brindi!"

Ellian could not hold his tongue.

"The Brindi stopped the attack on your nobles by bringing a stone mage and a fire mage to our side of the fight. If they had not come, then surely this tower would still be in the control of Shale, and you, Your Majesty, would be dead." Ellian stated the obvious and his frankness caught the king off guard. No one disagreed with the king, even a new king, no one, ever. He made a note of this moment. Either this young man had great courage or he was a fool. He would have to take time to decide which.

"Very well, young leader, the Brindi are your responsibility. You will lead them in my army. I will lead your Human troops. The elves are coming. I was given their word. It is true that they were not able to make it to the first battle, but they will make it to the next."

"And where, Your Majesty do you expect that to be?" Jaron asked.

He did not even look at Jaron as he answered while picking up a slice of cheese from the tray in front of him, "Temerrac."

*   *   *   *   *

The next three weeks were a flurry of activity. The elves had arrived. One thousand marched in rows of eight out of the roads from the East, crisscrossing the rocky trail between the low hills. They appeared as a giant snake with shimmering silver scales. Their armor held stone turquoise pieces on the shoulders, and their helms were marked with black obsidian inlay.

The High Elves of Taurminya were shorter than a man and slender as a birch tree. Their skin was as dark as the night and their eyes as green as the grass in spring. For three hundred years, their lives could span. A decade to them is as short as the fleeting vision of a sunrise is to men. A wise leader of Taurminya could be an advisor to generations of kings, knowing each from the moment of birth to the hour of death. They did not enter war often or ever willingly. Whereas men are hurried and impetuous in their affairs, the Elves are more relaxed in their responses. To Jaron their arrival brought the stories of centuries past into the present. Their long and vibrant history had often kept Jaron up, reading in his bunk at the library of Westmost until the light rose in the east.

Jaron walked alone in the courtyards of Holderness. He got an occasional wave from the brindi and some of the men that had helped take the city. He had been spending more time alone lately. His patrol disbanded and was King Gurrand's personal guard now. Everyone else had somewhere to go, something to do. It was true that he had practice with Anna and Keras every day, but then they went on to train others.

At one time he had felt scared, being the sole person that, it had seemed, everything would depend on. Now he felt insignificant. He could never be the natural leader that Ellian was. Men flocked to him, and held him in great regard and respect. Keras had made her name famous even before Ellian. She could master any fighting style with just a quick study. What did Jaron have to offer?

Absentmindedly, he reached to rub at his chest and felt a stinging pain. Wincing, he opened his shirt and craned his neck to look at his chest. The web was visible, a red outline for each strand. What could it mean? He had never been able to see it. Gentle as a feather, he poked at the web and rolled his shoulders forward in response to a searing hot pain. He pulled at his shirt to cover up and wished Arnor was there.

In the planning room, Jaron sat with Ellian, Rennek, Uhra, and Behra. The Brindi had set up a communication channel to Sandy River through the tunnel under the mountains. Every ten miles, a brindi waited to take information, either toward Holderness, or to the tunnels of Darrod. The latest news was not good. Sir William and Lord Baros had managed to escape the trap sprung by Neeva.

Behra held her hands together as she explained. "We knew we couldn't kill Mavius's knights. We thought this trap of Neeva's would contain them. Fearing they could escape, we left brindi behind.

"The living soldiers of Sandy River drowned like rats or were shot. However, the dead cannot drown. Without flesh for buoyancy, however, they also cannot swim. They built a ladder. It took some time to lash broken pieces of wood together, for most of the wood had floated to the surface already. Once one of the undead reached the rim, he needed only to drop a weighted rope to the bottom and the rest had climbed out. This is what they were doing when the runner left Sandy River."

"All of the brindi from Darrod's tunnels are on their way here," Uhra said, "another hundred."

"How do we stop the dead?" Rennek asked.

"Are the knights following Darrod? If so, we could get Neeva to close both sides of the tunnel under the mountains, after they've entered," Jaron answered.

"The knights won't allow themselves to be trapped again so easily," Ellian said. "Once they see the tunnel, they won't enter it. They won't follow the Brindi. They will use the main road through Temerrac or they will simply use the road of the minasts. The question we have before us now is: run or fight."

"If we run, then the knights will retain Holderness for the

eventual return of Shale. There were few goblins in his last army. He must have been holding them as reserve in Temerrac. We should expect them to accompany the knights. At least them we can kill," Behra said.

"Someone has to bring this to the King," Jaron stated. "I'm sure we're not the ones who will be making the decision."

*   *   *   *   *

Many sat outside the closed doors to the tower waiting for the plan going forward. Ellian opened the door from inside and shut it behind him as he left. His face was a mix of fury and despair.

"They don't believe me. We march for Temerrac in two days."

Chapter 27   Face of the Dead

The scouts came rushing back down the road, their mounts frothing from the exertion. Those troops in front, both brindi and men, made room to allow the riders to pass toward the rear of the line where King Gurrand and the Elven leaders rode.

"Your Majesty," one rider called from his mount, "an army lays ahead, goblins, Nargesh."

Gurrand looked back at the suspension bridge spanning the Besoth Gorge. Why hadn't Valcella's forces blocked the bridge? This would have been an ideal place to hold off an advancing army. "How many head?" the king asked.

"They are camped in the valley of South Besoth, five miles from here, and their numbers cover the wheat fields of six villages. We estimate three to four thousand."

Scouts, men of wood lore and stealth, went out to gather information on the Goblin camp while men skilled in battle tactics, nobles mostly, left to survey the land. The battle would occur somewhere nearby, and every advantage had to be considered.

Smoke curling around the horizon gave the sight of what was to come. Those weren't campfires burning. They were villages. The buildings and crops smoldered in the dusk as the bodies of any brave or foolish enough to try to defend them lay decomposing. The refugees had come carrying their children along with what belongings and food they could. Through the soldiers, they walked north, away from their homes.

Gurrand looked back at the bridge. The Elven forces were still crossing. Their knights had crossed with their leader. The archers were crossing now and the Elven footmen would cross last. Following the footmen at the back of the line were the women, children and servants that drove the food and supply carts.

Gurrand's army moved slowly, trying to clear the bridge, when a screeching cry came from the high ledge to the right of the road.

The hacked body of a scout and the dismembered body of his horse fell among the forward lines. Blood splattered off the carcasses as they struck the ground.

All eyes turned to the west to look up the steep hillside. There, running toward them in a disorganized mess, the goblins came, some of them small and mean, carrying daggers and short swords, layered in dirty leather studded with iron rings, others large and muscular, carrying maces or battle-axes as tall as a man. All of them had death in their eyes.

Jaron braced himself. The road could allow eight men to travel side by side and there was no area for the horsemen to maneuver. If the Goblin numbers were great enough coming from the ledge, they could scatter and separate Gurrand's army to defeat them in sections. Jaron gripped his shield and sword and waited.

The Elven archers traveling behind the army were trapped on the suspension bridge. Spanned out from side to side, they could not bring their numbers to bear on the attackers. Most of them were out of range, stretched out along the line of the long narrow bridge. Elves nearest the south side of the bridge took aim and dropped a number of the goblins rushing toward them. Those hit fell in agony to roll on their backs, grasping at the shafts, breaking them, or pulling them out to continue their assault.

The first to reach Jaron attempted a crushing swing over its head at full speed. Jaron leaped forward to throw off its timing and fell low, bashing into his attacker's knees with his shield. The large goblin crumpled over Jaron and was dispatched by Uhra.

Another goblin filled the space of the first and slammed into Jaron's midsection, leaving him gasping for breath on the ground. He was unable to defend himself and concentrated on breathing on his hands and knees. The goblin raised a sword over its head to finish him off with a mighty blow. Uhra scaled the Nargesh like a tree in the forest. The back of Uhra's left knee wrapped over the goblin's throat, and he threw his weight backwards, dragging the goblin after him. Jaron regained his composure and recovered enough air to aid Uhra, now stuck under the weight of the fallen goblin.

Over the clash of battle, Jaron could hear the king yelling commands while defending himself from attackers. His broken right arm hung slack at his side, but the blade in his left hand cleared the space around him.

The goblins kept coming. One after another fell to the arrows of the elves lining the bridge of Besoth. Those that came on faced men wielding spear and shield. The bodies piled up along the side of the road such that the blood coating the gravel became slippery underfoot.

Neeva's hands spun calculations in the air, but she looked drained. Stones rolled under the feet of the goblins, causing many to lose their footing. Her efforts during the duel of stone golems at the battle of Holderness had depleted her energy. She had nothing left. Her eyes were sunken in and her shoulders slumped. She whispered formulas, tracing calculations in the air, but she could perform only minor spells.

Verne was in much the same state. Only a junior mage, he weakened more quickly than Neeva. His magic would not answer his commands at all.

At Jaron's position, they had encountered over thirty goblins and lost four men. The goblins running from the forest were more concentrated forward along the marching line, and from his vantage point, looking downhill, Jaron watched the line of elves and men push back against the Nargesh forces pressing them.

The king rode past him with several other horsemen toward the still raging battle. "South, push south!" the King cried. Jaron, finding an unmanned horse, climbed into the saddle and followed as fast as he could. The area south of the bridge forced Gurrand's army to stretch out, like a string waiting to be broken. If Gurrand could get his men further away from Besoth Gorge, they would be able to organize.

They rode through the conflict behind the Goblin line, slashing their swords at the goblins' backs to ease the pressure on the footmen. Blades bounced off the ring mail armor as the goblins' tried to stop the horsemen.

The Goblin assault became thinner until the last few were hewn down easily.

Over the groans of the wounded or dying came a terrible crash from behind. Elves and men came rushing off the bridge. Those closer to the center fell to their bellies, gripping the wood and ropes tightly as the span danced oscillations. The bridge supports on the north side were beginning to lean into the gorge. Another catapult shot struck the bridge support again, throwing a cloud of dust into the air.

The elves were crawling toward the nearest side of the bridge when the whole structure gave way beneath them, swinging down to crash into the south side of the gorge. The falling let out sharp, short exclamations of terror, sudden intakes of breath, or silence. Over one hundred Elven archers fell to their deaths. The Elven footmen were still north of the gorge. Separated by the fallen bridge they were unable to aid their leaders. The Elven footmen rushed to secure ropes and cross the gorge, even without the bridge.

From the top of the ledge, the sounds of a battle rang. Ellian had taken Anna and hiked off in the direction whence the attacking goblins had come. With them went most of the brindi. They found, there on the hilltop, some surprised captains and lieutenants of the goblins.

With two hundred brindi behind him, Ellian halted the use of catapults against the forces of Gurrand. Nevertheless, the damage was done. The bridge was no more. *Perhaps,* he thought, *these catapults could be turned to their advantage.*

At the end of the assault, a count was made of over two hundred dead. Sixty brindi had died, as well as one hundred elves, and seventy men. The line had broken in fifteen separate places. A large portion of the front of the line was still missing. They were presumed dead. Gurrand estimated four hundred goblins had been killed.

He looked back to where the bridge should have been. This is why it was not guarded. A trap had been sprung, leaving his forces with their backs against a fall to certain death. To their right flank rose a tall hill, impassable for wheeled carts. And to their left flank lay a heavy bamboo forest that fell away once more into the gorge. There would be no reinforcements, no more supplies, and no retreat.

Gurrand began issuing commands. The archers who survived spanned out along the high ridge to the west and deep into the bamboo forest on the east. Against a large assault, they would not be able to fall back, but it did not matter. Shale, with this last effort, had given Gurrand only one move. The end was inevitable. Calling his nobles to him, he started to make plans for a final stand.

*   *   *   *   *

Jaron pulled at the straps on his armor. It had come loose around the chest and chafed him under the arms such that every move brought a sting of pain. His pants held a long stain, a result of wiping the blood from his hands. The water in his skin was warm and stale. It failed to quench his thirst.

Soldiers carried Goblin corpses to the south, stacking them across the road to create a barrier that would act as the first line of defense. The men and brindi that had perished in the assault were lined along the edge with as much dignity and care as could be afforded. All of the elves that had died were already at the bottom of the gorge.

Two hours after the surprise attack, and the destruction of their only means of escape, a cry came from ahead. The forces in the valley were mobilizing for the final assault. Two miles at a brisk pace and the goblins from the valley would be here in less than an hour.

A phalanx of soldiers stretched across the narrow gap of the road, spears stretched out in front. The goblins did not run into the assault this time. They came in waves, climbing over the gory wall of goblin bodies. Those goblins in front pushed against the phalanx, crushed by the advance behind them to die in pain on the spears of the shield wall. Twenty, forty, one hundred piled the road, a bloody reek of flesh, vomit, and excrement. As one soldier of the phalanx fell, another pressed into his position, often standing on the fallen body of his unlucky comrade.

A great mass of scattered shapes fell among the Goblin rear lines. Oilskins burst with a splash as they struck the road. Quickly following, lighted arrows struck the spilled oil under the feet of the Goblin ranks. They flailed in pain and panic, lighting one another on fire in their wild attempts to quell the flickering torture that engulfed them.

The Nargesh general of the Goblin horde, understanding the danger of the flames, yelled a command and the left flank turned and made its way up the hill. They climbed over bramble and stones, using the trees to pull themselves up the slope. Those struck by the arrows of archers were trampled underfoot by the climbing masses. They were moving to retake the catapults and oil supply.

Seeing the change in tactics from over the heads of the phalanx, Jaron dismounted his horse and called for Keras. Together they collected a troop of brindi, and led the race to the top of the hill. They were not as many as the goblins, but if the catapults were lost, it was all over.

Through the trees, Jaron could tell that he would not reach the top of the hill before the enemy. He doubled his efforts and the muscles in his legs and arms burned with the intensity. The brindi ran ahead, nimbly leaping over fallen trees and other obstacles with ease, their small frames exploding with the endless energy of a child on a holiday.

Above him, the sounds of clashing metal cascaded down the slope. He bounded over the last stone in his path and entered the clearing. Two catapults were in flames. Anna was on the far side of the clearing, battling against a steady supply of attackers. She swung a long bladed pole in a circle of death. The corpses of goblins piled up around her as she defended her position.

A great slash from a short goblin pulled Jaron into the conflict. His blade came up instinctively to deflect the blow so that his attacker's steel slid off toward the ground. Jaron's right fist came around to smash the jaw of the goblin, but the enemy blocked with his forearm. A foot followed the block, striking Jaron in the hip, knocking him onto his rear. Jaron's hands caught his momentum, leaving him, temporarily, undefended. The killing strike did not come. An arrow hit the goblin, piercing his neck and continuing on its path. Clamoring to his feet once again, Jaron jumped over the flailing strikes of the dying goblin to aid two brindi with their foe. A well-placed stab under the arm of another large goblin brought it down.

The wave of brindi pushed the goblins back down the slope where the fighting continued. Keras called for her forces to aid them in their counterattack.

"Keras," Anna called. She was standing, holding her bladed pole, over the body of a soldier. Around her in a wide circle were the bodies of Nargesh, dying, dismembered, or dead. From the fallen soldier's chest stuck three arrows. Blood smeared his face.

Keras ran to Anna, and seeing the face of the man on the ground, fell to her knees and lowered her head in grief. Tears streamed from her eyes, she screamed his name with a sob.

"Ellian!"

Jaron, from a distance, could not see the body, but he had heard Keras say the name. No, it couldn't be Ellian. He ran to Keras, his mind spinning in disbelief. Ellian had been commanding the catapult crew.

Jaron gazed down at the face of his friend. Ellian's eyes were open, and his expression showed no pain. Within one hand was his sword. Within the other was a burst bag of oil, ruptured so that he lay in a pool of it. So many memories flooded through Jaron, laughter at the library, training on the Aquilo, visiting the girls at the market, the first battle at Temerrac, the lesson of the bloody lip. He closed his eyes and wept.

Keras lay over Ellian, hugging him and kissing his lips, her tears falling on his face, her fingers stroking his hair. Sitting up, her breath shuddering, she closed his eyes and kissed him again.

The sounds of battle continued from the slope. Picking up Ellian's sword, Jaron locked eyes with Anna and Keras. Without a word, the three of them walked down the hill again into battle.

* * * * *

The brindi had pushed the goblins down the slope and were falling on them as they retreated, tearing holes with their sharp daggers through even the toughest armor. Other brindi that had climbed the hill set to work on resetting the catapults.

Ellian's blade in Jaron's hand bit deep into Goblin flesh as he swung, unleashing his grief. The three had worked their way through the brindi to the front of the downhill assault, cutting into the enemy and driving them back. Jaron fell forward with a swing, losing his balance, and caught himself against a slender tree. The roots shuddered against his weight. A goblin saw an opening and lunged, swinging his sword to strike Jaron's left knee. Pain erupted in Jaron's leg and he collapsed backwards.

Horns sounded from far to the south. The goblin hesitated. He was clearly torn between wanting to deal the deathblow and following the command of the distant trumpet. He sheathed his sword and fled back down the hill with his comrades.

Anna helped Jaron to his feet where he checked the condition of his knee. There was no blood, but it was sore to the touch. The armor that protected his shin came up high enough to have blocked most of the blow, but he could not walk without favoring it. Down the hill they trod, following the retreating goblins, wary still of a sneak attack from a hiding foe. None came. As they reached the bottom of the hill, they could see through the sparse trees. The road ran red with blood.

The goblins had not only retreated from the hill, but had fallen back along the road as well. Their wounded they left to die. The men made short work of them, killing them as quickly and painlessly as possible.

The goblins down the road milled about, readying for another assault. Some only stood there.

What are they waiting for? They could overwhelm us in sheer numbers, Jaron thought.

Another trumpet sounded from behind the goblins. This trumpet rang loud and hollow, different from the last that had signaled a retreat. The goblins did not advance, turning around instead toward the sound of the trumpet and moving slowly to the sides of the road. Something was marching toward them. *Not another dragon,* Jaron thought. *It could just fly for the attack.*

A standard appeared over the heads of the goblins, deep blue and gold around a golden falcon, Sir William's standard.

The skeletal army was coming.

There could be no escape. He was going to die, and Keras and Anna, just as Ellian had fallen up on the hill.

Anger welled up within him, for Ellian, for Anna and her son, for Chelle and Jihe, for the people of Temerrac and the children of Sotho Entollo. Grief and despair flowed through him. *What have I accomplished? Have I made any difference at all? Would it have all been the same if I had just remained in Westmost? Ellian would still be alive.*

Jaron remembered the tower encounter with Sir William and Lord Baros. He had vowed then to fight them, to do whatever was necessary to ensure their failure.

Despair became anger. He gripped Ellian's sword tightly in his hand. Picking up a shield from a fallen goblin, he strapped it to his arm and prepared for the coming attack.

Slowly, the knights of Sir William advanced. Eighty of them were here, out of over a hundred. *Where are the rest?* Jaron wondered. The creak of their joints, the suffering of their steps sent before them a wave of revulsion and panic that flowed through Gurrand's forces. Some men fled toward the gorge, throwing themselves off, choosing a sure death over the nightmare in front of them.

Men and brindi ran into the bamboo forest or up the hill. Hundreds turned to flee, making Jaron's walk to the road at the bottom of the hill more difficult as they brushed past him.

Those able to overcome their fear readied for their fate, and when the skeletal footmen came among them, they attacked with newfound ferocity. A long dead soldier would fall, to rise again a few moments later. The army that could not die began to destroy the army that could.

A man would fall, cut down from behind as he ran, and he would crawl in fear until a sword, swung by a fleshless hand, ended his life. Elven knights and the archers that had survived the bridge attack stood their ground. Those elves that did not run died, as did men, and brindi.

Jel fell to a soldier's swing, the blade penetrating his helmet to cut a deep wound above his left ear.

Jaron had reached the battle, bumped, and bruised by the panicked throng trying to escape. He fended off one attacking knight after another, knocking them down or decapitating them, only to have them stand and attack again. A block with his sword deflected the spear of his enemy, rolling it up and over, until the tip touched the ground. It snapped in half as Jaron stomped on it. He was tiring.

Yaru fought at his side, protecting king Gurrand, along with his personal guard. On the ground at his feet, mixed with the pooling blood, were bones, hands, arms, legs, skinless, still moving, trying to kill or find their way back to the undead knight that owned them.

A mighty swing caught Jaron in the shoulder of his sword arm. Shuddering pain and numbness bounced across each other as they rolled together down to his fingertips like the echoes of a ringing bell. Weaponless now, Jaron fell to the ground clutching the wounded arm. The skeletal warrior raised his axe for a mighty stroke, and in a futile gesture, Jaron raised his foot to push back the attacker and yelled, "No!"

The blue glow of the soldier's eyes focused on Jaron and the dead soldier stopped, letting his axe fall backward from his grasp. His glowing sockets stared down. Cupping his fleshless fingers around his mouth, the soldier raised his head to the sky, dropping his jaw in a silent scream.

Every skeletal foe ceased their attack.

The humans and elves continued, taking the opportunity to hit the still standing dead soldiers with their last ounces of strength. The skeleton would fall and rise again.

"Stop!" Jaron commanded.

Yaru was lost to the battle fury. Jaron pushed against him until Yaru's eyes showed recognition. "Stop!"

The sounds of battle subsided. Men, elves, and brindi fell back away from the enemy to wait out the new situation. The skeleton army stood motionless, waiting and looking at Jaron.

Through the mass of bones and bodies, Sir William approached, riding a living horse. Dismounting, he stood before Jaron, tall, menacing, and gruesome in his appearance.

Sir William held his hand over the chest of Jaron, as he had done before in the tower. The strands of Jaron's soulweb stretched out to the bones of his fingers and Sir William snatched his hand back in pain. He stepped back and drew his sword. Kneeling, he laid it at Jaron's feet.

Sir William's soldiers, those that had put away their weapons, drew them again. As one, they turned to face the Nargesh Goblin army. In disbelief and disgust, Jaron watched them walk away. Sir William rose and turned to lead his men in the slaughter of the Nargesh goblins.

"But, I'm not the king," Jaron said. Then, in sudden understanding, Jaron put the palms of his hands to his eyes. "My father is dead."

Chapter 28   Road to Nowhere

Three hundred dwarves filtered into Stenwood Den, settling down in houses to await the arrival of Mavius and his forces. Sarmas, Beshaa, and Mennan led patrols into the town through passages known only to the citizenry. Thargus, Loren, and Arnor followed as silent as they could, but Sarmas and Mennan were like ghosts in front of them, footsteps whispering along the path up the hill. This route would bring them to the square just outside of the building containing the gravity well.

Eyes peeled for any soldiers of Mavius, they lowered themselves down into the square. The street twittered with local birds. Finches, red as the evening sky, flitted between the trees. The dwarves moved without sound, ducking between houses, ever conscious to keep out of the sight of the enemy.

In the room of the well sat a single guard. He had not been expecting anyone. He was sitting, leaning back in his chair, whittling on a stick, curling slivers of wood away to the floor. His eyes widened in fear at the sudden appearance of five dwarves in the room, four of them holding murder in their eyes. With a cry, he stood, knocking the chair into the well, where it plummeted all the way to the bottom. He threw himself into the gravity well behind it. Arnor and Thargus did not hesitate in following him, leaving Loren standing at the top. Beshaa, Mennan, and Sarmas looked over the edge of the well in awe as the three fell slowly to the bottom.

"Yes," said Beshaa, "I have to try that."

At the bottom of the well, the soldier looked for an escape, and finding none, gave himself up to Arnor and Thargus. If Arnor had not forbidden it, Thargus would have killed him immediately, surrender or not. They did get information from him on Mavius's scheduled arrival. He was coming this day. They tied up the soldier and sat him in a corner.

"There's no way out of here, except through us," said Arnor. "Do you know what the other dwarves would do to you if I allowed it?" The man nodded. Arnor turned to Thargus with a stern look. "Don't kill him. I'll be right back."

Arnor arrived at the top of the well and stepped out of the air onto the ledge. "Loren, our best bet to get Mavius alone is to confront him near the door. You are going to have to come with me."

Beshaa touched Loren's arm looking at him, sizing up the human once more.

"You can stop him?"

"I don't know."

Beshaa, Mennas, Sarmas, and Loren stepped off the ledge behind Arnor.

*   *   *   *   *

In rows of four the men came. Four hundred men wearing the colors of blue and grey accompanied Mavius. Footmen walked both in front and behind the carriage. Human knights on horseback rode into Stenwood Den, confident in their superiority. Driven by two horses, the carriage in the middle of the procession was dark, its shutters hung closed to the daylight.

Their entrance into Stenwood Den went unchallenged. The soldiers that had already been in the city waved to companions, happy once again to be part of the main forces of Mavius. The sound of hooves echoed through the empty street. Soldiers assembled in the large square. Behind them, the dwarves entered the street and spread out to close off the city exit.

*   *   *   *   *

A reflection of the torches ensconced on the wall, glittered in the embroidery on otherwise dull black robes of the young man that entered the room. Brown hair draped his thin shoulders. At a motion from the black-robed man, two soldiers entered the well. He watched them as they fell away, allowing time for them to reach the bottom. At that moment, his bare feet left the ledge and he too began to descend.

Mavius watched below him as he dropped. His men that

should be at the bottom were not there waiting for him. *Something is wrong,* he thought. A crimson pattern stretched across the floor at the bottom of the well, pooling a dark red in one quadrant of the circle.

He closed his eyes for the remaining fall, allowing his mind to perform the elemental calculations required for defense, painfully aware of the limitations of his stone magic. He would be vulnerable to attack during the last few moments as he waited for his feet to touch the floor.

He opened his eyes to gauge his attackers as they came into view. Four dwarves stood over the bodies of his guards. Two of the dwarves hurled weapons, one axe, and one dagger. Both hit. The dagger struck his arm, cutting him but falling away. The axe careened off his shoulder, striking with the handle instead of the blade. Pain shrieked in his mind, pain, and fury.

His feet touched the stone bottom and his barricade came up around him, closing off the shaft from the rest of the room. He felt the strain of maintaining the shield wall. Weak, he was so weak. The portal held all of the strength he needed but could he reach it?

A wind whipped about him, striking him with the dust of the stone wall he had created. It had become as much a prison as protection. *I must get out,* he thought. However, when he tried to leave the floor to jump back up into the gravity well, the wind held his feet flat.

Unable to flee up into the well, Mavius reached out beyond his shield wall, feeling the locations of his attackers through the ground vibrations.

Spikes shot from the floor, impaling Beshaa and Arnor. Screams echoed the room, breaking through the wall to reach Mavius. He smiled.

Loren floated in the air outside of Mavius's protective wall. Holding himself away from the floor, using the air pressure, he avoided the blades. Seeing the danger of being the only one left to oppose Mavius, Loren reached out with his magic. He sensed the atmospheric ripples of the room, and whipped the air into a force that lifted Mennan and Sarmas from the floor, making them invisible to the vibrations in the rock that gave away their positions.

* * * * *

Dwarves fell upon the soldiers in the square, swinging axe and mace. They came from every street, attacking from all sides. Mavius's soldiers countered, using their numbers to drive the dwarves back into the side streets. The soldiers gained ground against this threat and chased them down lanes and alleys, foolishly spreading out their forces.

The dwarves waiting in those streets tore them apart.

Too soon, thought Thargus. He was watching the city entrance. If Sir William or Lord Baros had come with Mavius, they must be allowed to join him at the door to the abyss where Loren was waiting for them. As he turned to leave the city entrance, another group of soldiers marched the path to Stenwood Den.

Forty dead soldiers approached the entrance to the city. Their leader, his shoulders wide and strong, wore a tabard of blue and silver. The hood attached to his flowing cape covered his face and on his hip was a long broadsword.

Lord Baros halted his men at the gate. He could hear the sounds of battle coming from within. Thargus watched him raise his hands to his chest, stretching out his own soulweb, reading it.

At a silent command from their lord, the skeletal soldiers spread out into the streets.

Lord Baros was now alone astride his horse. He was not entering the battle.

I have to get him to the well, Thargus said to himself. *Maybe he'll follow me*.

A yank on Lord Baros's cape dropped him from his horse. Lord Baros hit the ground with a crack. His hood fell back, revealing the skull and glowing blue eye sockets underneath. Before him, with a mighty long handled axe and wearing a chainmail shirt, stood Thargus. Lord Baros drew his broadsword, saluted the brave dwarf, and advanced.

* * * * *

Intent on his escape, Mavius refocused his attention, allowing the shield wall to crumble as he stepped out of the well footprint. Before him floated Loren, surrounded by a blinding dust of swirling rock that stung at the eyes of both Mavius and the two remaining dwarves.

He's so young, thought Loren. *He looks like Jaron.*

"Many are the years I have fought to return to this plane. It is lucky for you that I do not currently possess my full strength." Mavius reached out with his magic and the ceiling fell six feet and held there. "Are you willing to die?"

"Don't you know me?" asked Loren lightly.

"I'm afraid that I don't. Are you only a fool from that false king in the North?"

"No," said Loren. "I am the king."

A great block fell from the ceiling to crush Loren, but he slid to the side, throwing another dust cloud at Mavius, only to have it deflected by a barrier of stone.

"I am the one you've been seeking to kill," said Loren. "Your 'allies' hid me from you. I've been tortured. I was to be the instrument of your defeat as they snatched away control of your army."

"You're dying," said Mavius, backing down the hall into the portal room. Loren followed him, still floating through the air like a spirit. "I can see the damage you've taken," Mavius held out his hands and Loren's soulweb glowed yellow. Strands of it fluttered in tatters, like an abandoned spider's web. "You won't survive the week." Behind Loren, hidden by the swirling of the debris in the air, Arnor stood up. Mavius reached the portal stairs. Drawing power from his proximity to the opening, he brought his hands together and the walls of the hallway collapsed in on Loren.

* * * * *

On the thoroughfare, Thargus spun away from the thrust of the knight's blade and drove the haft of the axe against Baros's arm.

The bone snapped with the blow. Baros did not slow. He kicked Thargus away, knocking him to the cobblestones.

The sound of battle carried from the side streets. The Dwarves had encountered the army of the dead. On the ground next to Thargus lay Nuala, his eyes staring away.

Thargus lifted himself from the road, rolling forward off his shoulder into the shape of a tripod, one knee, one foot, one hand. He stood, backing toward the square, and gripped the haft of his axe with both hands. The chainmail shirt Thargus had donned from the town armory weighed him down, but he could still move cleanly.

Baros stalked him, walking slowly, giving the bone in his arm time to set itself.

"I had hoped to find you, dwarf," Baros said. "You brought us the son of the king instead of the king." He held his sword nonchalantly in his gloved hand as he readied himself for Thargus's next attack. "Do you still bear the web given to you by Mavius?" He extended his left hand, the bones of his fingers spread wide inside the glove. "Yes, I can feel it. I have had mine for centuries. It has become a shield of a sort, against the darkness."

Thargus stepped in, dodging the upward swing of Baros's broadsword, and thrust his axe head at Baros's midsection like a spear. It caught the fabric, tearing away a thread.

Baros pushed down on the blade with his left hand and brought his broadsword back down across the chest of the dwarf. Thargus felt one of his ribs break as the wind left his lungs.

He fell on to his back, letting loose his grip on the two handed axe. He rolled in pain from his back to his stomach, trying desperately to regain his breath. *The well, get to the well.*

Baros kicked away the axe, and reaching down a gloved hand, rolled Thargus onto his back.

One black leather glove fell to the ground as Baros stood up again. His bony hand stretched out over Thargus, pulling the threads of his web, lifting him off the ground.

Thargus writhed in pain, but he was unable to break free.

Baros lifted him, clenching the threads in his skeletal hand. Baros shook off his other glove. Both of his fleshless hands now grasped the web strung across Thargus's chest. Baros's shoulders flexed as if the muscles still controlled them.

* * * * *

Loren's magic kept him alive, barely. The currents of air had thrust apart from Loren's center to cushion the blow. The blunt force of the attack still broke both of his arms. He was pinned.

Mavius stepped back away from the portal. He brought his hands up, summoning a thin drill-like blade to come spinning out of the stone floor. Slow and steady it bit into Loren's thigh, ripping away flesh. Loren twisted in pain, unable to escape the stone pinning him in place.

Arnor moved quietly around the stone walls pinning Loren. The mage was focused on Loren's suffering. Arnor climbed the side of the stairs, fearing that Mavius would hear him, or see him. Sweat dripped from his forehead. He drew a knife, and with a deep breath, drove the blade deep into Mavius's belly. Mavius's scream joined Loren's cries of pain.

Blood fell on the stones. Mavius pushed the dwarf away, magic incantations screeching from his throat as a mighty rock fell on Arnor, crushing his chest. Gasping for air and weak from the use of his magic, Mavius crawled through the portal.

Arnor pushed off the rock and stood up. "Ow," he said, "that hurt."

"Free me!" Loren yelled to him. Arnor pressed against the stones until they fell away and Loren landed on the ground. Jaron's father then rose, floating inches off the floor. He looked at Arnor, bloody and broken, but the resolve in his eyes was strong. He walked on the air toward the steps leading to the portal. "I can feel my power growing, Arnor, as I get closer. I'm healing," he said as he turned to look at Arnor again. Exhausted, Arnor could only stare back.

"You cannot close the portal from this side," said Loren. "I do this for Jaron. Tell him, I'm sorry."

Loren turned, entered the portal, and closed the door behind him.

* * * * *

Making his way through the debris of the hallway back to the room at the base of the gravity well, Arnor found Mennas and Sarmas working their way to him. Thargus was behind them, breathing gingerly.

"Where's Mavius?" Thargus demanded.

"Through the portal."

"Then I'm going through. Where is Loren? Is Loren dead?"

"Loren closed the portal. You can't go through."

Thargus stopped trying to get past Arnor and stared, unseeing, at the bloodstains on Arnor's shirt. *I failed. Is Mavius still alive?*

Arnor looked Thargus over. Blood was coming through the chain mail armor across his chest. His face held an unnatural pallor. "What happened to you?" Arnor asked.

"Baros," Thargus said. "He had me. I was done. Then, he just left, walked away."

Thargus sat down heavily on the steps, shattered. He put his head in his hands, cursing his failure. A hand went to the web on his chest. He could feel it through the armor. It was still there. With help, he stripped off the chain mail shirt. Unbuttoning the stained top, he looked at the web. The sores were gone, but the web remained.

Mennas pointed to the well guard tied up at the bottom of the gravity well. "What should we do with him?"

Thargus looked at the human. He had wanted to kill him only hours ago. He wanted to lash out, to feel that there was some sense of fairness in the world. This man was a member of Mavius's forces, but he wasn't Mavius.

"Let him go."

* * * * *

Thankful as they were that the gravity well still functioned, the thought of having to climb out from this depth unnerved them all, they wished that there was an easy way to return with the bodies of Mennan and Beshaa. Ultimately, they decided to leave them where they were. In the years to come, the Gravity Well became a shrine to the memory of the dwarves that gave their lives so that the portal could be shut.

Outside in the courtyard lay the bodies of men. They had fought bravely against the dwarves. The dwarves had driven the men into corners where their numbers became a hindrance instead of an advantage. Even so, half of the dwarves had been lost.

In the immediate aftermath of the Battle for Stenwood, as it came to be known, Thargus could only take note of the painful silence still looming over the town. Leaving Arnor, he found a shop that sold spirits and selected one that had a flavor of cinnamon and apples, for his wife's memory. Wincing at the pain in his chest, he opened it and sipped straight from the bottle, eyes rimmed with tears that wouldn't come.

The darkness of his house became his hiding place from the other dwarves celebrating the retaking of the town. He held a toy in his hand as he sat on the floor, drink between his legs. The joy this house once felt, the laughter, was a ghost memory. In his mind, he heard his children calling, his wife singing, his hands turning the pages as he read to them.

Standing, he walked to the bookcase and pulled a book from the shelf. Fumbling it with the toy and drink already in his hand, he dropped it.

A pair of small voices came from the bedroom, "Daddy?"

Chapter 29   End of the Road

This had been his home. The familiar smell of the books on the shelves welcomed him back, but it no longer felt like home. It felt small.

King Gurrand had assigned him a task, to aid an Elemental mage in researching a branch of magic that had long been thought impossible. To Jaron's delight, the mage was Neeva. Both Verne and Harris, the engineer of Temerrac, accompanied her.

After Neeva had gone with King Gurrand and his generals to close the tunnel she and the brindi had taken under the Fortunal Mountains, she was needed again to shore up fortifications in what was once the city of Temerrac, now a horrible ruin. Neeva expressed to Gurrand that she wanted to research the magic of the enemy. Gurrand ordered Jaron to assist her. He chose Jaron for a number of reasons. He was familiar with the library and the system of research needed. The boy was also to be protected as a valuable asset. So, assigning him anywhere far behind the battle lines kept him out of the enemy's sight. Last, he should be watched as a potential enemy.

The continent was divided. King Shale of Valcella, as he now called himself, held all of the land south of the mountain range. The engineers, to keep Temerrac out of the hands of Shale, had destroyed it, blocking the easiest pass through the range.

After the battle of Besoth Gorge, as it came to be known, the battalion of revenant soldiers had returned to Jaron for further instructions. He had found none to give. King Gurrand attempted to command them, but could not. For a time, it looked as if he would bring his forces to bear against them once more, but Jaron intervened and ordered the knights and their soldiers to consider their oath to Mavius fulfilled, and that they should take their rest as they so deserved.

Lord Baros and Sir William ordered their soldiers to inter themselves in the hill of the catapults at Besoth Gorge, where Ellian lay buried, incidentally. They did not dismiss their soldiers, saying that they would wait until needed again. When the last of the dead covered themselves over with soil, so did Lord Baros and Sir William.

King Gurrand was not heartened by this. Though Gurrand stayed at the new fortifications at Temerrac, the city of Westmost was now under the direct control of King Gurrand's men, leery as he was at Jaron's connection to the throne of a long dead king. He did not dare to kill Jaron outright, for fear of the return of the revenant knights. He, himself, had no ability to stop the knights if they were ever to return. This boy was either going to become an enemy or a powerful ally. Either way, he was to be watched.

Keras had remained at Temerrac with king Gurrand. Her performance in battle was the stuff of tales throughout the land. Although she longed to return home, she was now the official trainer of Gurrand's troops. She relished rising early every day and teaching her own personal form of combat. Her best pupil, Anna, was now her faithful assistant.

The journey to Westmost library, uneventful and boring though it should have been, held in Jaron's memory as one of the most interesting of his young life. Long conversations about the formulas and calculations hidden in the magic allowed him to see Neeva as happy as he ever had. She truly looked like an excitable teenager when she answered his questions. For the first time, he started to see her as a girl, and caught himself looking at her when she was preoccupied with other things, only to look away as she looked up. Her laughter made him happy.

Neeva was searching for a book by someone named Istilia Chonos. Jaron had never heard the name before, although there were many books of magic by various authors contained in one section of the library. "The master of air magic," Neeva explained, "wrote down his clues to the discovery." She was adamant that she would find the book, that it had to find its way to Westmost.

Ceryss was as much of a help in this matter as he could be, and on their arrival held a feast in their honor. Many new library acolytes had joined the library in the last year and Jaron could not get over how young they looked. Had he ever looked so young?

Rooms were chosen for them, and Neeva dove into the stacks of books before her, sometimes carrying four at a time, great tomes with dusty leather covers, to the table in the center of the room. She always seemed to read a page in the tomes that had her searching for another book to corroborate her thought patterns.

The day Thargus, with his daughter and Arnor, arrived at Westmost library was another joyous occasion. They came across the mountains instead of through the Temerrac pass. Thargus's wife and young son had stayed behind in Stenwood Den, the mountains being too dangerous for one so young.

The little dwarf girl, Nanca, Thargus had named her, was blond and attractive with big green eyes that shone with a light from inside. Jaron smiled as he noticed Thargus's eyes well with happiness as he watched over his daughter.

Arnor wore a new hat, bought the morning he arrived in Westmost, blue with a feather of bright green stuck garishly in the brim. After the greetings and hugs had subsided, he sat with Jaron over breakfast.

"I've something for you, from your father," said Arnor sipping his coffee.

"He's gone, isn't he?"

"Yes."

"Is he dead?"

"I don't think so. Mavius is still alive or these webs across our chests would be gone. Chances are that they are working together now, in the under-realm."

"Together?" Jaron was appalled. "Why would he work with Mavius?"

"To survive they may have no other choice."

Jaron frowned.

"You seem to be under the impression that Mavius is completely evil." Arnor reached for a piece of toast. "No-one is. Just like no-one is completely good, not even you. The lust for power often corrupts, blinding the powerful to the injustices they impose on others, even as they try in their own way to do the right thing." Arnor took off his hat and set it on the table. "Mavius wants to survive. For that, he needs your father alive as well. They are both powerful wizards."

"My father was a blacksmith."

"When you knew him, yes. That was before he read this book." Arnor pulled a leather bound book from his pocket and handed it to Jaron. "Your father sacrificed himself to close the door, to give you the power to stop the knights, to give you a chance."

Arnor proceeded to tell Jaron the natural ability of Jaron's father with the book called *Current Studies,* and that maybe Jaron should give the book a read.

Jaron turned the book over in his hands. "I wish I could have seen him."

"He fought for you," Arnor dipped his buttered toast in his coffee. This, for him, served two purposes, it made the toast taste like coffee, and it added a slight buttery taste to the coffee.

"Who knows? I believe he still lives," said Arnor. "You may see him yet. Mavius was able to return. It did take him a couple hundred years though."

Jaron frowned, looking at the back of the book. He had been so sure that he would find his father, so sure that he would speak with him again.

Arnor watched Jaron. He could see that this discussion wasn't making the boy feel any better. The dwarf finished his toast, stood, put on his hat, and picking up his travel pack, threw another one to Jaron.

"So, are you ready to meet your brother?"

Made in the USA
Middletown, DE
21 April 2017